Eternal Samurai

B.D. Heywood

B. D. Heywood

Eternal Samurai is a work of fiction. Names, characters, institutions, places, historical events and incidents either are the products of the author's imagination or are used fictionally. Any resemblance to actual persons, living or dead, or locales or events is purely coincidental.

Warning: This book contains sexually explicit scenes, violence and adult language that may be considered offensive to some readers. This book is for sale to adults only as defined by the laws of the country in which you made your purchase,

Sale of this book without its cover is not authorized. If you purchased this book without its cover, be aware it was reported to the publisher as "damaged" or "destroyed."

All rights reserved under International Copyright Convention. No part of this book may be reproduced or used in any form or by any means, electronic or mechanical, including recording, photocopying or by any information storage and retrieval system without permission in writing. Inquiries should be addressed to:

ICINI Publishing Co.
P. O. Box 39746
Phoenix, AZ 85069

Editor: Jacob Shaver

Cover illustration: Ben Gill

Cover design: Donna Conley

Copyright © 2012 by B. D. Heywood

First printing: November 2012.

Second printing: August 2013

ISBN-13: 978-0988300002

Printed in the United States of America

DEDICATION

For Hundi

Always run free.

And to all who suffer hatred, abuse and intolerance
because you stay true to yourself.
You are brave beyond words.
Your spirit will shine for all to see.

ACKNOWLEDGEMENTS

Ben Gill whose artistic vision and talent brought Tatsu Cobb to vibrant life on the cover.

Jessica Maxwell, my first beta reader, who dug out the errors and inconsistencies, and then encouraged me to continue no matter what,

Jacob Shaver, my editor who cut the dross from the metal to reveal the gold of the words shining beneath.

Kelly Wiggins who offered her patient and unswerving input that helped guide the book to its final version.

One

The Temple of Mii-dera, Nipon, 1180

It was a day of treachery. Of blood and gore and death. Of men shouting in triumph or screaming in agony.

It was the day the humanity was ripped from Saito Arisada's soul.

This was not Arisada's first battle, but it would be his last. He was Sōhei, one of Nipon's elite Buddhist warrior monks. Today, he was destined to die beneath an enemy's blade. He accepted that inescapable finality. In fact, he embraced it.

But he was incapable of accepting that the man Arisada loved more than life itself had betrayed him. Arisada's young, beautiful soul mate had chosen greed and ambition over honor and loyalty.

Hatred consumed Arisada's heart. Oh, no, not for the soldiers that had come to slaughter them all. His heart burned with hate for his lover, Koji Nowaki.

At dawn, Mii-dera's massive wooden gates burst inward, and twenty-five-thousand screaming warriors charged into the temple grounds. But hours before the assault, Arisada had received word of Nowaki's treachery. The youth had guided army sent to rescue Mii-dera along the wrong mountain path. Help could never arrive in time.

Oh, my koibito, my beloved, why? Why had Nowaki, one of Mii-dera's youngest and most feared warriors, chosen such a dishonorable path? Arisada's heart replied: Nowaki had chosen ambition over love, status over honor. He had become the lover of the enemy's most powerful commander.

Unmanned by a mélange of anguish and fury, Arisada dropped to his knees with a strangled cry. Ignorant of his lover's betrayal, Arisada was blameless for the terrible consequences. But none of that mattered. He was the traitor's bedmate. The only atonement for that lay in committing *seppuku*, ritual suicide. He tore off his leather chest plate and pressed his *tanto's* deadly tip against his naked abdomen. Arisada took a single, deep breath and steeled himself to drive the short knife into his belly.

The enemy's howls of "*Shi wa Mii-dera*," promising death to Mii-dera, shattered Arisada's single-minded purpose. His hand faltered and the knife skittered over his hipbone, leaving a bloody cut. Better to give his life defending his temple than waste it on his own blade. He sheathed the *tanto*, scrambled to his feet and tied on his armor. He pulled his *nodachi* from its sheath with a hiss. Brandishing the sword in one hand and his spear-like *naginata* in the other, he pelted to the front line.

Arisada would fight to save Mii-dera—fight with all his strength and skill, but not his heart. His heart was already dead. Fueled only by his anguish, he fought like a mad man. Fought and prayed. Begged all the Gods for the chance to find and kill his green-eyed lover who'd betrayed them.

Months ago, Mii-dera's ambitious abbot had forged an alliance with Prince Mochihito, an imposter to the throne. What did the bastard Prince care that the oaths of Mii-dera's warrior monks would bind them to a hopeless cause? The lust for power had ruled that day. Within weeks of the agreement, the Emperor retaliated, dispatching his massive army to Mii-dera with orders to take the heads of every Sōhei within its walls. The thousand Mii-dera Sōhei had no chance.

Surrounded by the screams of the dying and the enemy's triumphant howls, Arisada wielded his weapons with maniacal force. The hours blurred. His senses reeled from the battle's din, the clash of weapons, the berserk howls of warriors and the screams of the maimed. Sweat, and perhaps tears, flowed into his eyes, clouding his vision. Fatigue weighted his limbs. A fire burned through muscle and sinew. Dust choked his lungs. He slipped and skidded on the treacherous footing beneath his heavy sandals. The world narrowed until all that existed was the face and body of the enemy before him.

Around him, fighters caught in battle frenzy trod on the severed limbs or entrails of the fallen. Men shrieked in agony or bloodrage, slipped and slithered on the gore-covered ground. The air was fetid with the reek of shit. The ground turned to mud from blood and piss. The dust coating them all made friend and foe indistinguishable.

But even with their incredible skill with spear, bow and sword, the Sōhei of Mii-dera had no chance. By dusk, only a handful of the Temple's warrior monks remained alive. Then Prince Mochihito fled, abandoning his men to the slaughter. Now, all was truly lost.

A triumphant roar swelled over the battlefield. Arisada peered through the choking dust to see Hayato, commander of the *yabusame*, the Emperor's deadly mounted archers, gallop through the shattered gates. Hayato was the most powerful, and ruthless commander in the army—and Nowaki's seducer.

Red hate drove all reason from Arisada. Screaming, "Hayato," he charged toward the maroon banner fluttering above the commander's back. Blood streamed down Arisada's sword and covered his arms as he cut a swath through the commander's vanguard. Mere feet from Hayato, Arisada raised his *naginata*, and prepared to hurl it toward the handsome, arrogant face.

A panic-driven horse slammed into Arisada, knocking him into the muck. A hoof glanced off his head. Stunned, he struggled to his feet as a sword bit into his thigh. He ignored the pain and, without thought, slashed sideways at the shadow of an unseen guard. Heard with grim satisfaction his attacker's death gurgle. But Hayato had vanished into the chaos.

An unexpected lull in the mayhem allowed Arisada to rally his brethren. In a voice torn by raw desperation, he commanded those few to follow him. Exhausted, they staggered up the stone stairs into the Pure Land Garden behind the main temple. They boarded up the gate; praying the makeshift reinforcement would hold. If caught alive, every Sōhei knew the Emperor would extract a terrible and dishonorable revenge on them all.

Outside the stone walls, wild cheers punctured the air accompanied by the sudden and distinct roar of flames. Smoke billowed thick and black into the sky.

"They have fired the temple," Takanawa Ito moaned. His

broken left arm hung useless. The young monk dropped to his knees. "Saito-sensei, grant me permission to take my own life."

Arisada regarded the twenty-nine Sōhei—their armor and clothing torn and covered in filth, blood and gore. Their faces gaunt with fatigue. Some, too weak to stand, were supported only by their wounded fellows. But as one, they looked at him with proud, undefeated eyes.

His gaze, both terrible and calm, flashed with a momentary show of pride at their bravery. The last of the Mii-dera Sōhei. The last of Arisada's command. He knew this oasis would be a fit site for their final act.

"Life, death, they are the same, *neh*? You are samurai. You accepted your death the moment this battle began. Now, it is for honor you must complete that journey. I give you all leave to take your lives by *seppuku*." Arisada saluted them with his blood-drenched sword.

"I will be the *kaishakunin* for each of you. None will suffer a moment's more agony than your *karma* requires." He would take responsibility for *dakikubi*, the immediate decapitation of each warrior at the precise moment of disembowelment. Arisada would ensure each man died with honor.

Arisada ripped off his cowl and bound it around the bone-deep gash that ran from knee to hip. Not that blood loss was his concern—for soon he would be dead—but he needed to retain his strength just long enough to help his brothers into the next life.

"Saito-*senpai*, who will be your *kaishakunin*?" Takanawa's shocked voice reflected the horror in them all. With no one left to decapitate Arisada after he disemboweled himself, he would die in terrible agony. An end neither swift nor honorable.

"Honor demands my suffering before I go into the Void. Only this way can I atone for the shame of bedding the traitor and remove all dishonor from the house of Saito," he replied.

Twenty-nine died beneath his blade. Takanawa was the first. The last was the youngest, a boy of thirteen. Without hesitation, the youth plunged his *tanto* into his exposed abdomen. His face twisted into a terrible rictus of agony. He uttered no sound when he bowed his neck to accept the compassion delivered by Arisada's hand. On that final blow, Arisada's sword shattered in two.

The mercy killings took an hour. To Arisada it seemed mere moments; the time it takes for a butterfly's wings to flap once. He made no effort to staunch the tears flowing down his face, but stood panting and shuddering, drenched in the life force of his brothers. Their torsos lay like broken dolls, some bowed over their knees, some sprawled in contorted poses. Heads had toppled, rolled or bounced, often a far distance from the body. Arisada had neither the strength nor the time to place the severed parts near each other.

On the other side of the wall, Mii-dera, the Temple of Three Wells, burned. Pillars of roiling black smoke obscured the stars and the silhouette of Mount Hiei. The conflagration threw an unholy light up to the indifferent sky. Timbers fell with great cracks and sent spark-filled plumes into the air. The acrid reek of burning buildings and cooking flesh suffocated him.

A capricious wind cleared the smoke for a moment. With dulled, shock-filled eyes, Arisada stared at the now-defiled *ikinewa,* the pond garden. He was unable to recall the peace of its tranquil landscaping. Black grime from smoke and soot coated the foliage. His ears filled with the sickening buzz of flies gathering on the dead. The stench of shit merged with the choking miasma from burning wood. Thick rivulets ran into the pond clouding the water with crimson—defiling the emerald lily pads and white lotus blossoms. Golden fish thrashed on the surface in confusion, mouths and gills gasping for life.

He prepared for death amid the thunderous cheers of victory that reverberated through the air. The Emperor's troops were pillaging the vast temple. Summoning the last dregs of his strength, Arisada disrobed and placed his armor and clothing, drenched in gore from the enemy and his fellow monks, in a careful pile. The shattered halves of his sword rested beside his *naginata.* He folded his legs beneath him and bound them with his *obi.* Naked except for the *fundoshi* around his loins, he bowed, and pressed his forehead to the ground. Flames cast an ethereal luminescence over his sweat-drenched body.

"*Namu Amida Butsu.*" Arisada venerated the Buddha Amida for his mercy then called aloud the full name of his brethren whose lives he had taken. Their deaths had freed them from all dishonor. But if found alive, Arisada would be branded a coward and his head, placed on a pike, would be paraded in disgrace around the city. The centuries-old Saito name forever erased from all records.

He wept not for his impending death, but for the burning of his beloved Mii-dera and the annihilation of his Order. And he wept for his one and only love, Koji Nowaki.

"May I be granted another life, and the chance to revenge myself upon you, my betrayer, my beloved, my *koibito*," he prayed in a voice abraded by smoke and grief. He drove his *tanto* into his belly, pulled it left hip to right, then upward between the lower ribs. Arisada's face contorted at the excruciating pain, yet he made no cry.

Curled against his blood-drenched thighs, he welcomed the darkness eroding his senses. Smoke filled his nostrils. He coughed and the violent movement sent fire lancing through his body, forcing gouts of blood and ropes of intestine out through the wound. He prayed for death's sweet release before he lost control of his body, shaming himself.

Death came slowly, taking its sweet time, savoring every moment of the young monk's anguish. Arisada was unable to slow the spasmodic jerking of his chest. He panted like a trapped rabbit but not enough air reached his lungs. His limbs, covered with a clammy sweat, turned cold and heavy. His organs began to shut down with shock.

Arisada's nails cut into his palms while he fought the urge to pull the short-bladed knife from his bowels. But the agony radiating from his eviscerated belly paled compared to the anguish in his heart. The image of the face of his lover—his beautiful jade eyes, the sweet bow of his lips—eluded him.

His lover, Koji Nowaki, had deserted him even in memory.

Darkness washed over Arisada but he did not know if it was from true nightfall or his own closeness to death. He heard the garden door shatter followed by a triumphant grunt. At last, his suffering would end. He waited, strangely curious about how death would feel. Curious also about the warrior who would remove his head. Then peace embraced him and it no longer mattered. Soon he would cross over into the Void to begin a new life. To begin seeking his revenge.

An apparition loomed between him and the nightmare of the burning monastery. The warrior, dressed in the enemy's brown uniform, carried no weapons. The man knelt beside him. He pulled Arisada upright onto his haunches.

Crimson eyes appraised Arisada's contorted face. "You are truly beautiful." The soldier's breath reeked of copper and rotted meat. "You may desire death but it is not for you. Instead, you will serve me." Then he jerked the *tanto* free.

The movement fired fresh agony through Arisada's body. He writhed, his torso twisting, bound legs thrashing. His fingers scrabbled for the short blade, desperate to drive it back into his belly. His eyes bulged in their sockets.

Fingers, hawk-talon sharp, thrust into Arisada's wound and twisted a rope of intestines. "Swear by all you honor to serve me," the apparition demanded in an odd, sibilant voice.

Agony fired through Arisada, banishing the sought-after oblivion. "*Zettai ni*. Never," he bleated.

"No one refuses me," the samurai hissed and dug deeper into Arisada's tortured entrails. "I am Ukita Sadomori. I am *kyūketsuki*, a God of Blood. You will give me your pledge."

Never would Arisada denounce his oath to Mii-dera. He believed he heard his own refusal in his bleated moan. But the warrior took the sound for consent.

"You will bear the mark of my crest, my family's *mons*, for all to see." The voice was devoid of all human emotion.

Arisada's eyes locked onto the tip of his own blood-drenched *tanto* plunging toward his face. Fire burst across his left cheek. He ground his teeth so hard against crying out that he heard one crack. A tongue, wet and repugnant, lapped over his lacerated flesh.

With a curiously gentle movement, hands turned Arisada's head to one side. A sharp pain lanced his throat followed by the press of lips against the wound. He felt his blood drawn from his body by long, greedy gulps.

The man's pulse stuttered beneath Sadomori's lips. "You are close to death," Sadomori whispered. He bit into his own lip and fastened the wound to the monk's mouth in a bloody kiss.

Arisada tasted the bitter essence that trickled down his throat. He choked then swallowed. His body burned with a strange and terrible incandescence. Then ice crackled along his veins and froze his nerves. He fell insensate.

"Now, we shall be together for all eternity." Sadomori laughed with triumph for the monk was now his offspring, his first, his Primary. With no effort, he lifted Arisada and cradled him like a child. Ignoring the mayhem around him, Sadomori trod on the living and dead, bearing his conquest away from Mii-dera.

For months, Arisada's feverish mind wandered through evil places filled with unimaginable horrors. When he finally awoke, he no longer belonged to the gentle Buddha Amida. Forever denied reincarnation. Forever denied redemption. The creature's bite had infected him with an ancient, evil virus, which mutated Arisada's body into a monster torn from its humanity by the need for human blood. The oath forced from Arisada's lips now bound him to the *kyūketsuki* Ukita Sadomori.

Arisada's heartrending scream of loss drowned beneath his howl of primal bloodlust.

Two

The Seattle Quarantine, 2024

Sunrise's first pale hint kissed a sky gravid with storm clouds. For most people in the Seattle Quarantine, the pending light meant safety as the sun's rays drove the predators into hiding. For Tatsu Kurosaki Cobb, daylight meant the end of another futile night of hunting. Perhaps tomorrow he'd find his quarry. Find and kill.

He never wanted this—hunting creatures that until a few months ago he regarded with compassion. But he'd always known the way of the sword would become his destiny. *Bushido*, the Way of the Samurai commanded it.

Was he insane coming to this violent city with nothing more than the swords of his ancestors? For what? To kill one monster among hundreds in the name of *fukushū*, vengeance for the slaughter of his entire family?

Uncertainty flickered in his mind for a moment then sank beneath his conviction. He knew in the depths of his *tamashii*, his soul, his actions were just; still a ghost of misgiving haunted him. Was he as much a monster as those he hunted? In his quest to find one, he'd already killed many. And with every death he feared losing his own humanity.

Then the deep fires of hatred washed away any remnants of doubt. *Wakatta,* better hatred than heartbreak.

A *kyūketsuki* was not human. And a *kyūketsuki* that attacked a human forfeited its right to live. Tatsu could kill them with no repercussion.

For the last three nights, Tatsu had slipped across the bridge that crossed the river between Seattle's two species. Any human foolish enough to venture into the Quarantine courted an ugly death. Tatsu entered anyway. The first night a small pack had jumped him. He'd escaped, but not before he lopped off two predators' heads. Now the survivors had his scent. They would tear him to pieces if they caught him. No matter.

Tatsu hunched deeper into his beat-up motorcycle jacket, ignoring the February rain. By the Gods, if he believed in hell, this place was it. Unlike Japan, his native land bright with prosperity and promise, Seattle offered its citizens little more than bare survival. And the ever-present threat of a cruel death.

His nostrils flared at the acrid stench that was as indigenous to Seattle as its famous old landmark. The insidious odors of sewage, rotting garbage and the city's ancient methane plants were dangerous. They masked his quarry's scent.

The city wasn't always like this—grim and desolate. Even in Tatsu's short time here, he'd seen its elegance and charm. He'd also admired the beauty in the buildings and neighborhoods that had survived the volcanic eruption and subsequent massive earthquake. Only a few days apart, the twin disasters had devastated the Pacific Northwest.

Tatsu always had a strange affinity for this battered city. Perhaps because it was his father's birthplace. Perhaps because it was destroyed during *tatsu*, the Year of the Dragon. The year Tatsu was born.

In elementary school in Nagasaki, he'd watched the grainy, too-graphic videos of that belching, fire-breathing mountain spewing dust, ash and other terrible things into the sky. The lava tore down trees and drowned the green land under molten sludge while the massive earthquake ripped the ground apart, tumbling tall buildings like toy blocks. He recalled his naïve, childish clapping when he saw the great Space Needle still rearing proudly above the clouds of dust and smoke.

For three years, ash clouds had obscured the sun. Day turned into perpetual night. And Seattle became a haven for monsters.

He snorted. Fucking animals. Once, they were the stuff of myth; or so everyone believed. Five years before Tatsu was born, a pandemic swept the globe, devastating some regions, skipping others entirely. In its wake, the plague left millions dead and turned thousands into an entirely new species—one that preyed on human beings as food.

Japan had protected herself with ruthless efficiency by euthanizing people as soon as they became infected. But hundreds of *kyūketsuki* had escaped to the former United States, which, for an undiscovered reason, had suffered the worst from the plague. Half the population had died. The economy crashed, and the country fragmented into a handful of independent city states hostile to any outsiders.

Tatsu knew all about that hostility. He'd ridden two-thousand perilous miles from his adopted home in New Mexico to reach this dark city. Too many times he thought he'd never make it. The brutal winter weather, mechanical breakdowns and scarcity of gasoline made the trip a nightmare. Pushing the Kawasaki past guarded border crossings under the cover of winter storms nearly ended his journey twice. But that eighteen-year-old motorcycle with its near-bald tires and oil leaks got him here. Barely. Now, it was in dire need of a major overhaul. Nothing he could do about it; he was broke.

Tatsu shook his head, sending his choppy brown hair flying. *Baka! Idiot! Pay attention or you're dead.*

He picked his way around a collapsed house. His ears tuned out the scrabble of rats and feral dogs as they fled and focused only on that unique sound that signaled a much larger predator.

An easy leap over a crumbled wall dropped him six feet into a narrow, debris-strewn street. He crouched for a few seconds, all senses attuned for the merest hint of danger.

The bar's neon sign blinked strobe-like above the entrance a few yards away. He rolled his shoulders, let out the tension and slipped his weapons into the harness on his back. Brandishing a pair of Japanese swords was not the best strategy for making friends.

The Educated Whore, less than a half-mile from the Quarantine border, was known as gossip central for information about underground Seattle. Tatsu couldn't trust dumb luck that he'd find the one creature he sought. Someone in this sleazy dive had the right information. If he could get anyone to consider talking to a *bugaisha*, an outsider, that is.

A discordant bell clanked overhead as Tatsu pushed the door open. He heard an intermittent buzz from the beer sign flickering above the bar. His preternatural eyesight saw every detail of the room despite the dim cast of a single fluorescent light that hung by two wires from the ceiling.

The pub was an icon to the current decay of the human condition. A scarred wooden bar occupied the entire wall on Tatsu's left. Once, there might have been a mirror behind it, but now the unpainted wall was covered in a blanket of grime interspersed with moldy wallpaper. Beneath his boots, he felt the sticky squelch from spilled beer. The skunky reek of stale cigarette smoke, even staler alcohol and human sweat failed to cover the underlying stench of urine. Or the palpable smell of hostility.

A few tough-looking customers sucking down their cheap brew hunched over their tables. Conversation died as a dozen pairs of eyes swiveled to pin the newcomer. Tatsu felt the weight of their territorial glares. Clearly, outsiders were low on the welcome list. Especially *armed* outsiders.

Kuso, shit, no one looked the least bit friendly. Tatsu eased his fighter's stance into a relaxed posture. He knew what the barman and everyone else saw, or thought they saw. Some would notice the swords on his back and think *trouble*. Some would see a shaggy-haired Japanese youth in a scuffed motorcycle jacket, worn leather chaps and rundown biker boots and label him *drifter*.

And a few, those hate-filled few, would fix only on his slender body and gliding walk—the unconscious gait of a trueborn samurai—and label him *queer*. Not that Tatsu's preference for men was anyone's business. He just didn't care to broadcast it then have to fight his way out of a mob.

After a too-long stare, the bartender jerked his chin at a table near the door. This sent a signal to the rest of the crowd. The murmurs from the customers resumed as they turned back to their own concerns.

Tatsu spun the metal chair around and straddled it to

accommodate his swords. He groped in his jacket pocket and pulled out a crumpled pack of Canadian Kings. He sighed as he tapped it against his thumb then extracted a cigarette with his lips. Chikusho, *only five left. Looks like it's time to quit.* He lit the smoke with a steel lighter and inhaled a slow, appreciative drag.

From the corner of his eye, he watched the waitress approach. A slight hesitation in her step broadcasted her apprehension. Tatsu knew her eyes were riveted on the sword hilts visible above his leather-clad shoulders. At least his weapons would dispel any idea that he was another no-tip, rent-boy looking for a last trick before the night ended.

She placed a chipped ashtray in front of Tatsu and he acknowledged her with a polite dip of his head. All at once, the woman's tired countenance lit up with surprise. Her smile took years off her careworn face.

"I ain't never seen an Asian with green eyes before. They're gorgeous." A slight, sultry tone entered her voice. Tatsu sensed it wasn't really a pick-up line.

"*Domo arigatō gozaimasu.*" Flustered, Tatsu stammered his thanks in his native tongue.

"That's so cute." Giggling, she fussed with her notepad. "What'll it be, hon? We got a special on Red Vodka. Course, it ain't real but you'd never know."

Although he was almost broke, Tatsu ordered the cheapest stout in the house. Buying a drink might open the way to information. A minute later, the woman brought the bottle and a glass mug. Tatsu dug out a fistful of change and handed it to her with an apologetic shrug. "*Sumimasen.* I'm sorry. I don't have enough for a tip."

"Don't worry about it, hon. I'm Doris. You need anything more, just holler." She nodded at the dark brew. "You're one of the few men I see with the balls to drink that stuff. See that man over there?" She pointed toward a customer slouched over a table in the corner. "Always drinkin' it."

To hide his no-tip embarrassment, Tatsu glanced in the direction of her pointing finger. Two tables over, a dark-haired man reeled back in his chair and downed the last of his frothy brew. With a loud belch, the man wiped his wet lips with the back of his hand and levered himself up from the table. He mumbled about "needing the jacks" and lurched toward them.

"Hey, Bana. You oughta go home before you pass out."

"Sod you, Doris." The man elbowed past the waitress. Just as he reached Tatsu, the drunk lost his balance and fell. His flailing hand hooked Tatsu's shoulder and dragged him out of his chair. Both men crashed to the filthy floor in a tangle of limbs and furniture. Tatsu gagged at the man's rank beer-and-sweat stench.

The drunk's head lolled to one side. A thin trail of saliva ran down his unshaven chin as he peered at Tatsu. "'Scuse me." The man belched again, smacked his lips, and grinned as if he'd done something clever.

"Damn it," Doris cried as she grabbed Tatsu under his arm and helped him up. "You okay, kid? Sorry, he knocked over your drink." She retrieved his fallen glass. "I'll fetch you another."

Tatsu shook his head. "It's all right."

The woman grabbed Tatsu's sleeve. "Shit, I know you don't know him, but can you get him outta here? If the owner sees Bana like this, he'll burn him."

"Huh, why me?" A year ago, he would have been happy to lend a hand. Not now. Let the drooling idiot trying to prop himself against the table leg get his own ass home.

"You look like an honest guy. Bana's not a bad sort. Just loses it sometimes. He only lives around the block. Here's his address," Doris scribbled on a blank order ticket and shoved it into Tatsu's hand. She crouched, fumbled through the man's jacket pocket, removed a couple of crumpled bills and held them up. "'Sides, he's buyin' your drinks fer the next two weeks." She winked. Before another protest left Tatsu's lips, she dashed away to the other end of the bar.

He glared down at the semi-conscious man sprawled over the fallen chair. *Kuso*. Tatsu zipped his jacket, grabbed Bana under the armpits and hauled him to his feet. Hitching the man's arm over his own shoulders, Tatsu took a firm grip on the thick wrist and aimed for the exit.

ETERNAL SAMURAI

Rain drenched them within seconds as they stumbled into the street. Tatsu hunched into his collar as cold water ran down his neck. Bana mumbled under his breath, maybe a thank you, maybe a protest. Tatsu was struggling too much with the man's unwieldy body to care. Then to Tatsu's alarm, the man broke into a loud Gaelic ditty, off-key, no less.

Sweat broke out on Tatsu's forehead despite the cold as he lugged the heavy man along the slippery pavement. And with every unsteady step, the weight on Tatsu's shoulder seemed to increase until it felt like he was hauling a horse—a wet, drunk, singing horse—up a steep, rain-slicked hill. *Mochiron*, of course, Bana's home had to be at the top.

Ten cold, wet minutes later, they arrived at Bana's home. "Ish right up here." Bana wagged an unsteady finger in the direction of a narrow stairway between two small shops. "Upsie stairsie." He lurched forward, tripped on the bottom step and sat down with a thump. He didn't look the least bit inclined to move.

Kusho, Tatsu wondered if he could get the man upstairs before he passed out. Hauling the drunk to his feet, Tatsu tightened an arm around the man's waist and began the climb. Twice Bana swayed backward and nearly tumbled them both down the stairs. When they reached the apartment door, the man fumbled in his pocket, extracted a loaded key ring and dropped it. Tatsu propped Bana against the wall but his knees gave way, and he slid to the floor.

Tatsu looked at the deadbolts punctuating the wood. *Nande kuso*? What the hell? Three fucking locks. He tried several keys before he found the right ones. Grunting more with exasperation than effort, Tatsu lifted Bana under the armpits and maneuvered him into a darkened vestibule before kicking the door shut. The loud slam jerked Bana from his stupor. He muttered about needing another drink and staggered up to the bar in the living room. He pulled out a bottle, unscrewed the cap and took long gulps.

"Mr. Bana, maybe you shouldn't drink any more." Tatsu reached for the bottle.

"Ish Bana ... jush Bana." He clutched the bottle to his chest with both hands and leaned forward with a sloppy, wet-mouthed grin. He hiccupped once then vomited over Tatsu's jacket.

"Shit." Tatsu jumped back to avoid the putrid mess as it landed on his chest.

"Opps. S'my bad." Bana's grin held no real apology. He weaved over to the couch, reaching it just as his brain lost communication with his muscles. With a grunt, he collapsed and dropped the bottle. Its amber contents soaked into the plush carpet. Bana rolled onto his side and fell asleep.

Tatsu yanked off his jacket, found the bathroom and scrubbed the foul mess off with soap and a towel. At least the old leather was waterproof.

On the couch, Bana swam up out of his alcoholic fog. He swore and squirmed, trying to remove his hip-length leather coat. Tatsu, trying to ignore the rank odor of a man who smelled like he picked up a drink more often than a bar of soap, pulled at one sleeve. Bana flailed his arms with an uncoordinated intensity, heaved his thick body backward and disentangled himself. With a grunt, he fell back onto the couch and passed out again.

Tatsu dropped the coat in surprise when he saw a pair of semi-automatic guns held snugly in a much-worn shoulder harness. What the hell? Was this guy insane? Firearms possession meant an immediate death penalty in any Quarantine.

Gingerly, Tatsu removed both weapons—the drunk might shoot him. The guns were beautiful, a matching pair of Beretta 93 R2Xs capable of firing three rounds in a single burst. Tatsu could tell by the weight that each magazine was full, a round chambered in the slide. With quick efficiency, he unloaded the guns and placed them on the coffee table.

Tatsu picked up Bana's coat and draped it over the couch arm. A cell phone dropped to the carpet. He snatched it up half-fearing it had broken. Why the hell bother with a cell phone? Damn things were almost useless in a city so plagued by atmospheric interference that transmission was erratic at best. None of his business if the man wasted his money. Tatsu tucked the instrument back into Bana's pocket.

Capping the fallen bottle, Tatsu placed it on the bar and began to worry about leaving. The unconscious man might vomit and choke. A thin, grey light showed through the flimsy curtains. Tatsu knew he should leave but fatigue dogged him. He sure wasn't looking forward to that two-mile hike home in the rain. A cup of coffee would help. Hell, he was owed that much.

Tatsu rummaged among the kitchen cupboards until he found a round, silver can. This guy had expensive taste. Real Arabica coffee cost the average worker a week's pay. Soon, the brew's nutty aroma filled the compact room.

Blowing on the hot coffee, Tatsu wandered back into the living room and eyed the plush recliner opposite the couch. Maybe he could stay until Bana woke up, ask him a few questions. Maybe not. Good chance when the drunk roused he'd mistake Tatsu for a burglar. A man who packed that kind of firepower seemed like the sort who would shoot first, ask questions of the corpse later.

Bana snored away, occasionally grunting and farting. Tatsu guessed Bana was in his mid-forties with a blocky physique. The man was handsome in a grizzled sort of way with swarthy skin, dark brows and a head of unruly, black curls dusted with grey. The Irishman's large nose, clearly broken at some point, showed tracings of blue veins. A two-day stubble covered his florid cheeks. Not Tatsu's type but still attractive.

Still asleep, the man smacked his lips and scrubbed his palm across his mouth. He scratched at his neck, dragging down his knit collar. The action drew Tatsu's attention to the four symmetrical puckers just right of the Adam's apple, the exact place where the jugular artery pulsed. Only one thing left those kinds of scars—a vampire.

Feeling rude for staring at an unconscious man, Tatsu looked around the living room. A Chinese-made sound system and a wall-mounted screen were hooked to a computer, all high-dollar equipment. However, the shelves packed with books surprised him. So, the drunk likes to read?

Sipping his coffee, Tatsu scanned the odd assortment of

titles. Books on vampirology, medicine and Irish history shared space with tattered manuals on weapons, tactical warfare and urban combat. Graphic novels from Japan—rare and expensive—were crammed into a shelf. With an odd nostalgia, Tatsu leafed through a couple. It had been years since he'd read a manga.

A tall, steel cabinet took up the balance of the wall, and the doors hung ajar. Compulsively tidy, Tatsu moved to close them. At least half-a-dozen guns, a vicious-looking bayonet and a row of serrated survival knives were racked above cleaning paraphernalia and dozens of boxes of ammunition.

Intrigued, Tatsu couldn't tear his gaze from those Berettas. He wondered about their owner now lying insensate on the couch. Bana was either seriously paranoid or seriously prepared for a war. And he clearly didn't give a shit for any gun-control laws. Black-market arms dealer? The idea was absurd. There were easier, less instant-death ways to make money in this city. With a quick flare of hope, Tatsu wondered if Bana was a covert vampire hunter. That would explain the mini-arsenal. Perhaps he was the source of information Tatsu so desperately needed.

Quietly, Tatsu closed the cabinet doors and fired a quick glance at the couch. Time to get the hell out before the dangerous drunk woke up and started shooting.

Three

After dragging Bana home, Tatsu was too wired to sleep. The rich coffee made him jumpy. He sat on his only chair and stared out the rain-drenched window of his shabby room. The first rays of dawn fought their way through the grey clouds. The gloomy view reminded him how far he was from the warmth of New Mexico, his home for the last thirteen years. He couldn't believe only a few weeks ago his life was normal, his dreams about to be realized.

And the word *vampire* only existed in the news about distant places.

An unassailable loneliness made itself known with gut-wrenching insistence. What the hell was he doing here anyway?

With no warning, the loss of his one and only love crashed over him. Sage Neztsosie, the beautiful Navajo boy who took his heart. Who showed him the way of loving men.

Salty drops slid over Tatsu's lower eyelids. Shamed, he dashed them away. Foolish to grieve over a love that was never meant to be. A love forever lost in the unreachable past.

Santa Fe, The Pueblo Sovereign State, 2012

Rumors flew through Santa Fe Industrial High about the school's newest quarterback, Sage Neztsosie. School directors, desperate for a star player, lured Sage off the Shiprock Reservation with promises and bribery. They overlooked his juvenile criminal record and granted him a full scholarship.

Nobody escaped falling under this beautiful, copper-skinned boy's spell. His mobile mouth showed blunt teeth that flashed often in a brilliant, disarming smile. High cheekbones and sultry eyes the color of dark chocolate gave his face an exquisite cast. A scar across his right eye only enhanced his bad-boy glamour. Guys wanted to be like him; girls dreamed of doing him.

From the minute he arrived, the Navajo created his own brand of anarchy. He sped into the school parking lot on his battered motorcycle with one of his many cousins clinging like a monkey on the back. Brakes squealed and people yelled as Sage blithely ignored all driving regulations. One afternoon, the principal caught the Navajo rappelling down the wall of the high-school stadium. Before the homecoming game, the janitor found Sage dancing naked in the football-field end zone. Sage claimed he was doing it for victory. More than once, he faced expulsion for smoking on school grounds. No matter how often he broke the rules, Sage always charmed his way out of punishment.

Tatsu's school life was the opposite; a living torment. He was the only twelve-year-old in the school. Newly arrived from Japan and in shock from the loss of his family, Tatsu was *bugaisha,* an outsider. His genius mind coupled with his polite, shy manners, guaranteed he was every bully's target. His exotic, pretty face meant the *faggot* slurs began on his first day. It took all his self-control to ignore the vicious taunting. Even when physically attacked, he refused to use martial arts to defend himself. His grandfather would be angry if Tatsu revealed the secret martial arts handed down through the generations of Tatsu's family. And disappointing *Ojii-san* was far worse than anything anyone else could inflict.

Alone and friendless, Tatsu joined the track team. Running gave him a sense of purpose and power. And running gave him that magical moment when Sage Neztsosie captured his heart.

On that astonishing afternoon, athletes, cheerleaders and teachers froze when the football coach's rage-filled bellow ripped across the field. Coach and Sage faced each other like two bristling pit bulls. The coach screamed at Sage about his long hair, called him a queer, a fag and ordered the Navajo to get a hair cut "like a *real* man."

Everyone froze, waiting for Sage to erupt and slam his fist into the coach's face. Instead, the Navajo's wide I-don't-give-a-shit grin spread across his face.

ETERNAL SAMURAI

"Maybe I'm a fag, maybe not. But I'm the best fucking quarterback you'll ever see." He undid his waist-length braid, and shook his head. The obsidian mane flared free in the wind.

In his thin running shoes and too-large training shorts, Tatsu stood on the track, completely transfixed by that single, breathtaking sight. In an instant, one flicker of time, Tatsu's heart was utterly and irrevocably captured.

All that year Tatsu worshipped from afar. He learned they had the same birthday. Every day as he walked to the track, his belly quivered. The kind of quiver guys get when they're about to do something embarrassing or crazy like kiss a girl. His heart thumped painfully in his narrow chest each time he caught a glimpse of the handsome senior.

Tatsu didn't know he was in love. His body rollercoastered with bewildering fears and yearnings that frightened and thrilled him at the same time. On the days Sage was absent, Tatsu's running times fell into the toilet. On the days he saw the Navajo, Tatsu's world glowed golden.

He didn't care that Sage was a boy. Tatsu just knew he yearned for the gorgeous Navajo with a sweet, painful intensity. He imagined Sage leaning down, pulling Tatsu into an embrace and pressing their lips together. He fantasized about those strong, brown, Indian hands sliding down his back to squeeze his small bottom. Tatsu awoke to morning erections and the mystery of white stains on his sheets.

For the rest of the year, Tatsu suffered the agony of his adoration. Then came the moment he left boyhood behind. That day he stood beneath the locker-room shower, lost in his naïve fantasy. With a sudden, almost painful blast, Tatsu's young-boy spunk spurted over the wet tile. Confused and embarrassed, he looked down at his throbbing, dripping prick and knew the truth of his feelings for the Navajo.

They only spoke once. On this unforgettable day, Carl, the sadistic leader of the worst school gang, stuffed Tatsu butt first into a trashcan. The gang jeered as Tatsu flailed angrily about.

"We don't like slanty-eyed Chinks around here." Carl drew a knife from under his sweatshirt.

Tatsu's defiant, "I'm Japanese," triggered a fresh wave of

sniggers and taunts. A sick helplessness washed over him as his thin arms pushed with impotent fury against the sharp rim. The boys crowded around, spewing their hate. Tatsu's feeble kicks at Carl's arm drew more heckling. Tatsu fought back tears of frustration, unable to tear his gaze away from that approaching knife tip.

"Why are you all such goddamn assholes?" came a low rumble. Startled, the four spun around. A mixture of relief and shame washed through Tatsu at the sight of that voice's owner.

Sage leaned against a scraggly mesquite tree. Dappled shadows played over his face, hiding any expression. With lazy grace, the Navajo struck a match against the trunk then set it to his cigarette. His hair fell forward when he took a deep drag. He blew the smoke out from his nostrils in wispy trails.

"Shit, if it isn't our redskin football hero. Gonna save the little Chink?" Carl brandished the knife toward Sage. "Come on, pretty boy. Let's see if you got the balls." The bully, jaw set with murderous belligerence, lumbered toward Sage. The jeering gang crowded behind. He stepped from beneath the tree into Carl's path.

Fascinated and horrified at the same moment, Tatsu watched Sage square his shoulders and crook one finger at the group. Everyone knew one more infraction of school rules would get Sage kicked off the football team. These boys were determined to make that happen.

"*Sumimasen*. Please. Don't. I'm not worth it." Tatsu's plea went unheeded.

Carl, waving the knife in wannabe badass moves, lumbered up to the Navajo. "I'm gonna cut your nose off, Injun. Then let's see how many cunts think you're so fucking pretty."

Sage looked up into Carl's beefy face then flicked the smoldering matchstick at him. It bounced off his cheek. With an enraged bellow, Carl lunged, sweeping the blade in a clumsy over-handed stab toward Sage. The Navajo faded sideways, grabbed Carl's wrist, stepped behind the bully's back and rotated the arm outward. The joint left its socket with a sickening *pop*. With a shriek of agony, Carl collapsed to his knees, the arm dangling at a grotesque angle.

"Dammit, you made me drop my smoke." Sage's mild expression belied the fury in his dark eyes.

Tatsu's warning drowned beneath the angry roars of the other three boys. They rushed Sage in a pummeling, pounding, kicking pile. One pinned Sage's arms while another punched his exposed midsection. The Navajo doubled over with a painful grunt. He continued folding, dropping to one knee. Thrown off balance, the grappler lost his hold. Sage curled sideways, and drove his fist upward into the youth's exposed groin. The kid shrieked, grabbed his nuts and stumbled back.

Before Sage gained his feet, the third boy aimed the toe of his boot at Sage's head. The Navajo caught the youth by his airborne foot, sprang up and flipped the kid backward over Carl still howling and rolling in the dirt.

"Goddamn squaw." The fourth boy grabbed Sage by the shoulder, spun him around and punched him straight in the mouth. The Navajo staggered a moment, scarlet spurting from his split lips.

"Who you calling a squaw, dickhead?" Before the bully replied, Sage's fists thudded, delivering four fast blows into his gut. Clutching his belly and gagging, the teenager stumbled backward and shook his head. Sage shot him a disgusted look, spat out a stream of blood and spit then turned toward Tatsu.

Horrified, Tatsu heard the snick of a switchblade. His cry stuck in his fear-parched throat as the blade flashed toward Sage's back. But the Navajo spun, his leg kicking up in a high sweep. His booted foot connected with the kid's temple. The youth's eyes rolled up and he dropped with a single grunt to the dust.

Sage picked up the knife, snapped it closed and shoved it into his pocket. "You touch him again, I'll kill you all." He spat again toward the groaning boys then walked toward Tatsu.

"*Atsilí*, little brother, seems you've got yourself in a mess." Sage grinned and lifted Tatsu out of the trashcan with unexpected gentleness as if taking a sleeping baby from its stroller.

Delight shivered through Tatsu's thin body at the hard grip of Sage's hands under his wet armpits. Heat fired through

Tatsu's loins at the rich odor of the Navajo's sweat mingled with the smell of leather and tobacco.

Tatsu's knees wobbled at Sage's proximity. Staring up in adoration at the battered, beautiful face, Tatsu mumbled, "*Domo arigatō gozaimasu.*"

Not understanding, Sage laughed and shook his head. By the time Tatsu recovered enough to repeat his thanks in English, Sage was already striding away, that thick braid bouncing against his butt.

Sage disappeared the day after graduation. Tatsu hid his heartbreak. The years saw him immersed in college life and his grandfather's constant teaching of *Bushido*. Days, months then years passed. Time ran through Tatsu's fingers, taking with it his hope of seeing the Navajo again.

For the next seven years, Tatsu accepted his heart belonged to a myth. Until that bittersweet day a few weeks past his nineteenth birthday when Tatsu buried *Ojii-san.*

And the day Sage walked back into Tatsu's life.

Santa Fe dedicated the entire month of December to the Yuletide Festival. Ray Cobb, Tatsu's uncle, always embraced the holiday with gusto. His enthusiasm and delight over the pageantry, the music and the earnest gestures of goodwill, drew Tatsu and *Ojii-san* into the celebration despite their reserved upbringing. The house filled with the rich smells of Mexican, American and Japanese food, the laughter and crude jokes of Ray's friends and the sense of home and family. Their crazy mixture of cultures formed an international celebration that culminated with a day of feasting and sharing gifts.

And on that day, amid the pleasant turmoil, *Ojii-san* lay down for an afternoon nap and never woke. His ninety-five-year-old heart said, "enough," and stopped.

Three days later, Ray and Tatsu built a tiny shrine in the corner of the garden under the willow tree. Tatsu carved *Ojii-san's* full name in kanji on a wooden *sotoba* and drove it into the ground with savage grief. At *uma no kuku,* the hour of horse, they buried Shiniichiro Kurosaki's urn.

Dressed in white *hakama* and *keiko-gi,* Tatsu knelt on the snow-dusted ground. Grandfather's swords rested on his right side, their hilts pointing toward the shrine. Wisps of smoke from three sticks of incense in a prayer bowl carried the fragrance of sandalwood into the air. Tatsu placed the third and last oval stone before the brick *jinja* that housed the urn. He wrote his farewell prayer on a *fuda*, and tucked the rice-paper scroll beneath that last rock.

Unable to comfort the boy, Ray squeezed Tatsu's shoulder once before going into the house.

Tatsu knelt for hours, letting the sorrow take him. Tears slid unheeded down his cheeks, and numbness seeped into his legs from the near-frozen ground. Far away, noises of celebration mocked his anguish. He moved inside himself, sought his center, his *tanden*; wanting to hide there forever.

But *that* presence, that energy, that ineffable feeling of *him* reached Tatsu through his grief. Called to him. Mistrustful of his own senses, Tatsu rose on legs that trembled with hope and excitement. He turned and stared in mute disbelief.

Sage Neztsosie leaned against the wall. The dusky rays of the fading sun caught him, turning him glorious and bronze. He was the desert—flowing obsidian hair, burnished-copper skin and deep cinnamon eyes. In two long strides, the Navajo closed the space between them. He cupped the back of Tatsu's neck and rolled a thumb in light swirls beneath the hair at the nape of his neck. Comfort and understanding spread like a warm blanket from that hand.

"Your *shi'nali* has gone to the ancestors like a true warrior." Sage called Shiniichiro "grandfather" in the language of the People.

Absurdly, in this time of pain, Tatsu realized they were the same height. He stammered his thanks then fell silent and shy before that dark gaze.

"You've grown up, *Atsilí*. Couple of days, I'll come visit. We'll catch up. Okay?"

The grief that clutched Tatsu's heart softened as he looked once again into that beautiful, nutmeg face. "*Hai, hai,* I'll be waiting." He felt no shame when his voice cracked.

Amid the *pop-pop-pop* of a disgruntled engine, Sage pulled

into the driveway two mornings later. He climbed out of the battered pickup and leaned against the rusted fender. Beneath his shabby sheepskin jacket, Sage's tight black tee outlined the hard bulges of his chest. His hands, thrust into the back pockets of his indigo jeans, stretched the fabric over his magnificent crotch.

Awed by the raw beauty of the man waiting, Tatsu's heart pounded into his throat. Sweat prickled over his skin. Shyness took his voice. He felt like a teenager on his first date. Shit, this *was* his first date. School and his devotion to martial arts were his reasons to avoid giving himself to anyone. Now he knew, he'd been waiting for Sage.

"Hello. That your truck?" Tatsu felt the blush creep over his cheeks at the nervous squeak in his own voice.

Sage nodded while his gaze did a slow burn up Tatsu's body and lingered for a noticeable moment on his groin before stopping eye-to-eye. "Shit, *Atsilí*. All grown up and still blushing. Makes you the prettiest thing I've ever seen." Sage's voice rolled out like honey—deep, thick, warm. "Get in. Wanna take you for a drive."

Mouth bone dry, heart hammering, Tatsu climbed into the passenger seat. "Where are we going?"

"The rez. Want to show you someplace special." Sage winked. "Or maybe I'm just gonna kidnap you."

The wild fluttering through Tatsu's belly told him kidnapping wouldn't be a bad thing. Excitement turned his brain to mush and his mouth sand dry. Tatsu watched the town roll by until they reached the highway to the reservation.

"So, you're goin' to the U. now? What for?"

"I finished my Master's last May. I've been accepted for a doctorate program as soon as I finish my year of Border watch."

"You gonna work in the hospital?"

"Not a medical doctor. A Ph.D. In bio-engineering. There are so many things I want to do. Technology is improving constantly. The other day I read that...." Nervous to be sitting this close to his heart's dream, Tatsu stalled out.

"A Pee Haich Dee." Sage dragged out each letter with a

long pause between. "From what I hear, you gotta be pretty smart to get one of those. Hell, Ninja Boy, you're only nineteen and you're doing all that? I always knew you were a fucking genius. Those assholes that used to beat you up, called you shit names, they're nothing now. Maybe workin' in grocery stores, bars. A few in prison."

Tatsu squirmed under the profuse admiration, not sure how to accept it. "How have you been?"

Sage drove his stare through the cracked windshield. "I'm good. Life's good."

Suddenly, Tatsu knew it for a lie. Those deep lines around Sage's eyes and the way the muscles of his jaw jumped every now and then told Tatsu the Navajo was far from "good." But the question stilled on Tatsu's tongue. Sage would explain if he wanted to.

"How did you know my grandfather died?"

The truck veered slightly as Sage stared at him. "I had a vision." He burst into laughter. "Oh, *Atsilí*, you should have seen your face. My cousin told me. I keep an eye on the folks I care about."

Care about. Those two words sent an electric surge of want lancing through Tatsu's belly. He stole a glance at the Navajo, knew Sage also felt it, that core-deep desire that could only be satisfied one way. The need for it vibrated between them, expanded until it filled the dusty cab of the truck. Tatsu knew what he craved and knew Sage wanted it, too.

With a squeal of needy brakes, Sage skidded to a halt in a clearing among the scrubby mesquite. He shouldered a couple of plaid, wool blankets and two full, leather botas. "C'mon," he growled and strode into the brush. Tatsu followed with no question. Hell, he would have followed Sage anywhere.

Overhead, the New Mexico sky blazed the dazzling turquoise seen only in the desert. The pale sun warmed their bodies. Little puffs of dust from the winter-dry ground exploded from under their booted feet as they followed the winding trail.

Hours past, but Tatsu really didn't care. His hungry gaze remained fastened on the bunch and roll of Sage's butt beneath the worn denim. The sight sent want shivering deep within Tatsu's sex. His skin hummed with anticipation. He grew hard.

The path widened enough to allow them to walk abreast. "How are you holding up, *Atsili?*" Sage playfully bumped his shoulder against Tatsu.

"I'm fine now Sage," Tatsu replied. Better than fine, he was walking and talking with Sage Neztsosie. A happiness he hadn't known for years filled his heart.

"I've missed you, little Ninja Boy." Sage held a match to one of his homemade cigarettes. He inhaled deeply as he shook the flame out. "I don't give a shit what the *dibeh* thought; what they said." Sage always called outsiders *dibeh*—sheep. Only now Tatsu knew the word was used for those who reviled their type of love. "There were things I wanted to say to you but you were so young then. You know that now?"

"*Wakarimashita*, I understand."

"Good. 'Cause we're here." Sage pushed through a clump of creosote into a clearing. He indicated a makeshift hogan made from old wooden planks, canvas and tree branches. He lifted the ragged cloth door and crawled inside. A stone firepit sat in the center surrounded by piles of dusty, home-woven rugs. Sage squatted and lit the twigs. Smoke, redolent with the oil of mesquite, filled the tent. He added several round rocks inside the small fire. Then he stripped, casting his clothes aside until he stood bare-assed naked.

A pulsing heat spread through Tatsu, sending blood pounding straight into his prick. Before him stood this living sculpture of hard male flesh, the one who had filled every single one of his boy-love fantasies. Suddenly shy and embarrassed, Tatsu looked down at Sage's feet. They were long and broad, the toenails chipped and slightly dirty. Tatsu's gaze moved up the curves of the muscular calves and thighs to Sage's loins and froze. The globes of Sage's heavy sac dangled between his slightly furred thighs. The uncut cock hung semi-soft and long, the dark-pink crown pushing out from the wrinkled foreskin.

Sage tossed Tatsu one of the wool blankets. "Strip. Wrap yourself in that, it's gonna get real cold." He handed over a waterskin. "Drink only a little. Let your body feel thirst."

Tatsu shucked his jacket with feverish clumsiness. Boots next, tugged off with awkward, hopping pulls, then tossed into a far corner. He jerked off his socks. Shirt next. Ignored the couple of buttons that popped off and spun into the dark. His hands shook so much he thought he'd never get his jeans undone. The rustle of fabric as he slid the denim down his thighs was deeply intimate. He blushed as his hard-on slapped his belly when he slipped off his briefs.

"Not right now, *Atsili*, although I sure do admire what's offered." Sage winked. The promise in that wink shot Tatsu's heart halfway up his throat.

They sat facing each other, legs crossed Indian style. Tatsu draped the musty blanket over his trembling shoulders. He didn't know if he shook from the cold or his arousal.

Sage leaned over and touched Tatsu's right pec. "Different kinda tattoo. Complicated."

"It is the Kurosaki *mons*, my family crest. I got it last year in honor of the sacrifice *Ojii-san* made when he left Japan for me." Tatsu reached out, quivering fingers not quite brushing the long, angry line that ran up Sage's ribcage. Another ugly pucker of tissue arched over the Indian's right hip.

"What happened?" Tatsu's cheeks dusted warm at his boldness.

Sage's lips twitched up in a brief smile. "They're nothing. Just a little disagreement with a couple of unpleasant *dibeh*." He poured water on the rocks nestled in the fire. Immediately, the tiny shelter filled with steam and heat.

"Close your eyes. Just listen." He sat Indian-style across from Tatsu and started a rhythm on a small drum. His warm baritone rolled from his tongue, a chant in the language of the People. The notes rose and fell with each breath. The drumbeat matched the beat of their hearts.

Sweat ran down Tatsu's face, his chest, belly, under his balls and soaked the blanket beneath his ass. His body throbbed part in response to the rhythm of the drum, part with the constant awareness of Sage's raw sexuality. He closed his eyes as much to relax as to stop staring at those dark genitals—

large and pliant—between the Navajo's spread legs. The hours passed marked only by the occasional hiss of water on the coals, the hypnotic measure of the drum, the cadence of Sage's song. All led Tatsu into a deep, hypnotic state.

They walked through the brush again. Sage's calloused hand held his. "You are mine," that firm grip said.

Tatsu tilted his face toward that handsome nutmeg face and smiled to affirm Sage's possession. With the suddenness of a desert cloudburst, huge drops plastered Tatsu's hair to his head and slashed down his cheeks. Water slid chilly and ran in clammy rivulets under his shirt collar. He looked up into the brilliant azure sky of a New Mexico summer.

"Sage there're no clouds. Where's the rain coming from?"

"Inside your heart, *Atsilí*. Inside your heart." Sage stopped walking and pointed. "This is the place. Look over there."

Ojii-san stood beneath the spreading branches of a cherry tree, the color of its blossoms so intense they appeared purple. Strangely, winter snow lay thick on the ground and icicles hung from the bare branches of the nearby trees. In the distance, the multiple-peaked roofs of a majestic castle rose to touch an azure sky.

The old man was clad in a silk *kamishimo*—the perfect pleats of the hakama falling to just above his clad feet. Over this, he wore a wide-shouldered, sleeveless coat dyed in the burgundy and gold colors of the Kurosaki clan.

He watched his grandson approach. His ancient, wrinkled face remained stoic. Still, his eyes lit up when Tatsu showed his utmost respect by offering a waist-deep bow.

"*Konnichiwa, Ojii-san.*"

"*Konnichiwa, magomusuko.* Good day, grandson." The old man proffered his two swords. "These have been in the Kurosaki for five centuries. They are now yours. Use them only with honor, Tatsu-kun." Without another word, he turned his back and walked with the bold stride of a young man toward the castle.

Too late, Tatsu opened his mouth to call his grandfather back, but managed only an inarticulate croak. Sage's hard grip on Tatsu's arm turned him away. "The rest is not for you to see." The Navajo led them back to the mist-shrouded trail.

Tatsu opened his eyes and blinked at the dawn light filtering between the cracks of the hogan. Peace filled him. His grief quieted with the acceptance that *Ojii-san's* spirit rested in Tatsu.

The shelter reeked of the pungent tang of sweat and wood smoke. Tatsu's full bladder yelled at him its need to piss. His morning erection said something else.

With a noisy yawn, Sage sat up and stretched his arms up and wide, showing the wisps of dark hair under his pits. He unbound his braid and finger-combed out the tangles. An incredible eroticism and promise charged the simple gesture, turning it into pure seduction.

Lust went straight from Tatsu's brain to his cock. Desire warred with fear. In a panic, he mumbled, "gotta piss," and scrambled outside. Even after he relieved himself, his prick stayed hard.

"Shit, it's freezing out there." He pulled aside the door flap and stepped into the slight warmth of the hogan. His bobbing erection led the way.

"Better get dressed then." But Sage's burnished eyes smoldered as they riveted on Tatsu's hard rod jutting from the juncture of groin and thigh. Sage licked his lips. His wide, brown member stood up between his hips. "Or maybe we could keep each other warm." His words rolled out thick with want.

Tatsu longed to run his tongue over those taut cheekbones and bite those brown lips that promised so much. His sweet, secret need denied too long boiled through him. The dam of pent-up arousal burst. He whispered his plea.

Sage dove on him. Corded arms wrapped tight, hard body pressing, a tangle of legs as the Navajo bore them down onto the dirt-scabbed blankets.

"Do you know how long I've waited for that sweet ass of yours?" Sage's hot tongue, tasting faintly of cigarettes, stroked along Tatsu's lips, demanding and gaining entrance. Knowing fingers slid over Tatsu's chest, plucked at his exposed nipples, thrust between his thighs to the treasures between. A strong hand, scratchy with calluses, cupped his balls, caressed the smooth skin behind. Stroked up the length of Tatsu's prick.

Oh, the bliss of that first intimate male touch. With long-suppressed urgency, Tatsu clawed his arms around Sage's waist and pulled them together. Heated skin seared heated skin as Tatsu ground against Sage with the urgency born of unrealized fantasies and first love.

"You ever had a man before?" the Navajo asked in a voice gone smoky with desire.

"No. I've never... just couldn't if it wasn't you."

Sage's eyes widened. "Never? You're a...? Oh, *Atsilí,* I won't hurt you."

That simple promise shattered Tatsu's aching loneliness.

They surged together, mouths and limbs locked. Hungrily, they explored the deep recesses of the other. Flesh molded to flesh, cocks and nipples rubbing and rubbing together. Their tongues lapped each other's secret essence. Frantic hands danced back and forth exploring, teasing, grappling, gouging, learning every ridge and surface.

Sage's solid length rubbed against Tatsu's own pulsing prick. Breath that blew hot and cold passed over his skin, and a tongue trailed down his neck in a warm, claiming gesture; planting soft kisses over his heaving chest down to the begging peaks of his nipples.

A wildness suffused Tatsu. This was all for him! Just as he dreamed so often, he tangled his fingers in Sage's thick mane, urging that clever tongue to lap again and again over his engorged points each its own pebbled universe of delight.

Sparks danced over Tatsu's skin as long licks and kisses trailed down his clenched abdomen, teeth and lips combed through the dark nest around his prick. A demanding hand pushed between his trembling thighs, possessively fondled his sac, tugging hard before moving back up to squeeze his taut buttocks. Calloused and scratchy fingers curled around Tatsu's dick. Sage's thumb rolled over the slicked piss slit, spread the juice over the engorged head. The touched dragged a desperate groan from Tatsu's throat.

"Please, I want you in my ass." Tatsu hardly believed the desperation in the words tumbling out of his own mouth.

"First, let me play a little. Get you all juiced up. Then I'm gonna fuck your pretty hole until you can't stand." The Navajo kneed Tatsu's trembling legs apart. Gazed down at those vulnerable, enticing genitals. "So fucking beautiful," Sage breathed and curled his palm around Tatsu's cock.

Strong, workworn fingers teased down Tatsu's shaft, brushed lightly over his balls and lingered on that taut sensitive stretch behind. Then Tatsu's world exploded as a hot tongue took that first light lick over his cockhead. The wet velvet surface traveled up and down his swollen organ, lapped along the pulsing vein underneath, danced in circles over the ridge below his throbbing crown. Swift licks teased the slit. Stretched lips slid all the way down to the root as Sage, in one powerful gulp, took Tatsu all the way down.

Tatsu's head reared back as that wet heat enveloped him in a maelstrom of sensation. The exquisite suction of that burning mouth sent his hips jerking in hungry response. He arched off the blanket, driving himself deeply into Sage's throat. Fire and ice shivered over his skin. His cock hardened almost to the verge of pain. His balls threatened to blast their load with the next suck.

Cold air and disappointment hit Tatsu at the same moment as that mouth pulled off. Sage clamped his fingers tight around the base of Tatsu's prick. "Don't stop, please, don't stop," he cried. For so long, so freaking long, he'd dreamed of this. Even a moment's delay felt like an eternity.

"Ain't gonna let you come yet, little Ninja boy. Now, get that pretty ass in the air."

Tatsu flipped over onto his knees. He buried his face in the musty blanket that reeked with the vinegary scent of old sweat and horse dung. He didn't care. A breathy laugh of delight shivered against Tatsu's neck as Sage's warm weight settled against him. Silken hair fell in an obsidian waterfall around them, its tickle following the blazing trail of Sage's tongue down Tatsu's knobby spine to his crack.

"God, you've got a fucking gorgeous ass," Sage murmured

against the blush heating Tatsu's rump. The words vibrated through soft suctions over both cheeks. Kisses accompanied by nips, even a couple of painful bites made Tatsu jump with surprised pleasure.

"You like that? Good." Sage's honey-thick voice held dark, secret promises. His hands on Tatsu's buttocks—featherlight caresses, hard squeezes—sent shockwaves over his body. A gentle tugging on his balls, then an insistent pull as thumbs spread his crease. Brushes of heated breath travelled, deliberate and slow, down his crack. Then that slick, shiver-causing press of Sage's tongue, working deep into Tatsu's crease. Lapped and rolled around Tatsu's hole, slurping and tasting.

Tatsu quivered with want but his muscle remained clenched. He heard a quick spit followed by a gentle caress of slick fingers. The touch fired a wild frission that exploded from Tatsu's pucker through his balls, his cock his belly.

Sage teased and tapped over that resisting muscle until it pulsed with need and finally softened. "Ready?" He didn't wait for a reply, just pushed in his forefinger to the knuckle.

Tatsu gasped at the abrupt fullness; the unexpected burn. He fought the convulsion of his body trying to reject the foreign assault. A second finger vibrated in. Then a third, forming a wedge that curled against his walls, firing sparks deep into his gut. The first brush across the sweet spot deep within his core sent quivers of delight through his belly. Sage's fingers curled, brushed, twisted over Tatsu's prostate. The pulsing waves of pleasure consumed him and obliterated the last vestiges of pain and fear.

"*Dozo, dozo*, please." Tatsu clawed at the filthy blanket.

The Indian laughed with pure delight. "Sweet boy, don't have to ask me twice."

A muscular, sun-browned arm wrapped around Tatsu's sweat-slicked waist. Scalding skin pressed against his back. He felt a momentary chill as Sage's fingers slipped out. Then the hot, swollen head of the Navajo's cock pressed against Tatsu's quivering pucker, nudged hard and popped past the first ring. Sage stilled a moment then, in one powerful surge, the entire length of that cock drove into Tatsu's scalding core.

Oh, Gods, it was huge! It hurt; a deep ripping, tearing invasion of his vitals. Tatsu clenched his jaw against the painful stretching of his entrails, suppressed the urge to push out that strange fullness invading his guts. He didn't care. Sage's dick was buried in Tatsu's ass, and no matter what, he intended to keep it there until they blasted over that edge.

Sage smoothed his hand over Tatsu's chest, flickered his fingers over Tatsu's nipple. With each caress over those erect buds, Sage rocked his hips, his cock ploughing into Tatsu's sweet, virginal ass.

"Oh, Jesus, *atsili*, you're so fucking tight, so hot," Sage gasped. "If I move, I won't be able to stop."

"Waited. For. You." Tatsu panted, hiking back onto Sage's cock with every word. "Move!"

Sage moved. That thick rod burned as it pulled almost all the way out, then dug back in. In an instant, the pain dissolved into a sweet flame that burned all the way up Tatsu's spine. Then, Sage's cockhead stroked against Tatsu's prostate.

An indescribable burst of heat rocketed through Tatsu's entrails. Psychedelic lights danced beneath his tightly squeezed eyelids. Wicked fire sizzled over his body, coiled in his balls and burned across his lips.

Tatsu's throbbing prick, so close to its release, screamed for touch. He groped beneath his belly, reaching for his aching rod. Sage's iron grip jerked Tatsu's hand away.

"Wait, *Atsili*. I'm gonna make you scream when you come." Pleasure followed the burn when Sage eased out of Tatsu's core. A quick flip and his trembling legs rested on Sage's broad shoulders. His momentary disappointment at the loss of that cock inside him fled at the warm licks of Sage's mouth. Lips pressed hot, needy kisses Tatsu's quaking thighs and nibbled over his tightening sac and delivered several throat-deep sucks to his cock, leaving it dripping with saliva and precum.

"Oh *kuso*, Please Sage, fuck me. I can't wait any longer."

Sage's breath blew out in total astonishment. "Anything...anything for you" Sage rolled the head of his prick against Tatsu's brown, puckered hole, leaving a sticky trail over the pulsing muscle. With just a whispered, "ready?" Sage nudged in his first inch then the next, pushing slow and steady until his balls bumped against Tatsu's ass. A final hard thrust and Sage took Tatsu's virginity and his heart.

Tatsu bit his lip trying to stifle his cry against the excruciating pain. Fought not to expel that tree-thick fullness. The Navajo pulled out, his dragging exit stretching Tatsu in a delicious new way.

"Okay, *Atsilí?*" He bumped his cockhead, pushed it just inside the first ridge of muscle. Felt it relax and accept him.

"Fuck, yes. Do it now!" Tatsu curled fingers into the filthy blanket, and pushed against the Navajo's groin.

And Sage responded, rearing up, driving in; twisting and grinding.

Tatsu rocked against the pistoning body and gave himself in the shocking pain-pleasure of that invasion. He heard himself babbling, "*Fakku, fakku.*" Begging for the entire length of that wonderful, fat, Navajo cock.

Sage took Tatsu's prick, pumping it with merciless insistence from root to head in time to every pounding thrust into his chute. "Come for me, pretty Ninja Boy," he panted in a voice turned gravelly with sex and want.

That command fired sheet lightning from Tatsu's balls, through his pucker and out his cock. The climbing chill in his ass turned into blazing heat when Sage's wide crown rubbed over Tatsu's prostate.

Digging into the corded muscles of Sage's biceps, Tatsu arched up. He squeezed his ass around the Navajo's rod, and bucked with an erratic fury into Sage's hand.

"*Iku, iku!* I'm coming!" His orgasm ripped through him, taking him into a new, wild high. Spirals of glistening spunk spewed into Sage's palm and spilled through clenched fingers onto Tatsu's belly.

Sage slammed one final time into Tatsu's center. The Navajo's body froze for a moment. Then, his nuts emptied their load, driving his spunk out of his cock in pulses of pure, scalding heat.

"*Atsilí!*"

That cry shattered Tatsu's heart. He looked up at his copper-skinned lover, saw the eyes flaring with a wild radiance, the contorted face fiercely beautiful in its carnal pleasure. Sage flung his head back. His shining, black mane fanned the air like the wings of a great, obsidian bird. He was primal, untamed, gloriously savage as he poured himself into Tatsu's accepting core.

Spent, but not sated, they sprawled together, watching the smoke drift up through the hole in the roof. Sage dragged a blanket over their bodies, caked with dry sweat and sticky with cum. Lassitude, warm and heavy, spread through Tatsu. His ass throbbed with a delicious ache. His heart filled with a beautiful sense of the rightness of it all.
"Are you staying in Santa Fe?" Tatsu cringed at the grating need of his entreaty.
Sage propped himself onto one elbow and pecked Tatsu on the nose. "Maybe. For a while." Those mahogany eyes held no real answer. Sage rose and began dressing. "Come on, we'd better get back. Your uncle'll be worried."
For six days, they went crazy with each other. Sage took what he wanted, and Tatsu took what he needed. They fucked hard in messy and painfully glorious joinings. Tatsu complained of a sore ass from the Navajo's pounding dick. Sage merely grinned, told him to get his ass in the air and then rimmed Tatsu's hole until his spunk spilled over and over and his body had no more to give.
Tatsu had no words for his first taste of Sage's cock, that heavy weight, that rich male musk, the way the silky skin moved over the iron rod within. The taste of salty-sweet cum filling Tatsu's mouth and spurted down his throat. He loved that prick, taking it into his mouth and eager hole at every opportunity.
Late one night, frantic for reassurance, Tatsu rode his lover in the cramped cab of the truck while parked in the shadow of a store. A storm of desperation, touching the edge of insanity, gripped Tatsu. He drove his ass down so hard on the Navajo's cock that Sage joked they were going to break the shocks. "Just

like breaking the rules in high school," Sage panted afterwards.

Tatsu sprawled spent and sober against his lover's heaving chest. He whispered, "*Aishite imasu,*" too afraid to state his love in English, certain he'd never hear Sage say those words back in any language. Tatsu was right.

Four days later, it ended. Tatsu found Sage's Drifter parked in Ray's driveway with a note taped to its chipped tank.

"Atsilí, *we walk separate paths. Another waits for you. The bike is so you won't forget me.*" It was unsigned.

Oh, Sage, why? Pain—for his family, for *Ojii-san,* for Sage—sliced into Tatsu as surely as if he'd stabbed himself with his razor-sharp *tanto*. He clung to the cold steel of those handlebars, bit through his lip and suppressed the sob tearing its way up his throat.

"*Wakarimashita.*" He told himself he understood. But he really didn't.

Five years gone, those few precious days with Sage. Tatsu's hungry body had taken what Sage had offered. Time, not love, was their real enemy.

Staring out the grimy, bleak window over the alien Seattle skyline, Tatsu berated himself for his weakness knowing how foolish it was to grieve over a love that was never meant to be. His destiny lay along one path, *fukushū*. He would allow nothing else.

Four

The Seattle Quarantine, 2024

A clinging fog rolled off Elliot Bay the next night when Tatsu returned to the Educated Whore, determined to find the Irishman—the very armed and dangerous Irishman. A man like that only survived by knowing about every threat around him. And that meant vampires. Tatsu hoped Bana remembered his savior from the night before, and gambled that the Irishman felt somewhat grateful for his safe escort home. Even more grateful that his "good Samaritan" hadn't robbed him blind.

Tatsu entered the bar just in time to spot the Irishman ducking out the rear exit. Tatsu's, "Hey, Bana," drowned beneath the sudden blast of music. He darted across the floor, muttering his apologies as he shouldered aside customers who yelled their outrage. The steel door nearly broke Tatsu's nose as he slammed through it and stepped into total chaos.

A huge bull vampire held Bana aloft in a chokehold. The Irishman's fingers clawed at the tree trunk of an arm wrapped around his neck. Bana's eyes bulged from his florid, oxygen-starved face. With a growl, the vampire hoisted the Irishman farther off the pavement. Bana's legs flailed with futile desperation. A smaller vampire clung to the Irishman's thrashing legs. Bana's boot slammed into the creature's stomach sending him reeling into two more vampires, one Japanese, circling the struggling pair.

Tatsu whipped out both swords in mid-flight as he leaped over the railing to the alley below. At his war cry, the third vampire spun toward him and aimed a gun. Tatsu danced forward and sliced his *katana* downward through the bloodsucker's shoulder. A scream of agony bounced around in the narrow alley. The weapon fell from the nerveless fingers as the limb flopped to the ground. The creature staggered backward, clutching his truncated limb. Instantly, Tatsu whipped his shorter *wakizashi* across the vampire's torso, opening clothing, skin and viscera. Raw, steaming guts spilled out. Tatsu spared no glance for his eviscerated foe but whipped around to face the second attacker.

A Japanese vampire screamed a battle cry in *Kyotsugo* and charged. Two-handed, he sliced his *katana* diagonally across Tatsu's torso. The blade missed by a millimeter as with an imperceptible shift of his weight, Tatsu rolled into a half-crouch. He drove his *katana* upward. The creature faltered, eyes bulging in shock as Tatsu's sword slid between its ribs into his heart. Tatsu stood, pulling the blade free with a wet *pop*. The vampire staggered face first into the side of a rusted dumpster where he slid to the ground and lay twitching.

Distracted by the sounds of the fight, the large bull loosed his chokehold on Bana. The shorter bull lost his grip on Bana's flailing legs. With raw desperation, the Irishman twisted his head for air, jackknifed both knees to his chest and kicked out. His booted feet caught the short vampire in the solar plexus, hurling him backward. Tatsu sliced once with his *wakizashi*. The vampire's head bounced against the brick wall as the body toppled into its own scarlet pool, spreading across the alley floor.

Tatsu leaped over the corpse toward Bana just as the huge bull slammed the Irishman's head into the bricks. Bana's eyes rolled up and his arms fell limp. With a wet growl, the vampire jerked Bana's head sideways, and sank razor-sharp fangs into the taut skin above the collarbone. The pain woke Bana. Roaring with outrage, he bucked against the heavy body. One fist pounded against the vampire's nose, crushing it. Even as blood poured down his chin, the vampire ignored his injury.

"Fekkin' bastard," Bana screamed. His hand scrabbled beneath his jacket.

The blast of gunfire echoed loud and rude. The vampire reeled back, arms flailing, a look of disbelief on his face. Smoke and blood coiled from his chest. Bana freed the gun from under the jacket and fired again. The crown of the vampire's

ETERNAL SAMURAI

head disintegrated in a flaming ball. Cooked bone fragments and brain tissue sprayed into the night air. Slack-limbed, the corpse dropped to its knees then toppled over with an odd, hollow expulsion of wind.

The air reeked of cooked meat, blood, shit and the thick choke of gunpowder. Bana leaned against the moss-covered wall, eyes closed, lungs pumping in great, ragged gasps.

"Jaysus fekkin' Christ," he said several times like a mantra. After a minute, he pushed himself off the moldy brick. He poked his finger through the smoldering hole in his jacket. "Shite. Fekkin' rogues." Fingering his damaged coat, he walked over to Tatsu, grabbed him by one shoulder in a painful grip and spun him so they faced each other.

"Thanks, boyo. Thought they were gonna have me clackers fer dinner. Shite, what a stench. Now, do yerself a favor. Git the holy hell out of here."

Tatsu jerked away and pinned the Irishman with pitiless stare. "I just saved your life. You owe me."

"Yer making a mistake, boyo. Don't owe ya shite. Now I'm telling you, jist go into the bar, get a drink on me. Fergit all this." With a dismissive snort, only half-convincing, Bana shoved his gun beneath his jacket and pulled out a cell phone. He muttered into it; secret words for a secret act.

Tatsu looked over the carnage as he waited for the adrenalin rush of battle to drain from his muscles. He toed the nearest corpse, regarded the rictus on the face, the snarling lips turned rubbery and brown, the crimson eyes already fading into a mottled yellow-brown and the fangs—uppers longer than lower—holding the mouth agape.

A rivulet of crimson slid down one of Tatsu's blades and plopped onto the pavement, drawing his attention to it. He flicked blood from both swords before swiping the *wakizashi* on the nearest corpse. He sheathed it and bent over to clean the *katana*.

Standing immobile within the deep shadows of the alley, a slim, pale figure watched the fight with avid interest. The observer ignored the older man. Instead, his golden eyes fastened on the youth who killed three *kyūketsuki* in mere minutes. The watcher's breath caught in his throat.

"*Niten'ichi,* the Way of Two Swords," Saito Arisada whispered in awe. This hunter, this impossibly young hunter, fought in the style of Miyamoto Musashi, Japan's most revered *kensei,* sword saint. In more than five centuries since the great swordsman's death, Arisada had seen no fighter use this technique with anything approaching perfection. Until now.

Arisada's gaze devoured the young man. He feasted on the sight of the long, lithe legs and the hard mounds of the youth's buttocks moving in tight denim jeans. Arisada took in the hunter's delicate, perfect face, the high cheekbones, thin nose, the sensuous bow of full lips above a strong, slightly cleft chin and shaggy, chocolate-brown hair falling just above the collar of a leather motorcycle jacket. A defiant gold ring glittered from the lobe of his left ear. Defiant because men wore no jewelry in these times.

For the first time in centuries, the vampire's body burned with a scalding lust.

Then Arisada lost his breath at the sight of the boy's eyes. From their emerald depths shone the *tamashii,* the soul of Koji Nowaki. Deep anguish filled Arisada's golden eyes. He'd found his *koibito,* his beloved, his betrayer, reincarnated in the body of this beautiful boy.

Tragic the young man had to die. Even more tragic, Arisada would be the one to take his sweet, young life. An odd, strangled cry escaped the vampire's throat.

In that second, the fifth rogue, insane with bloodlust, attacked the young hunter from the shadows of a doorway.

Tatsu spun. Too late. Four fangs drove into his nape. He roared, arched his back and struggled to twist the *katana* backward into the monster. But the blade caught on the rogue's bulky overcoat. Tatsu reached over his shoulder, clawing for the *wakizashi,* but it was trapped between their bodies.

At any moment, those fangs would rip his spine in two. With a roar of desperation, Tatsu clawed at the vampire's head trying to gouge out an eye, tear off an ear, anything to pull that mouth from his neck. No good.

Then the weight fell away from his back. He spun around and saw a man brandishing a bloody *tanto* in one hand and holding the struggling rogue by the hair with the other. With one incredibly swift slice, the stranger cut the vampire's throat, avoiding the blood gushing from the corpse with a graceful step back.

The man wore a black *keiko*-gi and flowing *hakama* that fell in perfect folds from his narrow waist. A pair of split-toed *tabi* hid the small feet. A *katana* rested beneath his wide *obi*.

Tatsu was riveted by the beauty of his rescuer's face. Sensual, full lips that Tatsu wanted to kiss with a sudden, irrational passion. Above that mouth was a regal, straight nose with nostrils slightly flared. High cheekbones, the left marked by an odd scar, accentuated the face. What should've been a disfigurement only added an exotic allure. A trick of shadow hid the eyes, yet Tatsu mentally colored them a rich, chocolate brown. A face with that exquisite blend of the strength seen in the finest *katana* tempered by the delicacy of a sakura blossom.

"Who—?" The press of the man's mouth—warm and demanding—cut off Tatsu's question. He opened to those lips, felt the slide of a wet tongue, the taste alien at first then turning achingly familiar. An accepting moan slipped from his throat. Every cell in his body resonated with an inexplicable call to this man. Tatsu's heart, already pounding from the fight, dove straight down into his groin. He hardened so fast he hurt.

Those warm lips moved again, a briefer kiss filled with the sense of discovery and promise in the fleeting touch. Then, as suddenly as it began, it was gone. Tatsu opened his eyes and found he was alone, body pulsing with want, cock hard beneath his jock. Shit, had his adrenalin rush scrambled his mind? He turned to ask Bana if he'd seen the stranger, and saw with dismay the man was still talking on cell phone.

"You are *kurutteiru*." Tatsu called himself all kinds of crazy. Flustered, he snapped his *katana* into its *saya* and stepped toward Bana, who looked up in surprised confusion.

"Where'd that one come from?" Bana jerked his chin at the fifth corpse sprawled at Tatsu feet.

Tatsu's reply stuttered from lips that still sizzled from the tender press of that mouth. "Jumped me." What could he say? That a gorgeous, Japanese man wielding a *tanto* had just materialized out of the dark, saved his ass and then kissed him? And what a kiss!

Kuso, he must've hallucinated it, right? An adrenalin overload brought on by the intensity of a life-and-death fight. But the warm throb in his cock and burning on his lips told him otherwise.

Bana gave Tatsu a long, suspicious stare then shrugged. "Okay, c'mon then, I'm parched. I'll buy ya a billie-dee while I wait for the clean-up crew."

Determined to get answers and needing to hear the solid reality of another voice, Tatsu followed the stocky man back into the bar. They hunkered down in the booth nearest the back door and let their combat-strung nerves relax. Bana ignored the staccato of Tatsu's questions. Instead, he waggled two fingers in the direction of the waitress.

The Irishman muttered, "Thanks, luv," when Doris brought their tall stouts. He gulped his in three immense, thirsty swallows. "Keep yer gob shut, boyo," Bana menaced as he slammed his empty mug down hard enough to rattle the table. He fingered his throat above his collar. Deep purple blotches already blossomed around the wounds.

"Another word an' I'll personally slice off yer clackers. Go home. I'll find ya in the bye-and-bye an' we'll talk." His cell phone rang. Without another word, Bana shoved the instrument against his ear and stalked out the back door; leaving Tatsu speechless for the second time that night.

Mere minutes before the first glimmer of light touched the snow-capped Eastern Range, Arisada arrived at the sanctuary of his home on Mercer Island. He showered then locked himself in his bedchamber in the basement. Only able to think about the Japanese hunter fighting in that alley, he felt no urge to sleep. He had no doubt the soul of Nowaki lived in the body of the beautiful youth.

At first, the utter improbability of their meeting at this time, this place, stunned Arisada. But why not? That he'd been tracking those same rogues that attacked the older man was no mere coincidence. That the lovely green-eyed boy—the reincarnation Arisada had sought for eight centuries—just happened to be at that exact time and place, was also no coincidence. The timing could only be the result of *karma*.

Saving the boy's life was pure instinct. Kissing him was pure desire. After hundreds of lifetimes, Arisada's need had shattered his self-control, and within seconds he found his lips fastened to that pretty, surprised mouth.

He lay awake considering how to confront the emerald-eyed boy—for the vampire could only think of him as a boy. Should he tell the youth he is the reincarnation of Koji Nowaki, the traitor of Mii-dera? Should he give the boy a warning that he was a traitor and must die?

Arisada knew taking the youth's life would not be easy. Not with those incredible sword skills. No matter, perhaps there was a way to achieve the ultimate goal by means of an honorable duel.

But the satisfaction of realizing the long-awaited revenge mocked Arisada. The vampire recalled every exquisite detail of the boy from the alley. Every nuance of movement, every glimpse of flesh and expression even to the huff of sound as breath entered and left his delectable mouth.

And, oh, the taste of that mouth! Tender, sweet and heartbreakingly familiar. Arisada ached to claim this pretty youth. Drive his cock between those tight buttocks, into that pulsing heat, before death closed those peridot eyes.

The vampire looked down the planes of his thin body—the pale skin stretched over the stark arch of ribs, the angles of the hollows below his sharp hips, his large cock, responsible for as much pain as his fangs. His fingers, described by many as long and elegant, by others as cruel and talonned, tugged on his desire-hardened nipples before sliding down to curl around his hot, demanding flesh.

The fantasy took him as he pulled on himself with harsh, unforgiving strokes. In his dream, Arisada felt long legs settle their warm weight on his shoulders. Smelled the rich musk of arousal pouring from sex-flushed skin. He tasted every secret place on the youth's honey-colored skin, suckled on tender nipples—were they dusky pink or nut brown?—laved over the ridges and cuts of muscles down to that cock, pulsing hard and hot. His mouth taking that turgid, begging member deep into his mouth, until the boy bucked. Arisada's mind heard the raw noises of rut—panting, rasping breath, harsh groans, ecstatic mewls, entreaties for more and the slapping of skin on skin.

Arisada stroked himself faster, a punishing drag over satin-covered iron. He rubbed his thumb over his weeping crown with rough, desperate impatience. The other hand rolled over his balls, forefinger breaching his clenched hole and curling against his wet walls.

He imagined that beautiful boy's emerald eyes blazing with an incandescence of pleasure while the orgasm blossomed across his straining young face. Imagined that pure leaping cry, the hot, wet spurt as the boy surrendered his seed.

The image drove wild heat down Arisada's spine. His balls ached, his anus pulsed. His fangs tore through his gums. Then he reached that blinding moment when his spunk ribboned from his member trapped in his clenched fist. His harsh shout of ecstasy ended in a deep sob of sorrow.

On a tangle of sweat-soaked sheets, Arisada lay spent but unfulfilled. Anguish crushed his heart. A visceral honesty, more ingrained than his revenge, showed him the truth. He had fallen in love—instantly and insanely—with Nowaki's reincarnation. And Arisada knew would never be able to take the lovely boy's life. One glance from those jade eyes would shatter Arisada's heart and still his killing blow.

Nevertheless, *Bushido* bound Arisada to seek revenge for his Sōhei brethren. No matter that he'd fallen in love, that this love was deeper than his soul, he had no choice. Arisada needed to find a different way to take the youth's life. He thought about love, its lure, its seduction.

Hai, hai. Seduction—the very instrument of Nowaki's

betrayal. The idea held a certain sense of justice. Under the vampire thrall, the boy would willingly open his legs for Arisada. He would take the youth to ecstatic heights and, as they fucked, Arisada would let his own bestial nature take over. For at the moment of climax, Arisada lost all rationale, all reason, all morals.

As his orgasm ripped through him, Arisada would feed from the boy's succulent throat, letting their blood mingle. Over the centuries, the virus coursing through Arisada's veins had mutated into an irrevocable death sentence for any human being. The youth's body would be consumed while he wandered in a mindless fever.

Crimson tears seeped from beneath Arisada's slanted lids. His heart had already given itself to that unknown, beautiful youth who'd fought with the skill and grace of a Sword Saint.

One word slipped from the vampire's lips: "*Koibito.*" Beloved.

Five

"Two days since my *kyūketsuki* were cut down like dogs in the Seattle streets, and you have not found the human scum responsible?" Ukita Sadomori hurled his crystal wine glass against a painting on the wall. Rivulets of burgundy streamed down the Willem Kalf still-life.

Anger twisted the vampire Master's aristocratic features into a terrifying mask. His eyes turned scarlet, obliterating the golden iris. His thick lips wrinkled back from a large mouth. His hooked nose and high cheekbones added to the ferocity of his broad face. And his skin, now almost translucent, was beginning to match the color of the pure-white hair and mustache.

Sadomori reveled in the fear his appearance incited in other vampires. He knew they called him *Obake*, The Ghost, behind his back, and believed his power came from arcane blood rites. "Is there anything you do know, Arisada?"

"I believe they were hunters. I saw both had guns." Arisada spoke with care, fearing one misplaced word or gesture would reveal his lie. "We haven't found them. You know how hunters hide." He looked with sadness at the ruined, three-hundred-year-old, Dutch masterpiece. It reminded him of the hundreds of lives Sadomori had destroyed just as carelessly.

"Hunters are mere humans. Why didn't you kill them?"

"Daimyō, *gomen nasai*. I am sorry. I arrived too late. Before I could act, they went inside the bar. I dared not kill them in front of so many witnesses."

"You will find and kill these hunters, this human filth." Suspicion glittered deep within his red eyes. "How is it you happened to be there?"

"I was—"

"*Baka*. Idiot, You were looking for *that* boy." Sadomori interrupted with a sneer. "So many cities, so many *bishounen*, so many souls. It's pathetic, this obsession with finding the reincarnation of a dead lover." Sadomori's jealousy flashed. "You are a fool. But don't forget, you are *my* fool."

Arisada stilled his expression and prayed the slight increase of his heartbeat would not be noticed by Sadomori. He was only allowed limited freedom to hunt for Nowaki's soul. It was obvious that Sadomori believed the boy would never be found. That belief was now wrong.

To divert the subject, Arisada overstepped their long-established bounds, "Please *Seisakusha*, order the Clan to feed only from the indentured. To allow anything else will lead to our annihilation."

"How dare you question me? I do nothing except for my own pleasure." In the time taken by a single heartbeat, Sadomori moved across the room. He grabbed Arisada by his throat, and slammed him against the wall. The older vampire leaned up into the younger vampire's face. Sadomori's forefinger traced the spider-web scar marring Arisada's left cheek. "Never forget you belong to me."

Sadomori combed his fingers through Arisada's silky hair that rippled like molten fire over his shoulders. "This radiance of your hair; I know not if I like it more now that it has the brilliance of flame or when it was midnight black."

As always when this close to his Primary, Sadomori's mood shifted into lust. "There, my sweet, my anger's not for you. A few dead are not worth fighting over," he purred as he pressed up to bite the younger vampire's lower lip. The Daimyō's breath reeked from his recent feeding.

Arisada refrained from wiping his mouth with the back of his hand. He fought to quell his revulsion at the feel of his *Seisakusha*, his creator's, hand crawling beneath Arisada's shirt. Shuddered at the possessive slide across his chest, the sharp twist of one nipple. Against his thigh, Arisada felt the impotent grind of the Daimyō's flaccid sex.

Despite his own revulsion, Arisada's loins responded. Oh, how he despised his need to submit to this bestial domination. He pushed that exploring hand from his body and pulled away.

The Daimyō hissed a warning but allowed the rejection.

With his hands clasped behind his back, he walked across to the picture window. The view across the Bay was the sole reason he had appropriated the mansion above Alki Point. He fastened his avaricious gaze on the dark silhouette of the Space Needle. He regarded the monument as a symbol of human arrogance and had sworn the day he ruled this city, he would destroy that symbol.

"Several humans have violated their indenture and left the Alki compound. We give them shelter, food and protection. Still, they break their contracts. I will not tolerate this defiance. Order Nakamura-san to capture them and behead them as examples to the rest," he ordered in a terrifyingly flat voice.

"They are not cattle. I will not—" Arisada cried.

Sadomori's fangs distorted his face. "*Shizukani shite*! Be silent. How dare you question me, monk?" Sadomori stared at Arisada through a long minute of silence before shrugging. "Perhaps you are right. Have them flogged instead. And you need a lesson in obedience. My chamber at sunset tomorrow." Sadomori turned his back in dismissal.

"*Wakarimashita*, I understand, Ukita-san." Arisada gave a curt bow. After all these centuries, his vow of obedience still required him to come to Sadomori's bed. Arisada could have refused. To his shame, his own craving for his Master's domination made him acquiesce.

How many times had it been like this? Arisada agonized as he hunched over his swollen organ, pulling and twisting, muscles trembling and knotting with exertion. His panting increased with the effort to bring himself to another orgasm. Sadomori allowed no lubricant, and Arisada's cock was sore from hours of stroking. His mind willed his orgasm but the release could not be forced.

Twice Arisada had brought himself to a shuddering climax, but his *Seisakusha* demanded more. Arisada stroked the throbbing length of his member, squeezing the swollen length, pinching the foreskin. He rolled his thumb over the hot, purple head, teased precum from the slit, jacked himself faster, frantic to force that sweet, creamy juice, pulsing, glistening and hot, from his body. And when he did, when the sight of his cum stirred Sadomori's member, the torture would begin.

The Daimyō lay naked at the foot of the huge bed. He propped his head on one hand and fondled himself. His predatory gaze devoured the sight of the masturbating vampire, the exquisite creature he had created. Sadomori's body burned for that beautiful face with golden eyes framed by upturned lids. He lusted for those nipples now peaked with desire, that heavy prick jutting from narrow hips, those large balls within their sac tucked up hard and tight above Arisada's dark hole.

Arisada groaned and leaned forward, abdominal muscles clenched into ridges with effort. His sweat-drenched hair tumbled over his torso like a waterfall of flame, obscuring the view of his pumping hand.

"Do not hide from me," the older vampire hissed. Arisada flung his head back like a startled horse. His hair flared in a fiery arc over his back.

Sadomori licked his lips, his tongue rasping over his fang tips as he gazed greedily on the red tip of that engorged cock as it disappeared then reappeared within the clutch of slender fingers. He inhaled the heady pungency of male sex. His member remained flaccid.

"Use your fingers. Fuck yourself."

At the command, Arisada drove three fingers up to the last knuckle into his core. He massaged his walls, seeking that spongy gland. That first touch sent sparks straight up his spine. His scrotum tightened with a twisting ache. Close, so close. The vision of that Japanese youth fighting in that filthy alley rose behind Arisada's closed eyelids. The pretty hunter with eyes the color of jade, and a sweet, delectable mouth that tasted of cigarettes and human heat.

Arisada's orgasm scorched along every nerve and blasted out of his cock. His back arched, heels gouging against the mattress as gobbets of milk-white cum spurted over his chest. He bit his tongue to stifle his cry of pleasure. A pleasure made terrible by the secret that triggered it.

Sadomori inhaled the salty perfume of fresh cum. His

alabaster skin darkened as his blood reacted to the rich, heady musk pouring off the masturbating vampire.

"Arms above your head," Sadomori hissed.

Orgasmic aftershocks wracked Arisada as he raised his arms to the set of nano-steel shackles imbedded in the wall above the bed. Another pair of cuffs hung at the end of a four-foot chain secured just below the first. Sadomori snapped the shorter cuffs around Arisada's wrists, shoved Arisada's legs back and high, and snapped the second set just below the knee. The chains forced Arisada's legs so wide the tendons of his groin strained. His sex bulged outward in obscene prominence.

A thin cord brushed over the bulge of his balls. A shiver of fear mixed with a wild anticipation rocked throughout Arisada's body. Fingers stroked possessively down his prick, over his sac, teased at the sensitive skin behind, swirled around his rim. He pushed his haunches partially off the bed, thrusting out his vulnerable genitals in a move of pure submission. "*Kudesai. Please,* Master," he whispered.

A flicker of amusement crossed Sadomori's face as he grunted acknowledgement of the gesture. Then with swift, sure movements he encased Arisada's cock in an intricate knotted pattern. When finished, Arisada's erection jutted from his groin. The barely visible head pulsed, glistening and taut, above its constricting prison of red silk.

With a slow pulling motion, Sadomori stretched Arisada's sac, coaxing the rubbery skin to lengthen away from the groin. He rolled each orb in one palm before knotting the rest of the cord around the base of the scrotum.

"*Subarishi,* exquisite," Sadomori breathed as he sat back on his heels and admired the perfection of the *kinbaku,* Japanese rope binding. Those intricate twists of cord trapped the blood in Arisada's prick within a prison of silk and pulled the balls so tight that the skin stretched taut and shiny as a balloon. Sadomori relished the fear now pouring off Arisada that the cord would not be removed.

Sadomori opened a glass vial, poured a drop over each of his talonned fingernails then spread the remainder over his tongue. The liquid burned in his mouth. Centuries ago, he had concocted the aphrodisiac to stimulate his own flagging member. On him it failed. But the potion drove Arisada to uncontrollable heights of arousal, his pain and pleasure chemically enhanced to near madness.

The drug entered Arisada's system swiftly, scorching along every nerve with white-hot intensity, He quivered with anticipation for that first, feather-light slice from those talons. A single talon left a scalpel-thin line of pain from the naval to the fine curls bunched around the base of his cock. The cuts increased in length and speed, crossing his body multiple times. Arisada's chest heaved as he forged a bond with the pain. He reached for it, embraced it and turned it to waves of pleasure. Only in this way could he survive.

Never on any battlefield was Arisada as close to death as when his *Seisakusha* began this deadly play. This excruciating torment would not cease until the Daimyō's member came to life. Arisada knew that one night Sadomori's loins would refuse to respond. On that day, Arisada's throat would be torn out.

Sadomori cut, watched the younger vampire's agonized response, then cut again. Greedily, he lapped up each line of blood from groin to neck before taking a deep suck at the pulsing throat, not quite breaking the skin. He brought his thick lips up to Arisada's mouth.

"I crave your taste, my beautiful monk. You are as delicious as the first time I took you." His demanding tongue pushed between the younger vampire's clenched lips.

Arisada yielded with a defiant rush of breath, and that thick, wet tongue drove deep into his open mouth. He shuddered, waiting for the violation, choking a whimper as humiliation and pleasure consumed him. How well he knew that moans and inarticulate sighings, the sounds of sexual pleasure, stilled the older vampire's erection. This impotence triggered a murderous rage in Sadomori who would inflict pain until Arisada lay exhausted and all hope of climaxing drowned beneath the dark waters of exhaustion.

The Daimyō delivered a punishing slice across the tips of each peaked nipple. The nubs welled crimson. While suckling on those tender buds, drew his fingernails down Arisada's sternum leaving thin cuts. His mouth left red whorls when he sucked on the clenched abdominal muscle over each of Arisada's hips. He pumped Arisada's erection, hard, punishing strokes that twisted the velvet skin over the steel rod.

"Exquisite." Sadomori hissed at the sight of the head flushed rose-red with blood before pushing the tip of his finger into the slit. Arisada's twitch of pain brought a smile to Sadomori's pale lips. He mouthed over the balloon-taut skin of each ball, lapped the musky sweat pooled between Arisada's spread buttocks. His tongue rolled and lapped, teasing out spurts of precum. Greedily, he licked it up.

The heat boiled off Arisada's skin, a sign of the younger vampire's overwhelming need to climax. Sadomori's fangs sank into the tender flesh of Arisada's thigh. The bite a warning not to speak as much as a sign of possession. Blood welled. Sadomori slurped over it.

A talonned digit forced its way past Arisada's tight rim. Then a second and a third twisting deep into his vitals until one curled over the spongy knob of his prostate. His orgasm boiled through his body. His balls throbbed in agony, unable to release their load. Arisada bit his tongue. In begging desperation, he ground his ass against Sadomori's hand.

Sadomori's lips curled into a mockery of a smile. Writhing beneath him was the only creature ever to bring him fulfillment. The power to deny his beautiful Primary his climax drove Sadomori's lust to new heights. His cock pulsed into life. Sadomori grabbed his erect member, forced it against Arisada's hole then drove with fury past the clenched rim.

"I am your Master. Never forget it." Sadomori claimed Arisada as his property with each thrust of his organ.

The Daimyō felt his balls tighten. He hovered on that ecstatic edge for a few delicious seconds. But when he finally ejaculated, his spunk dribbled out. As for so many centuries, his body cheated him of that ultimate pinnacle of pleasure.

His scream of frustration echoed in the vast bedroom. His fangs emerged so fast they tore his gums. He fell onto Arisada and bit his chest. Greedily he sucked the seeping blood as he slammed his hips against Arisada's ass. No use, his flaccid member had already slipped from that pulsing hole.

With a snarl, Sadomori pulled on the end of the cord around Arisada's cock. The intricate bindings unraveled immediately. Arisada screamed as blood and sensation flooded back into his abused sex. The agony of his orgasm exploded through him, jetting frothy arcs of cum over his clenched belly.

Jealousy ripped through Sadomori as he plunged his mouth over Arisada's spurting prick. The Daimyō gulped down the thick, salty essence while his fingers mauled his own indifferent member. At last, he pulled off with a snarl as Arisada collapsed insensate, driven beyond even his *Seisakusha*'s reach.

The blood drained from Sadomori's eyes and his irises regained their yellow depths. He sat back on his haunches and gazed at the *kyūketsuki* who had been his for hundreds of centuries. He traced his forefinger over the symbol cut into Arisada's cheekbone, Sadomori's *mons*, and proof of his ownership. Yet, he knew he would never truly possess his Primary's spirit. Thousands had given up their souls as Sadomori sent them screaming to their deaths. But this one—this Sōhei monk—would never surrender his *tamashii*. It belonged to another. For that, Sadomori hated Arisada.

Sadomori viewed his Primary's sweat-slicked flesh. An echo of arousal flickered through his cock, but nothing more. Deep within his dark heart, he detested his own desperate need for this lithe beauty. That need held him in bondage.

With a massive effort, he reined in the rage that threatened to engulf him again. To unleash his anger now meant death for his monk.

Sadomori's expression verged on benign as he kissed Arisada's forehead. He released each of the abraded limbs, stretching them out on the futon. He smoothed his hands along cramped muscles, massaging life back into them. He brought a soft, wet cloth from the bathroom, and cleaned the fluids from the unconscious vampire's body. His hands gentled as he wiped over the groin and cleaned those softened genitals.

The action woke Arisada. He pushed himself onto his

elbows, limbs shaking, his hair hanging in wet crimson strands over his chest and back. Pain shadowed the golden depth of his eyes. A fine trembling possessed him as he climbed off the bed.

"Sadomori-san, may I dress?"

The Daimyō turned his back and ignored the request. He looked out the plate-glass window. His thin body looked emaciated, yet the lean muscles and pronounced tendons held a supernatural strength. His white skin stood in stark relief to the multitude of tattoos that blanketed his back and buttocks— Sadomori's life history rendered in ink on flesh.

"We are done, get your clothes." Sadomori poured a glass of wine before dropping into the Queen Anne chair by the fireplace. He regarded his Primary with a gaze that held the admiration of a connoisseur for a work of art. Saito Arisada was truly of the aristocracy with the pure features of a noble lineage. So perfect in form that Sadomori could easily believe the young vampire was a descendant of the Gods.

And Saito Arisada belonged body and vampire soul to Ukita Sadomori.

The older vampire indicated the carafe of wine. "Drink, renew yourself." He stroked over his genitals. The gesture was a deliberate invitation to feed at the tender juncture between the thigh and the groin where the femoral artery pulsed with life. As planned, the movement drew Arisada's attention.

Arisada's breath caught. His eyes locked on the inside of the older vampire's groin. The flaccid genitals dangling beneath were of no interest to him. But the unhealed scabs from deep puncture wounds on the insides of both legs made him tense with shock. "You are letting the young *kyūketsuki* feed from you? Are you insane?"

Sadomori held his anger at this outburst. His relaxed demeanor, the casually draped leg were a pose. He wanted Arisada to see the bites, and Arisada knew it.

"Jealous, my love?" As if to emphasize his indifference to Arisada's concern, he took another sip of his wine and stroked over the scabs. "Your alarm is foolish. I see no danger. Every vampire knows what an honor it is to feed from me."

"Why are you doing this? The disease in our blood is too

old," Arisada cried. "No *kyūketsuki*, especially the younger ones, should drink from us. You know how violent they become, how unnaturally strong. You will turn them into vicious rogues."

Abruptly, Sadomori stood, setting his glass on the bar so hard the stem shattered. He ignored it. His white eyebrows drew together. "Why would I care if a few of ours kill a human or two? It is time mankind feared us."

Fear rippled through Arisada. "I do not understand why you insist on this rash course of action. You are endangering us all. The people will turn on us."

Sadomori's lip lifted in a slight curl showing his fang tips in a subtle warning. "Hear me, monk. I will make those human cattle bow before us."

Arisada tried one last desperate plea not only for Sadomori, but for himself and their kind. "There is no need. We already control humans through their own vices, the drugs, gambling and sex trade. Our payment to the hundreds of indentured for their blood allows both our species to co-exist."

"*Â, sō desu ka*, that is right. We pay for what should be ours to by right. We are stronger and faster than the human vermin. But we have no real power. Men are bleating animals. To us they should be nothing more than cattle; mere fodder."

"They *will* turn on us. Have you forgotten what happened to you in Europe five hundred years ago? The same citizens who shouted their love for you sent assassins after you. You barely escaped. You could offer so much if you would relinquish your obsession for absolute power." Alarm ripped through Arisada. "Please, reconsider your actions. These times are far more dangerous to our kind than ever before. Stop this insanity, I beg you."

Sadomori ignored the entreaty. He took Arisada's hand, turned the palm up and kissed it. "Perhaps you are right, monk. Perhaps it is time for me to be magnanimous."

Arisada never trusted his Sire's mercurial moods, which too often hid a secret agenda. But the older vampire's gentle gesture tugged at Arisada's heart.

"You derided my anguish when I heard you had slain the

last of the Kurosaki family. You sneer at my beliefs in the benevolent Buddha. Yet, my vow is to bring redemption to the honorable warrior within your soul."

"Ah, my beautiful Sōhei, when will you stop seeking my redemption? You waste your time, I do not desire it." Sadomori shrugged and turned back to the bar to pour a fresh glass of wine. "You may leave me now."

Sick with defeat, Arisada dressed. At the door, he paused and defied his Daimyō one last time. "Remember Ukita-san, humans do not tolerate each other, much less other species. We exist only because they let us. Give them reason, and they will exterminate us all." In a sad silence, Arisada left the room followed by the echo of Sadomori's derisive laugh.

As he sped away, despair filled Arisada once again. Why did he endure this brutal existence? Not for an ancient oath forced from him centuries ago. No, he survived to find the reincarnation of Koji Nowaki.

But now Arisada had succeeded what justice from an ancient era would be served by killing the beautiful, green-eyed boy?

The voices of Arisada's long-dead Sōhei brethren cried out in answer. "For *fukushū*. There is nothing else. Only *fukushū*."

Six

Restless and frustrated, Tatsu paced the confines of his rented room. Four nights of wasted effort, of stalking and confronting vampires and questioning people had led him nowhere except three more dead on his conscience.

Then, despite his resolve, the memory of his mysterious savior from the Whore's alley rose behind his eye. Who was he? Was he a hunter following the rogues? And why the fuck did the man kiss him? Not that Tatsu minded. The harshness of those lips demanding entrance, the hot wet slide of the man's tongue, the taste of his mouth—all sent a wave of want shivering down Tatsu's spine straight into his cock. Hell, there had been only one other time in his life when a man stirred that kind of aching need.

Kuso, this pointless thinking got him nowhere. To quiet his confusion, he poured over the Nagasaki police files and his grandfather's journal but found nothing new.

He took out the faded photo from the back of the file. This was not part of the report, this was the sum of his innocence.

Five people dressed in the crisp, new clothing of holiday makers posed beneath the banner for the Tokyo Pan-Asia Tenjihin. Lights from the massive Ferris wheel in the background reflected a halo over the little family. The man was tall, Caucasian, with short blond hair and a shy smile. One arm draped over the shoulders of the petite Japanese woman—Tatsu's mother. A squirming toddler in her arms reached for her hat. The man held the hand of a boy, around five years old. Beside the youngster stood a taller boy with a shock of brown hair. Although trying to look serious and grown-up, the boy's sideways grin revealed his excitement.

Tatsu recognized none of them; not even himself. The small, intimate details that should make each face beloved remained a mystery. He couldn't recall the sound of his mother's laugh, nor of his father's voice. How did his baby sister smell fresh from her bath? Did his younger brother tag after him, pester him, call him *Onii-chan*? Although he loved them, his memories of them remained shrouded by a thick fog of pain.

He placed the photo on his dresser and looked out the grimy window to the street three floors below. There were no signs of life in the dark and silent predawn hour. Harsh gusts of wind promised rain. As if it ever did anything but rain here. Unexpected nostalgia filled him at the thought of Santa Fe's bright, arid air. Here, everything smelled of mildew and rot. Again, he wondered if he'd be able to fulfill his vendetta.

Screw it. Only one solution to these shameful doubts—a good workout with the sword. All concerns, all uncertainties disappeared under the sublime discipline of *shin-shin no tanren*, the samurai training of mind, body and spirit.

Tatsu changed into his practice gear and wrapped a tattered cloth around his head before grinning ruefully at the mirror. Even in the voluminous culottes and wide-sleeved shirt, he still looked like a skinny-assed kid.

As he trotted across the street to the dojo, he smiled, recalling his first day in Seattle when the owner, Morinaga Watari recognized Tatsu's Nagasaki accent. The old man presented the keys to Tatsu with the request to "honor" the humble establishment at any time.

As always, Tatsu kicked off his boots inside the entrance. He never turned on the lights when alone. Why waste the owner's electricity? He bowed before stepping across the threshold of the *shiaijo*, a room built for sword fighting. He racked his *katana* in a slot in the high wooden stand that held a dozen *iaito*. Carrying one of the blunt practice swords, he bowed again before stepping onto the mat covering the center of the room.

Kneeling, he closed his eyes and focused on the measured rhythm of his breathing, seeking the center of his being, his *tanden*. The turmoil in his mind melted away. Within a few minutes, he reached *zanshin*, a heightened awareness of all things around him yet focused on nothing in particular.

ETERNAL SAMURAI

At peace, Tatsu stood. Holding the sword in the classical combat style with both hands curled around the hilt, he warmed up with several basic exercises called *suburi*. He moved into left-and-right *katas,* the sword flying from single to double-handed holds. His measured shouts broke the quiet of the dojo as he practiced several solo forms.

An hour later, he was relaxed and focused, his breathing and heartbeat barely increased. He took a second *iaito* and moved into the difficult techniques of *niten'ichi,* fighting with two swords. In a blur of motion, he executed a flurry of cuts designed to eliminate multiple attackers at once. So deep was his concentration, he forgot the fundamental rule of combat—the enemy is always around.

Arisada's nostrils flared taking in the sweet scent of this boy, a distinct scent that had allowed the vampire to find the youth among the thousands of humans in this city. He marveled as the boy poised with both swords in the difficult combat-stance only used before by the great swordsman Miyamoto Musashi. Then Tatsu moved into a display of incredible swordsmanship that made Arisada's breath catch in his throat.

The way Tatsu's *hakama* flowed around the youth's lithe body woke Arisada's needy groin. He wondered if the boy protected his genitals with a Western-style jock or bound by a traditional *fundoshi.* Arousal shivered through the vampire at the thought of those naked buttocks outlined by a loincloth. Those buttocks would be firm, the muscles defined and rounding on either side of a deep crack.

Arisada sensed the suppressed loneliness in the young hunter. That loneliness could be used to lure him to his death. Unable to resist the challenge, Arisada would not use his vampiric thrall. Instead, he'd use Bushido. He licked his lips in anticipation of victory.

For now, he would savor the sight of this incomparable swordsman the same way he savored the perfection of an *ikebana* flower arrangement. Or the perfection of *seppuku.*

But as Arisada watched Tatsu become one with the Way of

the Sword, doubts ate like acid through the vampire's resolve. Arisada had never considered the eroding weight of *fukushū* on his soul. Or how time affected his conscience. Eight-hundred years. Too long. Far too long.

His vow of vengeance had been driven by grief and all that made him Sōhei—honor, tradition and his unswerving devotion to Mii-dera. But the centuries had eroded the meaning of that vow, and rendered it worthless in the light of the one thing Arisada believed was forever denied him: love.

With a searing flash of insight, love tore its way through the vampire's heart and destroyed all reason for *fukushū*. The vampire accepted the dishonor staining his soul. Accepted that his brethren would never be avenged. The mental force by which he repudiated his oath for vengeance nearly drove him to his knees.

Wakatta, better to exist with shame than destroy this lovely, vibrant youth for the events of a too-distant past.

Awash in an inexplicable mix of joy and sorrow, the vampire shifted his weight to leave. But his longing to touch this young man again, if only for a moment, stilled his step.

Just as Tatsu raised the *iaito* over his head in the *jodan* position, he sensed the presence of another. The air whistled as he began the descending cut. Instead of his weight landing on his forward leg, his body pivoted so he faced the entrance as he finished.

A silhouetted form moved against the darker square of the doorway. A man, maybe an inch shorter than Tatsu's five-foot ten, took a single step over the threshold and bowed. The man was dressed ready for *shinkendo*. A full-faced *menpo* hid his features. In his right hand, the stranger held a sheathed *katana* pointed forward and down in the samurai gesture of neutrality.

The stranger's commanding stance—weight always balanced on his forward foot, body held loose, with a deceptive stillness—could only be that of an expert swordsman. Perhaps even a sword Master. Tatsu believed he knew all of the dojo's students. Hell, over the past week he'd defeated every one of them. And no matter how skilled with a sword, no student would risk coming to the dojo at night.

A sense of déjà shivered through Tatsu. Something about the way this man moved seemed so familiar. Was this his rescuer from the alley behind the Whore? If so, Tatsu didn't know whether to thank him or ask what that kiss—that totally sweet fucking kiss—was all about? Unsure, Tatsu did neither, and covered his confusion with an impolite, "Who the hell are you?"

"*Sumimasen.* I do not mean to intrude. The owner, Morinaga-sensei, lets me practice here from time to time when I'm in town," the man replied in oddly inflected Japanese. "You are excellent. I haven't seen swordsmanship like yours in a long time. Would you honor me by opposing me in *tachiuchi*?"

Tatsu heard a smile in that voice. It held too much of a challenge. "A match? *Hai, dozo,*" he assented. "Besides, it looks like you're already prepared for one." He indicated the man's mask with a flick of the sword.

"*Watashi wa koiedesu.*" Again, in that odd accent, the man proclaimed his honor to accept. The stranger lifted his *katana* horizontally at face level, bowed beneath it, He repeated the motions in the direction of the *shiaijo* and then, to Tatsu's astonishment, bowed to him. The stranger placed his weapon on the floor facing the wall. Silently, he glided over to the rack of blunt steel blades and tested the weight and balance of several before selecting one.

They approached from opposite sides of the mat to the white lines that marked their starting positions. Carrying their naked swords on the left, both men performed *kiotsuke*, that formal act of stepping into position and bowing to each other. As one, they each dropped into *sonkyo*, a straight-back crouch. They paused as a flicker of energy sparked between them; an understanding.

With no outward signal they sprang up and apart, raising their swords. Tatsu opened with *jodan-gamae*, the sword raised above his head, while the stranger countered with *hidari seigan gamae*, the sword held point forward.

They stepped toward each other and their blades struck. In quick succession, each opposed and defended with authoritative yet classical moves. They sounded out the other's strength and styles, searching for any weaknesses. There were none. Their weapons met, slicing in rapid succession upward, downward, side-to-side. Each fighter mirrored the action of the other in split-second synchronicity. Thrusts at abdomens, cuts at heads, necks, arms or legs were effortlessly met by counter moves from above the head, from the side or upward from a crouch.

At first, they called out before each strike. Then the dojo fell silent except for their measured breathing and the clang of steel against steel.

Their slight difference in height gave Tatsu no advantage. He knew he didn't telegraph his moves. But the man always anticipated Tatsu's every strike and met it with a precise and flawless grace.

Kusho, this guy was fast. So fast and strong, almost superhuman. Tatsu admired how his opponent became a part of his environment. The stranger stepped on the mat as if he wished only to inflict the merest weight, like that of a butterfly, on its reed surface. Tatsu sensed the incredible strength in that compact frame hidden beneath those rippling garments. But those slender hands wielding the *iaito* with such perfect control looked too pale to be Japanese. *Bushi damashi,* the warrior spirit of the samurai, burned within this fighter.

As the minutes passed, Tatsu felt a growing sense of intimate familiarity. The man—every gesture, every precise move, every huff of breath, even his scent—was hauntingly familiar. With every passing second, Tatsu became certain that his opponent was the beauty who had saved him the other night.

The man's plaited hair licked the air like a flame. That beautiful braid, whipping back and forth with a serpentine virility, caught Tatsu's gaze. Irrationally, he ached to stroke that silky length. Imagined it moving across his palm, the living thickness of it, the satiny feel, like hot skin over a pulsing, rigid cock.

The momentary distraction should have cost Tatsu the match. Why hadn't it? Then he felt a minute restraint in his opponent's cuts. That puzzling reticence hurled a challenge more forceful than if the man had called Tatsu a coward.

"Dammit, fight honestly!"

The man answered with a barked laugh from behind the *menpo* then attacked with a new ferocity and a different style—the ancient techniques of the Seikanjito Shinden fighting sect. Secret techniques that had been Shiniichiro Kurosaki's legacy to his grandson, Tatsu.

Tatsu hadn't faced such an opponent since his grandfather died. Unbidden, a smile played over Tatsu's lips.

"*Wakatta*," the other man's exalted laugh reflected a similar joy. The sound danced along every nerve in Tatsu's body.

More determined than ever to win, Tatsu called on every iota of knowledge. The man countered with poetic grace and incredible strength.

Neither gained any small advantage over the other. Both men accepted the power flowing from the other, allowed it to infuse an unadulterated ferocity into their swordplay. The energy of their fighting coiled around them, shifted, and enraptured them in new meaning. *Suku*, the control and rhythm of their breathing, synchronized.

Tatsu reached out with his senses in the samurai's spiritual technique of *kami-hasso,* the technique of delving into the mind and the body of the other. Their energies met and melded into one as if both were of the same body.

Every strike and counterstrike delivered a subtle erotic promise. The whispering rustle of clothing promised the revelation of tantalizing secrets of the body beneath. The teasing susurration of their feet moving toward and away echoed the tentative questioning of two new lovers. The glissade of blade sliding against blade became as a caress over quivering skin. The repeated ring of weapon meeting weapon spoke of the two bodies, the one driving into the other, only to break apart again.

Tatsu knew this was no longer *shinkendo*. This was a

dance; a beautiful, deadly dance of raw lust. The yearning of a man for another man. His blood sang with arousal. The hairs on his arms lifted and his skin hummed. A shiver from his loins ran up his spine. He lost himself in the wantonness of his arousal, sensing that same arousal in the stranger.

"You feel it, too? That need to be taken, to take," the man whispered in a rich, sensual tenor. That voice sent a sweet thrill down Tatsu's spine. He heard the man's lust, that deep hunger. And for the first time, Tatsu became aroused in the middle of a *shinkendo* match. Turned on by a stranger wearing a mask. Uncaring of its outcome, Tatsu rode a wanton high, letting the seduction consume him, letting it course through every muscle, nerve and sinew of his body until it exploded in his brain and his groin. His cock filled; so hard it hurt.

"*Fakku.* Who are you?" Tatsu croaked in a vain bid to curb his blinding lust. Immediately, he regretted his question as the magic evaporated. His erection softened. He lost the discipline of the sword, and his next cut met only air.

The stranger laughed a melodious seductive sound. Then he attacked with a flurry of unusual moves so fast one blurred into the other. Savage moves straight from the battlefield that pressed Tatsu into a floundering defense marred by anger.

"Emotion is foolish, young one," the warrior laughed.

Young one? Tatsu's face flamed with embarrassment. *Kuso,* he'd just made a child's mistake. He choked back his self-disgust and forced away his anger. Damn, no way would he lose to this mocking stranger.

Tatsu dropped his weight forward, lowered his weapon diagonally across his body then slashed the blade upward with all the precision at his command. Before the sword reached its zenith, he reversed it in a curve toward his opponent.

The man responded with a soft cry. He inclined slightly forward, turned his wrist as if to cut across Tatsu's abdomen. Immediately, Tatsu changed the angle of his weapon to deflect the strike. Too late he realized the man's deception. With a continuation of the same delicate twist, the stranger flipped the *iaito* from Tatsu's fingers. The sword spun away before his hand felt its absence.

Tatsu froze in disbelief. The last time he lost, he was nine years old. His face colored with humiliation. He dropped to his knees, bowed his head to the mat and slapped it in surrender. As he stood and retrieved the sword, Tatsu realized they'd been fighting in complete darkness.

His opponent bowed low as if Tatsu had won the match. "*Gomen nasai*, that was not a fair move," the man apologized. He placed the *iaito* back in its rack, swept off his mask and bowed again.

"*Watashi wa* Saito Arisada."

Thrown off guard, Tatsu bobbed an automatic bow and gave his name without thought. "*Watashi wa* Tatsu Cobb." Then he looked up and froze. Before him stood the beautiful stranger from the alley, the man who'd saved Tatsu's life. The man whose kiss had haunted Tatsu's dreams.

With unexpected hunger, Tatsu's gaze swept over the exquisite face up to the beauty's eyes. Not brown, as he imagined, but golden; the color of the sun.

Before Tatsu took his next breath, the vampire stood before him, their chests almost touching. Fingers brushed a hank of wet hair from Tatsu's forehead and trailed gently down his cheek before the thumb grazed over shock-parted lips.

"Nowaki-kun, I have found you at last," the creature whispered.

The caress over Tatsu's mouth sent shivers of inexplicable desire rippling through his groin. That touch, so familiar, so welcome, delivered a memory he felt in every fiber of his body. He leaned into the seductive promise of those fingers and spiraled into a flaming well of hunger for just that touch.

"*Gomen nasai, yurushite, senpai,*" Tatsu blurted not comprehending why he asked for forgiveness. Nor did he understand the tears that stung his eyes.

Arisada's palm caressed Tatsu's cheek. "I have been searching for you for hundreds of lifetimes. Now, I find there is nothing to forgive." With those words, Arisada damned his honor and his redemption.

He cupped Tatsu's face in both hands and stroked both thumbs over his tender mouth. "So beautiful, my *koibito*."

The touch danced lightning over Tatsu's lips. He fell into eyes that were taking on the deep burnish of a sunset. The warm puff of Arisada's breath fluttered over Tatsu's cheek as the vampire leaned in.

Cradling the back of Tatsu's head, Arisada pressed his mouth against the boy's soft and pliant lips. Surprisingly, they opened. The unexpected willingness of Tatsu's response plummeted heat straight into Arisada's cock. His moan, thick with repressed desire, followed his tongue inside that moist cavern. Tatsu's taste was a delightful mélange of cigarettes, spices and human boy.

At the first touch of Arisada's lips, Tatsu drowned under the waves of want engulfing him. His body flared with blind need. Never had a kiss felt like this—so full of love. So bright with promise. So right.

Tatsu opened his mouth and invited the vampire's tongue deeper. He curled his arms around the vampire's back and drew him tight, groin to groin. Heat pooled into Tatsu's balls, his cock, his ass. Another moan rumbled deep in his throat as he felt the thickness of the vampire's erection press against his crotch. Desperate for something more, he ground against that hardness as he slaved his mouth to the vampire's.

Tatsu feasted on that kiss as if starved for it. He drove his tongue into Arisada's exotic mouth in a crude mating, a frantic slaving together of need. Mouth to mouth, exploring, savoring, remembering. With a heady urgency, the tip of his tongue traced the tender contours of the vampire's palate—and rolled over the ridges housing the vampire's fangs.

Awareness tore through Tatsu. His body recoiled and he tore his mouth from that source of ecstasy. He slammed his palm so hard against Arisada's chest, the vampire staggered backward.

"Get the fuck off me."

Dismay and hurt flashed across Arisada's face as he staggered. A sad, strangled noise slipped from his lips at the loathing contorting Tatsu's face.

"What the hell do you think you're doing?" Tatsu heard the disgust in his voice, not knowing if it was for the vampire or himself. He stepped back, scrubbing his mouth with the back of his hand.

"Claiming a kiss from the one I love." Arisada drew back, all sign of hurt gone.

"You're a vampire, an animal, you can't love."

"Oh, you could not be more wrong. Vampires do love, often deeply, destructively. The passions we felt as humans we feel now, perhaps even more because of what we have lost. Never underestimate our emotions, boy." Arisada glared, eyes flickering red.

"You lie! You have no heart. You can't possibly feel love."

"Feel this." Grabbing Tatsu's wrist in a punishing grip, Arisada slapped the open palm against his chest.

The steady pulse of a heartbeat thrummed beneath Tatsu's splayed fingers. *Fakku,* what was he doing? This man, no, this thing was *kyūketsuki,* a monster. A killer. He lifted the sword.

"Stay away from me. The next time I see you, I *will* kill you." But Tatsu's anger got caught somewhere in the wild tingling of his lips from the bruising force of that kiss.

Arisada's golden gaze darkened with sorrow. He raised his hand as if to brush his fingers against Tatsu's cheek but stopped mid-way. Instead, he combed his hand through the sweat-drenched tangles of Tatsu's hair, tugged off the *hachimaki* and took a single step back.

Tatsu dropped the impotent *iaito* and spun toward the weapons stand. Even as his fingers brushed his sword, the vampire was at the dojo's door. Arisada's eyes never wavered as he bent and picked up his *katana.* Then, to Tatsu's astonishment, the vampire pulled the blade free, held it horizontally above his head and bowed—honor and respect from one warrior to another. With blinding speed, Arisada snapped the blade into its saya and slipped it into his *obi.*

"We will face each other again. I promise." Arisada held Tatsu's ragged bandana up like a trophy. His golden eyes flared crimson.

"*Fakku!*" Tatsu lunged, raising his weapon to strike but skidded to a halt mid-stride, stunned by the deep sorrow that flitted across the vampire's face. Then, Arisada was gone.

Shouting for the creature to return, Tatsu shot through the door into the cold, deserted street. He stood transfixed; trembling. His mind reeled, seeking the hate he should feel for this Saito Arisada, this monster, this evil made flesh. The hate wasn't there.

"Next time, I'll kill you." Tatsu shouted into the empty, fog-filled night. For a moment, his stomach heaved as he recalled the arousal that flared through his body. Had Arisada used thrall on him? Bullshit. Tatsu was immune to it. But the alternative scared the hell out of him. No way could he be attracted to a *kyūketsuki*, a vampire, his sworn enemy. No. Fucking. Way.

So why for that brief, insane moment did that kiss feel like the answer to every yearning he'd ever felt? Why did it feel like it meant love? *Kuso, kuso, kuso.* Shit, shit, shit. He couldn't deny it. That balls-deep, cock-rearing need tore through his body and his senses.

Such fatigue filled Tatsu that the stairs up to his apartment felt like Mt. Everest. He needed to forget this insane night. He placed the *menpo*, left in haste by the vampire, on the table beside his bed but he couldn't help tracing his fingers over the fine molded leather. A thing of rare beauty, just like its owner.

He tried calling up the cold anger of his vengeance. Instead, the scalding heat of their kiss burned across his mouth. His tongue rolled over his lips seeking any last vestige of the vampire's taste.

As the tepid shower drizzled over his body, Tatsu stared down at his pulsing erection—the undeniable demand in its iron stiffness. He smoothed back the foreskin and a string of precum dribble off his cockhead and mingle with the water.

His hand moved faster, a vice around his cock, the strokes punishingly brutal. He found his hole and drove three fingers to the last knuckle deeply inside. He curled them against his wet, pulsing walls, found his spongy knob. His orgasm rocketed through him, slammed breath from his lungs and the sanity from his mind.

Chest heaving, he collapsed against the tiled wall. The

freezing blast from the shower shocked him back to reality. He shut off the creaky taps and dried himself with his single, ragged towel. With a strangled groan, he flopped onto his bed.

His loneliness was so deep, so ingrained, that he never gave it thought. Now, it made itself known as it reached out and tore apart his armor. He was starved for love. But if he gave in to that hunger, he would fail his family and dishonor *Ojii-san*. He would die before allowing that to happen.

Saito Arisada had made Tatsu accept that *kyūketsuki*—or at least this *kyūketsuki*—could tread the Path of the Samurai; could honor a spiritual tradition as ancient as Nipon herself. If this vampire was the one he sought, Tatsu would not hesitate to kill the beast but in a manner worthy of a true warrior.

Unbidden, Arisada's avowal of love echoed in his mind. Arisada spoke of love; of an undying devotion strong enough to survive centuries. A seductive promise. With an anguished sigh, Tatsu thrust his thoughts aside. No matter the cost, the Kurosaki blood debt must be paid. There was no room in his life for anything else. Especially not love.

Seven

"All right, all right, I'm coming," Tatsu yelled as he crawled from the rumpled covers of his cot to answer the loud thumping at his door. A hint of light at his window told him he'd slept less than an hour.

He shook off the fog of sleep. *Chikusho*, should he be angry or grateful that the incessant knocking had interrupted *the* dream? A wonderful, erotic dream that had left him with a raging hard-on coupled with a deep ache of loss. Except, strangely, the mouth of his dream lover felt and tasted like the lips of the vampire who had kissed him two nights ago.

Tatsu's erection wilted as he hopped around on the cold floor. He pulled on his jock and grabbed his *tanto* as the flimsy door shuddered beneath another heavy blow.

"*Matte kudasai*, hold on, will you?" Blade poised to strike, he yanked the door open and stared, dumbfounded, at the strange man grinning back. "Mr. Bana?"

"Course it's me, boyo, who else would it be? And bye-the-bye, me name's Murtagh, Bana Murtagh. But Bana's okay, just drop the Mister crap." Bana didn't waste a glance at the knife pointing at his chest, just pushed the tip aside and walked into the shabby, closet-sized room. He shoved his hands deep into his pockets and hunched his shoulders in an exaggerated shiver. "Shite, it's cold enough to freeze a whore's tit in here."

Bana noted those two swords—those amazing, deadly swords—lying on the narrow cot crowded under the window. A pair of worn motorcycle saddlebags leaned against the single wooden chair. In one corner, a rickety card table held a hot plate, dented saucepan, utensils and not much else. A tattered drape hanging from a metal rod did little to shield the dingy bathroom beyond. The Irishman's nose curled in an audible sniff. "This is a foin palace you're livin' in."

"It works for me." Tatsu shrugged and dropped the short

blade onto the cot. He hadn't chosen the boarding house for its creature comforts but because it was dirt-cheap and offered a shed where he could keep his bike out of the perennial rain.

Bana made a quick assessment of the kid's near-naked body. A fine layer of muscle there. No wonder he wielded those swords as easily as if they were a set of chopsticks. And fekkin' hell? Four distinct bite marks right alongside that Adam's apple. Bana would bet his sainted mother's silver crucifix those old scars were the legacy of a bloodsucker.

Tatsu grabbed his wrinkled jeans from the chair and pulled them on. "What are you doing here?" he demanded, the question muffled by the tee half over his head. Tucking it in, he turned to Bana.

The Irishman had intended to deliver only his thanks. But those wounds on the young man's throat changed his mind. There was a story here. Although Bana's nose itched with curiosity, all of that could wait. He was hungry. "Come on, breakfast's on me." He yanked open the apartment door and stepped into the hallway.

Tatsu stilled his protest. Instead, he pulled on his boots, strapped on his swords and shrugged into his jacket. The Irishman was the first friendly person Tatsu'd encountered in this hostile city. Best of all, Bana appeared sober. Sober might mean reliable information, especially from a man who kept an arsenal in his apartment.

They stepped from the lobby into a freezing drizzle. Tatsu hunched his shoulders against the rain. In stride, they hiked down the steep hill in the direction of a row of shops. Beside him, Bana grumbled how it was always, "bucketing in this fekkin' town."

"Where are we going?" Tatsu shouted over the gear-grinding clanks of the ancient garbage truck gathering refuse for Seattle's methane plants. Bana didn't bother to reply, but merely continued his short, powerful stride down the street—the set of his shoulders saying he was sure Tatsu would follow. Minutes later, the Irishman ushered them into the warmth of a hole-in-the-wall café filled with the hearty aromas of home cooking. Tatsu's stomach grumbled and his mouth watered.

"Place doesn't look like much but the breakfast here will warm the cockles of a man's stomach." Bana mangled the old cliché, hoping to make Tatsu smile. It didn't work.

They hunkered down at a table at the rear of the cafe. By habit, Tatsu turned his chair and straddled it. Bana unzipped his jacket letting it drop open, the butts of his two guns within easy reach.

Tatsu wondered if the Irishman didn't care who knew about his firearms. Or perhaps there was another reason for the man's casual disregard for the law?

"What's yer name, boyo?" Bana peered around for the waiter.

"Tatsu Cobb."

"Sod me. Yer only part Oriental. Coulda fooled me." Bana was not shy about his opinions. "You ain't got no accent. Where ya from?"

"Born in Nagasaki. Moved to the Pueblo Sovereign State, Santa Fe actually, when I was twelve."

Bana whistled. "Rich turf. Lotsa money, lotsa sunshine, no bloodsuckers. And you left it fer this hellhole? Pretty daft thing to do."

Before Tatsu thought of a response, the waiter placed a steaming pot of coffee and two mugs before them. The old man took their order, which Bana delivered rapid-fire as if he knew the menu by heart.

"How old are you, anyway? Seventeen, mebbe eighteen? An' no bullshit." Bana rubbed his forefinger down the side of his nose. "I can always tell. Ya might say it's a supernatural talent o' mine."

"Twenty-four." Tatsu grimaced, anticipating the inevitable reaction. This time it was delivered somewhere in a string of Irish profanity.

"No shite? Bugger me. You look like yer in fekkin' high school." Their food arrived, putting an end to Bana's questions. Bana ate with noisy gusto, washing down big bites with great gulps from his mug. His shrewd gaze never left Tatsu's face.

To a hungry Tatsu, the breakfast was absolute perfection,

and the food went down fast. He smiled his gratitude, a quick flash of perfect white teeth accompanied by unexpected dimples. "*Domo arigatō gozaimasu,* but you really didn't have to do that."

"Certainly did, boyo. You saved my arse. Most folks would take off, not even stop to call the coppers. Not that it would do any good, seeing as how they're strictly day-lighters. Not like in the old days."

Mochiron, of course. Bana was a young man in the old days—before the plague turned the world upside-down thirty years ago.

"What was it like, back then I mean?" Tatsu's mother would have thought it an impolite question. But polite wouldn't get him far in this world.

"Shite, boyo. Wasn't as good as some like ta think. In fact, this country was already on its way to the crapper even before me Mam spat me out. Economic hell, I heard. No jobs, millions, and I mean millions, o' homeless fightin' over scraps. The Feds tried to crack down and, Bob's-yer-Uncle, they got civil war. And that was even before we was hit by the fekkin' vampire virus."

"Do you remember the virus?"

"Lost half me family to it. Didn't know what the fuck it was. Before we knew it, couple billion died, thousands turned bloodsucker. Sod me, who knew vamps came from a fekkin' disease? So-called genius scientists couldn't figure out how something hidden for centuries suddenly woke up. This country was hit worse than any other. Dunno why. Other places not so much. The Dominion of Canada and the Greater European Consortium, pretty much untouched. All ancient history now, boyo."

Bana gave a little snort and got to the point of his breakfast invitation. "You snooped around my apartment the other night, didn't cha? Noticed a little more than ya bargained fer." He stared at Tatsu long enough that those honey-colored cheeks flushed.

"*Sumimasen*. You have a nice apartment."

"Sure do. And I gots the means to keep it."

"*Mochiron*, it appears you do, Murtagh-san. Several lethal means. Aren't you afraid of breaking the law?"

"Not me, I've got what you might call special dispensation." Bana evaded any further details by slurping his coffee with noisy relish.

"One of those vampires the other night had a gun."

"Yeah, lotta good it did him, eh? Stupid git shoulda remembered his best weapons are in his mouth. Along with super speed and strength. Makes life pretty crappy fer a lot o' citizens. But enough o' my blather. Christ on a crutch, you killed three bloodsuckers in seconds. Where'd you learn to use swords like that?"

Tatsu sensed more than friendly curiosity behind the man's question. Tatsu's innate reticence crumpled. Was it his dire need for information? Or just to talk with a man, any man, after so many weeks of painful solitude?

"*Ojii-san*, er ... Grandfather, started training me as soon as I could walk. I always thought it was because of family tradition, you know, honoring my ancestors, embracing the mysticism of samurai honor."

"Pretty efficient way o' packing 'em on yer back like that. I know that ain't traditional."

"I was taught Miyamoto Musashi's techniques, one of Japan's greatest samurai of the seventeenth century. He called it the Way of the Two Swords. It just means I adapt to whatever works."

"So, where'd you get them swords?"

"They've been in my family for five centuries."

Bana gave an admiring whistle. "Packing anything else?"

"*Tanto*. Short knife. Pretty handy. Used for many things including committing *seppuku*."

"Ugh, you mean suicide. Don't understand that at all." Bana scrunched up his nose. "You Japs take this sword crap pretty serious, don'tcha? Seems using a gun is a hell of a lot more practical, if you get my drift."

"Maybe for you. But I'm not breaking the law. And I'd put my swords against any gunman within twenty feet," Tatsu goaded, hoping to hear the Irishman explain those Berettas.

"Twenty feet. What the fuck's that mean?"

"Inside that distance, I can draw my sword and slice a man open before he can pull the trigger."

"Not for me to deny it, boyo. Not after seein' ya take out three bloodsuckers faster than shit through a goose."

Impatient with Bana's chatter, Tatsu pushed his empty plate aside. "Who are you? How'd you know where to find me? What do you want from me?"

"Whoa, slow it down, boyo. Me? I'm jist a simple Irishman, born and raised. As for finding you? Easy. Strangers are always noticed in this neighborhood—especially someone packing steel like yours." The amused crinkle fell from his weathered face. "The way you handled yourself other night, that wasn't yer first time. Been hearing a lot of shite 'bout vamps being chopped up by them swords. But you ain't no hunter."

"Perhaps I'm a different kind of hunter."

A loud guffaw burst from the Irishman's mouth. "There ain't no different kind o' hunters. You're either in the killing game or you're not. No middle ground here, boyo. Wannabe hunters always coming here looking to score kills. They're not encouraged to stay. I'd advise you the same. Move on. Vancouver's not such a bad place. Canadians are real friendly folks."

"I have something I must do." Tatsu refused to curb the edge in his voice.

"Yer a stubborn shite. But since I kin tell you ain't about to take my friendly advice, tell me whatcha really doing here?" Bana grinned, the friendly expression aimed at disarming Tatsu.

"I, ah ... it concerns my family."

"So, yer here to look up some long lost relatives. Lot of Orientals here. But something tells me you're not one for family reunions. Right?" Bana's deep grey eyes reflected more than idle curiosity.

Tatsu wanted to trust this man, needed to trust him. Needed a friend. The story slipped from his taut, reluctant lips.

"Two months ago, my Uncle Ray was murdered by a border jumper from Upland Mississippi." Tatsu's throat closed against the memory of his crippling grief as he scattered the remains of his only relative on a slope of the Sangre de Cristo Mountains, and of the tears that soaked the letter he wrote to Warren, Ray's former lover, now living in New York.

"When I sorted through his papers, I found a police report on my family's murders. The file says I was there but I didn't remember anything until I saw the photos."

Tatsu thought the pain of remembering was done. But mentioning those photos tore off the scab of forgetfulness and sent him reeling into the past. The noises of the restaurant faded as, with an implacable force all its own, Tatsu's mind catapulted him back to that night. A night of slaughter when a terrified ten-year-old Tatsu drowned in a sea of blood and terror.

Nagasaki, Japan, 2010

"*Kachan, mother. Tadaima,* I'm home!" Tatsu's usual greeting bubbled over with a rare excitement as he dashed through the front door of his house. He could barely contain his excitement at the amazing news that would fill his parents with pride. Just this afternoon, Chikamatsu-Sensei, the *shinkendo* master at the Nagasaki Boys Middle School promised Tatsu would be named captain of the lower-division team next term.

"*Kachan. Otoo-san.* Mother, father, I'm home," he called again in English, knowing it would please his American father.

He kicked off his shoes in the *genkan*, the tiny vestibule leading to the living area. Tripping and laughing, he jammed his feet into his slippers. He giggled with delight at the sight of his father's large, polished business shoes. Tonight, everyone was home to celebrate Tatsu's tenth birthday. Tomorrow morning, they were leaving for America. Tatsu felt his happiness would burst from his body and eclipse everyone.

Strange, there were no food smells, even though it was an hour past dinnertime. Perhaps they were having *Hiyashi chuka,* his favorite cold-noodle dish. He charged into the kitchen. Puzzled, he skidded to a halt just inside the door.

Where was *kachan* or his younger sister, Min-chan, who always pestered her mother to help with cooking? Tatsu stepped into the dining room expecting to see everyone seated and eating, but there were only five empty places at the low table. He giggled at his stupidity. *Mochiron*, of course, Tatsu, you *baka*. How could he be such an idiot and forget? Everyone must be upstairs packing for their holiday.

In his excitement, Tatsu failed to notice the eerie quiet of the house. He bounded up the stairs; his long legs—a legacy from his tall, American father—letting him take them two at a time with ease. Tatsu raced down the hall to his room, tossed his school satchel onto his desk, scrambled out of his uniform jacket and dropped it in a careless heap on top of his bed.

"*Onii-kun*, guess what?" He ducked his head into his younger brother's tiny bedroom and felt a twinge of disappointment at not finding his brother reading a book, as usual. Rikaru-chan must be in their parent's bedroom. He banged on the door to his little sister's room. "Min-chan, may I come in?" Silence. The door remained closed. No matter.

"*Kachan, Otoo-san*," he called for his parents again as he charged along the short, unlit hallway. For a moment, he wondered why he heard no happy chatter coming from his parent's bedroom. *Mochiron*, packing is hard work. Rudely, he slid the door open without asking permission but knowing his mother would forgive. She always forgave.

Tatsu bounded across the threshold. His feet skidded from beneath him. He crashed onto his back, slamming his head on the wooden floor. Bright lights danced in his head. Sticky fluid, like honey, coated the *tatami* beneath his splayed hands. A cloying, sweet smell, mixed with the rank stench of sewage, flooded his nostrils.

He felt a moment's confusion at the sight of a discarded pile of clothes. *Otoo-san*'s business suit? Why was it covered in red paint? He felt an odd disconnect before the horror hit him. The crumpled pile was his Dad, the tanned face now a sickly white, cheeks slack, the eyes open but unseeing. A hole gaped like a second mouth below the chin. Thick, crimson fluid covered his father's inert body.

"*Otoo-san* wake up, wake up." Tatsu cried, reaching for the hand lying open and unmoving on the floor. The fingers were cold. "Dad, please, look at me." He begged for his father's warm, green eyes to light with recognition of his son.

Tatsu lifted his head and stared blankly at the tangle of bedclothes spilling over the end of the bed. His cry for his mother turned into a shriek of agony as sharp claws dug into his calf with excruciating pain. With a neck-snapping jerk, his world flipped upside down. In terror, he twisted his body, flailing his arms, kicking with his free leg. One slipper spun in crazy arcs through the air and bounced against the wall. Someone screamed from far, far away. The screams were his.

The claws around his leg dug deeper, sending incredible pain up his leg as his attacker shook him. Tatsu's head flopped back and forth. A sick weakness swept through him. His cries drowned in a flood of bile that gushed out of his mouth. His eyes filled with tears, blurring the sight of his sister sprawled on the *tatami*; a mat that should have been sea blue but now was insanely red. Her crumpled body looked like one of her dolls with its blank, plastic face.

The world spun, everything going topsy-turvey. "*Kachan!*" His terrified cry came out as a liquid whimper. He saw his mother on the bed. Thick, red rivulets splattered over her torn neck and exposed breast. Her beautiful brown eyes stared unseeing up at him as he dangled above her too-white face. His little brother, Rikaru, sprawled immobile against her side, one of his small arms draped over her waist in a child's desperate and futile gesture of protection.

The room rocked again as Tatsu's body whipped from side to side. More pain as his head snapped back and forth. Then the vice around his leg vanished, and he dropped headfirst onto the blood-soaked *tatami*. He wanted to curl up and bury his head under his arms but was too stunned to move. He squeezed his eyes so tight that colored lights danced behind his eyelids. But he couldn't shut out the sounds of laughter bubbling thick and wet with a dreadful delight above him.

Hands on his ankles and neck dragged him flat onto his back. A terrible weight landed on his chest. He heard the sickening crack of his own ribs then he could not breathe. He clawed at the arm pinning him, scratched the hand clutching his chin. Then that hand twisted his head sideways. His neck was going to break!

"You're the last of that Kurosaki *onezimi*. The last vermin to ever carry that name." The animal growl rolled against the terrified boy's ear. A hiss of such hatred, Tatsu felt it would destroy his soul. Agony beyond comprehension pierced his neck. Excruciating pain ripped along every nerve in his body.

"Filthy *Kyuk*..." Grandfather Shiniichiro's blessed, beautiful voice ripped through the blindness of Tatsu's terror. The terrible scream of rage sounded like it ripped from the depths of the old man's soul. Another shout, this time the full battle cry of a Kurosaki samurai. Tatsu heard the whistle of steel cutting through air.

The monster gave an inhuman shriek of pain and fury. That terrible vice left Tatsu's throat. Another screech of agony, this time drowned out by Grandfather's victorious cry.

Thick fluid, rank and cloying, gushed over Tatsu's face and ran into his silently screaming mouth. His stomach heaved but couldn't expel the vile liquid burning its way down his throat.

Then the crushing pressure lifted from his body. He knew a terrible fight raged around him. But if he opened his eyes, he knew he'd seen his family drenched in blood. The horror of the gore-filled room would swallow him like the maw of a giant, evil dragon.

Tatsu curled into the tight ball of a terrified infant and buried his head in his arms. *Kachan, kachan*, his mind screamed for his mother. Why didn't she answer?

Above him, crashing and more cries followed by the tearing of a paper wall. The hiss of a sword sheathed into its saya. A sound Tatsu knew so well but seemed curiously out of place in this room.

Gasps, harsh and ragged, approached Tatsu. Terror made him curl more deeply into his body. The breathing changed into strangled sobs—a brittle sound like the splintering of glass. Trembling hands lifted him. His shattered mind recognized the familiar grip of *Ojii-san*'s strong, sinewy arms.

Those arms clutched him hard against a bony chest. Grandfather's chest, from which came only harsh sobs. Beneath Tatsu's cheek, he heard a heart pounding too fast and too hard.

"*Su-kun, Su-kun.*" Tatsu heard the endearment crooned in a broken voice. He heard other words that made no sense. A rhythmic, hitching movement reminded him of childhood. So strange to be rocked by Grandfather, the motion gentle and soothing, as if Tatsu was still a baby.

A vast abyss beckoned. All Tatsu had to do was step into it, and the horror in the room would vanish. He stepped. Silence and darkness enfolded him. The deep, black void took his pain and his childhood. For the next thirteen years he lived with no memory of that time save a sickening, copper smell that haunted him in his nightmares.

The Seattle Quarantine, 2024

"Real sorry 'bout yer family. Fekkin' filthy, murdering bloodsuckers." Bana's voice jerked Tatsu back to the present. He dragged his attention back to the Irishman.

"Lookin' fer a bit of revenge, eh?"

A terrible grief crossed the boy's face. Those remarkable green eyes glazed with unshed tears. Then, like a freezing storm, the expression turned cold.

"The police ignored the evidence, concluded my father murdered his family then committed suicide. Brought shame to our name because Dad was *gaijin,* an outsider. My grandfather kept a journal. He wrote that a *kyūketsuki,* a vampire, killed them. But vampires don't exist in Japan."

"Why here?"

"In his last entry, Grandfather had written one sentence. He believed the *kyūketsuki* was in Seattle."

"Kew ... kooo ...what the hell's that word?"

"Sorry, it's pronounced *cute-ski*. Japanese for vampire."

"Shite. Jist bloodsuckers by another name. Lotsa them poured in here years back; especially after yer country started exterminating them. Any luck?"

"No, couple of leads but they fizzled. Looking for you, hoping you'll tell me about the local vampires." Tatsu felt shame to admit to this stranger that he'd run out of options. He pulled out a cigarette, lit it and inhaled, letting the rush of nicotine dull the desperation that threatened him.

"What makes you think I'd know shite?"

"Why did those vampires jump you?" Tatsu countered, locking gazes with Bana.

"Wrong place, wrong time, I guess. Vampires are always looking for an easy meal." He frowned. "And you never explained to me about that last bloodsucker. Shite, ya musta moved like grease through a goose to frost his clackers that fast."

"Instinct. Didn't realize I killed him until it was over." Tatsu shrugged, grateful Bana had missed Arisada's timely appearance. But puzzled at why he felt he needed to protect the vampire. Was it because the flame-haired creature had kissed him—twice? And that those kisses had stirred a feeling deep within him he thought he'd never have again?

"You must have the luck o' the Irish, I'd say. Cept you're a Jap." Bana chuckled at his own humor for a second, then pinned Tatsu with a glare. "But enough o' that. Sounds like you're at a dead end. Maybe the bloodsucker ain't here. Maybe's he's dead. A bastard like that is bound to pile up a few enemies."

"He's alive."

Bana heard the utter conviction in Tatsu's voice. "Stubborn little bugger, ain't cha?" He felt pleased that Tatsu ignored the insult. Better and better. With those icy nerves, the kid could be of real use. "So, boyo, what are you going do if you find this monster?"

"Force him to tell me why. Then kill him." Behind his answer lay all the conviction of his samurai heritage. He suppressed a ripple of disgust. Perhaps he'd already met, and kissed, the killer. The warmth filling his groin told him his so-called disgust was a lie. Arisada had declared his love and kissed Tatsu with such passion that almost made him forget all about *fukushū*. Within those golden eyes, Tatsu had seen gentleness and a deep, ancient sorrow. That lambent gaze didn't reflect the cruelty of a killer.

Bana's scoffing laugh drew the startled glances of other customers. He reared back in his seat and grinned. "Sorry, boyo. But yer gonna *force* a bloodsucker ta spill his guts? How? Hack off his body parts one by one?"

Tatsu shot him chilling look. "I'll do what I have to."

"Seems ya might need help with that." The canny Irishman didn't look fooled by Tatsu's evasive reply. "Lots 'a folks think offing bloodsuckers is a good thing. Still, me nose tells me killing doesn't sit so easy with you." Bana probed.

Tatsu's lips turned white stark against his creamy skin. His jaw set and his eyes turned cold. He made no reply. The Irishman's comment hit too close to the truth.

"Shite, no law says you can't defend yourself." Bana signaled for more coffee. "This city was doing all right before the truce was broken. Now, bloodsuckers are hunting humans, sometimes fer food, mostly fer sport. I'd sure watch my back, boyo. Once they get yer scent imprinted on their wee brains, they won't stop until yer dead."

"Is that what happened to you?"

The Irishman's bushy brows wrinkled together, and he shrugged but gave no real answer.

Tatsu tried another track. "Do you hate them?"

"Bloodsuckers? Yeah, many folks got reason to hate 'em, boyo. Just don't care to share mine. Hate takes a lot out of a man but it won't leave ya until done is done. Some more than others..." Bana trailed off suddenly, then flushed as if he remembered what brought Tatsu to Seattle. "So, tell me where those scars on yer neck came from."

Tatsu bristled. "Are you going to give me any info or do I just thank you for breakfast and leave a tip?"

"Calm down. I got me reasons fer askin'. There's only one thing that leaves the kinds o' marks you got." He traced the four new wounds above the collar of his heavy sweater. "You got bit, got real sick but didn't turn, right? Now you're different, bit faster, bit stronger, maybe not quite human. Who knows?"

Tatsu shrugged and glared into those probing hazel eyes. Bana was right. Maybe his speed and strength just came from his training. Maybe not. He'd always known he was different, and his sexual orientation was not *it*. But no way had a vampire bitten him.

"No *kyūketsuki* live in Japan. By law, vampires are executed." Tatsu made no apologies for the actions of his native land that happened years before he was born. "New Mexico is safe; not like here. Although it seems most of the people here aren't that afraid."

"Oh, they're scared a' plenty, boyo. Make no mistake o' that. But life goes on. In fact, it's because of the vampires many of 'em stay. Folks can support their families by indenturing themselves to the Clan fer five years. Sort of like a human grocery store. Sure, it's a crapshoot if they get the bug. But what are they gonna do when there ain't nothing else?" Bana noted the restless shift of Tatsu's shoulders and realized the boy was about to leave. Time to spring his offer. "Speaking of money. Looks to me like you're skint considering the dump you're living in and the way you scarfed that food. Want a job?"

"What are you talking about? I don't need a jo—"

Bana cut off the speech with a dismissive wave of his hand. "Jist listen for half a mo'. I'm sorta in the security biz, get paid to kill the thing you're hunting." The Irishman winked and shoved the final bite of his bagel into his mouth. A sliver of whitefish dangled from the corner of his lip. He didn't notice and continued talking around the food.

"City ain't got the readies to handle the upswing in vampire attacks. So, my company was hired. Vamps are our specialty. We're real covert. My boss is very selective about hirin', but I'm thinkin' to meself you'd fit in right smart-like."

The kid also had another quality that would make him one hell of an asset to the company, but Bana was not about to mention it.

"Sorry, Murtagh-san. I'm just looking for information. Give me that and we'll call it even." Working for a company meant rules and restrictions. He had only one purpose for being here. Once that was done, he'd leave. Not back to New Mexico, he doubted if anything waited for him there. Maybe to Japan, look for his mother's family; if any remained alive.

"Yer a goddamn fool." Bana chewed furiously for a moment before swallowing. "Okay, boyo. Information it is. Best guess, there's mebbe a couple of thousand vampires living here. Ghetto is named Tendai fer some godfersaken reason by the Master. Him and his second-in-command are a couple o' sadists. Killed the old Master by choppin' off his head. Sorta like you." Bana laughed.

"What are their names?"

"Want 'em Japanese style, last name first, eh?"

"*Hai, dozo*, please." Tatsu hid his annoyance. Dragging information out of the Irishman would test the patience of the most enlightened Buddhist *ryoko*.

"Clan leader's Ukita Sadomori. His Primary is Saito Arisada."

Tatsu hid his dismay. He'd met—hell, he'd kissed—the very same Saito Arisada the night before. And during their *jigeiko* match, the vampire had shown his true spirit—the spirit of a *kensei,* a sword saint. Not exactly the beliefs of a vicious killer. But then Tatsu reminded himself that killers could be extremely cunning.

"You being Japanese an' all perhaps you've heard of 'em?"

"Not till now." Tatsu took a sip of coffee to hide any reaction to mention of Arisada. "What's a Primary?"

"That's the first human a vampire turns. They get bonded, like in bed together, ya might say," he leered. "Couple of other things ta put in yer noggin. When they use that thrall shite on folks, it's all over. Told it's something to do with pheromones. Plus, a bloodsucker fucks every time it feeds. The bulls are worse than the fems. Lot of times after that fuck, a human gets hooked on vampire mojo. Like an addiction."

"*Hai, hai*, I know that. What about these leaders?"

"They're old, mebbe the oldest that we know of anyway. Sadomori cut the heads off the city negotiators and dumped the bodies on the courthouse steps. Sadistic arsehole. Prolly his Primary is as bad but not much is known about him. He keeps to the shadows, sneaky sod."

Tatsu changed the subject. No need to appear too eager to talk about Saito Arisada. "So, is being in this security business the reason those vampires jumped you? They must have known you were armed, they can smell gunpowder."

Bana evaded the question. "Smart fer a raw kid. Sometimes a couple try to get lucky, or so they think. Them the other night behind the Whore weren't so lucky, eh boyo?"

"*Wakarimashita.*"

"Dunno what you meant by that. My Japanese ends at sushi."

"Sorry, I just mean ... I understand. Old habits die hard."

"Gotcha. Now, how about that job offer, boyo?"

Tatsu shrugged, rose and pulled his jacket on over his swords. "*Arigatō,* er... thank you, for the meal and the information, but I'm not interested." Perhaps he was *baka,* an idiot, for refusing. Yeah, he'd hit dead ends at every turn and he was nearly out of money. But a job like this could be a complication. Tatsu shook his head.

Undaunted, the Irishman slid a piece of paper across the table. "Big mistake, but iffn you change your mind, call me."

Just to be polite, Tatsu stuffed it into his pocket. "Thanks again for the breakfast."

"Sure, boyo. Consider us square."

"Square? Breakfast, even one with real salmon, is a small price for a life," Tatsu snorted.

"Lives ain't got much value in this city, kid. Don't forget it."

"Thanks, I'll keep it in mind." Tatsu zipped up his jacket and stepped into the rain.

Back in his squalid room, he looked at the name on the scrap of paper, *The Leper Colony.* What kind of screwball name was that? No address, only a phone number scribbled on the back. No way did Tatsu want to be a part of any vigilante-for-hire organization.

He dug into his pocket and pulled out the pack. With a regretful sigh, he took out a cigarette. Damn, only three left. He was broke, and without money, his hunt would end, probably well before he found the killer.

Three days later Tatsu was almost ready to give up. The Kawasaki hated the city's weather as much he did. Half a block from home, the bike had died. Tatsu crouched beside it, cursing the motorcycle, cursing the unending cold drizzle and cursing Seattle in general. He tweaked the choke and pressed the starter button. The engine turned over once, but refused to start. *Kuso*, he'd have to push the damn thing up the rest of the steep hill to the boarding house.

For four years, the motorcycle had been reliable, if cranky, transportation. Now, the bike's 1,500-cc engine ran with all the power of a two-stroke lawn mower. It needed new spark plugs and the carburetor rebuilt, probably new rocker arms and the valves ground. It ran so rough Tatsu's butt went numb after a few miles.

He pressed the ignition again. The motorcycle backfired, spewed a gout of oily smoke from its tailpipe and died.

"Sounds like you got water in the tank." The Irish lilt held a slight mocking tone. Surprised, Tatsu looked up. Only three feet away, Bana stood dry and smug inside a doorway.

"What are you doing here?" Tatsu pulled the fuel line loose.

"This is my neighborhood, boyo." He waved a half-chewed sandwich in the direction of the Drifter. "Need help?"

Tatsu tapped the line. "I'm good, thanks." He didn't mean to sound ungracious, but he was tired and cold, and in no mood for any wise-ass remarks. Seeing Bana reminded Tatsu their breakfast was three days gone, and he had only ramen noodles and some rice at home. But transportation, not hunger, was his problem. The night before, Tatsu had ridden ten miles out to the defunct airport chasing a rumor that ran out about the time the bike did.

"Gas is fulla shite, 'specially the black-market stuff."

"Tell me about it." Tatsu fastened the line back onto its nipple, tweaked the choke and kicked the motorcycle over again. Another defiant backfire but then the engine settled into a rough idle. Tatsu shut it off. Better save the fuel. He wiped his hands on a rag before wrapping his tools in it around and storing them in his saddlebag.

Bana pushed himself off the wall and sauntered over to the

bike. He handed Tatsu a paper bag. "Here, maybe this will help."

If that bag held a vacuum piston kit, Tatsu'd call the man a god. When Tatsu opened the sack, the mouth-watering aroma of corned beef assailed his nose. Maybe not a god, but definitely a friend of sorts. "Um, *domo arigatō*, Murtagh-san but you didn't—"

"Jaysus, boy. I told ya to call me Bana. And course I didn't, hafta do it, but you look like a starving rat. Hell, I swear you're skinnier than last time I saw ya. Now, do you wanna know where you can get top-grade gas fer free?"

Against his will, Tatsu gave the Irishman a hopeful glance. "Where?"

"My company, the Leper Colony."

Tatsu felt his shoulders stiffen. "I don't know."

"A job would sure help yer cir...cum...stances." Bana dragged out each syllable of the last word with a grin.

Tatsu stuffed the food inside his jacket, straddled the bike, and stomped down on the kick-start. The engine's rumble almost drowned out his, "*Arigatō*, I'll think about it."

"Don't think too long, boyo," Bana yelled at Tatsu's retreating back. He knew the boy had talent, the kind of major talent he could use at his side. Just then, the retreating motorcycle belched a noxious puff of black smoke from its tailpipe as if giving the Irishman a mechanical fuck-you finger.

A wolfish grin spread across Bana's face and his hazel eyes crinkled with amusement.

"Yer a stubborn little shite, but I'll be seeing ya sooner than ya think, boyo."

Eight

When his lips had fastened on Tatsu's mouth in that long, delectable kiss, Arisada knew he had been overcome by a sweet madness. His self-control, developed over centuries, nearly shattered. When the boy had responded with such intensity, the vampire was consumed by desire.

What insanity had possessed him to court attention then reveal his identity last week in the dojo? No denying he was consumed by desire for the young hunter; a desire that eclipsed all other emotions. Yet, no matter what his heart said, Arisada was oath-bound to destroy this young hunter.

The ache for Tatsu was a painful weight on Arisada's heart. And in his cock. He yearned to feel the youth's core pulsing and wet around his member. *Hai, hai,* he thirsted to drive himself deep into Tatsu's ass. Even more, the vampire needed to see the lust flare from those jade eyes moments before Arisada bit into that tender throat. Blind to all else but riding the crest of his orgasm, Arisada would drive his fangs into that vulnerable neck and drain the sweet, living blood.

Just like he had done countless times before.

Arisada detested the vile act of feeding. He recalled with horror the brutality of the first time the bloodlust possessed his body and senses. His first victim wailed for mercy. Arisada tore out the man's throat.

For an unaccountable time, Arisada killed wantonly until a tiny shred of conscience triumphed. Never would he forget the serenity of that blessed moment when he connected with his *tamashii,* his soul. After that, there were many times Arisada wished for his own death. But he had already taken so, so many lives. In his remorse, he stopped feeding.

His *Seisakusha,* Ukita Sadomori, intervened. He ordered Arisada to live. And, oath-bound, Arisada complied. He found a balance of sorts between his vampire instinct and his higher spiritual self. He took the lives of those who would never face justice—murderers, brigands and rapists. There were thousands of them down through the centuries.

With every death, Arisada begged for forgiveness from the Buddha Amida.

Now, in this modern era, no vampire needed to kill thanks to the indenture agreement. Some humans thought indenture was an easy life. Many did not believe they would catch the virus. Some did not care. And some offered themselves solely for the sexual high.

Arisada's soul rested no easier for it.

Driving to the indentured compound at Alki, Arisada cursed himself a fool. He hadn't fed in five days. In his near starvation, Arisada knew his lust for sex would overwhelm him. His fucking was no more than that of an animal in rut. No meaning and certainly no affection. That the human begged for it never justified the act.

Arisada spotted a young man—gawky, barely into his twenties—standing beside an open door. His posture indicated availability. Despite a smattering of acne and the fawning behavior common in the blood addict, the boy was pretty. His slim body and brown hair bore a slight resemblance to Tatsu.

The vampire approached the feeder and touched him on the shoulder. Although Arisada only chose men, not all were homosexual. A pleased exclamation escaped the man when he saw Arisada's face. The vampire felt no vanity with this reaction to his beauty. Beauty was a curse. His he used as a weapon.

Although strung tight with fear, his body reeking from adrenalin, the young man slipped under the vampire's thrall. Within seconds, the young feeder's cock tented his pants. With fevered haste, his hands groped at his waistband, jerked down the zipper. He dug under his tattered briefs for his prick.

"Not here, your utility," Arisada commanded.

While groping his crotch, the young man led Arisada into his single-room. The moment the door closed, the vampire lost all self-control. He struck, feeling his starved body burn with arousal at the first sip of the blood. As always, his hunger took him hostage.

Even before the vampire's saliva entered his bloodstream, the young man yanked out his own swollen dick and began jerking off with frantic strokes.

Arisada pushed the man's groping hand away from his dripping organ, and closed his own slender fingers over the hot shaft. He stroked the thick arc of flesh, once, twice before the sticky seed pulsed out. Then the vampire opened his own fly and pulled out his hard, angry prick. Blind to only his need, he smeared his organ with the young man's sperm then spun the human around and slammed him face first against the wall.

The youth rode his orgasm, his tumescent prick spurting with aftershocks. Arisada yanked the feeder's jeans to his thighs, and thumbed apart the cheeks of his ass to expose the tight, dark entrance. The vampire rammed in his cock into the feeder's rectum with brutal force.

The young man bucked back against him, crying his, "Oh yeahs," and, "Fuck me's" in the needy voice of the junky. Urged on by fingers pulling on his jutting hipbones, he ground his ass against the vampire's groin.

"*Gomen, gomen nasai. Yurushite, yurushite.*" Each thrust followed Arisada's grief-torn words that begged for forgiveness. With an anguished cry, he ejaculated, filling the youth with molten heat. At the same moment, he viciously drove his teeth into the sweat-slicked neck.

The boy uttered no cry of pain. Arisada fed with great gulps, his teeth and lips bruising the tender skin. Sated, he pulled out of the quivering ass. The thick cream slithered down the insides of the man's thighs.

Arisada laid his head on the young man's shaking back for a few moments. Alarmed, the youth turned around and saw red rivulets running down the vampire's face.

"What's wrong?" the young man asked, touching trembling fingers to the vampire's cheeks streaked with blood-tinged tears.

"Nothing you could ever understand, young one." Arisada kissed the young man on his forehead. "*Arigatō gozaimasu.*"

He touched the feeder's arm in an impotent gesture of gratitude then left. Remorse filled the vampire. The youth would be dead within a day, killed by Arisada's bite.

Hours later, Arisada walked along the tranquil paths of the Kuboto Garden. Beneath a rare, cloudless sky, the half moon cast a pale luminescence over the delicate Japanese landscape. The Garden was his solace and his bane—a poignant reminder of a land lost in time.

Arisada's refuge lay deep in a forested section of the Garden surrounded by Threadleaf cypress. Here was his secret place where he mourned Nowaki.

How he relished and hated his crystal-clear memories of his life at Mii-dera. A time when he was human, when he embraced the teachings of Buddha Amida and trained to be a Sōhei. His greatest joy came from that moment he fell in love. His greatest heartache from the moment his lover betrayed him.

Memories are supposed to blur with the passage of time, especially the long ages that mark a vampire's life. But his memory of Koji Nowaki remained sharper than the blade on his *kotagiri*. Thought it was hundreds of years in the past, Arisada's mind relived every moment, every nuance of the scents, sounds and feel of his time with his lover, his soul mate. His betrayer.

Relive it and weep.

The Temple of Mii-dera, Nipon, Spring 1175

Filled with concern, Arisada hurried through the monastery's vast grounds. At the age of twenty-one, he was a *gashira*, an officer in charge of training one-hundred foot soldiers. His status as their *sensei* made him responsible for gathering all novices to greet the visiting party. A display of strength was required, and all Mii-dera monks had been summoned to the great temple.

Tension rippled through every Sōhei of Mii-dera. This morning, the *zazu*, the abbot from Enryakuji, their sister monastery high atop Mount Hiei, arrived unannounced with a full complement of soldiers. It was no secret that he coveted control over the immense, yet independent, monastery of Mii-dera.

For decades, this concern had sparked violent conflicts between the two holy houses. Now, at the New Year, the question arose again. To counteract the threat, Mii-dera's abbot was considering an alliance with the clan of Prince Mochihito. This decision would determine the future of Nipon.

"Where the hell is Nowaki-kun? This is not the time for frivolous indulgences." As usual, when military training was suspended, his acolyte, Koji Nowaki, disappeared. Arisada's frustration grew while he searched through dozens of buildings on the vast temple grounds.

"He must be outside," Arisada growled, knowing how Nowaki enjoyed lazing in the warmth of the new spring. At times, Arisada wondered if the rebellious orphan would ever fully embrace the discipline of Sōhei life. The youth learned fast and was already leagues ahead of his class in nearly all fighting skills. Nowaki had seventeen summers, a man by all standards, but there were times—like now—when he acted more like a child. Although intelligent and fearless, Nowaki chaffed at the restrictions imposed by the Buddhist life.

The early morning sun suffused the orchard with a pale radiance. The blossoms from the sakura trees drifted to the ground to form a carpet of pink over the tender new grass. The air was redolent with their delicate scent.

Arisada sighted Nowaki lying under a sakura. Always a strange choice to Arisada who knew the boy had hidden in branches of that same kind of tree while his entire family was butchered. On silent steps, Arisada approached the sleeping form. In the stillness of the moment, he knelt beside Nowaki, all urgencies forgotten. Arisada allowed the peace of the orchard to quiet his annoyance at Nowaki's irresponsibility.

The older monk marveled how Nowaki-kun had grown in the few short years since he arrived at the monastery. The youth resembled an unbroken colt, not yet tamed by life, full of wild energy. The boy's exuberance often spilled over into little defiances like slipping off to doze under the cherry blossom trees when he should be cleaning the sleeping quarters.

One of Nowaki's arms formed a pillow behind his head, the other rested on his chest, the long fingers slightly curled. Despite the chill in the air, Nowaki wore only a thin *kimono*. He had kicked off his straw sandals and undone his *obi* to let the garment fall open. Pink petals had drifted down to dust his body.

A thin shaft of sunlight filtered down between the tree branches. It lit Nowaki-kun's face with a nimbus of golden light. The boy's slightly parted lips showed the tips of perfect, white teeth. There was no tension in his face, just the sweet look of slumbering youth. That unalloyed beauty of Nowaki's face had captured Arisada's heart.

Although four years separated their ages, Nowaki had already reached full manhood. He was taller than most men with a lean body that moved with coltish grace. The planes of Nowaki's chest showed the promise of the muscles beneath.

Arisada rubbed his hand over his own flat chest, knowing, with a little regret, he would never be as strong as the youth. Nowaki's skin was darker than Arisada's. Yet golden glints tinged the brown hair that dusted the youth's chest and trailed down his ridged abdomen.

Arisada's gaze followed the tantalizing concave of belly down to the boy's loins. Nowaki's thin *fundoshi* outlined every curve and ridge of his sex, more arousing to Arisada than a view of the naked treasures beneath.

A lone pink blossom drifted down to settle on Nowaki's forehead. Without thinking, Arisada reached out with trembling fingers to remove it. The gesture was an echo of his first caress when the boy came to him sobbing with fright and loneliness.

Arisada recalled that one precious time six months ago, when he held Nowaki in a loving embrace. A fierce winter storm tore through the monastery as if every demon sought to tear the place apart with supernatural forces. On that night, Nowaki had revealed the demons haunting his soul.

Why Nowaki's defenses fell, Arisada would never know.

The story had poured out in disjointed babble—the vicious mutilation, the murders, the rapes, the sheer helplessness suffered by an innocent who witnessed the slaughter of an entire village before suffering his own brutal violation. An all-too-common story yet singularly heartbreaking when spilling from Nowaki's lips.

Obeying his need to comfort the sobbing boy, Arisada had cradled Nowaki, rocking him while the youngster begged his *senpai* to protect him from the horrors of his young life.

Afterward, Nowaki burrowed, exhausted, into Arisada's arms, the undeniability of his need overwhelming the older monk's reticence. In the moment before sleep claimed them, Arisada professed his love for his young acolyte. But when Nowaki woke the next morning, curled within the protective circle of his *senpai's* embrace, the youth had recoiled. Cursing at Arisada, he had stormed out of the tiny room.

From then on, Nowaki had avoided Arisada whenever possible, and spurned any hint of affection from the older monk. Their voices filled with a harshness that could not quite obliterate the sound of their pain. Arisada became more brutal with Nowaki's training. He forgave no mistakes and wondered if he were seeking an excuse to kill the boy as punishment.

To deny his feelings for Nowaki, Arisada bedded others, hurried couplings during the night. However, each time left him feeling hollow and sad—emotions deemed unworthy of a Sōhei warrior.

The breeze fluttered the sakuras above Arisada. A bird gave forth with a joyous, full-throated song, and brought him to the present. His breath caught with the deep flush of that love washing through him. He ached to cradle Nowaki in his arms just for a moment. His long-suppressed desire emboldened him. He brushed his lips over the sleeping boy's mouth.

"No matter how you recoil from me, you are my *koibito*, my beloved," he whispered.

The need to lay with the youth, to console and comfort him, to love him in all ways shuddered through Arisada's thin frame. His erection strained against the coarse fabric of his *fundoshi*. Horrified, Arisada scrambled to his feet, losing one of his straw sandals, as he backed away from the youth and bolted for his sleeping quarters. Panting with fear and shame, Arisada propelled himself into his small cell. He slammed the door and barely made it to his night-waste bucket before his stomach expelled its contents.

Nowaki was an innocent. Arisada knew the youth's bravado and rebellion masked the deep hurt of a young child who had felt nothing but abuse. Nowaki's first intimate contact had been one of utter pain and degradation.

Arisada was Nowaki's senpai, his teacher in all things; yet, once freed of its shackles, his lust would murder the youth's spirit. Arisada crawled over to the tiny statue of the Buddha Amida and prostrated, forehead to the cold, stone floor. He vowed that he would never cause a moment of suffering for Koji Nowaki. A samurai in every fiber of his being, Arisada was determined to suppress his love for the boy.

No matter the depth of his feelings, Arisada would never take Nowaki to his bed.

The Seattle Quarantine, 2024

Eight centuries ago, yet it could have been last night. The diamond-sharp clarity of those memories never softened or faded. His yearning for the beautiful Nowaki, friend, lover, and, yes, betrayer, never abated. Over the centuries, the vampire had searched the faces of every youth he met. There had been thousands, yet none held the *tamashii,* the spirit, of his *koibito.*

Then, mere days ago, almost at the point when Arisada despaired of ever finding that soul, he saw it shining from the emerald eyes of the young hunter fighting for his life behind a bar. Using the boy's own delicious scent to find him, then sparring with him in such beautiful symmetry that the vampire was not only roused, but moved to tears. Never did he expect Nowaki's new form to bear the *bushi damashi,* the spirit of the samurai. Perhaps Arisada was *baka,* an idiot. He foolishly believed Nowaki would reincarnate in the body of a vile criminal, someone Arisada could justify killing. But not in a boy who was as beautiful in body as in spirit. A boy who bore the adversity of his lowly birth with grace and determination.

How the vampire wished to have never set eyes on Tatsu Cobb, never to have kissed him, pursued him, danced with him in the way of the sword. Never to have fallen in love with him.

"Oh you sweet, sweet boy. Why must I destroy you for the crimes of another?" Arisada moaned.

The tiny park was a solitary oasis in the dark. No one lived nearby to hear. Tonight, just like hundreds of nights in the past, Arisada howled his anguish to the indifferent sky.

Nine

Tatsu shut off the Kawasaki and dropped the motorcycle onto its kickstand. Hunched into his jacket, he cupped his last cigarette against the cold wind whipping in from the Bay. Even that first, slow drag tasted like crap thanks to the putrid stink of effluvia from the nearby sewage plant. He shivered then glared at the leaden sky. *Kuso,* between the ceaseless rain and the stench of shit, he wondered why a normal person would even consider visiting this godforsaken city. But then Tatsu no longer considered himself normal.

Puffing slowly, he leaned on the bike's seat and listened to the pings from his cooling engine as he considered the last few days. He'd been ambushed by the canny Irishman. Stuffed in with the sandwiches was a greased-stained piece of paper with the words, "Don't be a git," and a phone number. It only took Tatsu a couple of hours after eating the food to decide to look into the job offer. He might be a stubborn "git" but not to the point of outright stupidity.

When Tatsu called from the boarding house's ancient phone, the Irishman answered with a cocky chuckle. Directions to the industrial park on the Southside were easy. "Jist look for the foundry, can't miss it," Bana had assured. But weaving the bike through roads full of shattered concrete, wide fissures and treacherous potholes was a bitch.

Tatsu surveyed the massive structure, which sprawled over at least five blocks. Several smokestacks, covered with grime and soot, reared a hundred feet or so above the roof. Tatsu smelled old fuel and human ashes. Diamond-plate covered every window. Massive loading doors, at least six stories high, closed off one end. A set of double doors in a concrete-block wall at the other end looked to be the entrance.

Did he really want this job? If he agreed to work for this company, would he become nothing more than a hired killer?

What would that do to the legacy Grandfather had entrusted in Tatsu? Would he be shirking his karmic path? Yet, his encounters with the vampire Saito Arisada—no, the feelings about Saito Arisada—muddled Tatsu's thinking, derailing his singularity of purpose. Without some help and reliable information, Tatsu knew he was *fakku,* fucked and then some. Maybe this Leper Colony was worth a shot.

It was too much for him to admit he was lonely and tempted by the prospect of making a friend.

He took a last pull on his smoke and flicked the butt into a puddle. An unconscious shrug moved his swords into a more comfortable position. He mounted the short stairs to the grimy set of doors that looked fused closed by rust. Still thinking he was about to make a huge mistake, he curled his fingers around one of the jagged, metal handles. The hairs on the back of his neck prickled, the warning coming too late. The door jerked open so suddenly that he knew he'd been under surveillance since the moment he parked his bike.

"'Bout fekkin' time boyo," Bana bellowed. He yanked Tatsu into a decrepit lobby with such force the handle sliced Tatsu's palm. Even as Bana, chattering non-stop, dragged him down a narrow corridor, Tatsu felt the cut close and heal.

"Major Blenheim is a real combat vet, member of the elite British Royals. Twenty years with Scotland Yard's vampire-control branch. 'Course that was before Limey vamps got citizenship. 'Es cleaned up messes in more Quarantine cities 'round the world than you or I'll ever see. So, look sharp, me lad, and don't fuck up." Bana's babble alternated between outright admiration for his boss and admonitions to Tatsu to "look sharp."

The Irishman rapped once on a battered wooden door but didn't wait for a reply before pushing it open. He winked at Tatsu and pushed him into a small, airless room. "Meet Major Blenheim, our commander." Bana waved needlessly toward the room's sole occupant sitting behind a desk.

The man, dressed in black tactical gear, glanced up when the two entered. Tatsu guessed the Major to be around sixty although his trimmed mustache and intense, dark-grey eyes lent his weathered face a fierce vitality. This diminutive figure reminded Tatsu of Grandfather Shiniichiro—a warrior who could see into the true hearts of men.

"Major, this 'ere is Tatsu Cobb, the kid I told you about." Bana grinned with smug satisfaction and waved at two chairs facing the desk.

"*Hajimemashite.*" Tatsu bowed, offering the formal greeting between business associates. He took off his jacket then his harness, and held them in his lap while he sat.

"Welcome, Mr. Cobb. Mr. Murtagh tells me you're interested in joining the Leper Colony." The Major nodded to Bana. "Ask Mr. Cooperhayes to bring tea, thank you."

Bana muttered, "Sure, Guvnor," and ducked through a second door.

"I shall be with you in a moment." The Englishman turned back to his monitor until Bana barged back in with a mug of coffee in one hand and a bagel in the other. A tall, gaunt man carrying a tray followed.

"This is Mr. Cooperhayes, my adjutant." The Major waved his hand toward the newcomer. "Mr. Cooperhayes, this is Mr. Tatsu Cobb."

Tatsu fought the ingrained urge to rise and bow at Cooperhayes' nod of acknowledgement. In silence, the adjutant placed the pot on the desk, poured two cups of tea, handed one to the Major and the other to Tatsu. When Cooperhayes left the room, he barely disturbed the air as he closed the door. Bana slumped into the second chair and began gnawing on his food.

The Major removed a single sugar cube from its bowl and dropped it into his cup. He took a long sip, and regarded his visitor. "Mr. Cobb, I don't have a great deal of time. Because you saved Mr. Murtagh's life, you deserve my courtesy."

"*Domo arigatō gozaimasu.*"

The Englishman glanced at his computer. "In the past two weeks, you've killed nine vampires, including four the other night, defending Mr. Murtagh."

Tatsu felt trapped, hot and a little panicky. He stared at the Major then at Bana who just shrugged. "How did you know?"

"It's my business to know, Mr. Cobb. Now, please, tell me about your first kill." The Major pinned Tatsu with a hard stare. The youth's face blanched.

The question chilled Tatsu yet he knew everything hinged on his answer. Only moments ago, he was convinced he was making a mistake coming here. Now, sitting before the compelling authority of this small man, Tatsu suddenly wanted in. He shifted in his seat, hesitated, unwilling to share that single horrific moment when he crossed the irrevocable line that separated him from humanity.

Then the details of the hideous fight poured out in a disjointed slurry of words, Tatsu told about stopping at an abandoned park just outside Grand Junction, Colorado. It was nearly midnight, and he was exhausted. The Drifter was running rough, the engine sporadically cutting out. He needed to adjust the carburetor for the higher altitude. He dug out his tools while waiting for the engine to cool.

The vampire came screaming out of the night. Without thought, Tatsu whipped his *katana* from its *saya*. His first strike was clumsy, only cutting across the cheek. The vampire screeched with rage. Then, mouth stretched wide, it sunk its fangs through the leather sleeve of Tatsu's jacket and deep into his bicep.

Roaring with pain, Tatsu slammed the hilt of his sword into the vampire's temple. The creature opened its mouth to scream, releasing its bite. Tatsu twisted the razor-sharp blade against the vampire's nape and sliced once. The spine separated with an odd snicking. The body collapsed onto the carpet of pine needles littering the ground. It was only after the vampire's head came to rest against the rear tire of his bike did Tatsu realize he'd killed a woman. He spent the next hour vomiting against a tree.

To the Major, there was no mistaking the horror of that defining moment, the tremor in the young man's voice, the stare fixed inward to that irrevocable time and place. All good signs. Cobb may have thought he was a cold-blooded killer, but the Englishman could tell the boy wasn't hardened—not yet anyway.

The Major coughed once, a commanding sound that snapped Tatsu back to the present. He waved one hand at Tatsu's swords. "May I?"

Tatsu realized the man was giving him time to compose himself. With a look of gratitude, Tatsu placed his sheathed weapons on the desk.

The Major slid the *katana* from the polished scabbard, admiration for the blade clear in his eyes. "These are ancestral, I presume? But no longer the original steel composition. It appears the metal has been altered."

Although reluctant to reveal the blades' secret, Tatsu felt compelled to reply out of simple respect for the Englishman. "My grandfather had them treated with aggregated diamond nanorods. They won't break no matter what I strike."

"Thank you, Mr. Cobb." The Major handed the swords back to Tatsu with a visible show of reluctance. "Your background?"

"Entered NMU at fifteen, accelerated program, plan was to finish my doctorate next year."

"A doctoral program in what?"

"Urban-environmental engineering."

"Quite impressive to obtain a Ph.D. at twenty-four." Major Blenheim's initial doubt faded while he considered the young man sitting before him. A deep determination reflected in that young face. Intelligence and integrity. That Japanese code of honor clearly driving the boy. And, according to Mr. Murtagh, the youth killed with unparalleled efficiency.

"Military experience?" the Major asked. Tatsu hesitated.

"Go on boyo, open yer gob. Now's yer chance." Bana drove his elbow painfully into Tatsu's arm.

"One year, Pueblo Border Militia. Before I started my doctorate," Tatsu answered with a visible show of reluctance.

"Christ on a crutch, why'd ya volunteer for that?"

"It was my duty." Tatsu glared at the Irishman. The boy didn't feel he had to explain how there was no question about disobeying his grandfather's wishes. *Ojii-san* had said Tatsu needed the training to redeem their family honor. But *Ojii-san* died before revealing the mystery behind his words.

"Mr. Cobb, you are quite a surprise," the Major said. "That

Militia was formed for the sole purpose of keeping illegals from entering the Pueblo territory. And I know your only order was to shoot on sight. Perhaps—"

Bana interrupted, "Jaysus, boyo, the PBM? That's one of the bloodiest military units on this continent. Harsh fekkin' duty. Heard soldiers crack up, commit suicide, even—"

"How long were you in?" The Major cut off Bana's rambling.

"Normal tour, twelve months." Anticipating more questions, Tatsu steeled himself.

"Engaged in any combat?" The Major's eyes riveted on Tatsu's face. If the boy indicated any he felt enjoyment from killing, the interview would end immediately.

"Not much." The tick at the corner of Tatsu's mouth gave away the lie. He'd seen a lot of death in that brutal year, but none by his hand. He licked his lips, craving a cigarette, but even if he had one, he couldn't imagine asking permission to smoke.

The Major rarely changed his mind, but Tatsu Cobb was exceptional. "Mr. Cobb, if I employ you, your personal agenda must not affect any mission. Understood?" The Major pulled an ashtray, a pack of cigarettes and a lighter out of his desk drawer and pushed them across the desk to Tatsu. Gratitude flicker across the young man's face as he lit up.

Tatsu relaxed with the first deep lungful of nicotine. "*Domo arigatō gozaimasu.* But Bana wasn't really clear about what you do. I mean, are you some sort of a government or law enforcement agency?"

The derisive laugh bursting from the Englishman surprised Tatsu. Bana, who'd been lounging in his seat, snorted and muttered something that sounded like "we ain't fekking coppers."

"Not quite. I founded this operation to provide solutions for maximum-risk situations, primarily involving vampires. We contract with local governments and private clients. Occasionally, the work falls outside the definition of legal."

"Yeah, but legal or no, we're the ones who get the job done," Bana declared.

"If vampires confine themselves to the ghetto and feed only from the indentured, they're tolerated. Most Quarantines run somewhat peacefully under that arrangement. All quite civilized, what?" Tightness around the Major's mouth indicated his disapproval of that last social development.

Bana muttered, "Arsehole bleedin' hearts, living with a bloodsucker." He hunched lower in his seat with a muttered, "Sorry Guvnor," following the Major's sharp look.

The Englishman stepped up to a huge map of Seattle tacked to the wall. He traced an area delineated by a thick red line. "Everything west of the Duwamish to the Sound is the vampire ghetto. Paralleling the river is the Pipe, our red-light district. Many of the bars, brothels and pawnshops are vampire owned. The Pipe is the only area where vampires and humans mix legally." The Major returned to his desk, poured another cup of tea, took a sip and grimaced.

"Bloody hell. Mr. Murtagh, please ask Mr. Cooperhayes to bring a fresh pot."

"Sure, Guv, need a coffee refresher anyway. Cobb?" Tatsu refused. Bana slipped from the room.

"Ten years ago, Ukita Sadomori killed the former Master, abrogated the Quarantine agreement and eradicated any opposition, including all human gangs. Before that, things were fairly peaceful. We now have an epidemic of vampire attacks, There's also been a dramatic increase in human abductions, mainly from the Pipe."

"So, Seattle hired you?" Tatsu interrupted.

"One might say that. The local police force is vastly under-equipped to handle this rise in crime. There is no military force. The population is unarmed. Even if a few die-hard souls have firearms, ammunition is impossible to obtain."

Bana returned with Cooperhayes who placed a fresh pot on the desk. The tall, angular man placed a paper in front of the Major before gliding from the room.

The Major glanced down at the sheet. "Mr. Cobb, when were you infected by the virus?"

The question jarred Tatsu. "Never," he stammered.

"This report says otherwise." Major Blenheim stared at

Tatsu for a long moment, letting the prolonged silence push against the boy.

What the hell? The cut from the door handle? They'd tested his blood. Anger was quickly followed by apprehension. The scars on his throat. He had them since he was ten. Uncle Ray said they came from a dog bite during the time Tatsu's mind was shut down from grief. But there was that other bite from his first vampire kill.

He took a delaying drag on the cigarette while he recalled when he had hidden in a motel outside Grand Junction while he waited for the puking and shitting to run its course. "Maybe in Colorado. Was sick for a couple of days, nothing serious."

"Yes, quite." The Major took a long sip. He set the cup down with deliberate care. "Mr. Cobb, I hire only the best and only those with integrity. There is another quality I require. You must be a Leper."

"Leper?" The confused look in Tatsu's face made him appear about twelve years old to the Major.

"In medical terms, vampiral sanguine positive, one who recovers from the virus without turning. Rarely happens, still a medical mystery. People have a pathological fear of V-positives, even more than they fear vampires. Absolutely irrational, but prejudice is always irrational. We're outcasts. Ergo, Leper. You are one, according to this DNA report."

Tatsu shrugged. Perhaps he was a Leper, perhaps not. He didn't like the idea.

"From what Bana says, you're a formidable fighter, albeit somewhat unconventional. You have a code of honor. In addition, you are a Leper." A slight smile creased the corners of the Major's thin lips. "On your honor, will you set aside your personal concerns while working for this company?"

"*Hai, hai.* I promise." Tatsu nodded his agreement and his thanks.

"Any concerns about taking Cobb as your new partner, Mr. Murtagh?"

"Fuck no, guvnor."

"Jolly good. Mr. Cobb, you'll be issued tactical gear and communications equipment, full access to our files and the

DataNet, such as it is. Most of the team prefers small arms, like Mr. Murtagh's Beretta. We have a couple of exceptions, but these men are no less effective. You can, of course, use your own weapons. Although for a high-risk operation, I would prefer you carry a firearm. Will you have a problem with that?"

Tatsu balked at the idea of using a gun. He detested them, had seen the horrible results of quick-tempered idiots who fired first and never bothered with the questions. But then the words of Grandfather Shiniichiro slid into his ear, *"Koketsu ni irazunba koji wo ezu."* Nothing ventured, nothing gained. Tatsu bowed. *"Wakatta,* but I decide if and when I carry a gun."

"Fair enough. I'll allow that."

Two hours and a tour of the vast facility later, Tatsu signed the papers that made him a member of the Leper Colony.

"You'll meet the rest of the team tomorrow night at sixteen hundred hours. Oh, by the way, Mr. Cobb, I need not remind you of your agreement never to enter Tendai without authorization."

"Hai, wakarimashita," Tatsu replied, saddened that eventually he'd break that promise.

Bana slapped Tatsu on the back. "Come on, partner, let me treat you to a celebration."

The Irishman's idea of a celebration was great slabs of genuine beef served nearly raw in a pool of juice alongside mountains of fried potatoes. He surprised Tatsu by ordering coffee instead of a beer. "I'm too old to get pissed every night. 'Sides, the team don't like it much. Anyway, welcome to the Leper Colony, boyo." He clinked his coffee mug against Tatsu's water glass. "What's up? Havin' second thoughts about rollin' with us? Hell, laddie, look on the bright side. You get paid fer doing what you just did fer free. Plus, the Colony provides us with all the readies." He laughed.

"Iie, no. I have no doubts. I'm impressed. It looks like the place has everything you'd ever need for a war. *Jigoku!* Hell, you even make your own ammunition."

"Yeah, we got it all. Just gotta keep it hid from the

bloodsuckers." Bana stabbed a piece of meat and shoveled it into his mouth, the juice dripping down his chin.

"So, how long have you been with the company?"

"Goin' on twelve years. I used to be one of New York's finest. Was a fekkin' hero. Got medals ta prove it. Then got the virus."

"When?"

"Shite, boyo, nineteen years ago. 'Cept I didn't turn. Really bollocked my life. The fekking bastards down at One PPD gave me my walking papers. Said I was dangerous, too *unpredictable*. No pension, no Bob's-your-arse fer a great job. Just booted. Wankers!" He speared another chunk of dripping steak and crammed it between his teeth. Around the mouthful of meat, he continued, "What was I gonna do, become a night watchman guarding some fat cat's warehouse? Sod that. So, I did what any red-blooded Irishman would do, went home and offered my services in aid of the Troubles. Five years watchin' me own kind slaughter each other got old, so I came back here. Major found me, and here I be, an arse-kicking Leper." He finished his narrative with a wave of his bloody fork.

"Leper, huh? I'm not sure I am one."

"Sorry, boyo, yer blood says you are. You met our medic, Doc Wyckes. He's been researching this Leper thing fer years. He explained the scientific mumbo jumbo. Lost me. He makes us sound like we're more vampire than human. What I do know is we can turn without warning. People don't trust us. On the plus side, we can see in the dark, we're stronger and faster than the average bloke, don't catch diseases, sun don't turn us to charcoal. But we don't get to live fer centuries. Seems that's is the Universe's fekkin' joke; bloodsuckers get hundreds of years longer than us mortal men."

"Telomerase enzymes."

"Huh?"

"It is an enzyme on a branch of the DNA helix. Regulates aging in living things."

"Don't follow ya, boyo." Bana shook his head. "Where do you come up with that shit?"

"Just means a vampire's DNA lets them live longer than us.

That longevity is why they lose pigmentation in their skin, hair, eyes, you know." Tatsu shrugged and picked up his drink. "Immaterial, they're an aberrant species." He forced away the memory of the feel of the lips of one *aberrant species*, Saito Arisada.

"Shite, boyo, whatever you call them, you're gonna earn your keep killing 'em. Course it'd be the dog's bullocks if we had their thrall, but we don't. Immune to it. Thank the Holy Mother of God. And at least our insides don't burn up like theirs do in the sunlight. Another one of Nature's mysteries."

"No real mystery. Vampire virus is a mutated form of porphyria, a rare genetic disorder. Photosensitivity is so acute, they combust internally when exposed to sunlight."

"Bugger me. Don't give a shit why they burn up, just glad it happens." Bana winked. "On the plus side, Lepers can sure fuck like bloodsuckers. I got the prick of teenager. Go fer hours. Me willie gets sore drilling minge four, five times in a night. Never seem ta run out of spunk. Take my suggestion, boyo. Get yerself a girlfriend. Shite, get three or four. You're willie will thank you fer it."

Tatsu's mouth dropped open at the man's crude advice. Bana was right. Tatsu's hand and cock said *konnichiwa* to each other daily. He put it down to yearning for his one and only lover, ex-lover really. Sage was gone forever. But try telling that to his prick and his heart. And now this insane complication in the form of one flame-haired, gorgeous vampire who Tatsu had not only kissed but who now haunted Tatsu's dreams.

Abruptly, Tatsu's defenses reared up. It was clear Bana had no clue about Tatsu's sexual preference. And he dared not reveal his contact with Arisada. "Do you think we'll see action tomorrow?" He changed the subject.

"See action every night, boyo. Jist make sure you keep yer cell and combat gear handy at all times, got me?"

During the tour of the Colony, Bana had given Tatsu two sets of combat wear called dee-skin made from a flexible polyceramic. "These will keep yer insides where they belong." The Irishman grinned.

Tatsu had marveled at the clothing's light weight yet the fabric, which resembled chainmail, moved like silk over his body. The new shirt even eased the chaffing of his sword harness.

"This here's called a dog collar. Range ain't fer shit, half a klick maybe. But it'll keep you in touch with the rest o' yer teammates 'specially me, understand?" Bana had tossed him the communications unit buried inside a dee-skin neck choker.

Bana's next comment jerked Tatsu to the present. "Okay, partner, gotta go. See ya at the briefing. And tomorrow night, you watch yer arse at all times. Better yet, watch my arse."

Tatsu allowed a quick grin. Bana had no clue about the real extent of Tatsu's "arse watching."

Bana slurped the last of his coffee before he stood up. "Ya gonna need better digs than that crappy closet. I know the owner of the apartment over that dojo. I'll put in a good word fer ya."

"*Domo arigatō*." Tatsu flashed a quick smile, pleased with the idea of staying close to the dojo. When practicing *shinkendo*, he always entered an altered state where his heart didn't ache with regret and all doubt vanished. Who was he kidding? He wanted use of that dojo on the slight chance Arisada showed up again.

Bana paid the tab and left, declaring he was off to "shag" his girlfriend. Reiterated Tatsu needed to find a "bit o' minge" for himself. Tatsu pulled on his jacket and stepped out into the rain. Bana was right, Tatsu hungered for the intimate touch of a man. But he had no time for romance. Hell, he had no time for a quickie with some hot man's mouth around his dick.

Yet, his mouth tingled with the memory of Arisada's electrifying kiss *Fakku*, forget it. Tatsu was here for revenge. Period. He could defeat any vampire. Hell, he'd already proven it when he beat Arisada, who was not only *kyūketsuki,* but samurai.

Tatsu forgot those childhood legends of his native land. Especially the one that told of an immortal samurai who had slaughtered thousands throughout Japan.

Ten

"Hey, Chain, you hear the latest from the Mick? This kid came out of nowhere, killed four bloodsuckers with a couple of swords." Kaiden Galloway snorted and dropped into his seat alongside his partner. The two mercenaries were the first to arrive for the nightly assignment at the Colony's briefing room, fondly called the Snake Pit.

"*Vraiment*, the Irishman loves to bullshit." Chance "Chain" Passebon rocked his chair onto its back legs and propped both feet on the table with two loud thumps.

"Just heard he'd talked the Major into hiring this punk yesterday. The kid's some sort of real-life samurai."

"*N'importe*. The Major's never been wrong with anyone he's hired all the years I've known him." Chain shrugged while he lit a fresh Gauloises.

"Fuck, why'd the Major hire the punk even if he did save the Mick's drunken ass?" Kaiden sneaked a quick glance at the huge man now crossing his ankles with an easy stretch of his long legs.

"Four kills in one night. Can't argue with that." Chain tipped his head back and blew smoke in a slow trail toward the ceiling.

"But two swords? What the fuck?"

"As long as a weapon works." Chain poked a booted toe at his five-string crossbow resting on the table before him. Despite its bizarre design, the customized weapon was the instrument of hundreds of deaths.

Kaiden didn't hide his slight derision. "Shit, not sure I'd trust my back to any greenie, least of all a *swordfighter*."

At the far end of the room, the doors bounced open and Bana ushered said swordfighter into the room. When Bana hauled the young man over to the huge fish tank at the back of the room, Kaiden grinned. "Here we go, the big snake test."

"That *couillon* always tries to freak out the newbies. When's he gonna learn it never works?" Chain dropped his chair forward with a bang and crushed his cigarette out in a chipped ceramic ashtray. They watched the show.

Grinning like a man privy to the world's funniest joke, Bana rapped his knuckles hard against the glass. The six-foot long albino cobra reared up, flared and lunged over the open rim of the tank to within inches of Tatsu's face.

Tatsu stared, unflinchingly, at the reptile before turning to speak to the Irishman.

"Give the kid points for guts." Chain regarded Cobb through hooded eyes, at the thick shaggy mop of hair that flared in spikes each time Tatsu moved his head. "But *merde*, what's with that hair? Looks like a mop."

Kaiden wasn't listening. Shit, the kid sure moved pretty! Barely a swivel of those slender hips in that light, gliding walk, weight always over the forward foot. Graceful and pretty. The kid reminded Kaiden of an ex-boyfriend, a gymnast, who could, and did, bend his body in some of the most fucking interesting positions.

But this Cobb kid was definitely sexier. Not-too narrow shoulders tapered to a trim waist. Hips that just teased the edge of skinny were visible below a battered motorcycle jacket. His black TAC pants hugged the cheeks of a tight, come-fuck-me ass above lean legs, the kind Kaiden liked to feel draped over his shoulders. And unless Kaiden's gaydar was seriously broken, this kid wouldn't mind that position one bit, especially if it included eight-inches of cock buried in his chute.

"Heads up mates, this is Tatsu Cobb." Bana slapped Tatsu on the back with a head-jarring thump. "Have a seat, boyo, meet the family." The Irishman laughed then strode away in the direction of the coffee urn.

When Tatsu reached the conference table and pulled out a chair, Kaiden had to swallow hard against the heat spreading pleasure through his groin. The kid was fucking gorgeous. The boy's face mirrored a perfect blend of his Japanese and American genes. Strong chin with small cleft, a narrow nose above bow-shaped, dark-rose lips made for kissing. High, sharp cheekbones edged beneath a honey-kissed complexion. Almond-shaped lids, and, ah shit, the sootiest, sexiest lashes Kaiden had ever seen on a man.

But the kid's startling emerald eyes were cold and filled with a deadly purpose. Nevertheless, Kaiden caught a quick flicker of uncertainty in those jade orbs, something soft that said Tatsu Cobb didn't want the world to be this brutal and cruel place.

Some might call the kid a twink, but Kaiden knew this was no fem boy. Not by a long shot. That sinuous walk, the flat expression in those cold eyes, the cross-me-and-you-die set of his shoulders—all told Kaiden that Tatsu Cobb was a lethal weapon. A deadly hunter wrapped up in one lithe body of hot, man-flesh.

There would have been a time when this guy would have been high on Kaiden's fuck list. Extremely high. But not now. Kaiden sighed and glanced over to Chain, the man he loved— the unobtainable, *straight* man he loved.

Tatsu dropped his jacket over the back of a metal chair and shucked his harness, placing it on the table before him. He swung the seat around and sat aside it as if riding a horse before looking at the two mercenaries sitting opposite. He barely controlled his start of surprise. Was Bana playing a sick joke? Facing him were two of the most gorgeous men he'd ever seen. No way they could be hired killers.

With a sense of increasing unreality, Tatsu recognized one. "*Gomen nasai*, but you're... you're..." he blushed at his stammer.

The blond grinned, reached across the table and shook Tatsu's hand in a hard grip. "Yup that's me, Kaiden Galloway, big-screen phony and Hollywood reject."

For years, Kaiden had been the hottest commodity in action-adventure films. His stunning looks generated millions for the studios. He stood out as a muscular sex icon in an industry jaded from too many muscular sex icons. His incredible cerulean eyes and unruly blond locks powered the fantasies of women worldwide. Kaiden's not-quite-porn love scenes made them wet between the thighs and guaranteed his films outsold anything else the movie industry churned out. Then, six years after his first mega hit, he came out, breaking the hearts of his female fans from seventeen to seventy. Being gay didn't hurt his popularity, though, which soared to new heights when thousands of gay men flocked to his movies. Four years later, the actor mysteriously vanished.

"This is Chance Passebon, my partner." Kaiden hooked a thumb in the direction of the huge, muscular man lounging beside him.

Chain looked the same age as his partner, probably both in their early-thirties. In contrast to Kaiden's surfer-boy looks, Chain's face was all hard edges and sharp planes. Cheekbones so chiseled they looked carved from the side of a mountain. Bronzed skin. Eyes the color of obsidian. He radiated a deadly beauty, the kind seen in the cobra.

Tatsu's guess that Chain was Native American was close— Chance Passebon was full Cajun with roots that went deep in the Louisiana bayou.

Chain regarded Tatsu through a hooded stare, not hostile, merely interested. The Cajun took a long drag from his cigarette, tilted his head back and blew the fragrant smoke up to the ceiling. "Just call me Chain." The big man's soft baritone held no trace of the South. He stood, scooped up the full ashtray and sauntered over to the trash receptacle.

Tatsu's mouth watered. *Jigoku*, the man was tall, at least six-foot-four. Wide shoulders tapered to a narrow waist. His pants hugged his buttocks so developed they showed the dent in the side of each flank. The thick, black braid falling to Chain's waist filled Tatsu's gut with a quivery longing. He tore his gaze away and was mortified by Kaiden's playful wink that said the mercenary knew exactly what Tatsu was thinking.

Laughter came from three men entering the room. Clad in black tactical gear, each carried a firearm on one hip. One hunter headed straight for the coffee pot as the other two dragged back their metal chairs and sat across from Tatsu. He didn't waver when their eyes locked onto his with the territorial challenge of combatants.

"*Oi*, you wankers, this is my new partner, Tatsu Cobb." Bana interrupted the stare-off contest.

Tatsu heard a touch of pride in Bana's brogue. "Yeah, he's the dog's bollocks, so I don't wanna hear any shite from any o' you. You arseholes introduce yourselves, or I will. And no telling what fekking secrets I'll spill." Bana thunked a mug of steaming black coffee down in front of Tatsu before sitting.

A giant black man was the first to speak. His dee-skin shirt strained over his massive torso, and his thick arms resembled the thighs of a small heifer. The harsh glare of the fluorescent lights bounced off his naked head. The pin from a grenade dangled from his left earlobe. For a heart-stopping second, Tatsu wondered where the rest of the grenade was.

"I'm Pleasant Jones." The ebony giant leaned over the table and held out a bear-sized paw. Two of his fingers ended at the second knuckle. He grabbed Tatsu's hand and shook it hard enough to give him whiplash.

"Yeah, Jones is our demo man." Bana smirked at Tatsu's startled reaction to the mountain of black flesh towering over him. "He don't care about nothin' just so's he can blow up things." Jones glowered at the Irishman.

The second man placed a short-barrel shotgun onto the table with a deliberate clatter, sat and crossed his arms, head tilted to one side. "So this is the punk who saved the Mick's sorry ass. Hell, he's a fuckin' baby." The look he gave Tatsu indicated he wasn't buying anything Bana said about this skinny kid.

"Shut it. Phoenix, mind yer manners. Cobb, this is Phoenix Thunder Fuck. Don't ask." Bana jerked his thumb by way of introduction.

Phoenix propped both feet on the table. His hair and beard haloed his face in a frieze of red. Broad shoulders and thick neck spelled body builder despite the beginning of a pot belly. His sleeves, rolled up to his elbows, revealed tattoos down to his wrists. He looked at Tatsu through narrowed eyes. "That yer Jap crap outside?"

Tatsu clenched his jaw. Before he could reply, Phoenix continued, "No offense, just prefer old-style American myself."

Then he grinned, revealing his missing top front teeth. It made him look like an overgrown kid. "Meet Ma Bell." The biker jabbed his middle finger over his shoulder in the direction of the man approaching the table.

Bell ignored Phoenix's obscene gesture and sat down beside Tatsu. Even in combat gear, the thin man looked more like a corporate executive than a mercenary. Bell offered his hand but no smile. "Norman Bell. Welcome to the Leper Colony. Heard good things about you."

A shadow in Tatsu's periphery made him glance over to the newcomer leaning against the doorjamb. Young, mid-twenties, lean body. Curly brown hair capped a classical Mediterranean face. The man lit a cigarette with easy movements before turning his gold-kissed eyes toward Tatsu. The vampire's lips quirked up in a slow smile, showing just the tips of his fangs.

Tatsu's instinct screamed to whip out his swords. His rationale stopped him.

"This is Fornax." Bana stayed Tatsu's twitching hand with a light press of two fingers on his elbow. "Case you didn't notice, he's a vampire. He's also Bell's teammate. Play nice, Fornax."

The room hushed while every man waited for Tatsu's reaction. Tatsu's fist balled up, fingernails digging into his palms, when he looked at the vampire. Angry sweat broke out over his body, rolled down his neck, under his armpits.

Tatsu turned and glared at his so-called partner. "Bana, what the fuck is this?"

"Don't get your knickers in a twist. Just trust me." A feeble grin skittered over Bana's mouth.

The vampire took another drag on his cigarette then sauntered into the room and sat across from Bell. His golden eyes regarded Tatsu with a penetrating look. "You're very pretty." He smiled again; this time with no fangs.

Oh, *jigoku*, not only a vampire, but a *gay* vampire. Tatsu suppressed bristling at Fornax. The vampire was only hitting on him because he was the newbie.

The tension snapped when the Major strode into the room. Chain, loose-jointed and relaxed, rocked his chair back onto its rear legs, a newly-lit cigarette dangling from his mouth.

The Major looked around the table. "Gentlemen, I assume you've all introduced yourselves to Mr. Cobb. Just to verify, he's more than qualified to join this company."

Bana grinned as if he were solely responsible for Tatsu's kill record.

The Major placed two manila folders on the table, but remained standing, hands clasped behind his back. "We have two new assignments. Standard risk but you won't be disappointed by your commissions. First case: Three girls from the Queen Ann Preparatory Academy went into the Pipe last night. According to their friends, the girls ditched school to get hawked."

"Fucking idiot kids, think they're immortal. Think hawking ain't dangerous." Phoenix growled.

"Hawking?" Tatsu whispered to Bana.

"Comes from an old phrase, chicken hawk. Ya let vampires feed from ya so's you can get off. Aphrodisiac in bloodsucker's saliva makes you come till yer brains fry. Better'n any drug on the market," Bana muttered back.

The Major's discreet cough got their attention. He handed out photos of three teenaged girls. "A Gypsy cabbie dropped them a block from the Pipe at about twenty-three hundred hours Saturday. Said they were talking about Club Belladonna. Whenever the Club is involved, there's always the possibility of abduction by vampires. Therefore, we're sanctioned to enter Tendai if necessary. Fornax, see if your friendlies have anything. Mr. Murtagh and Mr. Cobb, you're are undercover at the nightclub. If the girls are bitten, bring them to the crisis center at St. Augustine's," the Major ordered.

"If they're alive." Chain's tone indicated he thought the opposite.

"Bloodsuckers always mean trouble." Bana grumbled.

"Think of it as job security, Mick." Kaiden flashed an insolent grin as Bana snarled to not call him "Mick".

The Major handed a set of glossies to Kaiden and Chain. "These boys have been missing about twelve hours. The parents say they usually find them in the video arcade in the old Gannon Center. This time though, they're afraid their children are in the Pipe." He looked over the room. "Also, gentlemen, be aware, the communication towers are out of commission again so don't rely on your cells."

Groans of dismay and a couple of, "What the fuck else is new?" followed the announcement.

"Seems like the goddamn system oughta be blown up. We'd be better off using fekkin' pigeons," Bana grumbled.

"You said it, Mick," Kaiden grinned. "If Seattle Telecomm ever gets the bucks to upgrade its system, we'll have one fucking big party."

Chairs clattered as men stood and moved toward the door. A the Major's cough, they stilled, all eyes turning in his direction.

"Mr. Kaiden or Mr. Bell, our newest recruit needs suggestions on a firearm. Please see to it. And, gentlemen, watch out for civilians."

In the armory, Tatsu helped load ammunition and medical packs. He couldn't resist a glance at Chain when the big man bent over to slide a serrated combat knife into his tanker boot. *Shimatta*! That was one gorgeous, mouth-watering hunk of a male flesh. Tatsu's flickered a quick look at the tall man's awesome glutes clearly outlined beneath his TAC pants. Then Tatsu caught Kaiden staring at the Cajun with look of such naked hunger that Tatsu turned away, strangely saddened.

"'Er, mate, You might want this." Bana offering Tatsu a gun. Tatsu shook his head. For him the best weapon was his swords. He risked another quick glance at Kaiden, saw the man was hiding any sign of his need.

Tatsu knew his best defense against that kind of raw desire lay in his quest. He had no armament against the longing that haunted his dreams. He locked those concerns behind his rising excitement when he climbed into the Hummer with Bana. There was no doubt he'd be facing *kyūketsuki* tonight. And perhaps, by fighting alongside these men, he'd be able to fulfill his blood debt.

A sick dread rose in Tatsu's gorge. A blood debt required nothing less than a death. What if Saito Arisada was the killer? Would Tatsu forfeit his honor by not being able to kill the gorgeous creature.

Eleven

Arisada detested bars and nightclubs, especially Club Belladonna with its pervasive reek of human sweat ladened with pheromones, adrenalin and desperation. Tonight, though, he suppressed his distaste. Tonight, he hunted his own kind, several *kyūketsuki* who had abducted three girls. For that vile crime, the rogues would forfeit their lives to Saito Arisada.

Dozens of humans milled around looking for sex, drugs, gambling, punishment—any kind of high. They were oblivious to the vampire hidden above in a dark recess of the loft.

Suddenly, Arisada's body thrummed with heat. He caught a scent forever imprinted in his brain: Tatsu Cobb. The sweet aroma was accompanied by the clatter of booted feet on the stairs. Arisada faded farther back into the darkest corner and watched Tatsu and the older, black-haired man at a table next to the balcony rail.

The vampire's groin filled, cock pulsing heavy with desire and excitement. He leaned subtly forward, wanting to catch every nuance, every movement from the adorable boy. *Á, sō desu ka*, Tatsu Cobb had joined the covert mercenary group. All vampires knew about them. Hated them. Feared them.

Arisada experienced a deep dismay. Tatsu was now a hired vampire hunter. And that made them mortal enemies.

The energy from too many people high on booze and who-knew-what-kind of chemicals assaulted Tatsu's senses the second he entered the club. Although only a couple of hours past sunset, the place was packed. Elbow-to-elbow, patrons jostled against the two bars lining each side of the room. Gyrating people jammed the floor. The music's thumping beat reverberated through Tatsu's chest. He curled his nose at the overpowering stink of fear and the musk of sexual arousal.

"This bar is one o' the most dangerous places along the Pipe," Bana bellowed over the noise. He slapped some change on the bar and scooped up a couple of bottles of fake beer before leading the way to the circular stairs and the dark loft. They found a table against the balcony and hunkered down. Tatsu leaned over the pipe rail and scanned the bar below and the front door. He sighed with relief when the band finished their head-splitting metal set.

Bana's voice dropped about five decibels. "We're just a hundred feet from the border. Bar's owned by vampires. Ya can get every kind of entertainment of the depraved sort, know what I mean? Lookit them *idjits*, getting stoned. They're cruisin' fer bloodsuckers. Hope ta get hawked. Some even wanna catch the virus and turn. Think they'll be fuckin' immortal."

Bana took a long gulp from his bottle, plunked it down with a thud. "Ya keep sketch now, boyo. Gotta earn our keep. I can hear ol' tightwad Cooperhayes howling about the hundred dollars jist to get into this joint." He jabbed a finger toward the crowd below. "Looks like we may get some action. This place always draws the bloodsuckers. Always happy to oblige the ijits who come here to get hawked."

"What do you have in mind?" Tatsu chaffed with impatience. So far, Bana hadn't said a word about how they were going to find the missing girls.

The Irishman took another gulp of his drink. "Simple, boyo. Bloodsuckers and humans mix here to get their little blood-fuck fix. We spot a likely suspect, lure his fanged ass outside and me and Fiona will get him to talk." He smirked and patted the holster that held his newest weapon—a Taser Shockwave modified by Wyckes to deliver an electrical jolt guaranteed to fry a vampire's eyeballs. Bana had named it Fiona the Instant Agonizer after one of his ex-wives.

He turned his gaze from sweeping the floor below to check his partner and caught Tatsu's frown. "Okay, kid, out with it, what's got yer knickers all twisted?"

"You said nothing about working with a vampire. Neither did the Major. I feel like I was suckered."

"Sorry, boyo. Fornax is one of our biggest secrets. If the wrong ones find out he's with us, he's dead meat."

"Why is he working for the Lepers?"

"Only the Major knows, and he ain't telling. It's how we operate, boyo. We trust him, no questions. He's never let us down, not once in the years I've been with him." Bana leveled a dark look at Tatsu, a look that said he'd better not ask either.

"So, he's an informant?"

"More'n that, boyo. He's one fatherfucking, hell of a fighter. He's mum on a lot of stuff. But if anything affects an operation, he's got our backs."

"Anything else I should know about?" Tatsu, feeling ashamed of his outburst, let his anger fade. It was pointless to fight with the irascible Irishman.

Bana shook his head before taking another swig of his drink. "See anything down there yet?"

Tatsu turned his eyes back to the crowd, *"Nani mo.* Nothing." He shrugged. The movement reminded him of the absence of his swords. On Bana's order, he'd stashed them in the Hummer. Unarmed, he felt naked.

"Nearly midnight, usually the time bloodsuckers come in. We got it in the bag if a fem shows up. She ain't gonna resist when she sees a pretty face like your'n. Just turn on the flirty-boy charm, waggle yer arse, and let her think you wanna get shagged." The Irishman leered and wiggled his bushy eyebrows up and down.

Tatsu blew out a huff. His looks. Every gay man's wet dream according to some. Nothing but trouble according to Tatsu. He was never sure whether to be grateful to his Japanese mother for giving him her delicate beauty or curse the genes that damned him to look like a perennial teenager—a pretty perennial teenager. And now Bana's latest target.

"Course, the way you blew off them girls, maybe a bull might be more up yer alley, eh? I seen several dudes eye you like you're the cherry on top of a sundae, and they want to lick it off. Or lick something else off." Bana took a deep, noisy gulp from his bottle then grinned wolfishly. "Shite, bet every single one of 'em got chubbed up thinking about giving it to ya."

Tatsu hid his irritation behind a swallow of his drink, recalling. Wyckes' warning about his new partner. In addition to the booze problem, Bana would torment a newcomer without mercy. Nothing was sacred, especially sex. "Sorry, Cobb, the way you look, he's gonna be a real asshole for a while. Ignore him. He'll get tired of it or you can knock him on his ass like Passebon did," Wyckes had advised.

But Tatsu hadn't expected it to happen his first day on the job. "*Shimatta*. Damn it, Murtagh, stuff it. I don't have time for that bullshit." Inexplicably, he recalled that first moment when Arisada's golden eyes caught him in a gaze full of want. The press of the vampire's need against his. Those soft lips. That tongue chasing its knowing way into Tatsu's mouth.

His cock stirred. *Jigoku*, where was an obnoxious, ear-shattering and equally distracting band when you needed one?

"Hell, I bet Kaiden would fuck ya in a heartbeat. Cept he's so in love with the Cajun, I don't think he'd do anyone else. They'd sure make a pretty couple, don'tcha think?"

Tatsu felt warmth of a blush spread across the tops of his cheeks. A picture of Kaiden and Chain—strong bodies pressed tight, hands rubbing, mouths devouring—flooded Tatsu with a smoky heat. "Chain is gay?"

"Not on yer life, laddie. The Cajun's straight, married once. But for a smart guy like him, he doesn't have a sodding clue. But me nose knows." Bana slid his thumb down the side of his broken nose with a sly wink.

"You know, you're asking for it. I heard Chain already took your head off once." Tatsu figured there was only one way to shut the Irishman up. "Hell, the way you keep talking, maybe you're into men."

Not the least bit perturbed, Bana chuckled. "Nah not me, got drunk once and let a dude blow me. Not too bad, but a pair of nice tittles and a good piece of minge... umm, now you're talking." He wet his lips.

Tatsu jumped at the loud clatter of chairs when Chain and Kaiden sat down. *Kuso*, that too-graphic picture of the two men kissing danced in Tatsu's mind again. Again, the heat crawled up his face when he looked from one man to the next.

"What's up, Mick? Ninja boy?" Kaiden smiled and winked at Tatsu. The smile took the sting out of the new nickname.

A waitress materialized by Chain's side. Her eyes fastened on his face. "Can I get you something?" she purred. Her nipples visibly hardened under the thin fabric of her blouse.

Although Kaiden was used to women going dewy-eyed and flirty over him, he loved to see his partner's effect on them. He grinned at the Cajun's slow, sexy smile mesmerizing the waitress.

"Sure thing, darlin'. Cervezas for me and my partner. And bring a round of whatever they're having." Chain waggled his forefinger in the direction of Tatsu and Bana. The waitress backed away, eyes still on Chain's face.

"Ack, ye got the luck o' the Irish with the lassies." Bana thickened his brogue for a moment before his voice lowered into a territorial growl. "What are you two doing here?"

"Don't sweat it, Murtagh," Chain snorted. "We're finished. Found the missing boys jacking off to porn flicks in a Sixty-Nine skin house about two klicks from the Mall." They stopped talking while the waitress placed their drinks on the table.

"Yeah, easy pay for us. *Salut*, partner," Kaiden and Chain clicked their bottles together.

"We just thought you may need backup," Chain said.

"Don't need ya. Me and boyo here got it covered," Bana growled.

Just then Tatsu spotted a likely target coming through the bar door. No mistaking that arrogant crowding or constant predatory movement of the head. A tall, beefy vampire on the prowl. Several humans scrambled to get away from the creatures, a few jostled closer.

"There." Pleased to be contributing so soon to the mission, Tatsu grinned at the other three men.

"Big bull. Can't mistake that arrogant, arsehole walk."

"Avec une femme, c'est bizarre." Chain added nodding his chin at the small female trailing behind the bull.

Kaiden smirked. "Looks like you're gonna need a little backup after all, eh, Mick?"

"Don't call me Mick." Bana's glare bounced from Kaiden to

Chain. "It's only two of them. Won't even need you guys."

"Are you both armed?" Tatsu saw no sign of weapons on either man.

"Couple of knives. K-bar in my boot. Bow's in the Hummer. Knew the dickhead bouncer wouldn't let me in with it. *Cochon.*" Chain muttered without taking his eyes off the quarry. Kaiden just grinned and flipped back the lapel of his hip-length leather coat to show his Colts snug in their shoulder holsters.

"Let's do this." Chain stood.

"Half a mo, got an idea. Boyo, give Galloway your jacket." Bana leaned close to Tatsu who waved his hands in protest. "Just do it, ya git," Bana barked.

"What are you thinking of, Mick?"

"Them's vampires, right? We all know they're horny and stupid. Way I figure it, the kid here is gonna sashay up to them, wiggle his cute little arse, and lure them outside." Bana sniggered as if he were about to pull the ultimate, killer of-all pranks.

"Me? Why me? Shouldn't Kaiden do this? He's the actor. No offense." Tatsu's protest went unheeded as Bana began tugging on Tatsu's tee-shirt, practically yanking it off his body. Tatsu slapped ineffectually at the Irishman's busy hands. "What the fuck?"

"Galloway's face is still seen on the telly. Vamps watch movies, same as us, might spot him. Besides, you look like you're jailbait. They'll go for that. Now, get this off, ya idjit." Bana continued to paw at Tatsu's tee.

Tatsu glared while he pulled off his shirt. He blushed at Kaiden's low, wolf whistle.

Bana ripped off the bottom half of the black tee with his combat knife and tossed the scrap to the floor. "Now, you're gonna saunter over there like you're on yer first hawking date." Bana winked at Kaiden and Chain. "He's cute, ain't he? Look at them cute abs and that little belly button. Don't think I've seen one this cute in a long while."

"Mick, you keep talking like that, and I'd think you've gone queer." Kaiden grinned, but couldn't take his eyes off Tatsu's naked flesh. The kid *was* more than cute. He was a total prick-teasing turn-on.

"Just shut the fuck up." Tatsu squirmed, feeling ridiculous in a ripped tee-shirt that revealed half his chest and the ridges of his abdominals.

"Needs more of a tease. Take off your belt and undo your top buttons," Kaiden said.

"Hell, no." Tatsu clutched waist of his cargo pants with an ineffective desperation.

"Stop whining like a girl, this is a mission." Bana grinned.

Swearing in Japanese, Tatsu unsnapped the first two buttons, exposing his navel and the tantalizing curl of dark hair trailing below.

Not satisfied with that, Kaiden popped two more buttons. He pushed Tatsu's pants further down to reveal the jut of his hips and the beginning of those sexy dips curving down under his jock's waistband. At the warm brush of Kaiden's fingers, Tatsu felt his blood pool into his cock.

"That's better." Kaiden's prick woke up to the answering heat in that same satiny skin.

"Alright, boyo, go over there and give 'em a chubby."

Tatsu flipped them off. Dammit, the three were having way too much fun with this. He trotted down the winding stairs, feeling naked without his swords. Hell, he felt even more naked with his ass hanging half out of his pants. Still, his gut fluttered with anticipation. This was his chance to prove himself, even if it did mean posing as sex bait. He moved toward the vampires leaning on the bar.

The two fanged predators had just become the prey.

Although his eyes were on Tatsu, Arisada sensed the two rogues the moment they entered the bar. Reluctantly, he shifted his gaze from the hunters to survey the scene below. The two vampires had ordered drinks and looked about to camp at the bar for a while. Arisada's lip curled over his fangs in a silent snarl at his quarry.

Arisada turned his attention back to the Lepers readying themselves for the action. A muted struggle was going on with Tatsu in the center. Whatever preparation the hunters were doing, it looked more like a forced strip tease than men arming for combat.

The older hunter, with much leering and profanity, forced Tatsu to remove his tee-shirt. Arisada sucked in his breath at the sight of Tatsu's chest, the ripple and bunch of defined abs. Creamy honey-kissed skin, with only a smattering of hair traveling down to the navel. A dark oval like a large bruise covered most of the mounded pec above the right nipple.

Even from several yards away, Arisada sensed Tatsu's arousal. When Tatsu's pants were tugged low enough to reveal his hips, a deep pulse of want throbbed through Arisada. His prick responded, began to plump. One button lower and the tip of Tatsu's semi-hard cock would be exposed. A frission of jealousy stabbed Arisada at the thought of the blond man's knuckle nearly brushing the top of Tatsu's cockhead, perhaps coming away slicked with precum.

The *kyūketsuki* couldn't tear his gaze from the boy. Staying a few steps behind, he followed the mercenaries down to the main floor. Arisada saw them split up and weave their way through the crowd, shifting closer to their quarry. He admired how effectively they used the cover of the jostling throng to mask their movements.

Tatsu's approach to the bar, however, was an aggressive strut, a cocky, shouldering aside of people, deliberately calling attention to himself. A young man trolling for some hot action.

In what he hoped was a good imitation of a horny, thrill-seeking teenager, Tatsu swaggered across the bar floor, hips swaying. He elbowed his way through the press of groupies clustered around the vampires. In a voice pitched high and nervous, Tatsu ordered a beer. The harried barkeep shoved the bottle over and scooped up his money. Tatsu picked up his drink and deliberately brushed his arm against the bull. The momentary contact made his skin feel as if it was crawling with ants.

The big vampire smelled the new human crowding beside him—young, nervous, male. Excitement washed over him in warm, delicious waves from the kid's skin. The vampire shifted his bulk and looked down at the nervous youth ordering a drink in that unmistakable trying-to-fake-adult kind of way.

The bull eyed his companion, the unspoken command in his eyes. The fem squirmed in beside Tatsu and rubbed her hip against his thigh. When she leaned over to pick up her drink, she mashed her breast against Tatsu's arm and smiled when he turned toward her. She was a head shorter than him. Thin-featured, maybe mid-twenties. Her auburn hair, swept up in a French knot, revealed an elegant neck. The sophistication ended there, sullied by makeup layered on to make her skin appear flush and pink. Her breasts spilled out of the low-cut, red blouse. A cheap micro-skirt and knee-high, faux-leather boots revealed nothing appealing.

"You looking for some real action, cutie?" She giggled and stared straight into those unusual jade eyes. Her tongue flickered over her thin lips. Her gaze roamed over the kid's gorgeous face, down the slim neck to the ripple of abs revealed by the torn tee. She had to snap her mouth closed when fangs stirred at the smatter of curly brown hair above his half-opened pants.

Tatsu licked his lips and pretended interest when he ogled her chest. He felt a slight revulsion at the sight of those fleshy mounds. He suppressed his gag at her too-flowery cologne that couldn't disguise her coppery vampire scent. "Umm, not sure," he said with a slight quaver in his voice. He prayed he sounded stupid and horny.

"Sugar, we got something you can be sure about." The fem smiled, no sign of fangs, just even, white teeth in a full, red-lipsticked mouth. "Don't we Cabe?" The bull ignored her. He couldn't take his eyes off the delicate curve of the youth's hipbones or the flat belly between them. Hell, this kid was prettier than his fem. The vampire's cock throbbed.

Sweat slicked under the hank of hair falling over Tatsu's forehead. His heartbeat revved up a few notches, and knew the male vampire heard it. But Tatsu's reactions were not from fear, they were from anger.

Playing dumb and gawky, he stammered out he was looking for action. He looked into the red eyes of the male and pretended to sink under the vampire's thrall. The bull's pheromonal power was strong; a normal human would be a witless idiot. Tatsu did his best imitation of dazed and stupid.

Tatsu suppressed his shudder when the fem hooked her hand around his elbow and guided him outside. He was aware of the bull crowding behind them. Feigning confusion, he looked up and down the street. "Um, can we get away from everyone?" He forced a dreamy tone into his voice and waved vaguely in the direction of the alley behind the club.

Giggling, the female wrapped her arm around Tatsu's waist and bumped her hip against him while guiding him into the shadows between the two buildings. The bull followed, amazed at their luck in scoring such tasty prey. He smacked his lips with anticipation, and his fangs slid from their channels. He crowded behind his fem and the boy, herding them deeper into an alley that was scarcely wider than the bull's shoulders.

"After we feed, let's add him in with those girls," he growled into the fem's ear, sure the youth was too caught up in the thrall to understand.

The electroshock from the Agonizer short-circuited the bull's sympathetic nervous system. He crashed face first on the wet pavement, his muscles frozen. His fangs retracted so fast they sliced through his tongue. He pissed himself and bloody saliva drooled from his mouth.

The fem spun around with a startled squawk. At the sight of her mate on the ground, she screeched with rage. Her fangs stretched her mouth into an ugly, lipstick-smeared maw. Howling with blood-rage, she launched herself at Bana. Two bolts from Chain's bow slammed through her breastbone and throat. The sodium fluoroacetate raced through her blood. Her convulsing body hit the ground with a meaty thud.

Kaiden tossed the *katana* to Tatsu who snatched it from the air and pulled it from its *saya* in a single fluid movement. Tatsu spun, the tip of the sword leveled toward the bull's head.

Bana reset the Taser and hit the vampire with another shock that sent him into spasms. With a sharp crack, the vampire's vertebra snapped. The air filled with the foul stench of excrement. The Irishman kicked the semi-conscious vampire over onto his back "Yer girlfriend's now a puddle of jelly, and you're in yer own shit. So talk." He squatted beside the convulsing body, the Taser hovering just over the vampire's face.

The vampire glared up at the crouching hunter through eyes filled with hate and fear. Bana zapped him again. The bull arched off the pavement, his back bowed at a strange angle. Blood poured from his mouth where he bit through his tongue. His hate spilled out in a wet burble.

"Doesn't look like he wants to make polite conversation with you, Mick." Kaiden grinned.

Bana shocked the vampire again then dropped the Agonizer, shaking his hand. "Ach, sodding thing zapped me, piece of shit." Bana yanked his serrated K-bar from his belt and jabbed the vampire in the crotch. "Maybe we'll turn ya into a eunuch. Or maybe we'll be nice and let you go with yer clackers still attached. Or maybe I'll let me little Jap friend have a go at ya." In voice ladened with menace, the Irishman listed each body part his "little Jap friend" would remove unless they got what they wanted.

The vampire's eyes jittered from Bana's sneering mouth to Tatsu's *katana* shining in the light. The terrified creature babbled out the information.

"Let's go. We're done here." Bana stepped back from the broken creature sprawled in its own waste.

"I'm not." The quiet menace lay thick in Tatsu's voice. He pressed the tip of the sword against the creature's cheek under the lower eyelid. Drew a minute, scalpel-thin line. Blood oozed.

"We ain't got time fer this shite, boyo."

Tatsu ignored his partner. With delicate precision, he moved his blade a fraction higher. "You know of a *kyūketsuki*, a Japanese vampire, with a scarred back?"

The vampire dared not shake his head for fear the blade would slice his eyelid. "No, never," he whined. "I swear."

"Convince me." That deadly tip hovered above the creature's dilated pupil. "Hurry up, my arm's getting tired."

The vampire cried his denial again and again. Truth filled those terror-widened crimson eyes. Tatsu relented and stepped back. "Now I'm done. Kaiden, where the fuck is my jacket?"

"Don't sweat it, Ninja Boy. It's in the truck," the blond replied.

The four Lepers turned toward the street. With a roar, the vampire levered his crippled torso off the pavement and flung himself at Bana's legs. His fangs sank into the back of the Irishman's calf. Bana howled and twisted around, pulling out his K-bar to drive it into the bull's neck. Before the serrated blade began its descent, Tatsu removed the vampire's head.

Bana jumped back, shaking his drenched leg. "Watch it, boyo. These are me new trousers!"

Tatsu said nothing, merely cleaned the sword on the corpse's shirt. Kaiden and Chain stared in dismay at the pitiless look on Tatsu Cobb's face.

The Lepers were oblivious to the observer hidden in the shadows at the far end of the alley. Arisada was still close enough to Tatsu that even over the pervasive reek of the city, he sensed the boy's rising excitement, the blood simmering, the adrenalin pumping high with the eagerness of a hunter.

Arisada felt no remorse at the death of two of his kind. The mercenaries had delivered a just punishment. But he was shocked at the passionless look on Tatsu's face when he decapitated the rogue. Tatsu Cobb was so young to be this heartless.

Sadly, Arisada remembered another youth equally coldblooded. Nowaki had that same single-mindedness. And it had destroyed him.

The four men circled the hotel where the girls were supposed to be prisoners. The building was a dark, boarded-up shell. No sign of life.

"I think the bloodsucker lied to you, Mick," Chain muttered and racked fresh bolts into his crossbow.

"No one lies to me when I use Fiona on 'em." Bana bristled.

"How do you know? This is first time you've tried it." Kaiden grinned and pointed with his chin in the direction of the defunct Taser now shoved in Bana's waistband.

"Sod you, fag."

"No thanks, you're not my type." Kaiden laughed.

"If you two girls are through with your bitch fight, we've got to figure a way in." Chain's gaze, all business, surveilled the building.

"That fire ladder's our best bet. 'Cept I'd lay odds it's rusted stuck." Kaiden gave his partner a lopsided grin.

"*D'accord*. It'll make a hell of a lot of noise. They'll know we're here."

"Shite, man, yer foul-stinkin' French smokes has already announced us," Bana grumbled.

Chain merely snorted and flicked the butt onto the wet pavement. Screams of terror ripped through the air. "*Merde! Les enfants.*" Before the others reacted, he'd covered the width of the street in two giant strides and vaulted. One hand snagged the lowest rung of the ladder at least twenty feet above the ground. With a painful screech, the rusted hinges gave way. He let his weight pull the ladder down until it locked above his upturned face.

"Sonofabitch, Chain, if they didn't know we're here, they do now." Bana waved at the darkened building.

The Cajun led them up the shaky ladder to the top-floor landing. They crouched before a grime-covered window. Bana drew one of his Berettas from its holster and chambered a round. His eyes glowed with anticipation. "Stay behind me kid," he ordered. Tatsu nodded and exchanged the *katana* in favor of the shorter *wakizashi*.

The Cajun smashed the window with the butt of his crossbow and climbed into the darkened room. Kaiden slipped in beside his partner a second before the door burst inward. Three vampires simultaneously tried to enter the room. They got stuck. Three bolts from Chain's crossbow punched into three chests. Gurgling in their own blood, the creatures fell in a tangle of limbs. Kaiden put a round in each vampire's brain.

As junior man on the team, Tatsu went through the window last. Despite his superior eyesight, he landed on Bana who was scrambling around, looking for the dropped Tazer.

"Get off me, ya clumsy git." Bana shoved Tatsu back. By the

time they untangled themselves, the enemy were dead on the floor.

"Shite, missed it," the Irishman snapped.

"Tough break." There was no sympathy in Kaiden's voice. Chain shrugged.

Another scream rent the air. Chain stepped over the dead vampires and scanned the hallway before darting across. The others followed, Tatsu still last. The Cajun shattered the opposite door with a powerful kick and leveled his crossbow. Before anyone else moved, Tatsu ducked under Chain's arm into the pitch-black room.

The two girls tied to the filthy beds writhed in terror. Their shrieks climbed to ear-splitting levels when a man brandishing a sword charged into the room. The third girl hung in the arms of a rogue bull. Her head flopped back from a neck bent in the wrong direction. Her unseeing brown eyes met her rescuer. "Too late," they accused.

The huge bull, deep within his feeding frenzy, ignored the Lepers. Blood and spittle spraying from his mouth, the vampire turned toward his attackers. The creature snarled and dropped the girl.

Tatsu sliced the *wakizashi* across the bull's torso, separating fabric and flesh. The vampire's roar turned into an unholy screech when his bowels slithered out of his slashed belly. The stench of offal and copper filled the room.

Twin thunders from Kaiden's Colts took off the top of the vampire's head. The vampire's torso folded on top of the dead girl, blood and intestines spilling over them both.

"*Merde*, it stinks in here." Chain stepped over the twitching corpse. He crouched between the cots and spoke nonsense in his singsong patois until the two girls calmed down. With a quick slash of his K-bar, he cut though their bindings. Lifting one girl in his arms, he turned toward the door. "Let's get *les bébés* home."

"Two of 'em anyway," Kaiden murmured looking down at the dead girl. "Cobb, call Cooperhayes for a clean-up."

Relief filled Arisada when the mercenaries escorted two of

the girls from the building and help them into a HumVee. The beautiful boy was unharmed.

Arisada knew his obsession with Tatsu could lead to both their deaths. Eventually, his Sire, Sadomori, would discover Tatsu's existence. Driven by jealousy, the old vampire would send rogue after rouge to hunt down Tatsu and kill him. Arisada knew he wouldn't be able to fight them all. Even now, he'd been reckless, lingering to catch the last glimpse of the boy. Arisada had barely made it to the safety of his home before the first rays of dawn touched his front door seconds after he closed it.

Sunlight filtering through Tatsu's window brought him no comfort. He lay on his rumpled bed, one arm covering his eyes. His other hand bunched the sheet in a white-knuckled grip. Images from last night's mission flashed strobe-like through his mind. Without thought, Tatsu had decapitated the bull vampire. Worse, he'd slain ten vampires in as many days, creatures who, at one time, were human beings. Where was the honor in that kind of slaughter?

Shivers racked his sweat-drenched body. Sobs fought their way up from his chest only to be trapped behind his teeth, biting down on his bottom lip. Just in time, he bolted off the bed and into the bathroom. His stomach tried to turn itself inside out, his vomiting so violent his belly muscles tore. Bile splashed into the porcelain bowl while his tears rolled down his drawn cheeks.

He knew by their looks and muttered comments, that his teammates already regarded him as a cold-blooded killer. They knew nothing of the guilt-driven evisceration of his soul. The samurai code, ingrained in him since birth, provided no relief from the remorse now tearing him apart.

Twelve

The staccato of automatic gunfire echoed through the vast foundry. Tatsu trotted the half-klick past the massive, unused equipment to the center of the building. He'd postponed this moment for three days since he joined the Leper Colony and couldn't put it off any longer. He punched in the code to the roll-up door that separated the firing range from the rest of the facility.

Tatsu paused and admired Kaiden's technique. The blond dodged among the wooden pop-up targets, firing short bursts before running or rolling to the next safe spot. With split-second timing, Kaiden hit every enemy dead center or held fire on a Friendly.

The gun spent itself with an empty rattle. Almost too fast for Tatsu to see, the blond switched magazines. Tatsu noticed Kaiden used a double-stack—two clips taped back to back that allows the shooter to reload in a fraction of a second. The automatic weapon discharged with incredible recoil, yet the Leper's arm barely moved.

A shiver of arousal rippled over Tatsu watching the lithe play of the blond mercenary's muscles, the bunch and roll of his ass and the swivel of his hips. Damn, no denying it, that was one gorgeous man.

Within a few minutes, Kaiden finished his run. He turned off the target program and sauntered over to Tatsu. "*Konnichi wa*, Ninja Boy." He grinned.

Tatsu hid his distaste of the nickname. The tall blond was just being friendly. "*Konnichi wa,* Kaiden-san."

Kaiden's grin widened. "Learned a little Japanese for my second movie. Here, you might like this baby." He tossed his weapon toward Tatsu.

Tatsu caught the assault rifle in mid-flight. He checked the safety before hefting the weapon, surprised by its light weight.

"Doesn't weigh much, does it? It's an Israeli Tavor; nice little assault piece. Perfect for urban combat. Doubt if we'll use them on regular assignment, but they may come in handy if things heat up." Kaiden winked at Tatsu's reaction to the latest in urban mayhem.

"The Pueblo Militia tried to acquire these. Never had any luck."

"Not surprised. If it weren't for the Major's contacts, we'd be fighting vamps with bows and arrows."

"Or swords."

"Yeah, or swords." Kaiden gave Tatsu a long stare that somehow was not at all about weapons. "Come on. Let's get you some range time. Heard you don't really need it but the Major knows you're not exactly fond of guns. Wants you to be a bit more accepting of the concept, so to speak."

"*Wakatta,* I agreed to his rules. And he isn't being unreasonable."

"Don't take off your swords. Get used to doing this with 'em on. We'll start on the silhouettes in the first lane and move over to pop-ups later. First, I want to outfit you with a sidearm." Kaiden took back the rifle and slung it by its strap over one shoulder. "Show me your hands."

Puzzled, Tatsu held out his hands. Kaiden held them for one sizzling moment and rubbed his thumbs over the calluses.

"Good, hard in all the right places." The blond nodded his approval.

Tatsu's face heated. He jerked his hands back, flustered by the rapidly growing erection crowding his pants. He saw Kaiden's pointed look at his crotch, the responding flare of interest in the man's blue eyes.

A strangled moan slipped from Kaiden's lips. He turned abruptly and marched over to the steel cabinets lining one wall. "I know you're stronger than you look, but my Colt is too big for your hands." He looked over the racks of guns in the cabinet then handed Tatsu a small automatic. "This should fit you better."

"Sig Sauer P230?" Tatsu racked back the slide and checked that it was empty before dropping out the full magazine and checking the ammunition. "Hollow points," he grunted. This kind of bullet was designed to tumble around inside its target, shattering bone and shredding tissue.

"Yup, stays inside what you hit. No dead bystanders. I know you don't want it, but take it anyway, or the Major will have my nuts in a wringer. Now, let's get some range time in."

Three grueling hours later, Kaiden called it a halt. They were both drenched in sweat and panting. The tall blond pulled cold water from a refrigerator near the range wall and poured them both a glass. "You're an excellent shot, Ninja Boy."

"*Arigatō*, Kaiden-san." Tatsu warmed at the compliment. "Still prefer my swords." He swallowed his drink in long, thirsty gulps. When he placed his empty glass on the nearby table, he realized Kaiden had been studying him the entire time. Tatsu felt that embarrassing pink dust the tops of his cheeks.

"What was his name?"

"*Sumimasen, wakarimasen.*"

"Don't give me that 'I'm sorry, I don't understand' crap. Who was he, the one who broke your heart?"

"No one. And it's none of your business."

"Probably not. You hide it well, but part of being a good actor is reading people. I see it in your eyes. A demon is riding you, and it ain't just that monster you're hunting."

Tatsu bridled. His life back in New Mexico had nothing to do with now. "I left Santa Fe for only one reason. To kill vampires."

Kaiden sidled over to Tatsu, leaned down almost nose-to-nose. "Bullshit, Ninja Boy."

Beneath the acrid smell of cordite, Tatsu caught the heady musk of male sweat with that sweet undernote that always meant arousal. Tatsu's heart revved up. Loneliness, coupled with a good dose of sexual frustration, overrode any cautious message his brain was hammering at him. His look skittered from Kaiden's deep-cerulean eyes to his full lips and back. No need to wonder if Kaiden was growing hard. Just as hard as Tatsu.

Kaiden sighed, shifted imperceptibly closer, placed one finger under Tatsu's chin and lifted his head. "Goddamn, you're so fucking pretty." He leaned in, clearly aiming for a kiss.

Tatsu knew he should pull away, yet his brain-cock connection screamed for that sweet contact. He closed his eyes and lifted his chin.

The door to the range beeped and slid aside with a screech.

"Shit," Kaiden muttered under his breath and stepped over to the bench. With a slight look of chagrin, he glanced at Tatsu. "Sorry, Cobb. Kinda forgot myself for a moment."

"*Mondai nai*, no problem," Tatsu nodded and knew it was all right between them. He also knew nothing was going to happen. For Tatsu could tell that Kaiden Galloway was plagued by his own demons.

It had been a week since Tatsu joined the Colony and already he felt like he'd made a mistake—two mistakes if he counted that dumb move with Kaiden at the range the other night.

Tatsu had learned a little about Tendai's vampires, but not enough. Bana was helping, in his shoot-from-the-hip way. Through an unspoken agreement, they'd developed a bizarre interrogation method of any rogue vampire caught during an operation. Bana enthusiastically applied Fiona followed by Tatsu threatening with his swords. So far, their tag-team approach ended in a couple of grisly deaths but no solid information. Tatsu despaired that their system was going to take more patience than he had. And he'd long left patience somewhere back in Santa Fe.

He shook off his misgivings. He'd give the Colony another couple of weeks. He owed that much loyalty to the Major. And the job did have its perks.

With his first paycheck, he'd moved into the tiny furnished apartment above the dojo. It offered only the bare essentials, but Tatsu liked that the bedroom had a balcony where he could look over the city while he smoked.

Tonight, the damp chill of a pending storm caught him

when he stepped out. He pulled out a pack of Canadian Kings, lit one and took a deep drag. He plucked a sliver of tobacco from the tip of his tongue and took another deep drag. But tonight the ritual failed to soothe. He leaned on the balustrade. A thin curl of cigarette smoke drifted into the air, drew his attention up to the silvery clouds scudding across the sky like the flying mane of a wild horse. Then the image of Arisada spun down his spine and straight into his prick.

Kuso, thinking of that damned vampire was not going to help! Tatsu flicked the smoldering butt over the railing and went back inside to change. He didn't need any cock-stirring, ball-throbbing fantasies. What he needed was a few hours of hard-assed sword practice.

Across the street, Arisada watched Tatsu lean on the balcony rail. Battling the craving to seek him out, since seeing him a week ago at the Belladonna, Arisada waged an internal war with himself against the Centuries of yearning inside his heart. Now, an unutterable joy filled him. For just one more taste of those tender lips, he'd embrace an eternity of dishonor.

The vampire ignored the growl of the incoming storm, his eyes riveted on the slim form standing three floors above him. Arisada stared with an odd fascination when Tatsu flicked away the used butt in a shower of sparks. Watched him turn and leave, resolution stiffening those young shoulders. The glass door slid closed with an odd finality.

Arisada lingered in the wet street and stared at the cigarette's thin paper dissolving in the puddle, the tobacco swirling around before sinking out of sight. His need for *fukushū* had vanished in much the same way.

He smelled the sea-salt of tears. When he touched his cheek, his hand came away red. Shame filled him, to be so emotional over the boy. Yet, that boy meant everything.

His gliding walk took him over the wet pavement in seconds. Silently, he entered the darkness of the dojo and made his way down the hall to the *shiaijo*.

Tatsu stood immobile, weapons held precisely apart to inflict the most damage on multiple attackers. He focused on his *tanden*, seeking that stillness a warrior needed before facing mortal combat. He was unable to find it.

The simplicity of executing every *kata* with precision and purpose usually drove all other thought from Tatsu's mind. His spirit vibrated on a higher plane dictated by the needs of the art of the sword.

Yet, since he'd met Arisada, an undeniable anticipation had tempered Tatsu's concentration. Could it have anything to do with the insane hope of seeing the vampire once again? Or the thick pulse throbbing in his loins at the memory of that braid whipping in the air? Perhaps it was the smoky tones of the vampire's voice, or the feel of that kiss burning across his lips every time he thought about it.

Just when Tatsu decided that tonight, like every night, Arisada was never going to appear, the vampire stepped into the *shiaijo*. As before, he held his sword in the position of neutrality. Dressed in a white *hakama* and *keiko-gi* with a scarlet *obi*, Arisada bowed deeply from the waist.

"You have been hoping I'd return." Arisada didn't wait for a reply but selected an *iaito* then stepped before the mat and bowed. "You are a superb fighter. Would you agree to *tachiuchi*." The challenge glittered in his golden eyes.

Tatsu gritted his teeth at the arrogance of the vampire's statement and at its truth. All consideration of the information-getting plan, submerged beneath that ineffable sense of connection, filled Tatsu. Perhaps because Saito Arisada was a Master swordsman, perhaps a Sword Saint. Face the vampire, defeat him, demand answers. Then maybe kill him. Hell, the opportunity was too much to refuse.

"We fight with real swords?" Tatsu knew the vampire was talking about live steel, the blades only allowed to kiss the opponent yet still offer the threat of a cut. The control and skill of both fighters would be a supreme test for both of them. Tatsu also knew Arisada would not temper his strikes out of any foolish regard that Tatsu was simply human.

"You may use two swords if you prefer, Cobb-san." Arisada's mouth twitched, almost a smile. His breath caught at the eagerness in those stunning emerald eyes.

"No. One will suffice." Tatsu bobbed his head. He took his *katana* and moved onto the mat.

"Perhaps we should place a wager on the outcome. If I lose, I will answer your questions. If I win, I claim only an honorable favor, *neh* Cobb-san?" Arisada suggested.

"*Watashi wa anata no chōsen o ukeireru.*" Tatsu accepted the challenge. This was what he wanted, a strategy to force the truth from the vampire. "Be prepared to lose." Tatsu had no doubt honor would dictate that the vampire answer Tatsu's questions with complete honesty.

"Your confidence is delightful, Cobb-san. Perhaps my curiosity about your request will slow my hand and make me careless."

The seductive note in that warm baritone sent shivers rippling down Tatsu's spine. Shivers that had nothing to do with vengeance and everything to do with a deep throb in his prick. "Perhaps I will surprise you with what I want." He heard the playful tone in his reply. *Kuso*, was he flirting with the vampire now? Embarrassed, he coughed to cover up the thought. He caught Arisada's slight smile. A smile that said the vampire was enjoying his effect on Tatsu's libido.

"First to draw blood, Saito-sensei."

"*Wakatta*, of course."

They crouched on the mat for a moment. A flicker of understanding rippled between them before they signaled their readiness by loosening their *katanas* an inch from the scabbard. In the same breath, they sprang to their feet and drew their swords. Tatsu raised his above his head in the *jodan* position. The vampire mirrored his pose. Air whistled. Their swords descended and met with a loud ring.

Tatsu fought as if all honor depended on the outcome of this match. Perhaps it did. His body hummed with exhilaration. Sweat formed a fine sheen over his skin and plastered his hair to his face. He met every cut of Arisada's blade, met and countered. But the longer they sparred, the more Tatsu's uncertainty grew. Why the hell was he observing the rules of *shinkendo*? Why did he not simply kill this creature? Yet, he knew why. He was hoping for a repeat of that earlier match—that incredibly erotic dance of their swords.

Arisada never allowed it. From his first move, it was clear he controlled the field. The vampire pressed hard and long, gave no quarter even while he admired Tatsu's instinctive mastery of the sword.

Step, strike, balance, defend, spin, attack. Every muscle ached. His breath came in shorter and shorter gasps. The *katana*'s weight increased with each cut. Knowing his human body couldn't outlast the endurance of a vampire, Tatsu delved deep within his determination and drew upon every last measure of strength. He lost track of time.

Arisada did not. He sensed dawn was minutes away. His concentration wavered for a split second. Tatsu saw it and drove into the offense in one last desperate effort. He shifted his weight forward and caught the vampire's *katana* just front of its square *tsuba*. With an unorthodox twist, Tatsu flipped the sword from Arisada's fingers and sent it spinning into the air.

Faster than any human, Arisada leaped up, grabbed the blade and slashed it diagonally downward toward the floor. Tatsu jerked his exposed foot away and faded to the side. He swept his sword in a counter cut. The *katana* met with a ring, slid together in a whispered glide and parted. Arisada's continued its descent. Tatsu dropped to one knee and whipped his sword into *jodansuki,* an uppercut toward Arisada's exposed arm. The tip caressed the cloth of the *keiko-gi*, cutting the garment and revealing the skin beneath, smooth and untouched. Tatsu savored a flash of triumph.

Arisada stepped back, moved his sword in a salute, signaling the end of the fight. "I believe I have won." He pointed his blade tip toward the mat. "Look at your foot."

Tatsu stared down in disbelief at the minute drop of crimson on his bare ankle. He hadn't felt the cut. "What happened to not taking unfair advantage?" Admiration coupled with shame caught him by surprise.

"My sweet boy, your lesson for tonight is who needed to win the most. I couldn't resist. I want my prize more than you." Arisada snapped his *katana* into its saya. A second later, he stood before Tatsu, so close they brushed chest-to-chest.

Tatsu breathed in the heady scent of the *kyūketsuki*'s body—the rich male tang musky, with a faint copper note. *Shimatta,* he had to be crazy. Arisada smelled so good. That scent sent a surge of arousal throughout Tatsu, boiling his blood with want. Instinct—or maybe it was his own need—told him what the vampire offered.

Fakku. He needed to kiss this gorgeous creature and all else be damned. Tatsu lowered his head a fraction and was met with the sweet press of Arisada's closed mouth, a kiss all the more arousing for its tender restraint. Tatsu's hand found that thick braid, silky soft, flowing, a life force beneath his fingertips. He stroked its satiny, knotted length, his fingers curled as if gripping a cock. A deep throated moan reached his ears.

Abruptly, hands pushed against Tatsu's chest and the delicious touch of those lips left. A slight breeze and the vampire was gone.

"Hey, boyo, get your fekkin' head outa your ass!" Bana's yell reverberated through the cab of the Humvee. Tatsu wrenched the steering wheel around but still sideswiped a rusted car parked in the narrow street. The screech of metal against metal drowned Bana's next string of profanity. Bana's insane driving speed often caused Tatsu to fear they would die in a tangled pile of metal and engine parts before dying on a mission. Tonight, Tatsu insisted on driving. Bad move. His urgent need to race back to the Colony had turned him into a demolition driver.

Before they left, the Major said the erratic DataStream was once again operable. At last, Tatsu could search for information on Seattle's vampire clan. He told himself he needed every scrap of intelligence for his quest. In reality, he knew he wanted to know everything about Saito Arisada. Because, he just couldn't get his mind off that enigmatic *kyūketsuki,* his exquisite face and thick, sensuous braid.

The creature's golden, almond-shaped eyes were so full of an undefined promise. Visions of the sensual smile played constantly at the edges of Cobb's mind. His brain wouldn't shut out the feeling of the vampire's soft, kissable mouth.

These thoughts about the flame-haired vampire were driving Tatsu *kuruu*. And being crazy put his team at risk. While on assignment two nights ago, a small pack of vampires jumped them. If not for Chain's incredible reflexes and that crossbow of his, Tatsu would be dead.

Bana grumbled again while they wrote their reports. "Dunno what's got inta yer head, boyo, but you'd better get back in the game before you get us both killed." The Irishman flung the warning at Tatsu before stomping out the door.

Dammit, Bana was right, yet Tatsu dismissed the warning the instant he punched the keyboard of the Colony's computer. Even knowing the DataStream was a mishmash of corrupt information, Tatsu hunted through the so-called global service with a ruthless obsession. It took several hours to scroll through hundreds of pages that amounted to a Vampire 101 course. Long lists of the names of those killed during Japan's *Kyūketsuki* Pogroms. Tatsu knew the records couldn't be complete. More than any other nationality, Japanese vampires were masters of subterfuge, able to remain hidden—much like ancient Ninjas.

He dug out any bit of information—fact, fiction, rumor, myth, he didn't care—on Saito Arisada. Many powerful vampires were open about their histories since the virus outed them. Not Arisada. The sparse data noted the crimson-haired vampire was Japanese—Tatsu knew that—of an ancient noble family from the Echigo Province—that was a surprise. Now second-in-command of the Tendai Clan. Knew that, too. Flagged him as extremely dangerous. No shit! Nothing more.

You're a secretive kono yarou, Tatsu sneered. *Secretive but fucking hot,* the horny part of his brain fired back.

Research on Ukita Sadomori yielded two pages in kanji from a Japanese history book about the Ukita family line annihilated a thousand years ago and a dozen alarming newspaper articles from the year Sadomori took over Seattle's vampires. Headline news about the decapitation of the three government negotiators. Several graphic photos of the bodies.

A long psychoanalysis treatise from a professor in Rostock University that postulated Ukita Sadomori was no ordinary vampire. As if there was such a thing as an "ordinary" vampire. The article stated Ukita had an antisocial personality, was definitely a sadist, torturer and mass murderer. It concluded with the hypothesis that some of the more despotic rulers throughout history were really Ukita.

No mention of a Koji Nowaki.

Tatsu shut off the computer, leaned back in his chair and lit a cigarette, considering his strategy. His instinct cried out that the killer was among this city's vampire population. And Sadomori and Arisada topped the list of probables.

He should have killed Saito Arisada the minute the vampire revealed his nature? Yet, Tatsu had no answer for why he hadn't. Was it Arisada's quiet demeanor, his calm, sincere voice or those serene, golden eyes that revealed the spirit of the samurai that dwelled within.

Perhaps this idea to force information from Arisada was foolish. At times, Tatsu felt *baka,* stupid, for even thinking of it. If Saito Arisada wasn't the killer, the fucking red-haired vampire must know who was. Next time Arisada showed his face, Tatsu would show no mercy. He'd enjoy seeing those freakish gold eyes fill with fear when the vampire realized he was about to die.

Ah, who the hell was he kidding? The pulse of heat in Tatsu's groin said he craved something else. Against all reason, against all sanity, against all honor, Tatsu's body wanted that beautiful creature pressing hot and hard and shuddering with desire against him.

He re-created every detail of that moment the vampire kissed him. Warmth coiled through his balls and his cock. He rubbed the bulge crowding his pants and was tempted to jack off right there.

Then shame engulfed him. How could he think of Arisada with anything less than loathing? Tatsu told himself he was angry for losing the fight and at being kissed against his will by his enemy. *Don't lie. You wanted that kiss.* Oh hell yes, he'd wanted that kiss and later, a whole lot more.

Two weeks after that kiss, Tatsu's flagging patience was rewarded. The moment Arisada entered the dojo, Tatsu fired a salvo of angry questions. "Why do you keep coming here? Who the fuck is this Koji Nowaki? What's he got to do with me?"

"I'll answer all your questions on one condition." Arisada's eyes glittered, the pupils large.

"What condition?" Tatsu noted the vampire did not place his *katana* near the door. Instead, it rested on Arisada's left hip, the combat side.

"*Tachiuchi?* Our own weapons. Again, whoever draws first blood wins. If I lose, I will do as you wish, *neh* Cobb-san? You lose, you grant mine." Arisada intended to make Tatsu promise to leave the city immediately, to give up his quest for *fukushū*.

They sprang into the fight. Tatsu took the offensive, pressing forward across the mat. A fierce joy filled him. The vampire met him strike for strike, giving no mercy. At the end of this match, one of them would bleed.

At first, Tatsu believed he was familiar with all of Arisada's techniques. Still, as the match wore on, he realized knowledge and skill were not enough. He had to be cunning. Tatsu stepped back into defensive mode trying to lure the *kyūketsuki* into a mistake. The vampire followed. In an inhumanly fast move, Tatsu drove his sword past his opponent's defenses, forcing Arisada's strike to glance aside. Tatsu reversed his sword and caught the center of Arisada's blade. So fierce was his cut, it sent Arisada's *katana* spinning into the dark. Tatsu's shout of victory ended in a bark of laughter.

The vampire dropped to one knee and pressed his forehead to the mat. The moment froze in Tatsu's mind. One swift cut against that vulnerable nape and Arisada would be dead. A heartbeat later, Tatsu knew he couldn't kill this beauty.

A second passed before Arisada slapped one hand on the mat and stood. "You have won, my young samurai. Ask your question. I promise to tell the truth."

Tatsu picked up the vampire's *katana* with his left hand. Suddenly, he realized he didn't care about Koji Nowaki or why Arisada sparred with him or even why Arisada had kissed him. There was only one question to ask.

"Nagasaki, fourteen years ago, four people slaughtered by *kyūketsuki*—my parents, brother and sister. On your word of honor, was it you?" Tatsu's voice grated with suppressed grief.

Unrestrained sorrow crossed Arisada's face. "*Gomen nasai*, Cobb-san. I am deeply saddened at the loss of your family. I offer you *bushi no ichigon*, my word of honor as a warrior, I committed no such atrocity. During that time, I was in Guangzhou negotiating a treaty between my kind and the people of Southern China."

"Prove it. Strip."

The edges of Arisada's lips crinkled up. "What is this, a seduction?" Before Arisada drew his next breath, the tip of the youth's sword pressed against his throat. The vampire smelled the miniscule drop of his own blood.

"I'm not fucking around." Tatsu increased the pressure of the *katana* a fraction. "Take off your clothes."

Showing no fear, Arisada stepped back and untied his *obi*. With a dignified grace, he slipped the *keiko-gi* from his shoulders and dropped the garment to the floor.

"*Nanimokamo*, everything." Tatsu gave a menacing flick of his blade.

Arisada removed the flowing black culottes then the silk under-trousers. Stripped to only his loincloth, he regarded Tatsu through a calm, curious gaze.

Tatsu stared at the curved planes of Arisada's body, the tantalizing joining of the underarm to the slightly defined chest. Smooth, alabaster skin with just a thin, teasing trail of hair above the waistband of the *fundoshi*. A white line, thin as a cut from a surgeon's scalpel, was visible from hip to hip. With an odd certainty, Tatsu knew that scar was the result of an attempt at *seppuku*.

His heart gave a disturbing leap when his eyes slid over the vampire's crotch and lingered. The bulge beneath Saito's white loincloth stirred. What the hell? The vampire was getting turned on, standing naked in the middle of the dojo with Tatsu's sword an inch from his throat. Worse, Tatsu's own cock showed interest, plumping up under a warm flow arousal. With effort, he wrenched his gaze away from Arisada's groin.

"Around." Tatsu flicked his *katana,* trying to hide his arousal behind anger. Arisada presented his back. Even at that critical moment, Tatsu's gaze betrayed him when it dropped immediately to the vampire's compact buttocks with their perfect indents on the outside of each glute. Smoky warmth spread through Tatsu's belly when he took in that rounded ass. His eyes traveled slowly, oh so slowly, up the twist of the *fundoshi* between the buttcheeks to the delicious dip of the spine. Then his look shifted upward.

For the rest of his life, Tatsu never forgot his first sight of the vampire's back. A tattoo covered nearly every inch of skin from the waist up over the right shoulder. A cherry blossom tree, so perfectly rendered that Tatsu reached out to touch one fragile pink blossom, expecting it to fall away in his hand. Instead of the softness of a petal, he felt warm skin. A hot prickle flared through him. He snatched his hand away.

Tatsu stared transfixed. Slowly, the image of a boy emerged from the depths of the art. A stereogram in which the tree slowly materialized into a beautiful youth—a *bishounen* with startling emerald eyes framed by long black lashes. A beguiling innocence reflected from those jade orbs, belying the boy's smile that was filled with a seductive promise. Then Arisada flexed his shoulders, turning the tattoo into a sakura tree.

No scars lay hidden beneath that beautiful skin art. Relief washed through Tatsu, puzzling in its intensity, its mere presence. His cock gave another throb when he took another long look at the vampire's hot—did he actually think hot—ass.

"Get dressed," Tatsu barked to cover his confusion.

Exhibiting no shame, Arisada bent over to pick up his clothes. The act gave Tatsu another delicious look at those tightly muscled buttocks. His body heated in a flash at the sight of Arisada's lean legs and the bunching of those fine ass muscles. Flustered, he lowered his sword. "*Gomen nasai*, I had to know"

"Know what?" Arisada ignored his clothing still scattered on the floor and turned to face the boy.

"The *kyūketsuki* who murdered my family is scarred, shoulders to hips. Do you know of any like that?"

Arisada had made the wager in honor. Yet, he froze, the reply turning to dust in his throat. "I cannot help you." Inwardly, he begged forgiveness from the Buddha Amida at the lie while he stared into Tatsu's peridot gaze.

"What about this Ukita Sadomori?" Tatsu persisted.

Arisada shook his head. "*Nani mo*, nothing. He is my *Seisakusha*, my creator. Nothing more." Arisada would do anything, say anything, to protect Tatsu from confronting Sadomori. The Daimyō would snuff out the life of this youngster with less effort than that needed to kill a fly. "What will you do if you find this *kyūketsuki*?"

"Kill him."

"*Â, sō desu ka*. It is a blood debt."

"The honor of my father's name must be restored," Tatsu retorted still pointing his weapon at the vampire.

"Honor is everything. Yet so many suffer for it." The vampire looked sadly at Tatsu. Again, he turned to pick up his clothing.

This time, the act held a finality to it that filled Tatsu with anger. A dark and perverse desire moved within him. It boiled over, shredding the tight band of control around his emotions. Frustration and disappointment, yes, but also the raw hunger of a man too long denied his most primal need. He wanted to inflict a lasting cruelty on this creature.

"Freeze!" Tatsu's sharp order surprised Arisada. He looked into that young face, the forehead furrowed into a scowl. The mouth, bowed lips bared over perfect white teeth. The eyes now turned sea-dark with lust. Saw with complete clarity that this was the true spirit of the warrior in Tatsu. The warrior who knew what he wanted and was going to take it.

The *katana*'s tip nudged into the indent just below the vampire's Adams' apple. It touched the pale flesh, and halted, its tip a hair's width from piercing the tender skin. Arisada froze. An incremental increase in pressure and Arisada felt the wound. Smelled the copper scent from that first drop of his own blood. He stepped back, weight on his rear leg. Still the *katana* kept up its relentless press. Arisada moved back again, his eyes never leaving Tatsu's face. Another step, then another.

With a hard thud, Arisada's back hit the wall of the dojo. Perhaps the boy was going to take his life after all. *Wakatta,* so be it.

The move, so fast it was a blur, stunned the vampire. The sword sliced through his *fundoshi* at the waist. The blade continued its arc straight into its saya. In the same moment, Tatsu's *tanto* replaced its brother at Arisada's throat. Seconds later, the loincloth reached the floor.

Arisada's pale cock bounced out—long and growing rapidly toward full arousal. The foreskin stretched back tight and thin revealing the head, tender as a ripe apricot, the slit glistening with precum.

The feral look that burned in Tatsu's eyes fixed on Arisada's erection. Tatsu licked his lips, the needy gesture clearly unconscious. His *tanto* never wavered as he moved chest-to-chest with Arisada.

Tatsu lifted his gaze to the vampire's face. "Don't fucking move."

Their eyes locked. Understanding rippled between them. Both knew the vampire could break free before Tatsu realized it. Both accepted that escape was not even a consideration. A tiny moan escaped Arisada. He submitted.

A fine quiver washed over the vampire's skin when the callused pads of Tatsu's hand trailed down his ridged belly. A harsh tug at the curls around Arisada's shaft, then the sublime, unutterable delight when those fingers took his cock in a hard grip. A painful squeeze as if to deny pleasure forced a gasp from Arisada. That pain blossomed into a sweet heat rolling up the turgid length of his prick into his belly. His eyes, now scarlet with lust, closed in sweet surrender. Arisada's top fangs slipped their channels and pierced his lower lip.

Tatsu smelled the blood. As if he were *kyūketsuki,* its scent captivated him, drove him into a pulsing, undeniable fever. His thumb pushed the silken foreskin back from Arisada's weeping crown and rolled over the slit. Pearly juice leaked into Tatsu's palm. He slicked it along the swollen shaft, used it to lube that iron rod. Rubbing, teasing, demanding. Tatsu's hand jacked the vampire's tender flesh with increasing fury. Yet he never released the relentless pressure of that knife tip against the vampire's jugular. Nor did he take his gaze from the vampire's face.

Heat scalded the vampire's cheeks. The white lines of his scar shone in graphic relief. The thin nostrils flared with every ragged breath. The full lips drew back over a mouth dropped partially open, fangs extended. Lust glittered from the vampire's eyes, turned them molten with excitement.

Pain from Arisada's cut lip sent want surging down into his groin. He gave free rein to his hunger, allowed his body to be engulfed in Tatsu's fury. The skin of Arisada's hardened cock stretched almost beyond endurance. Waves of fire spasmed from his sphincter deep into his entrails. Fingers pumped with punishing force, the friction sending a sweet, delectable pain through Arisada's sex. The rub of a thumb over his throbbing crown. A sharp drag of Tatsu's nail across the piss hole.

Every neuron in Arisada's ass, his prick, his balls fired at the same time. The blast of raw heat, bearing a thin edge of pain, shot from Arisada's rod. He rocked his hips, driving his sex a final time into Tatsu's hand. Uncaring of the danger from the *tanto*, Arisada's body convulsed, jetting his spunk through his slit into the torturous grip of Tatsu's palm.

With that first glistening jet, Arisada screamed. He twisted his head away, fighting the urge to tear into Tatsu's throat, to feast on the boy's rich blood and drain him of life.

Arisada, his cock still spurting with aftershocks, lunged sideways, away from Tatsu. He felt the *tanto* slice across his neck. Falling to his knees, Arisada dropped his head between his hands and fought off the urge to drink. His breath came in great shudders. His vision blackened. The muscles along his arms and legs knotted as he dove within himself, seeking that infinitesimal center of peace. He fastened on it and used it to drive back the lust for blood. When his body and mind at last belonged to him, he pushed himself to his feet and faced Tatsu.

The boy stood as if frozen, staring at the slickness of cum clinging to his hand with a strange fascination. Without lowering his knife, he sucked each digit one by one with slow, deliberate laps. With that final lick, the hunger on Tatsu's face dissolved. He shook his head, the primal glare fading from his jade eyes.

"*Sumimasen*," Tatsu croaked. The apology was bizarre, seeming a weak defense against the stricken rawness of the act between the two of them. He offered Arisada a confused, desperate look. Then, with a strangled cry, he bolted from the dojo.

On shaking legs, Arisada leaned against the chill surface of the dojo wall. He touched the thin cut across his throat and looked in wonder at the smear of blood on his fingers. Tatsu had stopped himself from cutting deeper and ending Arisada's life.

Many minutes passed before he felt the strength to gather his clothes from their tumbled heap on the floor. Minutes that left him filled with wonder of the power in this human boy who had brought him gasping and begging to such a total surrender. Fear filled Arisada at how close he had come to taking the young hunter's life.

With trembling fingers, the vampire fastened his clothing and tucked in his sword into his *obi*. Tatsu may have jacked him off as a show of dominance but Arisada knew the boy desired it as much. When Tatsu's fingers circled Arisada's tumescent organ, a covenant was fused. Tatsu had given himself to Arisada. Tatsu just didn't realize it yet.

"Next time, my *bishounen*, I won't allow you to win," Arisada whispered. He smiled, a beautiful human smile with no show of fangs.

That cock-pulsing, ball-throbbing, wet dream haunted Tatsu's sleep again. This time the hard body pressing with raw urgency against him was slim and wiry. The hair tumbling over Tatsu's body was the color of flame, not coal. The eyes above him reflected the gold of the sun, and the skin of his lover shone white instead of nut brown. Not Navajo but the ancient language of Nipon cried one word in ecstasy, "*Koibito!*"

He snapped awake, his cock rock hard, pounding with a painful, demanding insistence. With his left hand, the same hand that had wrapped around Arisada's prick mere hours before, Tatsu reached for the hardness between his thighs. He played with his chamois-soft foreskin, rubbed over the knobby head now slick with precum. His hand moved faster, quick, tearing strokes followed by merciless twists around the ridge. He felt the punishing scratch of his calluses on his cock, knew that same sensation had propelled Arisada over the edge.

He cupped the silky weight of his sac, fondled his nuts, rolling them, stretching the soft skin with hard tugs. His forefinger slid along his sensitive perineum sending cold pulses up his spine. He pressed his forefinger past the resisting rim. The tight muscle protested then yielded with a sweet rush. With a hiss of pleasure, he entered the heat beyond. Tight, wet walls clamped around him. Craving the fullness, he shoved in a second then a third finger before curling his knuckles against the wet, quivering walls of his chute. He finger-fucked himself until the sweet burn climbed up against his heart.

Tatsu hunched over his screaming groin, abdominal muscles knotting. His punishing jerks on his cock matched each deep finger-thrust into his ass. And then the vision of Arisada, face distorted by fangs, eyes crimson with lust, yet still stunningly beautiful, flashed into Tatsu's mind. The vampire's name spilled from Tatsu' lips as his cum splashed over his belly in arching spurts.

Chest heaving, Tatsu collapsed on the mattress. His shuddering, sweat-drenched body stank of spunk and shame.

"Oh, *fakku*." What the hell was he thinking? But he knew. The name bursting from his lips, the sticky mess clinging to his hand, the surging in his body—all told him.

He'd always faced the truth no matter how harsh. He wanted Saito Arisada, wanted to fuck him and be fucked by him. Craved him with a desperation that threatened all reason.

Thirteen

The double doors of the Snake Pit bounced open under a single heavy kick. Chain strode in outfitted in crisp combat pants that contrasted with his scuffed tanker boots. He braced his heavy crossbow over one shoulder. A dee-skin vest dangled from his other hand. His tight tank top barely contained the bulge of muscles across his massive chest. The fabric outlined every ripple of his six-pack abs. His unbraided hair cascaded over his shoulders in ripples of black silk.

The Cajun looked around for his no-show partner and raised one eyebrow before placing his bow on the table. He dug in his pockets—the act stretching his pants across his prodigious crotch—and pulled out a pack of Gauloises. He looked over the flame flickering between his cupped hands and winked at Tatsu. Then, cigarette dangling from his mouth, he braided his hair with swift moves made deeply sensual by their lack of guile.

Utterly captivated by the big man, Tatsu stared. His eyes fixed on the conspicuous bulge at the Chain's groin. *Shimatta*, he's pure, gorgeous animal. No wonder Kaiden's in love with him! Tatsu's curiosity jolted to a halt when Kaiden strolled into the Pit.

The blond mercenary dropped into his accustomed chair. "What's up, boss?" he drawled and shot the Major a smile that bordered on the insolent.

"Mr. Kaiden, what part of your employment agreement did you ignore that requires you to call in immediately on a Red Status?"

"Sorry, Major, didn't hear the page. Was in the middle of a hot date, if you catch my drift?" Kaiden fixed the expected leer on his face. In reality, he hadn't had his dick in anyone since he'd fallen for the Cajun two years ago. "Hey, partner, *comment ça va?*" he turned to Chain to cover his lie.

A frission of jealousy slithered into Chain's gut. Why should he care who Kaiden fucked? Never bothered him in the past. Lately, though, he could not stop thinking of his partner in bed with a man. Mentally, Chain shrugged. *Laissez-faire.* None of his business as long as the blond had his back.

The Major's words cut through Chain's distraction. "I apologize for calling all of you in during your two-day leave but this is top priority. Having stated that, Mr. Murtagh also seems to be among those who think dereliction of duty is a fine quality." He rarely displayed anger, but a scowl stayed his face while the minutes passed and Bana didn't show.

Kuso, where in the hell was Bana? Tatsu knew his partner would never ignore a Status Red. Hell, the Irishman lived for this stuff. Had Bana started drinking again? Tatsu's concern for his missing partner wiped out any other distracting thoughts, including Arisada.

The door at the far end of the Snake Pit opened. Tatsu's head snapped around expecting to see Bana. No such luck.

Two strangers followed Cooperhayes into the briefing room. The first was middle-aged, dressed in an expensive suit, and was clutching a battered briefcase to his chest like a shield. His not-quite-in-full-panic gaze locked onto the Major. A slim youth crowded nervously in behind the pair of men. The boy's letter jacket and tailored jeans were torn in several places and splattered with blood. Abrasions and deep scratches covered his face and hands. Bruise-dark circles under his eyes contrasted sharply with the sick pallor of his face. His shell-shocked gaze bounced around the room.

"This is Mr. Robert Terrance, President of Rainier-Scopes University, and Marshal Ortega, a student. Mr. Ortega, please explain what happened." The Major indicated with a nod of his head where the two clients should sit.

The youth, Ortega, stared at his hands, fingers knotted together in an effort to hide his trembling. In halting, garbled sentences he told how he and four others from the football team were enticed from Belladonna to an abandoned hotel by two female vampires and imprisoned. A vampire called the Daimyō showed up. Instantly, Sadomori had killed two of them after screaming that drugs polluted their blood. Ortega escaped but two students were still held captive.

The sound of Sadomori's name hauled Tatsu into the present. With a guilty start, he glanced at the wall clock. Two hours since the Red Alert and still no Bana. Tatsu turned back to the Major who was issuing orders for the rescue operation. Lepers separated into teams and left to collect weapons and munitions.

"Mr. Cobb, a moment." The Major's sharp command halted Tatsu halfway out the door. "Your partner isn't answering his cell. Find him and report back."

Tatsu's protest froze in his mouth at the withering look from his boss. "*Hai, wakatta.*" His angry strides took him past the others on his way to the motorpool and his bike. Shit, he'd miss the action—all because his damn partner couldn't stay away from the bottle.

Tatsu pushed the Drifter to insane speeds, redlining the engine until the machine howled. He ripped through the near-empty streets, jumping curbs and skidding around turns. Rationality returned when the Kawasaki became airborne for the second time as he crested a hill. He eased off the throttle but only a little.

Guilt replaced Tatsu's anger. Had his obsession with Arisada caused him to miss signs that Bana was in trouble? Tatsu had avoided his partner outside work. Hell, more than avoided. He bolted for cover any time Bana even looked like he was gonna say. "What's up, boyo?"

Tatsu checked the Whore first and felt relief when Doris said she'd not seen the Irishman for a few days. Said he might be shacked up with his new girlfriend.

"Thanks," Tatsu yelled on the way out to the street. *Shimatta*, he had no idea where this girlfriend lived. No, wait. A couple of days ago, Bana was grumbling that he'd been dumped. The man didn't exactly take rejection very well. Especially female rejection. Probably why he'd fallen off the wagon.

Tatsu skidded the bike to a halt in front of the Irishman's

apartment. Praying Bana was home, he took the stairs three at a time up to the second floor.

"Bana, open up! It's Cobb." He pounded on the door. No answer. He thumped again so hard the heavy door shuddered. *Kuso*, no one could sleep through this much noise. Bana must be out. Or out cold.

"Hey, punk, shut the fuck up. We're trying to sleep," one of the Chinese shop owners shouted from below.

"Is Mr. Murtagh home?" Tatsu yelled down the stairwell.

"Probably. That piece-of-shit truck he drives is still out back." An angry slam followed the words.

"*Fakku.*" Tatsu lost all patience, spun on one foot and kicked. With a satisfying crack, the wood splintered. Another slam of his foot and the door bounced open. He stumbled into the darkened vestibule.

The putrid smell hit him like a physical blow. It reminded Tatsu of a slaughterhouse—blood, shit and terror-filled animal sweat. He unsheathed the *wakizashi* and slipped silently through the living room and kitchen. No sign of Bana. Tatsu moved down the hall. The rank stench thickened. His skin crawled at the terror and pain that hung like a thick miasma in the air.

He stepped into the dark bedroom and saw the huddled form of Bana curled up, facing the wall. Tatsu crouched by the side of the bed and dropped to one knee. The Irishman was soaking wet. He'd soiled himself. Everything, including his guns, was drenched in sweat, piss and shit.

"Wake up, partner. You missed the Red Flash." Tatsu felt the back of Bana's neck. Heat poured off the man's skin like a smelter. "You don't look so good. Let me help you." He tugged on Bana's shoulder.

Bana rolled over. Crimson, feral eyes glared up at Tatsu with pure animal fury. Blood coated Bana's mouth and chin. His lips drew back over four long, glistening, white fangs.

The roar of an animal ripped from deep within Bana's chest. Faster than humanly possible, he lunged off the filthy bed and wrapped his arms around Tatsu. His heavy body drove Tatsu backward into the dresser, which splintered apart, showering them with wood and glass. They crashed to the floor, Bana on top, pinning Tatsu against the filthy carpet. Bana's mouth struck at Tatsu's throat. Instinctively, Tatsu blocked the attack with his forearm. Bana bit through the leather sleeve and deep into Tatsu's muscle.

"Stop, Bana. It's me, Cobb!" Tatsu ignored the searing pain.

With another mindless growl, Bana grabbed Tatsu's jaw, twisting it brutally sideways with neck-breaking force. Spittle sprayed the air. He lunged for the pulsing bulge of Tatsu's jugular.

Tatsu clawed his *tanto* from its boot sheath and plunged it toward Bana's torso. An instant before the knife penetrated, the horror of the action shot through Tatsu. He flipped the blade around and pounded its hilt against the Irishman's temple with all his strength—four, five, desperate, panic-driven blows.

With a sudden odd grunt, Bana's eyes rolled into his head, and he went limp. Tatsu lay for a moment, lungs pumping, adrenalin-flooded muscles shaking. The stocky body sprawled on top of him like a giant rag doll. He pushed Bana off. Retching from the adrenaline surge, Tatsu crawled away on hands and knees. *Fakku*, he'd nearly killed his partner. Tatsu dug out his cell phone and punched the Colony's emergency code.

"Come on, come on, come on," he muttered praying the service would connect. Miracle of miracles, he heard an answering click.

"Cooperhayes."

"I'm at Bana's, something's wrong with him," Tatsu shouted into the tiny speaker. A furious feedback screeched into his ear.

"Status, Mr. Cobb?"

"I think he's turned," Tatsu sobbed. Shakily, he climbed to his feet and sheathed his tanto.

"Copy that." Cooperhayes' usually dry, calm voice quavered. "ETA thirty minutes."

"Can't wait." Tatsu snapped the instrument closed, grabbed

the semi-conscious man under his arms and hauled him upright. "Get up, partner, we've got to get to the Colony." He snatched up Bana's truck keys from the foyer table.

In a grotesque parody of the night they met, the two stumbled down the stairs and out into the thick fog. Tatsu's desperate grip around Bana's waist forced the man to keep stumbling along. When they reached the truck, Tatsu struggled to open the passenger door and hold on to his disoriented partner—for he refused to think of the Irishman as anything else. He opened the truck door and shoved Bana halfway into the cab. They were seconds from leaving when the menacing growls rolled out of the fog. One by one, a dozen vampires materialized out of the mist.

"Hey, hey, what do we have here? Dinner and a drink by the looks of it." A squat *kyūketsuki* unsheathed his *katana*. "And look at those swords. That's the punk killing our kind." Mere hours ago, he'd fed from the Daimyō. Now, he burned with a rogue's insatiable killing rage.

"Sadomori will reward us good if we bring his head in," another snarled.

"Gets better. I can smell a new Clan member," the lone fem crowed and pointed to Bana. The pack's responding laughter resembled the yips and barks of hyenas circling their prey.

Bana pulled out of the cab and turned toward the pack. His low growl of recognition alarmed Tatsu. Tatsu grabbed him by the shoulder, spun him so they were face-to-face.

"I said we're going to the Colony."

With a strangled croak from deep in his throat, Bana tore from Tatsu's grasp. A moment of clarity filled those blood-red eyes. "Let me go, boyo, it's too late," Bana pleaded in fang-slurred words.

The entreaty spoken in that disturbing, wet voice devastated Tatsu. "You're not going anywhere but with me. Get in the truck." He shoved Bana against the truck again.

As if by an unspoken agreement, two vampires broke from the pack and leaped toward Tatsu. Unable to draw his swords in time, he grabbed the closest attacker by the front of his jacket, pivoted and kicked him in the gut, sending him reeling back into the second. The vampires collided and crashed to the pavement in a tangle of limbs.

"We're gonna kill you fer that, asshole," a short bull shouted, lifted a gun and fired. Tatsu ducked. The bullet grazed Bana's ear, shattering his daze.

"Sod it, no bugger shoots at me." Uttering a string of garbled profanities, he unholstered his Berettas and fired in all directions. One burst stitched flaming holes across the torso of the leader. Another took legs off another vampire, leaving it thrashing and screaming in a bloody heap. The vampires knocked each other down in a frantic scramble to put distance between them and the maniac with the guns.

"That's right, run ya cowardly wankers," Bana jeered. "C'mon, I'll take on all of ya."

At the first explosion from Bana's guns, Tatsu threw himself against the only safe place—his partner's back. "Shut the fuck up, you idiot, we're outnumbered," he hissed over his shoulder, even while a surge of hope filled him. Maybe Bana wasn't lost. The man was acting his old, cocky, Irish self.

Pressed against the solid muscle of Bana's back, Tatsu's eyes swept the enemy, counting the number left. Too many. No way were they going to make it out of this. *Kuso*, maybe he would die this night, but he'd take as many down as he could. He whipped out both swords.

"Ya dumb fucks." Bana fired both guns again, dancing forward, away from the protection of Tatsu's back. One gun clicked empty. The second jammed. Bana jammed the spent automatic into its holster. Ignoring the danger, he worked to free the other Beretta's slide. A steady stream of profanity about "fekkin' bloodsuckers" spilled from his mouth. Within seconds, Bana extracted the misfired bullet and chambered a fresh round. He finally lifted his head as the entire pack charged.

Screeching with blood-hunger, the fem landed on the Irishman's back, wrapped her skinny arms around his chest and sank her fangs into his neck. Bana thrust his gun over his shoulder into the slavering face. The Beretta stuttered once, sending blood, skull and bits of brain into the air. Bana bellowed with pain. The firearm's report had ruptured his eardrum. Enraged, he spun around, kicked at the female's body jerking on the ground and rolled her beneath Tatsu's feet.

Tatsu stumbled and fought for balance. At that moment, his shoulders were grabbed from behind. Fangs dug into the tender flesh above his dog collar. Tatsu jerked free, turned and drove the *wakizashi* into the creature's heart. He kicked the corps in its stomach, freed the short blade sword and spun. Windmilling his arms, he cut left then right, slicing deep wounds into the faces and chests of two more vampires.

An enraged *kyūketsuki* butted his head into Tatsu's midsection. He sliced the *katana* across the back of the vampire's neck, severing the spinal column. The convulsing body knocked Tatsu to the ground, pinning him and snagging the *wakizashi* between them. Tatsu lost his grip on the *katana* and heard it spin across the wet pavement. Gasping for air, Tatsu struggled to push off the heavy corpse with one hand while the other groped for the trapped sword.

Booted feet landed beside Tatsu's head with a hard thump. He stared up jean-covered legs into the crotch of a Japanese vampire straddling him. "You're mine, pretty boy," the *kyūketsuki* cried in triumph as his *katana* sliced down toward Tatsu. Helpless, Tatsu saw the bright steel of his own death arcing toward him.

The ring of metal on metal shattered the night air. A blade locked against that death-dealing sword and broke it in two, sending the broken steel spinning through the air.

Tatsu heard a scream not of triumph but fear. Those booted feet jerked off the ground. Tatsu looked up. Arisada held the vampire aloft by the neck. The vampire's eyes bulged, the face turning purple, mouth open wide in soundless terror. The creature's hands clawed futilely at the fingers cutting off his air. Arisada bit, drank then tossed the corpse aside.

Arisada, lips spread in a blood-smeared smile, pulled the corpse off Tatsu. "You seem to get yourself in the worst messes." He leaned down and offered his hand to help Tatsu to his feet. "*Daijoubu?*"

"Yes, I'm fine." Tatsu slapped away the proffered hand and

scrambled to his feet. Why was he not surprised Arisada had saved him—again? Tatsu picked up his *wakizashi* and turned back toward the last of the attackers. There were only two left, racing for a van a few yards down the street.

"Arisada, you traitor," one shouted over his shoulder.

"Gotta stop them. They'll know you were here." Tatsu tore after them. But not fast enough. The vampires had almost reached the van. With a cry, Tatsu vaulted; a huge, high leap, back arched, the *wakizashi* curving above his head. As he dropped, he sliced the weapon down in a screaming cut. The blade split the nearest vampire's head in half and buried itself down into the torso. The dead creature crashed to the ground, dragging Tatsu to his knees. With a desperate twist, he fought to free the trapped blade.

The last *kyūketsuki* roared as he smelled the coppery-rich blood. He spun around, fell on Tatsu and drove sharp fangs against the exposed back of the human's neck. Tatsu ducked sideways and felt the deadly incisors skitter over the dog collar. The move cost him his grip on the trapped weapon. Tatsu scrabbled for the *tanto,* pulled it free it and drove it toward the vampire's body.

With a screech, the monster clamped his hand around the blade haft, giving it a brutal twist toward the human's belly. Tatsu heard the brittle snap of his wrist bones followed by the cold slide of the knife between his ribs. In raw desperation, he slammed his head back into his attacker's face, breaking the vampire's nose. But the knife continued its relentless path into his vitals.

Arisada reached the struggling pair in time to see the knife enter Tatsu's side. "*Koibito!*" Arisada screamed in fury and decapitated the vampire. The jaw snapped open, releasing it hold on Tatsu. Arisada grabbed the head by its hair and tossed it aside.

Blood fountained over Tatsu's face. "*Fakku,*" he sputtered and pushed the body away from him. He shook his head to clear his eyes, and without thought pulled out the knife.

"Is that all the thanks I get for twice saving your life, Tatsu-san?" Arisada grimaced. He flicked the blood from his *nodachi,* then sheathed the sword. He crouched by Tatsu and wiped the remaining blood from Tatsu's face with the end of his *obi.* "Crazy boy, one day you *will* get yourself killed."

"Fuck, quit fussing and let me up." Tatsu pushed the vampire away and stood up. He looked down at the two corpses. The enormity of Arisada's actions hit Tatsu with the force of a sledgehammer. The flame-haired vampire had killed his own kind to save a human being. Wonder colored Tatsu's voice. "You've just killed a couple of vampires and you call me *baka?"*

"I do what I must for the survival of both our kind." Arisada's voice revealed no remorse from such killing.

With a grunt, Tatsu stumbled over to his last kill and jerked the *wakizashi* free. Then he looked down at the blood pouring over his hip and down his leg. *"Kuso,"* he murmured. He pressed against his bleeding ribs, and groaned at the stab of pain shooting up his arm. "Shit, I think my wrist is broken." He turned toward his partner. "Bana?"

Bana stood, legs-splayed, chest heaving, amid bodies littering the ground like so many fallen leaves. His sweat-covered face reflected confusion and battle lust. Through red-filmed eyes, he spotted Arisada. The Irishman growled, "fekkin bloodsucker," lifted his gun and aimed. The Beretta's slide locked open with a hollow click. Automatically, he ejected the empty magazine, fished another from his pocket and snapped it into place. He raised the weapon again for one more futile shot. Just as his finger curled around the trigger, Tatsu reached him.

"Murtagh, the fight's over, man. It's over." Tatsu's hand on Bana's arm asked him to lower his gun. "Come on, partner, we've got to report in. Understand?"

Bana stared around with blood-filled eyes that turned hazel as sanity slowly returned. His fangs retracted, turning his face human. He stared at Tatsu with a wrenching sadness. "Got to go, boyo. Things ain't so good fer me now." He spun around and, with vampiric speed, bolted into the fog.

Tatsu moved to follow but Arisada's steel grip on his shoulder stopped him. "Let him go," the vampire ordered.

"But he's my partner." Tatsu struggled to free himself.

"No longer. He is *kyūketsuki*."

"*Iie*, no! Must stop him." But everything began to blur. Psychedelic spots danced before his eyes. His legs trembled with a sudden, undeniable weakness. He couldn't breathe. A hot wet ran down his leg. He tried sheathing his swords but they waved above his shoulders as if they had minds of their own.

The weapons left Tatsu's trembling hands. He sensed Arisada step behind him. The comforting weight of the blades settled into the harness. Then the warm strength of Arisada's arm curled around Tatsu's waist, holding him. He staggered on rubbery legs to the shelter of the nearest wall and slid down. He barely noticed when his butt landed on the cold, wet pavement.

"Do not move, *koibito*. You are bleeding heavily."

"I'm fine. Now go away," Tatsu groaned. His gut heaved with waves of nausea. He peered up at the blurry figure crouched in front of him.

The vampire ignored the plea. He opened Tatsu's jacket and probed his wound. The sweet, copper smell of the boy's blood filled the night air, and the vampire's hunger flared in response. His fangs appeared so fast they nicked his bottom his lip. Worse was the nearly blinding lust to possess this boy, injuries be dammed. Arisada's gore rose in disgust at his reaction.

"Your jacket kept the knife from going deeper. You'll live." The vampire's voice was cold, but the backs of his fingers brushed warmth down Tatsu's cheek.

"Wait, don't... *Kudesai*. Please. Don't go, must talk..." Tatsu leaned into the haunting warmth from those fingers. Shouts approached; the words distorted and full of alarm. Another brief caress over his face, then nothing but the chilly night air. He opened his mouth to call out but the world swam away.

"You can talk to him now." Tatsu heard a muffled voice followed by the sound of a curtain being drawn aside. His mouth felt coated with sand. He opened his eyes, vision gradually sharpening until shapes separated and made sense.

He recognized the Colony's infirmary. His stomach, encased in a tight bandage, hurt like hell. His wrist throbbed with a dull, insistent ache underneath a cast. The room spun for a crazy moment when he pushed himself upright in the bed.

Wyckes, brows knit in a doctorly frown, hovered over him. The Major and Cooperhayes stood at the foot of the bed. Fornax, arms folded, lounged against the far wall. His inscrutable stare fixed on Tatsu.

"Bana?" Tatsu croaked, swallowed and asked again.

"Take it easy, Cobb. You have a hole in your side and a fractured wrist. Lost a lot of blood. Nothing serious. Thank your Leper constitution. Any normal human would be dead. You'll only be sidelined for a week." Wyckes handed Tatsu a glass and a couple of pills. Tatsu gulped the water; shook his head at the pills.

"Mr. Cobb, I'd like your report on the events that took place forty-eight hours ago," the Major ordered.

Kuso, he'd been unconscious for two days. Tatsu averted his face and fiddled with the cast around his wrist while he sought for a convincing explanation. In the clipped words required of a military debriefing, he reported the events of that horrific night. Steeling his expression against the lie, he claimed Bana's erratic shooting killed most of the pack. Perhaps some of them ran off, he was fuzzy on that part. He omitted the details about how a vampire, Saito Arisada, had saved his life. Relief washed through him when the Major nodded his acceptance of the story.

"What will happen to Bana?" Tatsu could not accept his partner was no longer human.

"Bana is fortunate. Tendai's border is only a kilometer from where he turned." Fornax stepped closer to Tatsu's bed and looked down at the pale boy.

Tatsu winced at the word *turned*. "How can you say he's fortunate? He's a vampire for fuck's sake, a bloodsucker like you." He glared at Fornax.

"Mr. Cobb, stand down. Fornax is here to help Mr. Murtagh, if possible. But have no doubt there is no cure, no coming back from the change." Sorrow filled the Major's voice.

"We don't know why the virus activates in Lepers. The change occurs without warning; the physical transformation is often within a few hours. It's the reason people fear Lepers as much as bloodsuckers." Wyckes' face reflected his frustration. He'd been researching a cure for the Leper disease for years and so found nothing. Now another of their own had turned.

Throwing off the covers, Tatsu climbed naked out of the bed. His legs wobbled as he struggled to pull on his shirt with one arm. Wyckes clucked at the boy's stubborn efforts then insisted on dressing him.

Tatsu turned to the Major. "We must help him." No way would he lose another person he cared about. No. Fucking. Way. "He is... *was* my partner. We can't just leave him out there."

"Either he'll adapt or he'll die. Normally, the newly turned are nothing more than ravenous animals. For some reason, Bana retained enough of his human senses to recognize you. It sounds like he tried to protect you during the fight," Fornax said.

"*Hai*, he did." Bana had certainly acted human, a least for a few minutes, when he fired at the pack. "So now we go fetch him, *neh*?"

"*Fukanō*, impossible Cobb-san. You know this." Fornax visibly curbed his anger. "There's nothing we can do. By now, Bana has fed and is no doubt inside Tendai. Ukita Sadomori always knows when new *kyūketsuki* arrive. He will ignore Bana as long as he believes he is in his animal phase. But once Sadomori discovers Bana was a hunter, Sadomori will send him against us."

The finality of Fornax's words sent cold shivers down Tatsu's spine. But the Major trusts you and you're a bloodsucker, Tatsu wanted to argue. He held his tongue, not knowing why Fornax worked for the Leper Colony. Whatever the reason, it had to be profound. Fornax had been *kyūketsuki* for more than four-hundred years, yet now he fought on the side of humans.

Tatsu thought of Arisada clinging to his honor and his faith even while his human side was ripped from him. Arisada walked between the two worlds, loving a human—yeah, Tatsu Cobb, the very confused human—yet owing allegiance to the monster Ukita Sadomori.

"I will speak with Murtagh. Perhaps he will respond to me, although I am not his *Seisakusha*." Fornax touched Tatsu on the shoulder in an uncharacteristic gesture of comfort.

Tatsu flinched away. "What does not being his Sire have to do with it?"

"There is a blood bond between every vampire and their creator, their *Seisakusha*. Some believe it is mystical. In truth, it is merely DNA recognizing itself in another. The bond manifests in a dominant/submissive relationship. Rarely, it becomes something more."

"Did that happen to you?" Tatsu asked.

"That is none of your business. I will tell you this, my real name is Fukashima Hideo. I was a *hasebe*, a potter, living in a village near Nagasaki during the time of Tokugawa shogunate."

"You don't look Japanese." Tatsu was surprised by the vampire's origin.

"I look like my father, a Portuguese sailor from a trading ship that came to Nipon in 1598. I never knew him. I was barely in my twenties when the Shogun's army conscripted me as *ashigaru*. The life expectancy of a foot soldier was short. I was mortally wounded at the Battle of Nagashino. Wars always draw *kyūketsuki* who feed off the wounded. I was bitten. My mother found me near death. She hid me from the army. Her blood was my first meal when I woke from the coma. A week later, my *Seisakusha* found me, and at great risk, protected me I during my animal phase. I gave him my loyalty and my love." Fornax said with no emotion.

"Who was your creator?" Tatsu's gut churned Why did he already knew the answer?

"Saito Arisada." Fornax replied.

The intense jealousy took Tatsu by surprise. Fornax and Arisada! Had the two been lovers? Were they lovers now? He hid his reaction behind a wince of pain yet knew he hadn't deceived Fornax.

"Why are you with the Leper Colony, Fukashima-san?"

"I prefer the name Fornax. My reasons for joining are none of your concern. Just know that we fight on the same side. Even though I am Saito-san's Primary and was in the Tendai Clan, I no longer answer to the Daimyō."

"Tell me, Fukashima-san." Tatsu deliberately reiterated the vampire's human name. "Do you know if Ukita Sadomori has scars across his back?"

Fornax recognized the ploy to remind him of his Japanese honor. "Ukita's back and left leg are covered by tattoos, If there are any scars on his body, I do not know of them." He exited the room, cutting off any further questions.

"Mr. Cobb, you're on medical restriction until Dr. Wyckes clears you. You'll assist Mr. Cooperhayes. Your motorcycle will remain locked in the motor pool. Under no circumstances are you to look for Mr. Murtagh. That's a direct order. Are we clear?" the Major said.

"*Wakatta.*" Tatsu gave the Englishman a curt nod of acknowledgement. Still, in that acceptance, Tatsu felt he was abandoning Bana. Despite his injuries, everything in Tatsu itched to search for Bana immediately. They had not known each other for long, but in that time, fighting side-by-side, Tatsu felt he had earned Bana's trust.

If he could reason with the man—now vampire—Tatsu knew he could talk Bana back to their side.

The place to start looking was Tendai. It was off-limits to the Lepers unless they were sanctioned by a mission, but Tatsu would break that rule willingly. Besides, he believed he had ace in the hole, Arisada. Maybe the vampire would help. *If* Tatsu could locate him.

Fourteen

Tatsu flexed his wrist, marveling how in only eight days it had healed enough for him to ride his bike. His ribs still hurt but no sign of a scar. Being a Leper had its benefits, he mused, while he wheeled the Drifter into the street.

Movement on the edge of his vision caught his eye. Moonlit clouds created eerie shadows around the figure lounging against a silver car. Tatsu dropped the bike back onto its kickstand. Even as he reached over his shoulder for the katana, Arisada had moved to the motorcycle's front wheel.

"*Konban wa,* Cobb-san. *Watashitachi hanaseru?*" He asked permission to speak intimately with Tatsu.

"*Konban wa*, Saito-san." Tatsu fell into the formal speech, curbing his impatience. He could count the number of days since he last saw the flame-haired vampire. Eight. The same number of days he'd jacked off while fantasizing about Arisada's lips, his mouth and his tongue.

Inadvertently, Tatsu licked his lips at the sight of Arisada. Tatsu's heart thundered its way up his throat. His body warmed all over, balls, ass, cock, nipples, armpits. All over.

"I've been trying to reach you. Where have you been?" Tatsu flushed at the rudeness of his question.

The corners of Arisada's mouth quirked up. "You've missed me?" He countered to evade Tatsu's question. He had fought his desire to see the boy, fought it and lost. Arisada's heart was held in bondage by his need for Tatsu. Now, standing next to the one he adored, his blood boiled, filling him with a throbbing want.

"*Iie*, no, I haven't *missed* you. I need your help." Tatsu snapped. Followed immediately by a bob of an apologetic bow. "*Sumimasen*. Forgive my lack of manners."

Arisada repressed a smile. Tatsu's rude speech followed by an apologetic bob of his head was so endearingly like Nowaki.

Arisada wanted nothing more than to stay. But he needed to feed. After five days, he was ravenous. "Perhaps we can meet later?"

Tatsu knew he heard more in that simple invitation. A powerful rush flooded his body, and he hardened with painful speed. Flustered, he mounted the bike to hide the prominent bulge beneath his fly. "Tell me where and when," he stuttered.

The sight of those tight, muscled buttocks—deliciously outlined by leather chaps—settled onto the motorcycle seat threatened Arisada's control. He wanted to take Tatsu; right then, right there. He moved to the Drifter's handlebars and wrapped his hand around those holding the clutch lever. Excitement raced through him at the slight tremor in the fingers beneath his.

"Are you familiar with Kuboto Garden?"

At that gentle touch, Tatsu's heart revved insanely up into the red zone. He knew Arisada heard it. Sexual energy crackled between them, wild and undeniable. One glance down at the prominent bulge in the vampire's crotch confirmed it.

"Haven't exactly had time for sightseeing," Tatsu muttered to mask the heat thrumming along every nerve.

"*Dozo*, give me your cell." Arisada held out his slim hand.

Unthinking, Tatsu, handed over the instrument.

The vampire tapped the keys. "This is my number."

"What, vampires have cell phones?" Tatsu blurted, fascinated by the graceful movements of those fingers.

"Phones, computers, cars, everything except a dental plan." Arisada smiled at the incredulous look on the youth's face. "Please, call me after you finish work. I will give you directions." He handed the instrument back with a bow, pulled on a pair of leather driving gloves and turned back to his car. In the act of opening the door, Arisada looked back at Tatsu. A sliver of moonlight cut through the clouds. It limned Arisada's loose mane, turning it into living flame.

Tatsu forgot to breathe at Arisada's sheer beauty. Driven by unaccustomed impulse, he lifted his cell and snapped a photo. He figured the Colony should have it for its files. Ah, who was he kidding? He wanted the image of the vampire for himself.

He stared at the sleek car pulling into the street. "The bloodsucker drives an Audi, go figure," he muttered before firing up the Kawasaki.

Tatsu's discipline was pretty ragged by the end of the night. Many times he had to force his attention back to the dull duty of guarding a warehouse. He couldn't keep his mind off the elegant movement of Arisada's fingers, picturing them touching his body, caressing his nipples, wrapped around his prick.

Tatsu turned down the usual post-work breakfast invitation. He flipped off Phoenix who'd made a weak Bana-style joke about "Ninja Boy's goin' for a piece of ass." Tatsu roared out of the motorpool and gunned the engine, wondering if he was doing just that—going for a piece ass.

A mile from the Leper Colony, Tatsu halted the bike. *Kuso*, he must be crazy even to think of fucking Arisada. His traitorous dick, pressing hard against the zipper of his pants, said he wasn't crazy enough. With quick, no-turning-back-now jabs, he dialed Arisada's number, nearly hanging up halfway through the first ring. The vampire answered at that moment.

The Audi sat alone near the entrance to the Garden. Tatsu parked his bike a couple of feet from the silver car, and sat for a while looking over the area. The wind stirring the leaves of the surrounding trees was the only movement. Sensing no threat, he lit a cigarette, leaned his ass against the bike, and tried to figure out why the fuck he was here. Sure, he hoped Arisada would reveal knowledge about a scarred vampire. But that only was part of it.

He looked down at his new leather pants. They were tight in all the right places, outlining the bulge at his crotch, molding the hard lines of his thigh muscles and hugging his ass. They left no doubt he was cruising for the vampire.

"Dammit, I'm totally *baka*." He ground the cigarette beneath a hard twist of his boot. Against all reason, he wanted Arisada and knew he trusted him. He drew out the *katana*. There was trust and there was stupidity.

Slipping from shadow to shadow, Tatsu moved under the

wooden archways of the entrance that resembled the Shitenno-ji Temple in Nagasaki. The Garden reminded Tatsu of the popular Tsukiyama or hill-garden landscaping so popular in his hometown. Its small hills and circular paths meandered among massive trees and groomed foliage.

He moved into the deep stillness, avoiding the gravel path, using the damp grass to muffle the crunch of his footfalls. Tranquility stole over him. His naked blade seemed an affront to the peace of the tiny park.

Tatsu lingered at a Shinto shrine, brushed his fingers over the cold stone and felt a moment's guilt that he had nothing to offer. The sound of running water guided him to the rendezvous spot. He paused several feet from the wooden Japanese bridge arching across the stream.

He sensed the vampire seconds before the figure materialized from the mist. The vampire had discarded his trench coat. His black sweater and tight pants molded his compact, hard body, accentuated his narrow waist and the lines of slim, athletic legs. Part of his hair was knotted samurai-style on the crown of his head. The rest flowed in burnished lengths over his shoulders.

Breath blasted from between Tatsu's parted lips. *Shimatta, nothing should look that sexy.* His fingers tingled with the urge to comb through that silken mass.

"*Domo arigatō,* Cobb-san. I am honored you chose to meet me here." Arisada bowed. Such formality when he really wanted to blurt out the love he'd suppressed for eons.

Arisada's drew slow heated look drew up those long legs encased by supple, black leather. He made a point to let his gaze linger on that prominent bulge of sex at the groin that left he liked what he saw.

"Why here?" Caught in the desire vibrating between them, Tatsu abandoned any show of politeness.

"I find tranquility and peace here. The Garden exists only because of the devotion of the Asian people living nearby. Although this place is a mere echo of home, an echo is all most of us have."

The vampire's nostrils flared. "The sakura are blooming,

but not for much longer. Their blossoms are so delicate, their beauty so fleeting." He plucked a handful of pale petals then cast them free, watching them drift from his fingers. Without another word, he walked to the center of the arched bridge and stared down at the tumbling water. Tatsu moved beside him.

"People say this bridge represents the difficulty of living an honorable life; hard to walk up and hard to walk down. Do you believe that?" Arisada murmured while stroking the worn, red wood of the railing. Without waiting for Tatsu's reply, the vampire crossed to the other side of the bridge. He turned north deeper into the garden.

"Where are we going?" Tatsu demanded before realizing he was ogling the play of muscles of the vampire's ass. "*Jigoku*, I'm nuts," he muttered. Still, he couldn't tear his gaze from movement of those rounded, compact glutes each time they bunched under the linen of the tailored trousers.

The vampire smiled when he heard Tatsu's self-admonition. He knew exactly where the youth was looking. Within a few strides, they were walking side-by-side. Arisada felt the emotional conflict radiating from Tatsu's body, the nearly imperceptible catch in the boy's breathing. Tatsu's lust warred with his hate. Arisada wondered which would win.

The burbling of the stream faded when they entered a copse of Cyprus trees. The mist left shimmering droplets on the leaves. Large stones stood in stark relief to the lushness of the verdant landscape. Just then, the fog thickened, enveloping them in an ethereal cloak. The real world melted away.

Arisada caressed the side of a huge slab of granite taller than a man. "Do you know these stones were left in this area more than twelve-thousand years ago by the last glacier?" His voice became hushed.

"This park is an enduring monument to the perseverance of your kind. Even in the midst of this chaos, even while their lives are consumed by pain and despair, they toil to keep beauty alive. It is for this reason I love humanity."

"It reminds me of Nagasaki, my birthplace." Yearning gripped Tatsu, disturbing in its intensity.

"Like our ancestors, our roots are always with us." Arisada

plucked a winter-dried lavender bloom from its slender stalk. "Pity our memories can't wither like this flower."

Tatsu shrugged off the mesmerizing promise of the peaceful garden. He grabbed Arisada by the shoulder and pulled him around face-to-face. Oh shit, the fluid move of that taut muscle sent all thoughts straight into Tatsu's prick. "What do you want to tell me?" he asked with forced anger.

"Perhaps there is something you want to tell me first," Arisada evaded. "When we first met, you wanted to kill me. Now, your enmity is all but gone. Why is that?"

Tatsu dropped his hand as if burned. "You're mistaken. I despise your kind." But even to his ears, his voice lacked conviction.

"But not me, right?"

"*Wakatta*, makes no sense, but I don' hate you," Tatsu stared into the vampire's eyes. "I'm asking you, Saito-san, as one warrior to another, for your help."

"What do you want from me?" Oh how he longed to hear Tatsu say, "Your love."

"Help me find Bana Murtagh."

"Why?"

"He's my friend."

"You can do nothing for your friend. He is *kyūketsuki* and no longer feels any loyalty to humankind. Leave him alone."

"*Wakatta*." Tatsu's nod did not look sincere. "My family's murderer. He's here somewhere. You've killed rogue vampires. I believe you're motivated by an honorable reason. *Dozo*, please, extend that same honor to my quest for *fukushū*. Do you know anything about the monster I hunt?"

The vampire's eyes flickered red with suppressed anger. Anger at Tatsu's obstinacy. Anger at himself for being forced to lie to the boy. He heard the unforgiving harshness in his reply.

"I cannot help you."

"Cannot or will not?"

Arisada shrugged off the question. "Stay out of Tendai. Some of my kind would like nothing better than to drain the blood of a hunter."

"What the hell? Were you following me?"

"No. But others saw you. You were lucky. Not all of my Clan is your enemy."

"I can take care of myself." Tatsu's sea-green eyes glared ice at the vampire.

"*Baka*, reckless boy. I am the most powerful vampire in Tendai next to the Daimyō, yet even I cannot prevent your death if you persist in this foolish action."

"The blood debt commands I do this."

"You think killing will bring you peace?"

"I don't care. I'll do what I must to restore my father's honor."

"I know firsthand the tragedy of revenge. The futility of it. I have seen how it destroys the *ki*, the spirit. Will you continue this even at the cost of your own soul?"

"My life means nothing if I don't."

Arisada's eyes deepened to goldenrod with sorrow. "Never say your life means nothing, *koibito*. It means everything to me."

"Don't say that, I—"

"Is killing that easy for you now?" Arisada made an impatient gesture with his hand.

"And it isn't for you?"

"Make no mistake, young one. I brought terror-filled death to thousands. But know this, each time a human dies by my hand, it diminishes my *tamashii*, my soul. I only kill to feed, yet those acts make me a monster. A monster who can never atone."

Tatsu shook his head in disbelief. "No, you are good. I see it in your eyes. I felt it in your warrior's *ki* when we sparred. You may have killed, but so have I. The difference is, you only kill to survive."

"You are wrong, Cobb-san. For decades after I turned, I murdered thousands wantonly often for no reason except that I could. I made no effort to control myself such was my rage. Now, every death takes a part of my soul. But you have a choice."

"I cannot turn back." Conflict ate its way through Tatsu like acid through rice paper. Could he give it all up? Would the spirits of his butchered family rest if he stopped right now?

"*Wakarimashita.* I understand. If you give me your word you will not enter our territory alone again, I will do what I can. Do not expect to hear from me unless I have news."

"*Domo arigatō gozaimasu.*" Tatsu remembered his manners, offered a short bow but made no promise. He would not leave his revenge in the hands of this vampire. A confusing mix of hurt and gratitude was followed by the irrational impulse to touch Arisada in some gentle way.

Arisada sensed it, shifted closer, looked into the slightly flushed face, the clenched jaw muscles, the swallowing Adam's apple. Knew how Tatsu fought against his conflicting emotions. The vampire brushed aside the tumble of chocolate-brown strands over Tatsu's forehead. His nostrils flared at the pheromones rolling off the boy's skin. Pure sexual need.

"My young hunter, do you know how beautiful you are?" The vampire whispered, Gently, he trailed the backs of his fingers over in the faint stubble on one cheek.

At the delicate brush of those fingers, Tatsu shivered, *Fakku, why did that touch turn him on so much?* Tatsu fought to deny his arousal but his traitorous cock was already a throbbing weight in his groin. "Stop that." He forced a growl yet leaned slightly into that touch.

A smile tugged at the corners of Arisada's lips at Tatsu's struggle. "Your body is honest. You grow hard for me."

"Bullshit, I have no desire for you. You're *kyūketsuki* and my enemy." He stepped back, shaking his head with unconvincing denial. But he blushed at the lie.

"I'm not your enemy. Centuries ago, we were lovers. You are the reincarnation of Koji Nowaki, the one I adore."

"Like hell. I'm not the reincarnation of anybody; especially your so-called lover from hundreds of years ago," Tatsu blustered. He tried anger to crush his arousal but knew it wasn't working. His desire for Arisada moved within him, deep, visceral. He realized he *had* desired the vampire from the moment they met.

"You are Shinto, are you not? You believe in reincarnation?"

"I practice my mother's religion. But I'm not all that sure about reincarnation."

"Whether you believe or not, you existed centuries ago. You were a fierce warrior."

Tatsu shrugged. "The only past I care about is my own. It gives me reason to kill your kind. One day I may kill you." His threat sounded feeble even in his own ears.

"Perhaps I should kill you. You did betray me, after all." A thin smile flitted across Arisada's face

"I won't accept that." Tatsu's retort trailed off when another wave of desire obliterated the final remnant of his hostility. He gazed at Arisada—the delicate upslanted lids and long lashes framing those deep golden eyes. Tatsu licked his lips, suddenly aching to kiss those wide lips.

At the desire radiating from Tatsu, the vampire's restraint threatened to slip its cage. Being this close to the one he loved was dangerous. Abruptly, Arisada turned down the narrow path. "Please, walk a little further with me."

Kuso, Tatsu's body went nuts. His head was at war with his heart, and both were overridden by his cock. He followed Arisada up a steep hill into a willow-tree grove. The grey fog rolled in and turned the glade into a mystical bower.

Arisada's fingers grazed along a mist-drenched branch. "This forest reminds me of Mii-dera before Taira no Kiyomori destroyed it." Coyly, he turned to watch the young hunter's reaction. The sight of Tatsu's mouth agape in surprise sent the vampire into deep laughter.

The laugh, so carefree and light, delighted Tatsu even while his mind reeled at the thought of the vampire's incredible age. Completely stunned, he stared wide-eyed at the vampire. Mii-dera, home to one of fiercest sects of Sōhei warrior monks.

"Mii-dera? Just how old are you?" he stammered, feeling foolish. Every child in Japan knew the of destruction of that famous temple, and how the last of Mii-dera's warrior monks committed *seppuku.*

"I was born in 1155, the year Go-Shirakawa became emperor. That year began the loss of my family's fortune when many clans fought among themselves for power. I was the son of a noble family that chose the wrong side. To save me from execution, my father sent me to Mii-dera when I was nine. And yes, Cobb-san, I am Sōhei. As was Koji Nowaki."

"You're an eight-hundred-year old Sōhei?" Tatsu stuttered, trying to grasp the immensity of the vampire's age. "So much time. What have you seen? Learned?"

"*Hai*, so much time. Throughout my indecently long life, I've witnessed humanity at its worst and at its best. I learned that love is the only thing worthwhile. It matters not who we love, just that we love."

"What does that have to do with me?"

"My story has everything to do with you." Arisada sighed. "For most, life in that time was harsh, short, brutal. You worked in the fields and became a soldier or a servant to a noble family. If lucky, you married and had children before you turned twenty. If you were exceptionally fortunate, you lived to be venerated for your old age at fifty."

In the quiet, droplets of mist gathered at the ends of willow branches and fell with individual plops into the koi pond. Arisada stared into the widening circles on the surface as if strange spirits moved beneath the dark water. When he glanced at Tatsu, lifetimes of suffering reflected from those golden eyes.

"Do not judge my story by today's morality. Same-sex bed partners was an acceptable part of society. There was no shame in it. In the monastery, our first sexual experiences were with an older man. But it was Koji Nowaki, four years my junior, who showed me the joys of love." The sharp planes of Arisada's face softened. "You cannot imagine my happiness. For five years, we reveled in the pleasure of each other's bodies. I believed we shared a unity of mind and spirit. I was wrong."

Shivers rippled over Tatsu's skin at the pain and yearning in the vampire's voice.

"My Nowaki-kun was beautiful, a true *bishounen*, just like you. He had your eyes, the color of jade. Such unusual, beautiful eyes. His hair was also different—a deep chestnut with touches of gold. He had a brilliant smile with full lips and perfect, white teeth. Dimples, too, as I imagine you have when you smile. He grew unusually tall for that time. Taller than me. Still, he moved with the grace of a young deer and fought with the bravery and strength of a tiger."

The vampire's gaze clouded, and his voice quivered with repressed grief. "I loathed him at first—of peasant birth, so angry, so ignorant. But then he became the most precious thing to me, more than my faith or my brethren. Perhaps that is why he was taken from me in such a cruel manner."

"Taken from you?" Unable to tear his gaze from the vampire's face, Tatsu watched the eyes turn terrible with anguish. The sense of an immense history about to be revealed filled him with a sick foreboding. He didn't want to listen Arisada's confession about the loss of his lover—a traitor, no less. Didn't want to know his connection to someone who had perpetrated such a vile betrayal, and caused the deaths of hundreds of Sōhei.

Yet, how could he refuse?

The Temple of Mii-dera, Nipon, Summer 1170

Sōhei novice Saito Arisada despised the scraggly boy on sight. He sneered with disgust at the worthless mongrel struggling and howling with rage. The child kicked shamelessly at *Hanshi* Michinaga Kiyosura's legs. The teacher ignored the blows and dragged the squalling brat over to Arisada.

"You will be his *senpai*. Mold him as I have molded you. Make him worthy," Michinaga-sensei ordered, and threw the filthy child down onto the bathing hall floor. "First, clean him."

Arisada's hands clenched against his anger. How could his *sensei* order him to turn this *gaki*, this brat, into a suitable acolyte for the Sōhei? Wasn't he, Saito Arisada, destined for a worthy position among the Sōhei? Wasn't he, at fifteen summers, already one of the most respected clerics and fighters of Mii-dera?

Revulsion filled Arisada at this clawing and spitting savage. Why was he charged with taming this feral boy who had no name?

The child's thin, scabrous body clearly crawled with vermin and reeked of urine and feces. With a shudder of disgust, Arisada grabbed the front of the youngster's threadbare kimono and tore it off. He threw the naked child into the stone bath and held him under the freezing water. The youngster fought like an alley cat, clawing Arisada's hands and arms, biting him, spitting in his face and wasting precious oxygen to shriek vile profanities.

Driven by his escalating anger, Arisada repeatedly forced the boy under the freezing water; almost drowning the youngster. Finally, realizing his emotions were ruling him, Arisada relented. He pulled the boy out by his neck and threw him onto the stone floor. The child crouched, naked, wet and shivering.

Arisada could see the defiance boiling from those alien green eyes. He threw an old robe at the youngster. The boy who glared pure poison, but pulled on the garment. "I will tell you this only once. You will drop to your knees and press your forehead to the ground whenever you are in the presence of your superiors. Do not speak without permission. When you do, address your superiors by their honorific sensei. Now, dress and follow me."

"But I'm hungry. When do I eat?"

That whining tone infuriated Arisada. His blow across the youth's face knocked the boy to the dirt. Undaunted, the youngster glared up, shivering inside the too-large kimono.

"You will address me as Saito-senpai every time you speak to me. Otherwise, you will do what is asked in silence. You eat when you are told, sleep when told, shit when you are told. Do you understand?"

The scruffian's jaws clenched. He gave a small shrug in acknowledgement but the defiance did not leave his eyes—those strange, memorizing, green eyes.

"First, though, we are going to rid you of that disgusting, lice-riddled mane of yours." He did not tell the youngster to follow him, merely turned and stalked off. This was the first test. If the boy stayed where he was, Arisada would strangle the child and toss the body outside the gates.

Arisada hoped the boy would refuse to follow. Disappointment filled the monk at the sound of the youth trotting behind, still muttering obscenities. Arisada's rage threatened again. He knew he was not acting honorably. With effort, he suppressed his emotions in the manner of a true Sōhei and resolved to tame this feral youth. Tame him or kill him.

Perhaps this would not be too odious an experience, Arisada hoped. The *kami* had given him one of lower status—one who would be subjected to Arisada's every order, who would accept training and bow before Arisada's wisdom and status. In his youthful arrogance, Arisada dismissed the twinge of compassion in his breast.

No one, including the boy, knew his true age—perhaps eleven or twelve summers? Brigands had slaughtered his family. Illiterate and starving, his body riddled with vermin, he would not have survived into adulthood. Michinaga-sensei named him Koji no Nowaki, which simply meant orphan of Nowaki, the village where he was discovered beside a still-smoldering hut.

So many times Arisada despaired of ever making Nowaki into a true Sōhei. Rather than showing gratitude for his new life, Nowaki resented it. He railed against the restrictions of the monastic life. He yelled in anger when woken the hour before daylight and grumbled every night when not allowed to eat until he had finished all his duties.

However, by his third year, Nowaki had accepted his life as an acolyte. He absorbed and then excelled at every skill imparted by the Sōhei masters. But, most of all, Nowaki emulated his *sensei,* Arisada, in all things involving the arts of war.

Saito Arisada was one of Mii-dera's most skilled warriors. He excelled with the *naginata* and the longbow called a *daikyu.* He had long been acclaimed a true Master of the art of weaponless fighting called Budo. Many claimed Saito-sensei's prowess was even superior to that of *Hanshi* Michinaga. Yet Arisada's pride in his own fighting skill was far exceeded by his pride in his novice, Nowaki.

ETERNAL SAMURAI

The young orphan boy had surpassed all other acolytes in fighting skill, able to use every length sword and master every technique for wielding the long, halberd-like *mikoshi*. He embraced the skills of warfare with a ferocity that impressed even the seasoned Sōhei warriors.

One day, Nowaki's sparring opponent stepped on a Mamushi, the most lethal viper in Nipon. The snake struck at the monk's naked leg. Before those fangs touched skin, Nowaki had sliced off the head before continuing his upward movement, sending his opponent's sword flying through the air.

From then on, Nowaki was called Mamushi, the Viper.

And Arisada was smitten by the Viper. He believed Nowaki perceived the social issues of the country with a maturity far beyond his age. During their philosophical debates, Nowaki analyzed the political and military climate with rare maturity and intelligence. The boy's admiration of the Taira Clans—whose actions threatened the peace of all Nipon—appeared to be driven by a rare perception of politics coupled with youthful enthusiasm.

With increasing boldness, Nowaki also voiced his resentment of the traditions of Mii-dera, which for years had avoided committing military support to any of Nipon's warring Clans. He advocated success in warfare as the only true measure of a samurai's worth; the only path to honor. Like many warrior monks throughout the land, he had begun to covet power, wealth and prestige, the worst characteristics of far too many Sōhei.

By contrast, although Arisada was one of the most feared warriors of Mii-dera, he also was one of the most spiritual. He followed the Pure Land teachings, the Buddhist's gentle way of seeking enlightenment and peace. He despaired for the incredible suffering of the people and often argued with Mii-dera's leaders for more aid for the peasants.

"How foolish you are," Nowaki stated during one of their debates. "It is *karma* that people suffer and die. It is fitting that the strongest take what they want. And we are the strongest in this region."

"Buddha says all life is suffering. Don't you see, Nowaki-kun? It is our duty to use our power to help ease the plight of those less fortunate. Mii-dera is a wealthy monastery, we have more than we need and should share it with others," Arisada countered.

"You will give our hard-won wealth to those who do not deserve it, who grovel in the filth, begging rather than working?" Nowaki sneered. "This is the way of weakness."

"It is not the fault of the peasantry that recent famine and earthquakes have destroyed their homes, their crops, their livelihoods. We only grow stronger by our benevolence."

"*Baka*. You are a fool, Saito-san. A fool who will bring down this great monastery and all in it with your stupid generosity." Nowaki spat his derision at his *senpai*. "I will have nothing more of your weak-willed beliefs. I am a warrior not a priest." He stormed out. From then on, he avoided Arisada, save for their military training sessions.

Despite the youth's hostility, Arisada never believed Nowaki's avowed selfishness. By their fourth year together, Arisada had fallen deeply in love with the boy. Arisada hid his love by meting a harsher discipline on Nowaki than to the rest of the Sōhei novices. Only within the safety of dreams did Arisada dare caress and kiss Nowaki.

He believed his love was unrequited until that wondrous and fateful night when Nowaki came to the bedchamber, not in anger or fear, but in boiling need. A slight stirring of the thin blanket woke Arisada. Nowaki crawled onto the sleeping mat and pressed his warm, naked skin against the length of Arisada's side.

"*Senpai*, I must speak with you. Please, it is urgent." A puff of heated breath from Nowaki's whispered entreaty caressed Arisada's ear. Nowaki pressed his fingers rudely against Arisada's lips to still any protest.

"*Sumimasen*. Be at peace. Please, just listen, Saito-*sama*." Nowaki blurted out the intimate honorific.

The acute awareness of warm, smooth skin against Arisada's hip did little to slow his heart slamming in his chest with dread.

Was Nowaki going to leave Mii-dera? By rights the boy could choose another mentor, even go to another temple. Nowaki had not yet dedicated himself to the temple, and for the past two years his behavior screamed that he wanted nothing from his sensei.

In sheer panic, Arisada scrambled upright, pressing his back against the freezing wall of his cell. His eyes closed against the impending devastation of the next words he would hear. He prayed he could become deaf in that second. He wished he were on another plane of existence instead of sitting naked on his futon facing the one he loved.

Shivering from apprehension, Nowaki knelt on the thin mat. His words tumbled out. "*Senpai, Gomen, gomen nasai, yurushite.* Please, forgive me. I have treated you with nothing but disrespect. My feelings for you are so powerful, they unmanned me. Yet shame filled me for revealing the details of my cursed life. Still, I was afraid. Now, I feel your anger, see you turn away. I fear my hatred has destroyed your love. When I couple with others, I am not fulfilled. My member gets hard every time I think of you. I want to... I *need* to share my body with you. *Daisuki senpai*, I love you. Please, *senpai*, say you have even the smallest amount of affection for me."

Arisada's heart thundered so hard he thought his ribs might crack. He desperately wanted to know he heard what he longed for most. But fear stopped him. He inhaled a single, deep breath, forcing calm. "You do not know what you are saying, Nowaki-kun. You are still so young. Your feelings are misplaced, youthful lust." Arisada trembled, cold sweat limned his body. His stomach knotted with unaccustomed fear.

"I am coming up to eighteen winters, a man by every standard. And I do know what I am asking of you." Nowaki, arms wrapped around the older monk's neck, straddled Arisada's exposed loins. The wet head of his cock pressed into Arisada's clenched stomach, his balls nudged warm and soft against his throbbing prick. Before another protest escaped Arisada's mouth, Nowaki slaved their lips together with such force their teeth clashed.

At the touch of Nowaki's mouth, long-suppressed arousal

obliterated Arisada's pretense of resistance. He drowned in the promise of the youth's emotions, embracing them all—devotion, tenderness and the incandescence of Nowaki's passion. Arisada's groaned at the sheer need in his beloved's face. Those sea-green eyes flaring with heat, that creamy-dark skin sweat-flushed, that bottom lip sucked in under perfect white teeth.

Their arms enveloped each other in an uncertain, careful embrace. Their lips pressed, soft, exploring, asking for acceptance from each other. Arisada yielded first, opening his mouth to welcome the deep intimacy of Nowaki's tongue. It was many minutes before they pulled apart.

"Oh, *koibito*," Arisada breathed, and buried his head in the crook of that tender neck, kissing along under Nowaki's jaw. Tears slipped down Arisada's face and over the tender bump of Nowaki's collarbone. He inhaled the heady musk of the youth's arousal. The desire boiling off Nowaki's skin melted the last of Arisada's resolve. He surrendered to the shackles of the boy's need.

"Let me taste you," Arisada murmured, "just taste you." He thought he heard only love in the boy's whispered, "*Hai, hai, senpai, dozo.*"

Fifteen

The splash of a koi slapping the surface of the pond snapped Arisada out of his reverie and back into Seattle's fog-filled night.

"My adoration of Nowaki blinded me to his true nature—until he became *uragirimono*, a traitor. Because of his single, shameful act, the Emperor's army overran my temple and burned it. History records no Mii-dera Sōhei survived that day. Most died in battle, the rest committed *seppuku*. Except me. I was cheated of an honorable death and condemned to become a demon, *kyūketsuki*." His eyes glittered with a film of red.

"But that means you were only twenty-five when you died," Tatsu blurted.

"*Hai*, but I didn't exactly die, did I? Karma dictated another path for me. Perhaps when I awoke as a monster, I should have allowed the sun to take my life. But I chose to live, praying for my own redemption while I searched for Nowaki. I killed his seducer, Hayato, but not before he confessed he had taken Nowaki's head the same day Mii-dera fell."

An irrational ache to wrap his arms around the suffering vampire gripped Tatsu. How could anyone bear so much sorrow for such a long time? He hid his sympathy behind a question.

"Do you still love him?" Tatsu whispered the question into the night. Apprehension turned his mouth dust-dry. Why did he want to know?

The vampire gazed at the pond. "Part of me will always love him. There were times I felt a purity, a joy in him that could not have come from someone evil. He was an innocent once."

"You're telling me I have this person, this Koji Nowaki, inside me that evokes these feelings I have for you?"

A brilliance danced in Arisada's golden eyes. He smiled. "So, you admit you have feelings?"

"*Nani mo!* None! You know what I mean." But Tatsu could not denying the wild throbbing that pounded through his balls and swelled his prick every time he thought of Arisada.

"There is no one *inside* you, Tatsu." Arisada used Tatsu's first name without permission.

Tatsu's heart quickened at the intimate address. He shrugged to disguise his pleasure. "I'm don't buy that whole reincarnation thing."

"Imagine the spirit is a flame that is passed from the dying candle to the wick of a fresh one. The flame is the continuing essence of the person's soul. The candle is a new entity with its own properties and makeup. It is subject to a different time and place. The flame on top of the candle is there to learn what was missed in a previous lifetime."

"I'm not a fucking candle. And I sure as hell have enough shit to deal with in this life without worrying about a previous one."

The vampire smiled with a flash of brilliant white teeth, No hint of fangs. "No, you certainly are not a *fucking* candle. You are the beautiful soul I feared I'd never see again."

"I can't be the only one who ever looked like this Nowaki," Tatsu stuttered, stunned by the beauty of that smile.

"I have met hundreds of *bishounen* who could pass for Nowaki's twin, but none had his soul. Your physical resemblance is superficial, although you are truly an exquisite boy. The soul within you is who I love. His *tamashii* has returned in you, perhaps for the redemption of us both. Perhaps to accept my love."

"Who I fall in love with will be my choice. I'm not a mindless vessel for another."

"*Wakatta*, you determine your own path. But you cannot deny me my love for you." Arisada's fingers ached to caress Tatsu's cheek.

"I can never love a monster like you." Tatsu covered his lie with a show of anger. It failed. Caught in the raw need vibrating between them, he shifted his weight and leaned in until he pressed chest-to-chest with the vampire.

Arisada inhaled Tatsu's unique scent, now pungent with

the undeniable smell of an aroused man. The vampire dropped his gaze to the bulge beneath the slick leather. His eyes held there for a long, deliberate moment while Tatsu's cock stirred then hardened into a rod that curved up to his left hip. "*Â, sō desu ka?* You say you feel no desire for me, yet your body tells me different, Tatsu-kun."

"Whatever twisted ideas you have, forget them. And don't call me *kun*. I'm not a child."

"You prefer I call you *koibito*?" Arisada leaned closer and drew the pad of his thumb slowly over Tatsu's lips, leaving a trace of lavender scent.

The vampire's touch scalded Tatsu's skin. Want—wonderful yet terrifying—shivered up from the center of his vitals.

"If I'm your so-called beloved, why don't you kiss me?"

The want in that demand destroyed Arisada's resolve. Tangling both hands in that chocolate-brown hair, he drew them close. He traced over Tatsu[s mouth, asking for entrance. Those pretty lips parted, and Arisada plunged into his beloved's delicious cavern.

A kaleidoscope of pleasure and confusion ripped through Tatsu. What the fuck was he doing? The kiss should have been a short experiment to prove he felt nothing for Arisada. Instead, his tongue answered by chasing even deeper into that fanged cavern. A groan of want rumbled up from his chest.

That sweet, yielding sound swept through Arisada's senses, obliterating all caution. Grinding their mouths together with savage need, Arisada forced Tatsu back until he hit the tree with a brain-rattling thud. He grabbed Tatsu's jacket and dragged it half off, trapping the boy's arms in a leather vice.

Tatsu jerked back from the kiss. His head hit the tree trunk. "What the fuck?" He thrashed futilely against the unyielding leather. His cock hardened him so fast it hurt. Even as he struggled, the sense of helplessness, of being bound, fired a thrill deep into his ass. He wanted nothing more than to submit to this creature's savage sexuality.

"Don't fight me, my beauty," Chest-to-chest, Arisada pressed hard. At the sweet sigh of Tatsu's surrender, the vampire began to press kisses over the flaming cheeks, the edges of that pretty mouth, under each earlobe, and down to the sweet curve of the neck. His lips pressed against Tatsu's jugular, feeling the *lub-dub-lub-dub* of the heartbeat. Smelled the rich blood coursing through the vein.

"Just this one time, I will possess you." Then Arisada struck.

Tatsu had no time react before fangs shredded the front of his combat shirt. Thousands of polyceramic rings rained onto the grass. Cold air bit his nipples. Dumbfounded, Tatsu looked down at the so-called indestructible fabric hanging in tatters around his harness straps.

A groan escaped him. He didn't know if it meant surrender or protest. He just knew he was desperate to feel Arisada's flesh pressed against him, chest-to-chest, loins against loins, bare cock rubbing bare cock. Wanting oh-so-much more.

A demon of primitive hunger possessed Arisada. Hunger fueled by eons of unrequited need. He had to taste Tatsu's flesh. Nothing would stop him; not the fast-approaching dawn, the immorality of his assault or Tatsu's hate that would come later.

Arisada mouthed over honey-kissed skin. A taste of salt and man-flesh hot with desire burned his lips. With feverish impatience, his tongue roved over the planes and valleys defining each muscle of the sculpted chest, leaving a wet trace along the edge of a tattoo showing from beneath the harness strap. He blew a cool stream over Tatsu's deep brown aureoles, the skin puckering around the engorged nipples. The vampire drew one hard button between his teeth and bit softly. A shuddering gasp of delight rewarded him. His fingers played over the second nipple—soft, circular rubs, hard flicks, pinching, pulling, tugging the nub erect.

This loving should be slow, tender, an aching exploration of his beloved. But the vampire had no time for that. His true enemy, daylight, already stalked him. Yet, for these precious moments, he would risk death.

"*Gomen nasai. Yurushite, koibito.*" Arisada begged for forgiveness even while he yanked down chaps and pants. One tug ripped Tatsu's jock in two and his erection bounced out. At the sight of that pale arch of flesh, a gasp of delight escaped Arisada. He closed one hand around the hot tube, knowing every wrinkle, every ridge, every pulsing vein. He pumped from root to crown, thumbed over the weeping head. Every stroke pulled precum from the slit and ragged moans from Tatsu's mouth.

The just-perfect touch of Arisada's hand sent jolts of pure lightning along every nerve to the top of his head. Shudders ripped through him. Pleasure consumed his loins. His thighs trembled, muscles gone weak with a fine trembling. Only his desperate clutch on the tree held him upright.

"*Dozo*, do it. Suck me." He jerked forward, presenting his rampant cock, demanding and eager.

Arisada dropped to his knees. Tenderly, he gazed at the hollows slanting down from the jut of Tatsu's hips. The sweet dip of tendons into his groin. That curling of hair at the root of his iron-hard member. The trace of blue veins beneath saffron skin. The perfect helmet glistening with precum.

All these sights, tastes and scents were Arisada's for this night only. He seared them into his memory.

Quivering with want, Arisada rubbed the heated length of Tatsu's throbbing prick over his cheek and lips. His thumb rolled over the tender, ripe cockhead. Oh, the silkiness of the skin, the steel beneath it, the heat, the musky male odor.

"*Koibito,* let me taste you." The plea of centuries ago.

Astonishment filled Tatsu when the taut head of his prick was kissed with a tender reverence. Hadn't he wanted this from the moment he stared into those golden eyes? A begging permission slipped from Tatsu.

Arisada licked the shaft from the round head to the tight curls at the root. At the salty taste of Tatsu's skin, a ravenous hunger possessed the vampire and he plunged down, engulfing the slippery weight to its root. He pulled off with a loud suck, flicked his tongue over the piss slit and drew forth a fresh, sticky offering. He teased, plying Tatsu's rigid length with delicate licks, long slow swirls, tiny touches of human teeth under the shaft, to the pulsing vein underneath. His velvet tongue lapped over the glistening purple head, the tip digging into the piss slit, bringing forth a fresh spurt of briny nectar. Greedily, the vampire sucked up the slick juice. Spit ran from the side of his mouth, mingling in rivulets with cock juices.

He laved all the secret, tender places, knowing they were right by the mewls being pulled out of Tatsu. Adorable, delightful, loving pleadings. The boy's thighs bunched, tendons standing in stark relief. A tentative thrust of his hips and Arisada pulled off Tatsu with a loud *pop*. Tears glittered in the vampire's eyes. No blood feast could ever compare to the delectable taste of that cock. Nor any sound compare to those sexy and oh-so-begging noises from his beloved.

Arisada looked up into the boy's lust-consumed face. Such absolute beauty was stunning—the wild glitter of jade eyes barely visible beneath lids weighted with pleasure, the lashes fluttering against flushed honey-colored cheeks. Swollen, kiss-bruised lips slightly open. The white reveal of perfect teeth.

"Oh, *fakku*, what are you...?" Tatsu's moans slipped from lips gone slack with need. Searing chills drowned him when that warm, wet tongue travelled along his throbbing flesh. The wet heat surrounded his prick. He stared down at lips stretched wide around the girth of his cock that was engulfed to the root by a creature that could ravage him within seconds.

Nerves screamed with every slide of the pebbly surface of Arisada's tongue, each delicate scrape of teeth. The hard press of the vampire's ridged palate, the convulsive suction from his demanding throat—all delivered a universe of scalding pleasure.

A delicious pain coiled in Tatsu's ass and pulsed into his chute. The wicked sensations set his body aflame. Like the helpless swimmer caught in a tsunami, he tumbled over and over, drowning in sensation. Every nerve vibrated, driving him in boiling waves to that razor-edged peak.

Tatsu writhed against the construction of the leather sleeves. His helplessness inflamed him with an alien pleasure. And, in that bondage, a truth blossomed through him: he wasn't the prisoner of this vampire's love, he was its master. In that rushing firestorm of awareness, he surrendered. Wonder filled him. That it was Arisada's mouth meant everything. That Arisada was *kyūketsuki* meant nothing.

Tatsu's legs quivered, his thighs straining to their utmost. His ass muscles clenched, drawn tight by spasms of pleasure. His balls crowded tight and hot against his body. Fire and ice ripped through every nerve from his toes to the top of his head. So close, so incredibly close to that sweet, flying release. Just one more swirl of that tongue, one more stroke, one more dragging suck and he'd plunge over. Tatsu's whimpers escalated, moving up the octave range into sweet, high mewls.

At the knowing touch of Arisada's hand, that frost climbed Tatsu's chute. His balls boiled with the need for release. His hips bucked desperate thrusts that drove his cock to the back of the vampire's throat. Moans vibrated around his steel-hard prick.

Fakku, one more pull from that mouth and he'd come. An insane craving to feel Arisada's bite hammered at the back of Tatsu's skull. As if from a far distance, he heard his own harsh pleas. "*Kudesai, kudesai.* Please, bite me."

As much as they thrilled him, Arisada ignored those pleas, instead dug one hand between Tatsu's straining thighs to cup his chamois-soft sac. Kneading the twin orbs, Arisada's forefinger circled along that silky ridge of skin behind them. Teased and massaged around that clench rim until the muscle softened. Arisada pushed his knuckle deep into Tatsu's pulsing, wet core. Arisada added in his second finger and vibrated along the soft walls.

Pain and pleasure blasted through Tatsu's gut. He thought he moaned for more, but he wasn't sure. Those probing fingers curled against his pulsing chute, pushed in deeper until it found his gland, brushed and pressed. With every caressed on that sweet spot, the vampire's mouth sucked harder.

Lightning fired through Tatsu's nerves. Gasping mewls tore from his vocal cords at the climbing, sweet hurt. His release boiled up from his balls into his heated shaft. Then he was flying, spurting huge, gouts of jizm into that hot, accepting mouth.

Tatsu's ecstatic cries nearly plunged Arisada over the edge

into his own orgasm. The wild pumping of Tatsu's hips drove his prick deep into the back of vampire's mouth, nearly choking him. Arisada groaned with delight as he swallowed every glistening drop not letting a single drop spill from between clamped lips.

With that first taste of spunk, a ferocious need for possession gripped the vampire. He's yours. Claim him! The demand pounded along every fiber of the *kyūketsuki*'s body, echoed in his heartbeat and throbbed through his sex and his mind. He's yours. Claim him!

Arisada's iron control almost shattered. The unthinkable filled his mind. A desire so reprehensible, yet so undeniable. After all, Tatsu had begged for it. One bite. One tiny bite into that tender flesh. The tips of his fangs emerged, brushing the taut skin of Tatsu's shaft—a delicate touch that left no mark but the one in Arisada's heart.

With the strength of raw desperation, Arisada pulled off and stood. Regret scalded him. Even though sweet, Tatsu's cum was a poor substitute for what he the really craved—the boy's blood.

Chest heaving, Tatsu fought for air. Suddenly, his legs gave way, and he sagged against the solid trunk of the willow.

"Tatsu-kun!" Arisada grabbed him around the shoulders, and pulled him against his chest. "I've got you." The vampire kissed the hollow above Tatsu's collarbone, felt the runaway beat racing beneath the sweat-soaked skin. Arisada's fangs stirred. He pulled back, and hastily he tucked Tatsu's softened member into his pants. A last intimate touch.

A deep lassitude turned Tatsu compliant with trust. Why couldn't they stay just like this? His spent cock stirred at the warmth of Arisada's palm. Tatsu heard his zipper close and wanted to protest. His mouth ached to wrap itself around Arisada's cock, and taste his spunk. Tatsu longed to hear his name cried out by the vampire in ecstasy.

"Please, let me suck you." Desperate want grated in Tatsu's voice. He ground his thigh against the vampire's hard-on.

Despite his sorrow, Arisada's heart soared. He heard the note of love in that plea.

"Never forget you are my soul's chosen. *Sayonara, koibito.*" His lips brushed over Tatsu's sweat-drenched brow. An immeasurable grief over parting with this precious youth warred with his joy. He would cherish those words and this time—his only one with the boy—in his heart forever.

Tatsu smelled tears. The scent moved him in a way that nothing else could have. Then, the warm press of that body vanished. His frantic gaze swept the empty glade.

Through the branches of the tree, a pale, pink light tinged the clouds on the Eastern horizon. Daylight, a stark reminder that his lover—*yes, his lover*—was not human. Fear filled him. Would he ever see the vampire again? The loss threatened to shatter him.

"*Ojii-san*, what do I do now?" Inside his heart, where Grandfather had never died, he heard, *"The answer always lies in the Way of the Samurai."*

Sixteen

The purple smudge of dusk filtered through the thin drapes of Tatsu's bedroom. He dragged himself from the embrace of a deep sleep, yawned and stretched the contented stretch of the well-blown. He lay still for a moment, enjoying the lassitude and the memory of a hot mouth around his cock.

Shimatta! He bolted upright and looked down at his prick. Still there. He groped his groin, balls, asshole and skin between. No bite marks. His dick gave a happy throb, recalling every detail of the night before.

Groaning, he flopped onto his back. *"Jaysus, what the feckin' hell you gone an' done boyo?"* Bizarrely, Bana's voice asked the telling question.

What the fuck had he done? More to the point, what the *fekkin' hell* had he allowed to be done to him? Tatsu had no answer.

His cock had been buried to the root in that fanged mouth. He'd fucked the vampire's throat, needing and taking and loving every second of those scorching lips. It was difficult to believe it was Arisada's throat sucking him in deep, bringing him to the most mind-shattering orgasm of his life. Arisada the vampire.

Tatsu's body surged at the memory of that mouth's deep, stroking pull, those elegant fingers drilling into his core. And Tatsu knew he'd begged for it. Not just with words, but with his body, with a kiss—with a prick that hardened under the vampire's gaze.

"*Kusho*, I am so fucked," Tatsu groaned. His growing hard-on said he hadn't been fucked at all.

Since Sage, there had been no one in Tatsu's heart or in his ass. After a couple of attempts with sad, little endings, Tatsu accepted he would remain loveless. Until last night.

With a groan, he rose and headed to the shower. He shivered beneath the stinging water, deliberately keeping it cold. Letting the freezing blast distract his mind and his prick from thoughts of the flame-haired vampire with a mouth that could suck cock through a tailpipe.

Now it had been a week since they'd met at Kuboto Garden. Twice, Tatsu had visited the park. He'd wandered through the darkened landscape hoping to find the vampire. The second time, Tatsu found himself stroking the rough bark of the willow, recalling every detail of their moments together. Arisada's lips on his mouth, licking his nipples, sucking his cock.

Until Arisada pinned him to that tree and gave him that blowjob, Tatsu never believed anything could be more important than revenge or more complicated. The confusion rioted in his head. How could he have fallen in love with the enemy? Fear had kept him from answering his own question. With a muttered curse, he'd torn away from the tree and fled.

"*Yatta.* There, you sonofabitch, done." With a grunt, Tatsu tightened the last bolt on the Drifter's manifold. A few days ago, Phoenix had handed Tatsu a crate of grease-covered Kawasaki parts. "Heard you was looking for this shit. One of my Bros down in Oakie was gonna trash 'em. Figure they'll keep that Jap crap of yours running until you get some real wheels." The biker's sudden show of concern rendered Tatsu speechless.

He had taken advantage of the Colony's repair shop to fix every problem on the bike. But, shit, he didn't know how to fix the turmoil in his mind. Was he falling in love with Arisada?

Tatsu stood and pushed his hand into the small of his aching back. *Jigoku*, he needed out of here. He pulled on his chaps and gloves, and fired up the Drifter. Fifteen-hundred cubic centimeters of power thundered with new life. He gave the throttle a hard twist. The Drifter's fierce snarl gave voice to Tatsu's unexpected anger. He slapped the control button to open the massive steel doors, and burst through with less than an inch to spare on either side.

He roared away from the foundry, trying to outrun his confusion. Not caring where he rode, only craving the thrill of speed. The wind tore his hair loose from the confines of his headband. The vibration of the engine sent shivers all the way through his ass—his wanting-to-be-fucked ass.

Throttle cranked wide, Tatsu raced along the broken highway toward the distant, snow-capped peaks. The bike thundered its approval. Riding the wrong side of reckless, he crouched over his handlebars, taking the broken road climbing the mountain. Dodging potholes and piles of rocks, his knee mere inches from the cracked asphalt, he powered the Drifter through the hairpin curves.

A drunken thrill shivered through him. He balanced on that emotional edge where one mistake would send him tumbling over the precipice and rode the bike the same way. One tiny slip and they'd both hurtle into the abyss. But the exhilaration was a pale shadow compared to remembering the wild ride on Arisada's mouth.

When he hit the top of the mountain, Tatsu's chest pumped as if he'd climbed to the summit on two legs instead of astride a powerful machine. He leaned his ass against the bike and took a deep drag on his cigarette. The clouds parted and a single stream of sunlight bounced in playful glints off the slate-grey water of the Sound. Such a breathtaking sight now lost forever to Bana and Arisada. The knowledge curled into a hard knot in Tatsu's stomach. Then, despite his sorrow, Tatsu's entire body quickened with lust for the *kyūketsuki*.

Baka! He'd fucked up. He'd lost his mission and fallen under the spell of a creature he should've killed on sight. Yet even if his throat was about to be ripped out by the vampire's fangs, Tatsu knew, with a helpless certainly, he could never slay Arisada.

He snatched up a rock and hurled it off the side of the mountain. "Damn you, Saito Arisada!" he screamed over and over. The fierce mountain wind whipped away his screams and carried them into the unheeding sky.

Riding full-throttle back to the city, he reveled in the bite of the air that dashed tears from his eyes and froze the muscles of his face. The Drifter devoured the treacherous mountain road. The snarl of its engine gave voice to Tatsu's fury.

A blind dogleg loomed ahead that promised death to those who ignored its danger. What the fuck? Ignore the vicious curve and hold the Kawasaki straight. *Seppuku* by motorcycle. The impulse mesmerized him.

He felt himself flying, flying, flying off the edge of the cliff. The Drifter's engine roaring, its tires spinning uselessly for lost traction, the sucking grip of the road suddenly gone. The handlebars tearing from his hands as the motorcycle obeyed gravity and dropped toward slate-grey water. His ass lifting from the saddle, the heavy bike dropping away, tumbling over and over beneath him. The freezing shock when he hit the water, his studded boots and swords dragging him under despite his body's instinctive struggle to live. Perhaps moment's panic, then a merciful blackness taking all his pain.

Would his *tamashii* reunite with his ancestors? Would his parents smile and greet him with loving arms? His brother and sister; would they run toward him with cries of joy?

Suddenly, Ojii-san appeared, body rigid with disapproval. With a cold, yet sad stare, the venerated old man spoke. "Su-kun, you have dishonored our name."

"No, Ojii-san, I did my best!"

"Then finish it!" The old man cried, and vanished.

Tatsu's defiant cry bounced off the mountain. He rejected the false promise of that hungry curve and leaned with the bike, the symmetry of man and machine conquering the road. In a flash they were through, easing onto the highway leading like an arrow toward the city. Toward *fukushū*.

Closer to Seattle, he curbed his speed. Absurdly, his stomach rumbled, reminding him he hadn't eaten all day. Death—his or others—be damned for the moment. Tonight, he wanted food from home, his true home: Japan. He pointed the motorcycle toward the hub of the city, the Olympia Freetrade Market.

Flanked by the fishing docks on one side and a dozen warehouses on the other, and spilling between a half-dozen high-rises, the market was the economic lifeblood of the city.

During the daylight hours, it thronged with people hunting bargains among hundreds of mom-and-pop stalls, buying and selling life's necessities. When dusk approached, merchants dropped their prices and engaged in furious competition to separate a few more coins from shoppers.

The cacophony of this enterprise filled Tatsu's ears. He locked the Drifter to a steel fence post and went in search of edible bargains. He found the stall that sold Oriental food, and bought miso, Soba noodles, fresh vegetables and a small fish. On impulse, he added a bottle of sake. Maybe if he got drunk, this crazy obsession with Arisada would magically go away.

On his way back to his bike, Tatsu passed one of the many second-hand shops. He looked idly through the cracked window displaying a jumble of cheap knickknacks and tarnished heirlooms. Obeying an impulse, Tatsu wandered into the dingy store. His eyes fell on an open box of pastels. He traced his fingers over the chalky surface of the crayons. He used to love sketching. A sudden, unexpected memory caught his heart—his mother holding up one of his drawings, praising it to the family.

He never drew after he left Japan.

Chattering in Mandarin, the shopkeeper waddled toward him. She clutched a large sketchpad, which she shoved against Tatsu's chest, forcing him to take it before it fell. She nodded toward the art box. He stammered his refusal. She pointed to the crayons and held up four fingers. A real bargain, her gapped-tooth smile urged.

Before the enthusiasm of the old woman, Tatsu caved. "*Hai, hai, obaa-san,*" he said, even though he knew she didn't understand Japanese. Grinning sheepishly, he handed over the cash and walked out with the pad tucked under one arm and the pastels stowed in his backpack with his food and the liquor.

After dinner, Tatsu changed into his yukata and curled up in his easy chair with a cup of wine. The sketchpad rested on his knees. He ran his fingers over the pebbly surface of the first page. The corners were yellow with age but he rather liked that. Using one of his favorite colors, burnt umber, Tatsu sketched an oval, letting his hand wander where it willed. A second oval evolved into a pair of wire spectacles. He perched them halfway down a button nose. Two quizzical eyes peered over the bridge. His hand moved faster. A pointed chin and a narrow face topped by a shock of thick hair chopped ragged and straggling over largish ears came next. Another quick couple of lines, and a beloved, almost forgotten, face emerged.

"Hello, Hisoka-kun." Framed by the frayed edges of the paper was Watanabe Hisoka. Tatsu stared at the portrait and allowed the doors of his memories to open. He'd met Hisoka in grade two and they became inseparable. They shared secrets and joys, and a friendship that might have led to more. After he moved to New Mexico, Hisoka became lost in the fog surrounding Tatsu's memories.

Just for fun, Tatsu drew a pair of *neko* ears peeking above Hisoka's spiky hair. The cat ears and glasses gave Hisoka's face a whimsical look endearingly combined with a deep wisdom. Tatsu took a long sip and stared at the drawing.

"Soka-kun. How could I have forgotten you?"

Their favorite boyhood game was to make up plays about the other's future, which usually resulted in wild, outlandish stories. Tatsu's dramas involved bookish Hisoka defeating evil aliens and giant robots that ran amok in the city. Tatsu acted as the giant robot. Hisoka's stories always ended with Tatsu wielding his swords to save the kingdom and its imperiled princess.

One rainy afternoon, Hisoka demanded the hero kiss his princess to break the evil spell cast upon her. Caught up in the game, Tatsu agreed. In an awkward, bumping of noses, they mashed their lips together in an imitation of passion.

Hisoka pulled away. "That was weird." He giggled and straightened his crooked glasses.

Tatsu touched his mouth, tingling with a strange wonderment. His body flamed prickly hot. Kissing another boy wasn't weird at all. It felt amazing.

The next time, Hisoka insisted that the story ended with Tatsu falling in love with a beautiful samurai. Tatsu thought Hisoka was twisting the game to cover his embarrassment of their princess-kissing episode.

"*Baka,* Hisoka-kun." Tatsu punched his bespeckled friend in the arm. "Men don't fall in love with other men."

"You will." They ended up tussling each other to the floor in mock anger. Despite Tatsu's protests, Hisoka insisted on ending every story with Tatsu in love with a beautiful samurai.

Tatsu stared at the portrait of his friend as if it could give him answers. Watanabe Hisoka, you were right, he mused. Unfortunately, the beautiful samurai is not only very much male but *kyūketsuki.*

Tatsu flipped the page and began a new image. His mind drifted, absorbed in figure and form. Half an hour later, he looked at his creation. The vague lines depicted a view from atop a mountain. In the valley below, mist drifted over a cluster of buildings. A man carrying a loaded basket on a pole over his shoulder climbed a narrow path into a line of trees. Deep weariness bowed the man's shoulders and sorrow weighted that single, heavy step. With an odd shock, Tatsu realized he'd drawn the Temple of Mii-dera.

He shook his head, forcing himself out of the melancholy created by the sketch. He tacked the picture on the wall behind the *kake* stand before curling in his chair. Sipping on his glass of sake, he stared at the drawing.

He remembered his history lessons. How every Sōhei of Mii-dera died in one brutal, bloody day. How they were betrayed by their leaders. Tatsu recalled Arisada's pain when he talked of his lover's betrayal.

"You coward, Arisada," Tatsu muttered. "Why are you avoiding me?" He emptied the bottle into his glass. *Fakku,* getting drunk seemed like a great plan about now.

Like individual beads on a prayer necklace, each memory of his time with Arisada slid one-by-one through Tatsu's mind. Absently staring at the drawing of the monk, he let the warm drink take him down into an alcoholic whirlpool.

The Temple of Mii-dera, Nipon, Spring 1179

Cold, tired and frustrated, Koji Nowaki trudged through the wooden gates of Mii-dera alongside his exhausted brethren. They had finally finished the backbreaking task of felling hundreds of trees. The denuded forest was now a sea of stumps. Tomorrow, they would hack the logs into stakes and place them facing outward to form a barricade around the monastery walls. Other massive timbers lay in piles ready to roll down over the enemy. The path to a narrow bridge—the monastery's only vulnerable point—had been hidden by a seemingly impenetrable pile of boulders.

This year had been brutal for all in Nipon. A bitter winter left snow and ice on the ground far longer than normal. Food supplies were depleted and starvation threatened. With the coming of spring rains, rumors of warfare among the clans compelled the Sōhei to fortify the temple. In addition, fighting practice had been extended far into the night hours.

Despite his pride in the work to fortify the temple, Nowaki's resentment flared. He resented that he was compelled to toil with the younger acolytes. He should be commanding the combat drills. Instead, he'd been relegated to the status of supervising the woodcutters.

Was he not one of the elite Sōhei warrior class? Just a few weeks ago, he killed two men during practice with the *ninjato*. His sensei, Michinaga, offered only a curt nod of approval before signaling for the bodies to be carted away.

Just inside the massive gates, Nowaki shouldered his way through the crowd of peasants huddled together like a gaggle of frightened geese. Their chatter bordered on hysteria. A peasant had been killed last night, the corpse found drained of blood. The villagers showed less fear of the impending war than that an *oni*, a demon, stalked them.

Nowaki snorted with derision at the peasant's superstitious babble about a *kyūketsuki*, a blood-sucking *oni*. Starvation and fright turned reasonable men's minds into those of frightened children.

"Koji-sensei." A boy of about eight dropped to the ground and pressed his forehead into the mud. "I beg you to forgive my interruption of your thoughts. Saito-sensei says he wishes to meet with you after the hour of the Rat when the bathhouse is no longer in use."

Nowaki acknowledged the information with an ungrateful grunt. He was hungry. Mud caked his clothes and wooden *geta*, chilling his feet. He wanted to bathe before eating. But today he would have to wait. The bathhouse was reserved for the guests from Enryakuji until the hour before midnight.

Enryakuji, their supposed sister monastery. More like traitors, he sneered inwardly. The leaders of Enryakuji supported the Emperor Taira no Kiyomori. For the last year, a contingent from the temple on Mount Hiei visited every month trying to usurp the leadership and end Mii-dera's alliance with the Taira's enemy, the Minomoto clan.

Nowaki chaffed at the conventions requiring that he honor people considered the enemy. He regarded every visitor as a spy sent to ferret out weaknesses in Mii-dera's fortifications—weaknesses his station in life would not allow him to address.

Daily, his respect for the competence of Mii-dera's leaders diminished. Despite his youth, he instinctively understood large-scale military tactics. He only needed a chance to prove it. Unlike his brethren, he lusted for the war to begin so he could show his courage and prowess.

Loud conversation interrupted his disgruntled thoughts when dozens of men emerged from the abbot's house. In defiance of his lowly rank, Nowaki stared openly at the Enryakuji monks. Those of the highest status were dressed in *kamishimo*, the richly decorated court garb that contrasted with the drab garments of the Sōhei. He envied any with status and power. He also despised his brethren who deferred to the visitors.

Behind the contingent, another group of monks followed, crawling along on their knees. He saw Arisada. As always, Nowaki admired how Saito-sama conveyed great dignity even when offering respect in this manner.

Then Nowaki caught the magnificent warrior standing cold and aloof apart from the group. The strikingly handsome warrior bore the haughty look of nobility. He regarded the group with the unflinching gaze of a seasoned commander.

He was short, perhaps only reaching Nowaki's chin, but with wide shoulders and a powerful, stocky body. The warrior stood impassive, yet his posture was that of a coiled viper ready to strike. Unlike the colorful attire worn by other samurai, the *mons* of the Taira Clan was all that decorated this man's obsidian armor and horned *kabuto*. That lack of color and ornamentation exacerbated the samurai's fierce countenance.

Nowaki sensed the man's impatience with the chattering delegates and monks. Then, the warlord's cold eyes narrowed, and, sensing Nowaki's scrutiny, fell on the youth. The samurai started for many moments, frowned and Nowaki heard his derisive mutter about a "green-eyed bishounen."

Aware of his terrible breach of etiquette, Nowaki bowed several times while moving backward, away from the group. He bolted to his cell and flung himself down on the thin mattress. His cock was hard, his loins pulsing. He groaned with desire, recalling the lustful glint in the warrior's eyes.

This was not the first time Nowaki felt interest from other men. Until a few months ago, no lover existed for him except Saito-sama. Lately, though, he had found himself considering the advantages of coupling with another—such as this commander in black armor.

Later that night, when Nowaki arrived at the bathhouse, Arisada was already there lighting a single lamp.

"*Sumimasen.* Forgive my lateness." Nowaki lowered his gaze and bowed.

Arisada swept Nowaki up and planted a quick kiss on his lips. "Waiting for you always feels too long. But never apologize. Now, help me." He released his young lover and turned away, but not before Nowaki saw the concern clouding Arisada's face.

"You appear tired, Saito-sama."

"Please, Nowaki-kun, after four years of sharing our bodies, call me by my first name."

"*Arigatō,* Arisada-sama. I am deeply honored by the intimacy." A trembling emotion filled his words.

They opened the heavy control gate to the hot spring that fed the huge stone tub in the floor. They stripped and washed themselves clean, a requirement before entering the bath.

Nowaki's cock hardened at the sight of the supple play of

muscles along Arisada's lithe legs, the rounding of his buttocks and the heavy fall of the tea-colored scrotum hanging below.

Arisada sighed, showing a small wince of pain when he eased into the bath. "We only have an hour. I am leaving before moonset to take messages to Prince Mochihito. Emperor Taira will not negotiate. And to complicate matters, the abbot of Enryakuji states he has the Taira's support to seize control of Mii-dera from our own *zazu*."

"Your responsibilities are so many. Let me massage your neck, it is the least I can do to ease you before your long journey," Nowaki murmured.

Despite Arisada's protests, Nowaki slipped behind and wrapped his long legs around his *senpai*'s hips. The swell of Arisada's buttocks nestled against his groin. Nowaki's cock throbbed and he worked it between Arisada's ass cheeks. Nowaki dug his fingers into the corded knots of muscle along Arisada's neck and shoulders.

The water's soothing heat lulled Arisada into drowsy contentment. He closed his eyes and lay against his lover's chest. "*Domo Arigatō*, Nowaki-kun," a deep weariness marred his otherwise clear voice.

Nowaki wanted to hear more about the afternoon's negotiations. He exploited that fatigue and the trust between them. Gently, he cajoled many details about the meetings between the two monasteries and Emperor Taira's delegates. Between teasing butterfly kisses and soft caresses, he learned many secrets. A thrill shot through him—he could be executed for this knowledge. But he craved the power he'd get from the information.

"There will be war, I feel it." Arisada ran his hand over the muscle of Nowaki's thigh in a reassuring caress. "Do not embrace fear, Nowaki-kun. It is a samurai's goal to die in battle. And we will reincarnate. Whether it is on this plane or another, we will find each other." He closed his eyes with a deep sigh at his absolute conviction of his belief.

Nowaki murmured his agreement, and pressed his lips against his lover's neck. "There are considerable nobility among the samurai guarding the abbot." Nowaki probed for intelligence about the black-armored warlord without it seeming obvious.

"True, many of our visitors are from the royal court." Arisada described the samurai who had caught Nowaki's eye and roused his lust. "The delegates from Enryakuji are most fortunate. Their escort is Hayato Kazan, the commander of Taira's *yabusame*, and a nephew of the emperor. Many say he is the greatest mounted archer in two-hundred years. Certainly, he is a brutal warrior, ruthless in his defense of his uncle."

Nowaki's cock began to harden even more, the arousal driven by this information about Hayato. The warrior had noticed him, had called him *bishounen*.

"If there is war, there will be many opportunities to show bravery. You will be recognized as the great commander you are." Nowaki flattered Arisada to allay any suspicion of his interest in Commander Hayato.

"I do not care for a leader's role, only that I will always do my best defending Mii-dera."

"As do I. But enough discussion of politics and conflict. It is all maneuvering and posturing, *neh*?" Nowaki knew it was time to divert his *senpai*'s attention. He ground his prick against Arisada's ass. "My rod yearns for your touch."

Arisada's prick was already hard, throbbing with want beneath the hot water. "*Dozo*, face me," he asked.

Waves sloshed over the rim when Nowaki squirmed around to straddle Arisada's waist. Their cocks rubbed together, pressed between their ridged bellies. The weight of Nowaki's balls pooled against the root of Arisada's prick.

Arisada clasped the sides of Nowaki's face in a possessive grip, hands hot and wet from the bath. At the naked hunger in Arisada's face, Nowaki groaned and shivered with delight. Their lips slanted together with desperate hunger. A long intimate kiss, tongues probing, tasting the fleshy flavor of each other. The scent of their arousal floated on the steam from the water.

Nowaki chased his tongue in deep, exploring, claiming. Even as they kissed, the youth groped beneath the steaming water to wrap his fingers around Arisada's cock. He pulled gently on the heated skin before flicking a thumb over the engorged tip. It would be dripping with precum if the water were not washing it clean.

"*Senpai*, how I delight in knowing your organ as well my own," Nowaki murmured. Again, he thumbed over the slit, teasing forth more nectar.

Still gripping Arisada's cock, Nowaki bent down to suckle on the dark nipples. The hot water washed over his shoulders. Each caress of his tongue over the hard pebbles drew inadvertent mewls of pleasure and need from Arisada. Nowaki nibbled up Arisada's chest, over his collarbone, his face, brushing a soft kiss over each closed eyelid.

Nowaki cupped Arisada's sensitive scrotum. "My Master, open yourself to me. Let me give you release." The young acolyte rolled the satin-enclosed balls within his fingers, tugging and kneading, matching each caress with a stroke along Arisada's cock. The older monk writhed as his body responded to every touch like a sensitive, well-trained hawk. His ragged gasps echoed around the bathhouse.

Desire took Arisada as his beloved explored every pleasurable place of his loins—his cock, his balls, the sensitive perineum—all were teased to throbbing heights. Arisada's entreaties escalated at the first scratch of Nowaki's calloused thumb around his puckered entrance.

Breath exploded from Arisada's mouth. He spread his knees wider and arched his ass to expose more of his quivering bud. Long, begging moans slipped from his lips as Nowaki worked three fingers deep within his *senpai*'s anus. He finger fucked Arisada's hole, pulling out, rolling around the quivering rim, scraping his nails over the tightened scrotum before plunging back into the heat of Arisada's chute. The rhythm increased, fingers always going deeper until they skillfully caught that nub of a gland.

Arisada threw his head back against the rim of the tub, groaning at every thrust of his young lover's hand. "Oh, my beloved. Give me the clouds and the rain. Make me come," Arisada begged for his release.

The youth plied his hand, stroking hard, then agonizingly slow. He tugged up and down the thick heat of Arisada's shaft, squeezed the mushroom-shaped head, rubbed over the swollen slit. At the same time Nowaki teased over Arisada's gland. Multiple times, his impeccable timing brought the older monk to the brink of orgasm then curbed it back, much like curbing a runaway horse.

"I beg of you, by all the Gods, let me come."

But Nowaki ignored the gasps spilling from the sex-slackened mouth. Ignored them until his *senpai* begged in complete submission.

Nowaki drove his hand with full force into the pulsing chute and vibrated his thumb over the cock slit with the exact pressure he knew Arisada craved.

Arisada's hips arched and his leg muscles locked. With a long howl, he ejaculated, his cum spurting from his prick into the swirling water.

"*Oh, koibito, koibito.* You please me so much," Arisada murmured as he slid down from the pinnacle. His body resonated with aftershocks. His arms wrapped Nowaki in a crushing embrace, lips nuzzling against the youth's neck.

"Now, it is my turn." He pushed his hand between the spread ass-cheeks, found Nowaki's hole. The tight ring of muscle quivered then welcomed him as he pushed in one expressive finger. A second finger followed, then a third, stretching the tight rim. Arisada dug deeper into the hot channel, pulling a shocked gasp from his young lover.

"*Domo,* my *senpai*, please, fuck me." Nowaki groaned and ground his ass harder onto Arisada's hand. "Tonight, give me more than your fingers. I want your cock."

Surprised, Arisada tensed and withdrew from Nowaki's ass. "Are you sure, *koibito*? We have never done that. It will hurt."

"The pleasure will be in the pain. Your fingers and clever tongue have given me so much joy but now I want your member deep within me. Besides, from a practical view, you can hardly suck my cock under this water. You might drown." Nowaki laughed as he nipped Arisada's lips. The steam from the water obscured the hungry look in his eyes. For Nowaki's desire to take Arisada's cock into his body came not from love, lust or desire, but from ruthless ambition. He craved the power he would gain from his lover's submission.

Before his *senpai* refused, Nowaki rose over Arisada's taut prick, holding it against the wet rim of his waiting hole. With a soft grunt, he sank down onto the hard, slick shaft. He gasped with pain as his core stretched around the thickness of his *senpai*'s rod. Then an exquisite sensation followed mere seconds later as that round cockhead slid against his prostate. The pain and pleasure merged. Koji Nowaki exalted for now he owned Saito Arisada.

"Oh *koibito*, you do not know how I have longed to do this," Arisada whispered. Lightning surged along every limb and his body shuddered with delight as the heat from his young lover's core enveloped Arisada's cock. He dug his fingers into Nowaki's slim, strong hips and urged the boy faster.

Pleasure rolled up from deep within Nowaki's vitals each time he drove down onto that iron-hard rod. Deliberately, he constricted and relaxed his tight anus, milking Arisada's prick. As Nowaki's climax coiled in his balls, he bucked onto the thick shaft harder and faster. The water sloshed with every thrust, spilling over the rim onto the flagstones. The bathhouse walls echoed with their ecstatic cries.

"Stroke my organ," Nowaki pleaded as he impaled his hole onto his *senpai*'s cock. With a low moan, Arisada gripped him and began pulling, hard and fierce, then soft and loving. Nowaki clung to Arisada's shoulders as if for life as his supple young ass sucked in every inch of Arisada's organ.

"Oh my, *koibito*! Your center devours me with its heat." Legs straining, thigh muscles knotting, Arisada lifted his hips and drove his cock in to its root. With an explosive howl, he tumbled over the pinnacle. As his cum flooded his young lover's chute, Arisada jacked Nowaki's member with frantic, hard jerks, rolling soft skin over iron.

Molten lava filled Nowaki's core. Everything but the sweet need for release fled his mind. Caught in such a rising tide of pleasure, he rode that thick, invading member until he lost control. Fire shot into his balls. The pulses of that cock in his chute triggered a monumental release. His cock emptied its load in long, hot splashes into Arisada's hand.

Panting, Nowaki collapsed into the enfolding embrace of his lover. He smiled at the muffled murmur of love from Arisada, "*Aishiteru.*" From that simple declaration, Nowaki knew his complete dominance of Arisada was assured.

For a few moments, they rested, curled together, their panting echoing harshly in the small room. Nowaki felt the racing of Arisada's heart slow, but still the older monk held on. Tender lips brushed Nowaki's cheek.

"I must go now, young one. I will not return for at least eight days, and already I am missing you."

"I shall miss you too, *senpai*. Travel safely back to me." As Nowaki whispered the words into his lover's ear, an odd foreboding touched him. He dismissed it.

They dried off and dressed. With no other words between them, they opened the drain and let fresh spring water wash into the bath. The hot flow washed away all signs of their passion.

Arisada stepped up to the heavy, wooden door. Suddenly, he spun back and caught the youth in a tight embrace. "*Aishite imasu.*" He pressed his lips to the top of Nowaki's head. The kiss became a benediction. Then, the older Sōhei slipped out into the cold night.

The lips of Nowaki's rectum burned and his entrails ached, but it was worth the price. Through allowing that simple act of penetration, he had asserted his dominance over Arisada. For a single heartbeat, Arisada's words of love—so intimate in their honesty—stilled Nowaki's ambition. But only for a heartbeat.

Ever since bandits had destroyed his home and slaughtered his family, Nowaki had vowed never to be helpless. Only power over others would keep him safe. Now, he had it.

Shivering in the freezing night air, he rushed back to his tiny cell. He slipped off his muddy *geta* at the entrance and slid aside the door.

Clad only in his *fundoshi*, Hayato stood with regal expectation in the center of the room. His armor and clothing lay folded in a neat pile at the foot of Nowaki's sleeping mat. Still, he held his *katana* combat-ready in his left hand.

"I've been waiting for you, my green-eyed *bishounen*." The warrior removed his *fundoshi*. His dark, semi-erect cock dropped low between his furred thighs.

Nowaki spared no thought for Arisada, Mii-dera or honor. Did not even notice the slight leak of his lover's spunk from his hole. With swift, eager motions, Nowaki discarded his clothing. Naked, he dropped to his knees, forehead pressing against the *tatami*. His hands spread his buttocks, offering his dark sphincter in an invitation to his new Lord's rod.

When this night was done, Nowaki would have access to the power and status he craved.

The Seattle Quarantine, 2024

The cell phone's piercing ring jarred Tatsu out of his daze. His asshole hurt and his chute pulsed as if recently fucked. Cum smeared his crotch and thighs. Judging by the size of the mess, he'd ejaculated more than once. And still his cock throbbed hard with a painful want.

The demanding ring continued. Through blurred vision, he peered around. A modern living room—not a tiny cell in a Buddhist monastery—swam into view through the pounding headache from his alcohol-driven, self-pitying indulgence.

He hauled himself up on numb legs, staggered over to the table, groped for the cell, fumbled it open and stared at the screen. If the Red Alert hadn't burned through the fog clouding his brain, the needle-sharp spasms shooting up his legs sure as hell would.

"*Moshi, moshi*. Cobb here," he mumbled past a thick tongue. Gods, he hope he didn't sound as fucked up as he felt.

"Mr. Cobb?" Cooperhayes' flat tone crackled from the tiny speaker. "On the double, if you please."

"Copy that, Mr. Cooperhayes. I'm on my way."

Stupidly, Tatsu looked around, still holding the cell. Wind and rain blew into the room, leaving a puddle on the floor. *Jigoku*, he'd left the damn window open again. He slammed it shut and leaned his forehead against the cold glass. His face burned as if with a fever.

The sketchpad lay on the floor beside the chair. Tatsu scooped it up on the way to his bedroom. Right before he reached his closet, he stalled out and stared at the image.

The simple drawing showed the head and torso of a young man—a youth really—turned to look over his shoulder. A *naginata* rested over one bare shoulder. Clouds of thick smoke boiled above his shaven head. Remorse marred the beauty of his face.

Koji Nowaki.

Fear shivered through Tatsu at the undeniability of the dream. The truth slammed into his gut. He'd experienced every moment—every exquisite touch, every scent, every taste—between Nowaki and Arisada.

With utter conviction, Tatsu knew he'd betrayed Arisada and the Mii-dera Sōhei. He was truly Nowaki's reincarnation.

"*Ojii-san*, I understand now. There is so much more to my debt than family honor," he whispered to his grandfather's spirit. Tatsu was in this life to remove the bloody stain of *uragirimono* from Koji Nowaki's soul and give that spirit peace.

Seventeen

The weight of Tatsu's new insight brought him little peace. Time after time, he jerked awake, his heart thundering in his chest, his body drenched in sweat. Nightmares filled with moans, screams of lust and pain, smells of blood and shit, demented laughter and mocking words plagued him. Bana morphed into a blood-drenched Sage who begged Tatsu to kill him. Distorted images of Nowaki blurred into Arisada, face distorted with hate, as his engorged cock took Tatsu in the ass before the vampire's fangs ripped out his throat.

The meaning of those dreams was so clear: He'd failed Bana. Only a few days ago, Fornax had reported that the Irishman was fast becoming one of the most vicious vampires in Tendai. The single time Fornax approached, Bana blindly attacked him.

"It's to be expected. Like all newly turned, Bana's memories of his human life affect his vampire instincts," Fornax explained. "He was always an angry man. That anger is now exacerbated by his *kyūketsuki* nature. Still, despite the danger he poses to us all, I don't want to be forced to kill him."

Major Blenheim, ever the realist, stated it was only a matter of time before the identity of the Lepers was uncovered. Still, he was loath to take Bana's life. "Leave him be," he said. "I have faith that Mr. Murtagh's human integrity will win out, what?"

In direct disobedience to the Major's order, Tatsu sneaked into Tendai. He told himself he was searching for his lost partner. In truth, Tatsu knew he was hoping to find Arisada. Several times, Tatsu questioned the indentured in the Alki compound but received only guarded stares or outright hostility.

Then he was caught by Fornax deep within Tendai. "You

can do nothing for Murtagh. Now leave, boy." For an unknown reason, the vampire did not report the incident to the Major.

Tatsu tried convincing himself he needed the *kyūketsuki*'s help. Knew his reason was bullshit. He wanted to find Arisada, wanted one more chance to look into those golden eyes. One more embrace of those arms, the soft press of those lips, that mouth around his cock. Hear Arisada say, "*koibito.*"

Feeling as stupid as a lovesick teenager, Tatsu dialed Arisada's number just like every night for the past two weeks. But it was always the same—no answer.

By the great god Hachiman, this craziness had to stop. Tatsu had to talk to someone. There was only one person he trusted. He prayed the man thought they had enough of a friendship to listen without judgment. If not, Tatsu would face the consequences, no matter what.

He punched the numbers without listening for a dial tone and felt a wash of relief at the sleepy voice at the other end. "*Gomen nasai*, sorry to interrupt you but can you meet me before work? Got to run something past you?" He let Kaiden believe the discussion would be about Bana.

That evening, when Tatsu entered the armory, he found Kaiden hunched over trays of dies for large-caliber bullets. Boxes of brass cases flanked two sets of scales. The far end of the workbench was laden with green ammo bins filled with new incendiaries. The bullets reminded Tatsu of Bana, who always used them in his precious Berettas.

"Why so many incendiaries?" Tatsu asked, unbuckling his harness and dropping it on the table. He spun his chair around and straddled it.

"Where's your head been? Didn't you hear about the major operation coming up? Chain just left. Been cranking out bolts all day." Kaiden looked up. Tatsu's honey-colored face was pale and covered with a fine sheen of sweat, despite the chill of the room. He noticed how the kid's eyes skittered about, landing everywhere except on him.

"Hey, Ninja Boy, lighten up. I mean you elevate brooding to an art." Kaiden focused on measuring the cordite. He decided to try a different conversation track when no response came from the too-edgy Tatsu. "Meet any of the Snake Eaters yet?" The Chicago Leper team had arrived yesterday, bringing with them their vehicles and enough armament to win a war.

Tatsu shook his head, sending his mop of dark hair flying, but at least he looked directly at Kaiden. "Do you know any of them?"

"Yeah, a couple. They're all mean motherfuckers. You gotta be that way to survive in that city." A tightness around Kaiden's eyes cast a harshness over his handsome face.

Tatsu fumbled his cigarettes out of his pocket and pulled one out with his lips. He flicked open his lighter, then realized he sat beside an open canister of cordite. "*Chikusho!*"

"Shit is right, Cobb. Dump the smokes. You wanna blow up the whole damn building, mess up my gorgeous face and piss off the Major?" Kaiden watched Tatsu, looking stunned at his own stupidity, tossed the unlit cigarette into the trashcan and pocket the lighter.

"How about clueing me in before you send us both to a fiery hell?" The blond continued his painstaking task during the five minutes of silence that stretched like an eternity between them.

"Sorry about the smoking. By Hachiman, I must be *baka*. Got things on my mind, I guess." Shit, more than *things,* more like a crazy-in-lust-for-a-certain-vampire thing.

"Dunno from Hachiman, but you're *baka* alright. You still blaming yourself for what happened to Murtagh?" Kaiden no longer called the Irishman Mick. "Nothing you could've done. Nothing anyone could've done. Hell, it could be any one of us at any time, even you. Gotta accept that."

"*Hai.* Turning like that was horrible. But then I couldn't stop him from going into Tendai. Couldn't catch him and bring him back here for help. I keep having nightmares about it. Like he's calling for us to get him out of a box, and just when we reach him, he starts screaming like he's in agony. Then, we jerk open the lid, only we forget it's daylight, and we burn him up." Misery etched deep lines in Tatsu's face.

"Holy Christ, Tatsu. Let it go. For what it's worth, we've

lost five others like that since I joined the Colony. Could be any one of us next."

"*Â, sō desu ka.* I just feel so guilty."

"Nothing to be guilty about. Still, no matter what others say, losing someone never leaves you. Worse if you're close. And as a team, we are. Most of us, that's all we've got." Kaiden's voice turned gravelly. "I know more than I want about guilt. How it can eat you alive. It was my fault my lover, Bryan, died."

"Your fault? How?"

"I killed him."

Tatsu stared in horror at Kaiden, shocked as much by the reply as by its flat, clinical utterance.

"Bryan was incredibly talented but he'd only done theater. I leaned on a couple of producers to give him the lead in this movie on location near the Detroit Quarantine. Wanted realism, even hired vampires to be extras. Fucking insane idea. Next thing, he's been bitten by a bloodsucker. He survived and came home to me in California. We thought he was gonna be fine."

His eyes turned cobalt-dark with pain. "When he turned, he slaughtered half his family. I thought he was a monster. I tracked him here. By then he was out of the animal stage and swore he still loved me. When I told him vampires can't love, he attacked me. I shot him. The Major saved me from eating my gun."

Tatsu floundered for a suitable reply. "*Gomen nasai.* How long were you and Bryan together?"

"Five amazing years. We met right after I came out."

"When did you know you loved him?" Tatsu flushed. He felt rude prying into a deep and painful part of another person's life, yet sensed the other man wanted to talk.

Kaiden sighed but his look said he was okay with the question. "First time we fucked, I knew we were meant for each other. No hesitation. Bryan knew it, too. If we're lucky, it happens that way. It's more than just sex, it's a connection between the two of you that makes you just know." The shimmer of unshed tears told it all. "I was convinced there'd never be another. Until—"

"You fell in love with Chain Passebon?"

"Yeah, blindsided by the oldest, gay cliché of 'em all, falling for a straight man. My friggin' partner no less. Go figure. But who the fuck understands love?"

Hai, hai, who understands love? But maybe Kaiden would at least sympathize with Tatsu's utterly, incomprehensible dick-twitching, ass-throbbing desire for a vampire. He drew in a deep, unsteady breath. "Do you think love can really exist between human and vampire?"

"Why the fuck are you asking me?"

"Because you know, you..."

"My boyfriend turned bloodsucker and still said he loved me. I couldn't accept it." The blond mercenary skewered Tatsu with a sharp look. "Where are you going with this, Cobb?"

Tatsu gulped through a throat gone desert dry. Too late, he wasn't *going* anywhere, he was already there—hot and hard and crazy. And about to share his secret with a killer elite who would slay Arisada in a heartbeat.

"I ain't got all day, Cobb."

Tatsu wanted to lie, to find a quick meaningless excuse for his questions. He swallowed hard, realized his face looked guilty as sin. When his eyes locked onto Kaiden's, Tatsu knew nothing but the truth would suffice. This may be the only guy who could help figure out this insanity.

The lump that was I-let-a-vampire-blow-my-cock stuck in his throat. The bigger, heart-skipping confession that he was in love with that same vampire, stayed lodged in his heart.

"I've met this person that I might be in love with."

"Might be? What the hell, Ninja Boy? I can't believe you've never been in love before."

"Yes! Once." In a dragging whisper, Tatsu told about Sage. "I'd fallen for him years before we um... ah—"

"Fucked," Kaiden interjected with a slight smirk. "If you're gonna do it, you better be able to say it."

"Yes, *wakatta*. Fucked! We were only together for one week. After he left, I looked for him for years. His grandmother said if he didn't want to be found, he wouldn't be." Shame filled Tatsu at the moisture filming his eyes.

"Ah, man. We never forget our first love. Bet he topped 'cause you are one tasty-looking bottom. Don't argue, I can always tell."

Fine pink dusted the top of Tatsu's cheeks. Yeah, he was a bottom all right, a bottom whose ass craved the wrong thing—the cock of one flame-haired vampire.

"So this long lost love, Sage? He show up?"

"No, he's gone." The flicker of remorse in his eyes changed to an odd pleading.

Kaiden finished the tray of bullets and began on another. "Another hot guy from your mysterious past?"

Tatsu shook his head. "Nothing like that."

"So, I'll take a wild guess and say this beat-around-the-fucking-bush conversation is really about a new love thing? Not that you've exactly come out with it. Crap, Ninjas and their sneakiness."

Tatsu gave a mirthless, coughing laugh at Kaiden's half-assed humor. "Yeah, new love, kind of like that. And if I don't figure it out, I'm really going to fuck up. Someone will get hurt."

"No shit. You nearly blew us both to hell a minute ago." Kaiden's voice softened with sympathy. "I know in a world like ours, it can be hell even finding a moment of joy. But if what's going on makes you a liability to the team, you'd better talk." His penetrating gaze never left Tatsu's face. "Tell me he ain't one of these animals on our team." For a second, Kaiden feared Tatsu had fallen for Chance Chain—or worse, for him.

"*Iie*, absolutely not." Tatsu sat back, startled at the absurdity of the thought. "Somethi... someone else..." Tatsu's voice trailed off.

"How long has this been going on?"

"A few months. We met shortly after I got here. Before I joined the Lepers."

"No shit? You fuck him already?" Kaiden grinned, getting a kick out of watching Tatsu squirm with embarrassment. For a stone-cold killer, little Ninja Boy sure got shook up talking about doing the dirty deed.

"No, I haven't *fucked* him; but every time I see him—"

"You wanna jump his bones." Kaiden's grin widened.

"Oh, yes." The affirmation came out on a long, throaty breath. "But it's more than sex. I'll always love Sage. This feels the same but more intense. I've never believed in *unmei no hito*, you know, soul mates. Figured it was load of bullshit before now. But this is special. This is it. The one. And it's really fucking with my head. I've always known what to do, been taught to control my feelings. Now, it's like I'm drowning." Tatsu heard himself babbling and tried to rein in his chaotic thoughts.

"Falling in love is a lot like drowning, I guess." Kaiden's voice softened with concern. He smiled, a quirky sideway lift of his lip.

Tatsu dragged his hands through his hair, leaving it a tousled mess. "This is absurd. I have no time for anything else. Especially love."

"Crap, Tatsu, just cause we're killers, doesn't make us machines. Even you with your swords and samurai code. Love, companionship, sex, all has a way of making itself known. We need what we need, love who we love." He knew he'd said the right thing. The confusion faded a little from the kid's eyes.

Kaiden got up and walked over to the giant press to snap more ammunition into the autoload vault. He held off pushing the start button. The old machine made a terrible racket, and he didn't want to give Tatsu any excuse to stop talking. Instead, Kaiden went back to the table and began assembling another tray. "So, tell me about him."

Misery etched lines in Tatsu's face. It wasn't the look of a man about to reveal a happy secret. "I'm not sure I can explain it," Tatsu muttered. "It's er... it's complicated." His voice trailed off.

"It's always complicated, Tatsu. If thinking about him makes you hard maybe all you need to do is nail him. But if your damn heart aches when you don't see him, and you only feel complete when you're with him, it might be love."

"I haven't known him long enough." Yet Tatsu's soul had known Saito Arisada for eight-hundred years.

"Hell, time's got nothing to do with it. Can happen in an

instant." Kaiden flashed back to an undeniable moment two years ago when he fell for the gorgeous Cajun. "Sure you don't need just to get a good fuck outa this guy and move on?"

"I'm certain I don't want to just *fuck* him. And the only thing I *am* sure of is he's not a guy."

Kaiden reeled back in pretended shock. "Huh, a chick? No. Fucking. Way. You ain't hardwired fer pussy."

Tatsu gulped, embarrassed, suddenly reluctant to reveal more. "*Gomen nasai.* I'm sorry I shouldn't have bothered you about it." He pushed up from the table but iron fingers clamped like a vice around his wrist and yanked him back onto the chair.

"Sit your butt down, Ninja Boy, and shove that Japanese apology crap up your cute, tight ass." The blond's fierce cerulean eyes locked onto Tatsu's jade ones. "You're not just my teammate, you're my friend. You can trust me with anything, and I mean anything. So, spill. It can't be that bad."

"Oh, yes, it's that bad." Tatsu's misery-filled eyes skittered off Kaiden's stare. Without thinking, he rolled a brass casing between his thumb and forefinger. "He's a vampire." The words eked out in a whisper as if to deny their reality.

"Huh? A what? You're telling me a bloodsucker got you so horny you want to fuck him? You're immune to their thrall so's as long as you're in control, no big deal. A quickie never hurt anyone no matter whose cock is involved."

Tatsu gulped. "I want more." How could he explain about the huge hole in his heart that disappeared every time Arisada called him *koibito*?

"He ain't the one you're hunting? I mean maybe you're suffering from that freaking Stockholm syndrome."

A shocked expression crossed Tatsu's face. "No, it's not him. I'm positive. Grandfather almost severed that monster's spine. This one has no scars. I made him show me."

Kaiden's laughter bounced around the cold room. "A bloodsucker stripped just because you asked? Man, you're one talented little Ninja." He leaned across the table and skewered Tatsu with an intense, definitely not friendly stare. "Now, what the fuck are you hiding from me?"

The events of the *shinkendo* bet, Arisada's tattooed back, even the blow job, tumbled out of Tatsu's mouth in a confused rush.

"A blow job? He sucked you off? You sure this vampire's not playing you? I mean, you're still a baby to the Life. I'd hate to see any bloodsucker getting his teeth in my friend's adorable, not-quite-virgin ass."

"He's not playing me. And leave my ass out of it," Tatsu snapped. "I can't stop thinking about him. How he looks at me, his arms, his kisses, his voice. *Jigoku,* he didn't just blow my cock, he blew my mind."

"What about your vendetta? He's still a vampire."

"I don't think of him as *kyūketsuki*. He's... he's just mine. Shit, just listen to me. I'm pathetic."

"You're not pathetic. Maybe just this side of crazy, but not pathetic. Not all of them are vicious animals. Look at Fornax. People hook up with vampires all the time, live with 'em, some even marry them on the down low." Kaiden floundered to a halt. Damn, how many times he had listened to guys lament the I'm-in-love-with-the-wrong-cock conversation? But this one was way out of his league. "You think this vampire knows the one you're hunting?"

"Maybe." Tatsu sounded unconvinced.

"You too afraid to ask him? Sounds like you're not sure you can trust him."

"I trust him." But did he really trust Arisada? The vampire hadn't contacted him since that night in Kuboto Garden. "Only he's not been around for a couple of weeks."

"Maybe he got what he wanted from you."

Tatsu glared. "He wouldn't do that. He's honorable in a way you'd never understand. Says he loves me. *Aishite imasu.* Said it every time we met."

"Cool it, Tatsu. Just trying to help." Kaiden held his hands aloft in mock surrender. "Shit, it's going to be a cluster fuck no matter what happens. Mind telling me his name?" He resumed his careful loading of empty shells. Breathed soft and quiet during the long minute of silence that hung between them.

"Saito... Saito Arisada."

The measure crashed to the table, scattering priceless gunpowder over Kaiden. He stared in shock at his younger teammate. "What the hell? Saito Arisada? The second top dog in Tendai? You have *got* to be bullshitting me. Saito fucking Arisada says he loves you. And you love him. You don't do anything half assed, do you, Ninja Boy?"

Eyes downcast, Tatsu nodded but quelled another apology. Suddenly, he wished he'd never confided in Kaiden.

"Shit, you're messing around with Ukita Sadomori's Primary." Kaiden leaned over the table and gripped Tatsu's chin, jerking his head up, forcing the younger man to look at him.

"Tell me everything about him," the blond demanded. "You owe us that."

"I don't owe anybody anything." Tatsu jerked his head out of Kaiden's hand. "He's no threat to us." Yet he knew his actions went against the every code of the Leper Colony.

Ignoring Tatsu's hostility, Kaiden sat back with a sigh. "Maybe, maybe not. I know you won't deliberately endanger any of us. I trust you. But you gotta admit, you've dropped one big-assed bomb on me."

"I have to know if what I feel is real. Sage said there was another waiting for me. Maybe Arisada is it. My life can't just be about killing."

"This has really gotten your dick tied up in knots. Tell me, is he hot?" Kaiden faked his best actor's leer, hoping to deliberately luring Tatsu into revealing everything he knew about one of the most secretive but dangerous vampires in Seattle.

Tatsu dug his cell out of his jacket, flipped it open and spun the instrument across the table. "Here, Saito Arisada. He used to be a Buddhist monk."

Kaiden let out a long, low whistle. No mistaking that translucent skin or those golden eyes. Whether vampire or man, this one transcended mere beauty.

"Man, this guy's drop-dead gorgeous. Look at that incredible hair. It looks like living flame. Don't Buddhists shave their heads? And those eyes. Should creep me out but they're beautiful. Like they're promising something wonderful if you just ask for it," Kaiden murmured. He snapped his eyes from the cell to stare at Tatsu. "And he says he *loves* you?"

"I already said that." Tatsu felt a wash of pride at the blond's frank admiration of the vampire. "He says I'm the reincarnation of his long-ago lover, Koji Nowaki. After I saw Nowaki's memories, I'm convinced."

"Sonofabitch." Kaiden shook his head, looking once more at the image. "Don't know about the reincarnation shit but if you think this love is real, it'll be hard to turn your back on it. Just be sure you can trust him."

"I trust him. I think he's really on our side. I just don't know if I can trust myself. I'm fucked."

"No, we're both fucked." A sardonic smile twisted Kaiden's features. "You've fallen for the enemy, and I'm in love with a straight guy. Dunno know which one's worse. You gonna try to find him?"

"You know I will."

"Bad idea. You gotta back off, Cobb. Tell the Major. He doesn't give a rat's ass who you sleep with, but he should know you're close pals with the second-top dog in Tendai." Kaiden's look said he sympathized but regulations were regulations. "I'm sorry, kid; you got one day to log that pretty picture in along with a report. *Wakarimasu ka*?"

"*Hai, hai. Wakarimasu.* I understand. I'll inform the Major immediately." Tatsu stilled his expression to hide the lie. Only one path lay open to him now. The path of *fukushū*.

Reassured, Kaiden left the table to lock trays of brass into the reloader. "Holy shit. You and Saito fucking Arisada."

"*Kuso*, will you stop saying it like that?"

Kaiden snorted with laughter. He pressed the start button on the noisy machine, drowning out Tatsu's next comment.

Eighteen

"So, Mr. Cobb, I can't persuade you to reconsider? You're a valued member of this organization."

"*Gomen nasai,* Major Blenheim-san, but it can't be helped. I must resign from the Leper Colony." Tatsu dropped his eyes, afraid they'd give him away. Against Kaiden's suggestion, Tatsu hadn't revealed his association with Arisada to the Major. Hiding the intimate connection with the second-in-command of Tendai was a clear betrayal of his agreement with the Lepers. Revealing it would be a betrayal of Arisada.

"Very well. I asked for one week's notice and you've honored that." Disappointment dragged in the Major's voice. "I expect you to be out of Seattle within twenty-four hours after your last assignment."

Tatsu nodded his acceptance in silence. Head bowed in misery, he followed Major Blenheim into the Pit.

"Gentlemen, last week I asked you to prepare for a major assignment. It begins tonight. Dr. Wyckes will explain the details."

The doctor limped up to the head of the table. "There have been major outbreaks in Europe and Western Russia of a new strain of sanguinae virus. Unlike the original, this bug, designated SAE-49, is airborne and extremely viral. The bad news: Full physiological change occurs within twelve hours after infection. The really bad news: There's a seventy percent survival rate—as a vampire."

The room buzzed with "what the fucks" and "oh shits." Wyckes ignored them and continued, "One of the nasty side-effects, other than becoming a bloodsucking monster, is the total destruction of the ventromedial area of the brain."

"Okay now you're fucking with me," Phoenix barked. "In English, man—"

Wyckes ignored Phoenix's interruption. "Victims lose all

sense of morality. They become killing machines. Think shark with a tad more brainpower. Moreover, their mutated DNA puts them immediately under the control of any alpha vampire, a Master such as Ukita Sadomori."

"So you're saying we'd be totally fucked, without the dinner and a movie first." Kaiden's joke bombed. No one laughed.

Not to be outdone, Phoenix added, "We're gonna be looking at an army of zombie vampires."

"Sounds like an oxymoron to me," Kaiden retorted.

"Who you calling a moron, you mother—" Fist clenched, Phoenix rounded on the grinning blond. Kaiden raised his hands, palms out, in fake surrender.

"Stand down, gentlemen." The Major's quiet order stopped Phoenix's next retort cold. "The Jiangxi-Dai Pharmaceutical Corporation opened a new research satellite in the old Olympic Hill Hospital. Their program starts next week with the first shipment of SAE-49. We've been hired to provide protection."

"The Chinese have an entire army. Why'd they need us?" Bell asked.

"Unfortunately, a typhoon has delayed the Jiangxi-Dai teams. Until they arrive, we'll protect the center." The Major turned to the large-screen monitor behind him. "The labs are on the ground floor. Only three access points: the front to the lobby and two rear doors for the loading docks and parking areas. The rest of building is sealed. Four teams of three, nine hours on, overlapping coverage. I don't see the necessity of automatic weapons for this job. Now, Mr. Cobb has a rather regrettable announcement."

"*Gomen, gomen nasai.* I... I must leave the company right after this mission." Tatsu bowed, holding it a fraction longer than necessary, hoping to avoid looking anyone in the face. When he raised his eyes, he caught the look of hurt accusation in Kaiden's glower. Without a word, the blond stood and stomped out. Tatsu prayed Kaiden would say nothing to the Major about Arisada. Not immediately, anyway.

On his last night as a Leper, Tatsu parked his bike beside the Humvee at the rear of the research facility. The tedium of the assignment left him with too much time to think. Already he'd discarded several ideas to hunt in Tendai without the Major finding out. Even the idea of becoming indentured didn't seem remotely workable.

It didn't help that Tatsu's body surged with desire every time he thought of Arisada—his deep voice, the exquisite brush of his fingers, the fierce possessiveness of his mouth. Tatsu had come to Seattle to settle a blood debt, not find a lover—a *kyūketsuki* no less—who had seduced him with gentle words and an amazing, cocksucking mouth.

And then dumped him. *Fakku*, maybe when this was over, he'd head back to New Mexico and look for Sage. The Indian can't hide for—

An explosion followed by the ear-rending screech of alarms, ripped Tatsu's musings apart. He snatched both swords from their scabbard and raced along the corridor to the central laboratory. He skidded to a halt outside the double doors handing askew. Smoke billowed out into the hallway. When he entered the lab, utter carnage met him. Scientists lay amid the smashed glass and broken instruments. Many were missing limbs. One had been decapitated.

Almost on Tatsu's heels, Chain burst in, sweeping his crossbow side-to-side. "*Merde*, what the hell?"

Kaiden halted just outside the room and took in the devastation with one look. "Holy fuck! Anyone alive?" He remained in the doorway, guns sweeping the hall, while other two men ran from body to body.

"This one's alive." Chain crouched beside a man curled against the scorched wall. The scientist stared around with glazed, uncomprehending eyes. A scarlet stain blossomed over his white lab coat.

"Don't move. Can you tell me what happened, *mon ami*?" Chain soothed the dying man.

"Grenades came through doors... techs took virus. Another guy with...." He lifted a shaking hand and pointed to the back of the laboratory. Blood bubbled from his mouth. He coughed several times and died.

With a jerk of his head, the Cajun indicated the receiving

doors leading from the laboratory to the loading docks. Weapons raised, the three Lepers slipped toward the rear of the complex.

In the lead, Tatsu pushed one of the swinging doors ajar with the tip of his *katana* and glanced into the parking lot.

Three men, one clutching a steel container, scrambled into the back of a white panel van. Another man leaned out of the driver's side door. No mistaking that curly black hair or the string of Irish obscenities spewing from his mouth.

"*Kuso*! It's Bana." Tatsu kicked the doors open and dashed through. He sheathed the *wakizashi* and charged toward the van.

"Bana, wait." He pounded on the driver's window and twisted the door handle, trying to pull it open.

Bana snapped his head around and stared at Tatsu through the glass. An angry look flitted across Irishman-turned-vampire's face.

"Boyo, get away from me," he spat, and stomped on the gas pedal. The van fishtailed, the back bumper knocking Tatsu to his knees. Before he recovered, the vehicle careened out of the parking lot and skidded around the end of the street.

"*Fakku*, Bana stop!" Tatsu leaped to his feet, sheathing the *katana* while dashing toward the Kawasaki.

Kaiden and Chain scrambled into the Hummer. The roar of the Drifter's engine drowned out Kaiden's, "Cobb, in the truck, now."

With a recklessness that bordered on stupidity, Tatsu cranked the engine. The surge of power lifted the heavy bike on its back tire and Tatsu single-wheeled across the tarmac. At the gate, he dropped onto two wheels, and roared into the street after the van.

"Cobb, what the fuck are you doing, man?" Kaiden's bark crackled through Tatsu's dog collar.

"Bana's driving that van," Tatsu yelled unnecessarily. The dog collar screeched with feedback at Chain's string of profanity and "*Mon Dieu's*."

"Bana, gotta catch Bana." The demented mantra pounded through Tatsu. Twisting the throttle wide open, he raced through the twisting, littered streets. No thought on his mind except intercepting his old partner.

He caught a glimpse of the van cresting a hill less than a block away, cranked the throttle wide open and felt the Kawasaki leap under him. He was close enough to see one of the thieves peering through the back window when a pack of feral dogs darted in front of him. Reflexively, Tatsu swerved, it was a second too late. His front wheel clipped the dog's haunches.

The impact sent the Drifter into a skid. Even his Leper reflexes and strength weren't enough to control the heavy motorcycle. The rear tire lost traction and the bike spun out, sliding several feet along the street. Tatsu barely kept his ass on the seat. Man and machine crashed against a mountain of garbage covering the sidewalk.

Cursing, he scrambled to his feet and hauled the bike up. The front fender lay crumpled against the tire. He tore off the useless piece of metal and tossed it. A breath of relief escaped when he kicked the starter pedal and the engine roared to life. He thanked all the gods for Japanese engineering, and thanked them again for the dee-skin that had saved his ass from a world of hurt.

But when he looked down the street, the van was long gone.

"Cobb, what's your ten-twenty?" Kaiden's voice crackled out of the dog collar.

"Near the West Bridge. Harbor Island."

"We're about half a klick behind you. Wait there. Do you copy?" Do. Not. Cross. That. Fucking. Bridge."

Tatsu couldn't wait. The hell if he gave up on Bana now. He kicked the bike into gear and rode across the bridge. Keeping his speed down to a wobbly crawl, he rode through darkened streets. Derelict warehouses and factories lined either side. His eyes swiveled back and forth. The back of his neck crawled with the feeling that any second he'd be surrounded by screaming, out-for-his-blood monsters. Yet he saw no sign of life. No sign of a white van. *Kuso,* where the hell did it go?

Just when he was about to give up, he rounded a corner

and spotted the tail end of a white vehicle entering the gates of a massive power plant. The van halted with a squeal of brakes. Bana and the thieves clambered out and headed toward the facility.

Tatsu cut the engine and pushed the Drifter behind a dumpster. He dug into his pocket. *Kuso*. No cell. He must've dropped it when the bike went down. Hoping it worked, he spoke softly into his collar. "I found them. Need back up."

Chain's welcome drawl rumbled beneath Tatsu's ear. "Where the hell are you, *mon ami*?"

"Harbor Island. Bana's here, at least a couple dozen vampires."

Kaiden's voice filled Tatsu's ear. "Harbor fucking Island? Bad place, Ninja Boy. Wait for us. ETA about ten minutes." And Cobb? If you disobey me again, I'll personally kick your pretty ass back to Japan. Do you copy?"

Screw orders, he had to get inside that plant. He wriggled through a tear in the chain-link fence and crouched beside one of the mountain of garbage that dotted the lot. Tatsu wondered how the human workers stood the stench. Even breathing through his mouth didn't help. At least the reek would hide his scent from any *kyūketsuki*.

A thin, pale light from the moon filtered through the clouds, letting Tatsu see most of the complex. Conveyors ran up to a giant, smoke-spewing furnace in the center. Steel pipes, larger than a man's body, connected the furnace to several gas kilns then to a single tower that loomed hundreds of feet into the night sky. The whole assembly looked like a monstrous, angry spider surrounded by its eggs. Tatsu shuddered; he hated spiders!

A dozen methane tanks sat on the perimeter. Steel ladders ran around each tank connecting the entire plant in a criss-cross of catwalks. Those catwalks were his way in.

Time was running out. The vampires would scatter before the coming daylight. He needed to get directly above the pack, hear what was going on and get word back to his teammates before having to fight.

And he knew there'd be a fight. No way would he leave that

virus in vampire hands. And he sure as hell was going to save Bana's ass.

In a low run, he dashed past a stinking mountain until he reached the nearest tank. Silently, he clambered up to the first catwalk then belly-crawled along it until he was crouching above the milling group below. He peered through the metal grill. Things looked like they were getting ugly. The vampires were growing more edgy as they prowled around Bana and the thieves. Bana, legs braced in a combat stance, had drawn both guns.

Tatsu felt a twinge of hope. Perhaps Bana was recalling how he protected people; not killed them. Or maybe he was just guarding his next meal. Regardless, Tatsu knew that even with vampire speed and strength, there was no way Bana could survive that many attackers.

Tatsu bunched his legs under him and braced himself to drop into a fight. He ducked when headlights swept across the plant. A car came through the gate and stopped a dozen feet away. The driver climbed out, slammed the door and strode toward the plant.

The vampires grew silent. A few shifted away from the figure walking toward them. Their sly, uncertain moves reminded Tatsu of a pack of coyotes waiting for a signal from their leader.

Although shorter than anyone else, the newcomer emanated incredible power. The creature's alabaster skin shone with an eerie translucence. His silver hair was tied in a samurai top-knot. The classically Japanese face, with it flowing mustache, could have been noble. But the sneering arrogance of the lips rendered the face ugly.

The vampire's ankle-length coat blew back and revealed a full *hakama* bound with an embroidered *obi*. A sword, so long it almost reached the ground, hung down the vampire's left leg.

With a sick certainty, Tatsu knew this was Ukita Sadomori, Daimyō of the Seattle Vampire Clan, and Arisada's *Seisakusha*.

"You have the virus?" Sadomori signaled to a heavy-set bull to take the biocontainer from the frightened thief. The bull popped the lid and examined the contents before tossing a canvas bag to the cowering man. "Quarter of a million, as agreed. You breathe a word, I'll pay you with something different." The monster cupped his crotch and thrust his hips out with a fang-filled smirk.

With trembling eagerness, the thief opened the sack and pulled out a wad of cash. Greed flashed across his face. When he waved the bundle at his partners, it split apart and scattered. Shouting with dismay, the men scrabbled about on their knees, stuffing bills into their pockets. Several vampires jeered and showed their fangs. One of the men pissed himself, and the pack roared with laughter.

Taking advantage of the chaos, Tatsu squirmed back into the deeper shadows of the tank. He pressed his dog collar against his throat and whispered, "Found virus. Twenty or more hostiles. Ukita is here."

"Sonofabitch. Copy that. ETA five, six minutes tops." Kaiden's response broke up.

Kuso, five minutes was too long. Tatsu squirmed back along the catwalk. The pack circled the thieves, who jumped and skittered like terrified deer about to be eaten alive. Sadomori stood apart, staring at the tableau with a look of disdain.

Headlights flashed at the far end of the street and raced toward the refinery. Tatsu' knew it was too soon for the Hummer. His throat went desert-dry when the sleek, silver Audi pulled up outside the gate. Arisada climbed out of the car.

Scalding hurt filled Tatsu when, for the first time in nearly a month, he beheld the one he loved.

Arisada's gaze swept the scene—the quivering fearful men, the dozen slavering vampires, the smug satisfaction in his Daimyō's face. He slipped his sword through his sash and strode toward the pack.

The stench of human fear and piss, coppery vampire tang, rotting garbage and old oil assailed him. Then he caught the merest hint of Tatsu's scent. His belly clenched. *Shimatta*, what in the name of the Buddha Amida was the boy doing here? He suppressed his reaction and continued his unhurried approach.

A few paces from Sadomori, he stopped and bowed. "*Seisakusha*, you sent for me?"

The Daimyō knew his Primary with an intimacy forged by centuries of fucking him. He immediately sensed the miniscule change in Arisada body. Fear coupled with arousal.

The Daimyō's nostrils flared, and he peered up into the spider web of steel above. He separated the new scent of life from the thick smell of blood-hungry vampires and cowering thieves. A youth—battle-ready, sexually aroused. A body filled with anger and grief. He could only be Arisada's soulmate!

Stark jealousy flashed through Sadomori. His lips lifted in a snarl, fang tips flashing white. He greeted his Primary in a voice ladened with venom. "Saito-san, you show me no respect by arriving late."

Arisada offered a sketch of a bow. "*Gomen nasai*, Daimyō. I only just received your message."

"Take charge of this matter for me, Saito-san." Sadomori nodded at the three frightened men. Relief flooded their faces. "I will deal with your disrespect later." He knocked Arisada aside with his shoulder when he strode to his waiting Mercedes. He tossed the container into the backseat before turning back to the group.

"Arisada, there is a hunter up in the scaffolding. Bring me his head." Sadomori smiled with a cold twist of his lips at the shock distorting his Primary's beautiful face.

Sadomori's departure signaled the pack. The vampires surged toward the humans. Blood howls rent the air. In a panic, the thieves bolted away from their van beneath Tatsu's hiding place. The pack surged after them.

Shit, now what? The sweep of wide-set headlights lighting the far end of the street answered Tatsu. Heedless of the danger, Tatsu jumped up, waving the *katana* in the direction of the departing car. "Mercedes. Sadomori has the virus! Go! Go! Go!" he screamed.

Chain slammed on the brakes, the truck leaving long, black skid marks. "*Merde*. Cobb or the car?"

"Little Super Ninja won't last long on his own. Needs backup." Praying for a signal, Kaiden dialed his cell. "But don't lose that fucking car."

Laughing, Chain jerked his chin toward the vanishing Mercedes. "You insult me, *mon ami*. This one is a *cochon*, and we know pigs can't drive." He skidded around the corner and caught a glimpse of the red tail lights of the Mercedes a block ahead. He stomped on the gas. The Hummer ploughed between two derelict cars, smashing them aside like toys. "This is easier than taking *grande-mère* on her Sunday drive to church."

"Stop being a wiseass and drive."

The Hummer took a hill, tires screaming. The Mercedes was mere yards ahead.

The second he saw the Hummer accelerate, Tatsu dashed back to his position. Some of the vampires were already running toward the ladder leading up to the catwalk. Others circled the cowering men, toying with them, feasting off the palpable wash of terror now filling the air. Directly below him, Tatsu spotted a distinct head covered by a thatch of curly black hair.

Shit, no sense in waiting. Howling the war cry of the Kurosaki Clan, Tatsu vaulted over the railing. His free hand folded around the thick links of the chain hanging from the gantry above his head. Brandishing the *katana*, he dropped twenty feet to land beside Bana.

"Hey, partner." Tatsu grinned. "Need help?"

Bana stared with surprise. The crimson glare in his eyes dissolved back into their hazel, human shade. "Boyo, what the fekking Christ you doin' here?"

"Saving your ass." Tatsu laughed at the familiar obscenity spitting from Bana's fanged mouth. Out of habit, the two moved back-to-back. Tatsu drew his second sword. Let out another war cry and began the fight of his life. Beside him Bana's guns began their distinctive chatter.

Arisada halted, stunned at hearing the ancient war cry of the Kurosaki Clan. Dismay filled him at the sight of Tatsu dropping into the slavering mob. Oh, my *koibito*, you possess such foolhardy courage. Arisada whipped out his *nodachi* and waded into the melee with only one purpose—to save the boy. One after another he cut down his own kind, fighting his way toward his lover.

Tatsu caught a flash of the fire-colored hair. A moment of fear filled him. Would Arisada fight alongside his Clan? Then Tatsu caught the silver-bright arc of Arisada's blade as it cleaved through one, then another of his kind. All Tatsu's doubt evaporated. Even if he died this night, he would be at Arisada's side.

"Come on, partner. We can take 'em." Tatsu turned to Bana. His mirthless grin dissolved in dismay at the distortion of Bana's face. Nothing of humanity remained in that fanged visage.

The scent of blood obliterated the last of Bana's rationale. He saw the red-haired vampire wielding a gore-covered sword. In a confused jumble, Bana recalled another night, another fight, when he'd tried to kill this same bloodsucker. With a scream of blind rage, he aimed his guns at Arisada's head.

"Bana, *kudesai*! *Kudesai*! Stop!" But the din of the fight drowned Tatsu's shout. In desperation, he slammed the back edge of his short blade across Bana's wrists. Too slow. Too late.

Bana pulled both triggers. White-hot bursts of incendiaries stitched across the torsos of several vampires and punched into the wall of the nearest gas tank.

Night turned to day in a blinding instant. The second tank exploded, then the third. Huge gouts of flame and black smoke boiled into the sky. Sheets of flesh-shredding metal spun like confetti over the site, raining death over everything. Then, with a mind-shattering roar, the world disintegrated.

Searing pain ripped through Tatsu. He didn't hear his own scream. The ground spun up to meet him and everything turned black.

Warehouses around the plant shook then collapsed as walls split. Roofs fell in. The road bucked like a rollercoaster, bouncing the speeding Humvee into the air.

"Earthquake!" Kaiden yelled a second before a massive

explosion tore the night apart. He spun around with a cry of utter horror.

The Cajun looked into the rearview mirror, eyes widening at the sun-bright ball boiling into the sky. "*Mon dieu, mon fucking dieu!*" He wrenched the steering wheel, fighting the bucking truck. With a scream of tires, the Hummer spun through a-hundred-eighty-degree turn and clipped a wall. Sparks accompanied the shriek of metal when the bumper sheared off.

Kaiden's temple smashed against the passenger-side window. His grunt of pain turned into several "fucks" at the sight of flames and roiling black smoke billowing hundreds of feet into the air.

The Mercedes forgotten, Chain careened insanely though streets filled with blinding smoke back to the plant. He skidded to a halt half a block from the raging inferno.

"Oh, Jesus Christ. No, no, no, not the kid." Kaiden leaped from the Hummer even before it came to a full stop.

The two Lepers were driven nearly to their knees by the heat. Thick, oily smoke choked their lungs and tore away their breath. The roar from the conflagration deafened them.

Angry flames lashed over acres of twisted metal and mountains of shattered concrete. Only the lower part of the central tower remained standing. The roofs of every tank had blown off and lay like bizarre, giant bowls. Both men ducked when the loaders exploded, flipping high in the air like chaff to crash upside down, their smoldering tires spinning.

Bodies, scorched beyond recognition, lay scattered about. The smell of burnt meat engulfed the two horrified men, the stench made hideous by the knowledge that it came from human flesh.

Dashing dangerously close to the inferno, Kaiden screamed Tatsu's name. Nothing. In grief-stricken resignation, the blond Leper staggered back to the Hummer. His hands shook when he punched in the emergency number on his cell for the Colony. An eternity passed, or perhaps a millisecond, before he heard Cooperhayes' calm voice. "Situation, Mr. Kaiden?"

"Mayday. Mayday. Mayday. Harbor Island power plant.

Explosion." Kaiden's cry tore into the tiny speaker. "The kid! Oh, God, the kid! He's..." His voice ended in a strangled cry.

"Copy that. I shall inform the Major. Back-up ETA, twenty minutes." Cooperhayes' voice shook with unaccustomed emotion.

Anger clouded Chain's senses while he scanned for any sign of the kid. "*Merde*! No one could've survived that!" He caught his partner around the shoulders, holding the distraught man against his broad chest. Murmuring in French, he said everything and anything to stop Kaiden from running into the inferno.

Over that blond head, Chain spotted a shard of steel glittering on the ground near the gate. He released Kaiden and, with a shaking hand, picked it up, realizing in shock, it was the lower half of Tatsu's *katana*. Light from the fire danced along the shattered blade.

"*Mon Dieu*. It's the kid's." His deep voice grated with anguish. Then he let his tears fall.

Nineteen

The sole survivor of the explosion writhed in agony, his face twisted into a hideous rictus. Blood and body fluids soiled the rich Persian carpet. Most of the creature's clothes were burned off, and the flesh beneath rendered to blackened meat. His wounds were so severe even his unnatural healing ability could not save him. "I saw Saito-san...fighting...slaying our kind—"

"Did you see a boy with him?" Sadomori interrupted in suppressed rage.

"*Hai, hai.* Bishounen...jade eyes, brown hair. Fighting...two swords...style of *niten'ichi.*" The vampire's scorched lungs labored but found no air.

Sadomori's gorge rose. His Primary had lied to him, disobeyed him and not killed that boy. The Daimyō knelt and stroked the matted hair away from the suppurating face. "Tell me, did you see Saito-san after the explosion?" The fury in his voice gave lie to his gentle caress. The mutilated vampire opened his mouth to reply but only gasped out a foul breath.

The door burst open and Nakamura Omi rushed into the room. He blurted out his news without waiting for permission to speak. "Daimyō, I believe Saito-san survived. When we arrived at the plant, his car was gone. A large group of hunters was already there."

"Why didn't you kill the filthy swine?" Sadomori glared up at his cowering underling through death-filled eyes. Blood-flecked spittle sprayed the air where his fangs sliced his lips.

The terrified *kyūketsuki* dropped to his knees, pressed his forehead to the floor. "*Gomen nasai.* I feared a fight with them would delay me. I deemed it was critical to tell you of your Primary's actions."

"I see the fear in your eyes, fear of mere humans. Your cowardice will not go unpunished. But, for now, I have more pressing matters." Without looking down, Sadomori drove his *tanto* into the burned vampire's eye. The creature's body convulsed once and its chest collapsed with an obscene rattle.

Sadomori wiped the blade on the corpse's clothing and stood. "Nakamura, get off your knees. Remove this offal. Pack up what we need. We're moving." Body vibrating with fury, he strode over to the window. He stared at the smattering of lights surrounding the silhouette of the Space Needle.

He spun around, catching the group of anxious *kyūketsuki* in a ferocious glare. Every vampire backed away, bowing. Sadomori smiled, the expression grotesque, twisted by his fangs.

"Destroy these hunters. But bring the traitor and that boy to the Needle. Do not harm them. The pleasure of their deaths will be mine alone. Do you understand?" His voice was all the more deadly for its sudden calm.

As one, the *kyūketsuki* exited the chamber. Their inhuman growls rising in anticipation of the hunt for blood.

Sadomori stared again at the tall spire above the night-shadowed skyline. Soon he would rule this miserable city, just as he ruled countless others in the past. He savored that thought of triumph and the killing that was about to come.

He was right to trust no one, not even his Primary, the one who swore to serve him until death. A thousand years ago, Sadomori Ukita was betrayed and now, again. Betrayed; always betrayed.

Satsuma Province, Nipon, Winter 798

The old woman shrieked when the apparition loomed out of the swirling snow. Her foot skidded in the frozen mud, and she dropped her straw basket of wood. Fagots scattered everywhere. A yard away, a horse crashed to the ground. Its cracked hooves scrabbled against the frozen ground leaving long gouges. The beast's final breath escaped its lungs in a wheeze when its gaunt ribs slowly collapsed. Steaming red-flecked foam dribbled from its stilled nostrils and turned instantly to pink ice.

The crone backed away from the beast, tripped and landed on her bottom. Her screeches of, "*Oni, oni*, save me from the demon!" reverberated through the small mountain village. The echoing shrieks drew the brave and foolhardy alike. Shivering in their thin cloaks, several men tiptoed closer to the fallen beast.

"Fools, stop your hysterical chatter. This is not the *oni*." Jurou, the village elder, hobbled through the crowd, shoving the gawkers aside with his staff. He knelt beside the brown, shaggy horse, and saw the rider pinned partially beneath the animal's gaunt flank.

"It is a samurai!" Jurou gasped with dismay. His trembling fingers pointed to the colors of the man's once-splendid *yoroi-hitarre* so tattered it no longer concealed the armor beneath. Jurou picked up the horned helmet from the snow, wiped off the slush and held it up to the crowd. "See this crest? It is Emperor Kurosaki's *mons*."

"It cannot be," a doubting voice cried from within the crowd.

Jurou stood as fast as his arthritic, old body allowed. "Dare you question me? While a youth, I saw this crest carried by his army when it marched out of Nara." All nodded their acceptance of this statement. Only Jurou had ever been out of the village.

"Only a real samurai could have endured crossing the winter sea and been strong enough to climb our mountains," a villager said, voice tinged with awe.

The head miner stepped beside Jurou and looked down at the fallen man. "But we sent our petition to the Shogun at the beginning of spring before planting began. Why send someone now, after the first winter snow?"

For the past year, an *oni*, an evil monster, had been brutally killing villagers during the night. Week after week, cries of horror had rent the morning air at the discovery of another body drained of its blood. So far, ten had perished.

"It is not for us to question the wisdom of the Shogun. He does things in his time. But he knows the iron we supply is the purest. He values us. He sent this warrior," Jurou said.

The old woman pushed herself to her feet. "There won't be any value if the man is dead," she snapped, reclaiming her dignity through her sharp tongue.

Jurou leaned over the inert body and placed his ear against the warrior's mouth. "He is alive. I feel his breath."

"We are saved," a young woman cried with joy. Smiles spread over the faces of the villagers at her announcement. They all bowed toward the unconscious man.

"Not if we let him die," Jurou shouted. "Stop this foolishness and get him to my home." Gesturing with flapping hands, he instructed several younger men to lift the horse from its rider. Villagers clustered around, clumsily pulling on the warrior's arms, tugging him from under the bulky carcass.

Jostling each other for the honor, the villagers carried the warrior up the icy pathway to Jurou's wooden hut. They maneuvered through the front door and lowered the injured man to the thin, straw-filled futon. At Jurou's impatient gestures, they dragged the rough bedding closer to the smoldering fire pit.

The crone, silent now, banked her meager collection of fagots onto the coals and fanned them to life with the edge of her ragged shawl. The wood was damp, its smoke making everyone cough.

Jurou's grandson lit the small oil lamp. It cast a dim circle around the room. "Hurry, we must see to his injuries. Fetch the *isha*, she will know how to heal him." Jurou regarded the warrior with deep alarm. The samurai's gaunt, wind-chapped cheeks and the dark hollows beneath his closed eyes attested to his starvation. The right leg bent back at an odd angle, perhaps crushed by the dying horse.

By now, eight villagers crowded into the small room. "He will need food, warm soup, meat," one woman said, wringing her chapped hands with fear of the privation everyone faced.

"But how? We barely have enough for ourselves. There was so little rice this year, and our few chickens would not go far to sustain one so injured." The pregnant wife of the chief mine engineer voiced the entire village's concerns.

"Our children will die," another woman echoed and

triggered a babble of frightened voices that filled the tiny hut.

"Silence!" Everyone cowed at Jurou's bellow. "Even if we starve, if our children die crying with empty bellies, we must save this man." Mutters of dismay rippled through the crowd.

"What about his horse? Can we use it?" The old woman suggested in a quavering voice.

"*Iie, baka.* No, you idiot. A samurai's warhorse is sacred. We cannot eat it," a man replied, calling the old woman a fool.

Jurou glanced down at the unconscious warrior and saw, not just an injured man, but the death of the entire village. *Wakatta,* he understood. Everything lay in Jurou's hands, including the consequences of his next words.

"Lord Kurosaki would demand we save his samurai at any cost. He will find it in his heart to forgive us using the warhorse to do so. After all, we did not kill the animal. We are not *eta's*, we do not normally butcher animals. But we must make an exception. Strip the carcass. Let no part go to waste. Take the marrow and boil the hooves into a jelly. Bring me the heart of the beast. I will make a rich soup for our guest. And surely the Shogun, in his wisdom, will not begrudge the bones to feed the serfs who are saving his valued warrior's life."

Three men volunteered to butcher the horse despite the sheer repugnance of the act. They shuffled out of the hut to get knives.

The candle burned away another hour before a harsh order at the door caused the villagers to crowd apart. Sanba, the *isha,* elbowed her way through the crowd to the injured man. Her eyes widened at the sight of the samurai's broken body.

"Everyone out. No one should view this man's indignity," she ordered. The villagers shuffled through the door, grumbling while they pulled their ragged cloaks tight against the fierce, winter wind. The last man out slid the door into place, leaving Jurou and his young grandson hovering behind Sanba.

She knelt on the worn *tatami* and, without looking at the headman or the boy, ordered them to undress the warrior. Together, they unbuckled the man's armor and stripped him to his *fundoshi.* She clucked with disgust at the filthy state of the undergarment, then cut it off and threw it in the fire. A foul stench washed over them. The boy scrambled to open the door and let in the freezing but fresh air.

"Fetch me another *fundoshi*. Make sure it is your finest," she commanded. Jurou bowed in her direction before scuttling into the back room of the house.

While her gnarled fingers examined his body, Sanba felt a certain admiration for the samurai's virile physique. Perhaps thirty summers, he was taller and stockier than any man in the village. His broad chest, covered with black hair, tapered down to a slim waist. When returned to full strength, the warrior would have thick, muscular thighs and calves. The samurai's head was narrow with a high brow and wide-set eyes. His face, covered by stubble, was not handsome, but his elegant nose, sensuous lips and cleft chin spoke of nobility.

Though Sanba no longer desired what hung between a man's legs, she admired the long cock curled against the samurai's large, dark balls. Then, feeling shamed by how her thoughts violated this nobleman, she turned her mind to the business of her craft.

Sanba sighed with relief when she found the knee was dislocated but not broken. "Hold his foot. Twist it the moment I say," She ordered Jurou, with no pretense at formality. Together they moved the limb back into place. She splinted the samurai's leg with bamboo staves and secured it with hemp.

Then, she turned to the source of the rank stench that filled the room. The samurai's left calf was inflamed from ankle to knee by a deep, festering wound. Sanba prayed the man would stay unconscious while she scraped away the putrid flesh and washed the leg with hot water and salt. Despite his deep coma, a moan of pain escaped the man's lips.

Sanba chanted healing prayers to her *kami*. When satisfied she had removed all the rotten flesh, she applied a poultice of mashed herbs and roots before washing off the soiled privates. Finally, she and Jurou wrapped the man in the clean *fundoshi* and covered him with blankets.

"We must do everything within our power to save his life. In turn, he will save ours." She handed Jurou a packet wrapped in a dockleaf. "Make him drink this in a tea at least four times per day. Force it down his throat if you must. Burn everything you own if you have to but do not let him get chilled. Keep him still. I have a child to deliver in the next village, but I will be back tomorrow at the hour of the dragon. Pray that he lives. If not, Shogun Kurosaki will not be forgiving, no matter how much iron we mine for him." Sanba bowed then hurried into the storm.

Jurou and his grandson looked at each other in fright. Yes, they feared the *oni*, but they feared the Shogun's wrath even more. If the samurai died, Emperor Kurosaki would execute the entire village.

The murmurs of voices dragged Ukita Sadomori away from the soft pillows of the courtesan's jasmine-scented breasts. Before his eyes opened, his nostrils told him he had only been dreaming he was in the Pearl House of Pleasure. The poor incense failed to mask the unpleasant odors of a peasant's hut. Sadomori opened his eyes to peer into the wrinkled face of a woman looming over him.

He struggled to sit up, but the old woman pushed him down with a gnarled hand on his chest. He opened his mouth to berate her for laying her coarse, peasant hands on him but his voice came out like the croak of a summer frog.

"Please, rest, noble lord. Here, drink this tea." Before he could refuse, Sanba placed the lip of a bowl against his lips and poured a small sip into his mouth. It soothed his parched throat. He swallowed. A warm lassitude spread through his limbs, and he slipped into a deep, natural sleep.

"He will live now." Sanba sat back on her heels, pleased at the success of her ministrations. "Tell everyone our lives may be spared."

With a wide smile, Jurou hurried from his home into the snow-laden streets. Shouts of joy soon filled the air as the villagers rejoiced in the reprieve from the fear that had gripped them for days.

He ordered the warrior's armor and *yoroi-hitarre* be cleaned and repaired. The *nodachi* remained sheathed in its scabbard. The law of the samurai—no, the law of the land—decreed instant death for any peasant who touched a samurai's weapon without permission. But, all this reverential care of the warrior's weapons might mean aught. Despite an exhaustive search, the man's *naginata* had not been found.

Jurou feared several in the village, including him, would pay the ultimate penalty for the loss of the spear. He forced those worries down. Life was life and death was death, *neh*? They would do what they could.

He demanded every household offer what valuables it had to replace the horse. Small coins, family heirlooms and ornaments filled a cloth sack. Men went in search of a mount suitable as a warhorse. If the animal were fine enough, maybe the samurai's anger would be mollified. If not, the warrior could demand a man's death—probably Jurou's—for authorizing the horse's consumption.

Five days later, Ukita Sadomori sat up. Although weak, he vented his anger at the loss of his horse. Then acknowledged the condition of his armor—fastidiously cleaned by Jurou—with a reluctant grunt of approval. He gulped down his first meal with no show of courtly manners. A villager brought a clay jar of sake, which the samurai downed in one long gulp. With a huge belch, the sated warrior rolled on his side, away from the peasants serving him, and fell asleep.

Since that day, the village had struggled to feed the warrior who healed with surprising speed. Within a week, he could hobble around the hut using a bamboo cane. Then, he demanded pillow rights. Jurou sent his young niece. The girl was a virgin. Nevertheless, the next morning she told her uncle that Ukita-san praised her creamy skin and shy obedience.

Ten days later, Sadomori summoned the village elders to Jurou's hut. The five men pressed their foreheads to the *tatami*. They trembled, afraid, yet prepared, to die under Ukita Sadomori's blade. True, they had saved the samurai's life, but they had butchered and consumed his horse. After a wait of many interminable minutes, the samurai grunted permission for them to raise their foreheads from the floor.

Jurou's face reflected nothing but calm although his heart

pounded with fear. He cast a sideways glance at the samurai who was truly resplendent in a new kimono sewn by Jurou's daughter. Yes, her work was above reproach and the fabric the finest the village had to offer. Jurou's satisfaction further increased when each man groveled before the warrior. Surely, the honor of his village would increase.

Sadomori sat immobile on a stiff cushion with his healing leg extended straight out. His *nodachi* rested by his left hand. The blade faced away from him, ready for use at a moment's notice. He was not pleased with the new *yukata*. The garments were crude, the silk not fine. The undergarment scratched each time he moved and bunched awkwardly around his waist. He had the right to kill these simpering men for this affront alone. However, Shogun Kurosaki needed them.

Jurou's daughter entered on her knees, her back bowed flat, her eyes downcast. She placed cups and a steaming teapot before Sadomori and backed out of the room. The samurai nodded to the headman to pour.

"Tell me about this *oni*, every detail. Leave out nothing, not even your own cowardly actions. Only then can I form a plan to rid my Lord of this nuisance." His impassive expression revealed none of his doubt in the villagers' story.

One-by-one, in order of social rank, the miners told of the fifteen bizarre deaths since the previous spring. Over the next few hours, Sadomori listened implacably to their tales of horror. He searched for inconsistencies as much as facts, winnowing out embellishments that arose from pride or fear.

"Get out. I have heard enough of your simpering." He dismissed them with an annoyed wave.

The miners shuffled out of the hut. "What if he doesn't believe us?" One man voiced the fears of all.

"*Hai, hai,* he showed no emotion when we told our tales," another replied.

"*Baka,* fools. Of course he believes us. But samurai never show emotion. Now get back to work and stop these foolish musings." The head miner Hideke stomped away to hide his concerns. Ukita-san had snorted with derision at their fears that the killings were caused by an *oni,* a demon.

The next morning, Hideke's eldest son was found drained of blood. The villagers' wails of sorrow echoed off the mountains while they carried the body to Jurou's home.

Ignoring the grieving family, Sadomori examined the corpse, taking his time with the four puncture wounds in the throat. "Bring me your maps of the mine."

"*Hai, hai*, most noble lord." Still sobbing, Hideke dashed from the house to return a few minutes later with a worn rice scroll. He dropped to his knees, lowered his head until it pressed against the *tatami* then, at Sadomori's grunt of acceptance, scuttled closer to proffer the precious map.

Sadomori spread the fragile document across his lap. "Tell me about this mine."

"As you see, most noble Lord, these are the adits we use to enter the mine." The engineer's grimy fingers shook when he pointed to lines branching from the central chamber. "This is the central chamber. From there the tunnels go deep into the belly of the mountain. Some collapsed during last spring's snowmelt and can only be entered with great difficulty. Perhaps the *oni* is hidden in one of them."

The samurai studied the scroll for a full candlemark. During that long hour, the miners knelt immobile, held by fear of making even a whisper of sound and interrupting his concentration.

"Tomorrow, give me a torch bearer. I kill this demon. I shall bear its head to my Lord Kurosaki. My family and my descendants will have proof of my prowess and my honor."

"My grandson will accompany you, most noble Lord." Jurou bowed, head pressed hard against the tattered mat. His voice trembled with pleasure at this rare opportunity to gain status for his family.

The next morning, the anxious villagers huddled inside their huts. None would venture out to watch the warrior leave on his mission. Through their paper-thin walls, they heard the samurai order the youth to follow, and the fading crunch of their footsteps in the snow when the two entered the forest.

At the entrance to the iron mine, Sadomori squeezed through the narrow opening of the adit into the main chamber.

He squatted and studied each branch. The minute but odd displacement of fallen rubble at the entrance to one tunnel spoke volumes to the seasoned warrior. This tunnel hid the lair of the *oni*.

Ignoring the bone-deep chill permeating the air, he avoided the many pools created by the constant drip of water from the ceiling down the scarred walls. They inched down the incline deeper into the bowels of the mountain. Soon he and the boy were ankle-deep in freezing water.

Twice, Sadomori cuffed the youth for lagging. Sadomori gave a small, grudging approval when the boy accepted his punishment with no noise. Frequently, Sadomori halted, held his breath and let the darkness speak to him. But he heard nothing save the groans and creaks of the mountain and the pervasive drip of condensation down the walls.

The incline of the slime-wet floor increased and made their feet slip. The tunnel narrowed, forcing even the boy to crouch. Sadomori discarded his helmet and cursed the bandits who had stolen his *naginata*. However, in the confines of the mine, the long spear would have been a hindrance. Hours passed while they moved ever more deeply into the mine.

At every deep fissure and juncture, Sadomori paused and scrutinized the shadows before moving on. He grunted with a deep satisfaction. He estimated it was now night and the monster should be awake. In his pride, Sadomori desired to fight the demon, not slay it while it slept.

The torch flame guttered when a sharp gust of air blew past them. Sadomori smelled the hint of an odor not natural to man nor beast. Then he heard the merest exhalation of a breath. It was the only warning he had.

The boy shrieked once before death took him. His body fell with a splash into the stream, extinguishing the torch with a hiss, and enfolding Sadomori and his attacker in complete darkness.

Sadomori, trained to fight blindfolded, spun toward the enemy, locating the *oni* by the wet sound of its breathing. With lightning moves, Sadomori slashed his blade back and forth. Snarls of anger and pain followed every strike.

He felt his blade tip graze along some part of the creature's ribs. Sadomori lunged, putting all his strength into driving the sword home. When he shifted his weight to his front leg, his sandaled foot slipped, only a little, but enough. His death-dealing thrust skidded along the monster's ribcage. Before Sadomori recovered his balance, talons locked around his throat.

Sadomori tucked his chin to gain a little air, but already the pressure around his trachea was excruciating. His lungs heaved for even the smallest gasp of air and his vision blurred.

Iie! No! He would not surrender his life to a demon. With blind desperation, he pounded the rounded, metal end of his *saya* against the creature's temple—three, four, five brutal blows. The monster grunted with each clout yet his deadly stranglehold did not loosen.

"I shall take you for my own, warrior," the *oni* growled in the impeccable dialect of the Imperial Court. He tore Sadomori's sword from his hand.

Stark horror possessed Sadomori at hearing the cultured language of the nobility. Teeth, sharper than any known weapon, punctured his neck. He ignored the pain while the scalding heat of his own blood gushed down his chest. He pulled his tanto from his *obi*. With mindless desperation, he drove the razor-sharp edge into the demon's thick neck. He heard a deep growl, but still those teeth never slackened their deadly hold.

In rank desperation, Sadomori twisted the blade, sawing it back and forth, praying to pierce the monster's brain. Unconsciousness threatened the samurai. A comforting black void that promised peace. Only his fierce will drove his blade.

The creature thrashed but its jaw refused to loosen. Blood—samurai and monster—sprayed the air, streaming down their thrashing bodies.

Suddenly, the monster's head separated from its shoulders. Jets of arterial blood drenched Sadomori's face. The body dropped to the floor with a splash, but the fangs remained buried in Sadomori's neck, the head resting on his shoulder like that of a hideous lover. He clawed at the rigid jaw and tried to pry it open. It was no use. Every tug threatened to tear out his jugular.

Exhausted, Sadomori sank to the ground, ready to embrace the Void. He prayed word of his triumph would reach home and enhance the honor of his family name. His last thought was for his Emperor.

Sadomori did not know how long he lay in the brackish water while he faded in and out of consciousness. There were times his body raged with fever, other times he shivered so violently he thrashed against the walls. He should have died; perhaps the utter cold in the tunnels sustained him.

When he finally woke, his throat was swollen, his mouth dry, tongue pressing thickly between his parched lips. No thought existed except to slake his thirst. He scooped up a handful of the filthy tunnel water. He retched at its foul taste but forced himself to sip a small amount. His body cried for more. Yet, he knew, to drink too much would bring death from belly cramps.

During his delirium, the putrid head had dropped from his neck. The wound from the monster's bite had festered, the stench of the pus one of many among the rank odors including his own shit. Exhausted, he sank once again, insensible, to the wet floor of the tunnel.

The second time consciousness returned, Sadomori knew he must quit the tunnel or die. The compulsion to bolt from the claustrophobic tomb of the mine nearly took his reason. With incredible strength, he controlled his panic. He would not leave until he found his sword.

Gagging on the putrid stench of decomposing flesh, Sadomori groped beneath the corpse and retrieved his *nodachi*. He located the monster's head, wrapped it in remnant of his coat and fastened it to his waist.

Time lost meaning. Sadomori inched his way up the incline. He ignored the decomposed remains of the boy when he passed the corpse. All that existed was the act of dragging one knee forward, then the other, repeating the move, all other thought subsumed by the metronome of that simple act.

He heard voices crying out for him only to fade away when

he called out. Other times, it was the whisper of a soft spring wind blowing through the sakura tress or the delight in his children's laughter. When at last the tunnel widened, he was too weak to stand. Babbling with delirium, he inched over the last pile of rubble and collapsed in the main chamber.

Many hours later, Sadomori awoke and stretched his limbs. He felt as refreshed as if from a deep, restful sleep in the most luxurious bed. New vigor pulsed through his body. He explored the hideous wound in his neck but could not even find a scar. Was the *oni* merely a terrible nightmare? No, the evidence of the creature's existence was a lump of decomposing flesh tied up in his cloak.

He exited the mine, stretched his arms and inhaled the clean, mountain air in great, intoxicating gulps. The sliver of a new moon showed through the clouds. He had been under the mountain for three weeks.

Despite his weakness, Sadomori found an icy pool. He dove in and scrubbed himself and his soiled clothing. This was no vanity; an enemy could detect a warrior who smelled. Then, he staggered toward the village. The steady beat of a human heart sounded as loud as a taiko drum. In fact, the sounds and scents of the forest were overwhelming in their intensity.

The smell of fresh blood assailed Sadomori's nostrils with such force he staggered. The delicious scent made him reel with hunger. His mouth flooded with saliva. He lurched from the last of the underbrush surrounding a field. In three swift strides, the samurai reached the man rising from his squat. Sadomori intended to demand succor from the peasant. Before the words left his lips, he embraced the peasant like a lover. His mouth pressed against the warm skin of the man's neck.

"My Lord, we... we feared you were dead," the man stammered in utter surprise.

The rich scent of blood filled Sadomori. One thought—feed. His fangs ripped from his gums. Driven wild by smell of his own blood, he struck, his teeth piercing the pulsing vein.

Never had he experienced such sublime joy as that of his first sip of hot, human blood. The coppery, sweet-salt taste filled him with ecstasy. Heedless of the body writhing in his grasp, Sadomori drank with feverish thirst. His member leaped awake, grew tumescent with painful desire. He had to fuck his prey. He tore his clothing aside, and freed his cock.

Too late, the life force had left the peasant's body. Sadomori held a cooling corpse. Lust fled the vampire. With a frustrated snarl, he dropped the body. He ran his tongue over his lips and razor-sharp fangs, licking away the last drop of blood. He had never tasted anything so sublime.

Then the horror flooded him when he understood the truth of his actions. He had not slain an *oni,* a demon. There was no *oni.* He'd killed a greater evil, a *kyūketsuki,* a monster that fed off the blood of men. And in that act, the samurai Ukita Sadomori lost his life and his humanity. What was left was a monster cursed never again to walk in the light of day. He raised his head to the indifferent stars and screamed his rage and loss.

Instinct kept him alive during his treacherous journey home. Instinct drove him to find shelter before the day's first light. Weeks of hiding, hunting, learning the ways of the night, honed a new set of killing skills for the cursed samurai.

His body hummed with its new supernatural strength. At first, the intensity of every sense was painful. He saw colors never before experienced. No sound within a hundred field-squares escaped him. There were times he recoiled at the fetor hanging over all human habitation. However, he could scent blood, or hear a heartbeat, from vast distances. Insatiable, he fed four or five times in a single night, not caring if it were man or woman. But he could not feed from a child. That first taste of a child's blood sent him reeling with revulsion.

His need for blood was matched only by his sexual hunger. Every time Sadomori fed, he fucked his prey. His climax was more intense than any he had ever known.

As his strength grew, so did his ambition. Before his transformation, Sadomori desired only to achieve the rank of *Hyoe no Suke,* captain of the Imperial Guard. Now, he wanted nothing less than the throne. It was his right. More than man, more than *oni.* he was *chi no kami*—a God of Blood.

Weeks later, during a cold spring rain, Sadomori arrived at the outskirts of the new capital Heian-kyo. Taking advantage of the storm, he slipped past the guards and travelled unseen through the city. His estate was but an hour north. When he crossed into his own *shoen,* a modest-sized holding of a few hundred acres, an unexpected peace settled in him. He noted with satisfaction that the fields were in order and spring planting was under way. His trusted overseer and wife would have kept his property in perfect order no matter how long he was absent.

Body thrumming with power, Sadomori planned his triumphant return. First, he would bathe. His most beautiful serving girl would dry and scent his body, then help him dress in his best clothing. He would tell the tale of his success to his entire household but not reveal the demon's rotting head. The next night, he would answer the summons of the Emperor Kurosaki no Gitako. Sadomori planned his tale to be eloquent yet thrilling, a story designed to validate his bravery. He pictured the Emperor commanding his generals to acknowledge Ukita Sadomori as the most-honored of all warriors. As a sign of his imperial favor, Kurosaki would grant Sadomori permission to climb the pedestal and sit on the right of the golden *takamikura*.

However, the moment Sadomori reached the side of the throne, he would pull out his rotting trophy and hold it aloft. He imagined every man rendered immobile with horror. Before anyone could react, Sadomori's fangs—the fangs of a God of Blood—would tear open the Emperor's neck and drain the royal blood. Then, he would slay every warrior present. Death would come with such swiftness that none would have time to react. There would be no honor in the killing, but Sadomori's ambition left no room for honor. None would be left to challenge Ukita Sadomori's right to the title of Emperor.

He climbed the final hill to his home, eagerly seeking the first glimpse of his ancestral banners. He halted, puzzled by the alien flags fluttering in the night wind. Why were the standards of Lord Oshahito flying above the main gate to his home? Where were the banners of the Ukita clan?

Sadomori crept around to the back wall, opened a hidden gate and slipped into the garden. So silent was his approach, he did not disturb the croaking of the young frogs. All appeared in order, the delicate sakura trees on the verge of blooming, his prized cypress trimmed to perfection, the plum trees were green with new leaf and tiny buds. He listened to the trickle of the streams connecting each pond and the distinctive "tock" of the *shishiodoshi's* bamboo tubes filling then emptying with water.

But the scent of his home was wrong—alien and rank. with foul odors of dozens of unknown males. One stank with the unwashed odor of a meat glutton. Sadomori knew of only one man who disdained the ritual of the bath—the brutal Commander of the Guard and the Emperor's first cousin, Oshahito no Kano.

Sadomori crouched lower among the bulrushes. He could not sense his wife, his children or his concubines. Brays, laughter and drunken revelry replaced the normal, orderly sounds of his household.

A *shiaijo* slid aside and a drowsy man, scarcely more than a youth, stumbled out. He made his way to the bamboo privy reserved for the lower castes. He fussed with his clothing and pulled out his penis. With a long sigh, he let out a hot stream of piss. The acrid tang of his urine filled the air.

Before the soldier tucked his prick away, Sadomori grabbed the man by the neck and threw him to the ground.

Sadomori stood astride the stunned guard. "Where is my family?" He leaned down and showed his fangs.

The man's eyes bulged at the hideous demon looming over him. "*Oni. Oni,*" he shrieked, and covered his face with his hands. He shit himself.

Sadomori dropped down, driving one knee onto the man's chest, hearing the sickening crunch of broken ribs. Snarling with fury, Sadomori gripped the guard's shoulder and ground the joint until it parted from its socket. The guard's eyes rolled into his head as he nearly fainted.

"Again, why do Lord Oshahito's banners hang from the walls of *my* home?"

Garbled phrases spilled from the man's lips. Within moments, Sadomori knew everything he valued—his lands, his family and his honor—was lost. Emperor Kurosaki no Gitako had murdered the entire Ukita line. Sadomori's wife had slit the throats of her three children, including his infant son, before taking her own life. His consorts had committed *seppuku* and his loyal guardsmen had died defending his household and his name. Every serf had been sold to the slavers from China.

"When did this happen?"

Only blubbering noises came from the guard's mouth.

"When?" Sadomori snarled, spittle dropping from his lips.

The soldier defecated again. "The week after you left for the mining village. The Shogun decreed you *dassōhei,* a deserter."

Cold hatred filled him when he realized the monstrous extent of the betrayal. The moment he left on his mission, all he valued was stolen. What a fool he had been! A trusting fool who believed his Emperor valued him. Sadomori's mind raced, recalling tiny clues and minute insults that should have alerted him. When a band of well-armed brigands ambushed his vanguard, he should have sensed treachery.

He considered the law of the land, which dictated all samurai live or die at the will of the Shogun. But to take lives and property without justifiable cause was immoral, an act of pure greed.

And to brand Ukita *dassōhei* was unforgivable.

With less effort than breaking a straw, he snapped the young guard's neck. He would not deign to drink the blood of one who served the Kurosaki name. In pure rage, Ukita Sadomori threw his head back and howled into the night sky.

Dozens of guards poured from the house, brandishing their weapons and shouting at the unknown threat. Sadomori leaped to the top of the high palisade and crouched on its thin edge. His face was a hideous mask, all trace of humanity gone.

"I swear by all Gods, all *kami,* all *oni,* I will exterminate the House of Kurosaki from this land. Not a single soul will escape. Not the highest general or the lowest of the *eta* will live. Bear witness, oh God of Blood, the last breath of air to fill my lungs will be free of the taint of these names, these vilest of scum." He hurled the vampire's putrid head toward the house. It splattered against the wall, leaving a foul, black stain.

"That is now my new *mons*, the mark of *kyūketsuki*." He screamed before disappearing into the night.

Not even time could stand in the way of his revenge.

Twenty

The Seattle Quarantine, 2024

Tatsu was drowning. His lungs burned, breath gone. The wave inundated him, tumbled him deep into the freezing murk. Rocks battered his body, every jar wrenched a cry from his numb lips. Each time Tatsu broke the surface, another black rush thrust him back under. His arms and legs thrashed with blind desperation. Mindless, he fought for the elusive surface.

His head broke free. With great gasps, he sucked in a precious lungful of air. His leaden legs kicked furiously against the undertow that threatened to drag him down into the abyss of terrors yawning beneath him. A wave pummeled him under, then another, in unending rolls. Exhausted, he surrendered and sank to the bottom.

"Wake up *Atsilí*!" Sage commanded. Tatsu dragged his eyes open against the weight of the dark water. The Navajo stood before him. Sage's hair swirled like black seaweed in the green murk of the water. "Fight! It is not your day to die, my little Ninja Boy," he commanded.

"Sage, I want to go with you."

"*Atsilí*, your journey is not yet done. Your love waits for you. Now, swim!" The Navajo, eyes full of sadness and regret, smiled and drifted away.

Tatsu reached out, his fingers clutching, eager to grasp his boyhood love. From far away Tatsu heard Sage's voice; or was it that of another?

"Come back to me, *koibito*. Come back. Please, for the love I bear you."

Tatsu fought for the heaving, distant surface.

"He fights hard, that one." Fornax held the writhing Tatsu

facedown by his shoulders. The vampire ignored the stench of blood, sweat and bodily fluids each time the injured youth thrashed beneath his hands.

"Please, keep him still. He mustn't open his wounds," Dr. Amos cautioned as he debrided the suppurating flesh before spreading ointment over Tatsu's hands. He began wrapping a fresh dressing over Tatsu's weeping skin. "On first examination, I thought he would die. But the internal bleeding stopped spontaneously, and the fractured bones are knitting at an incredible rate. As for the burns, I've never seen skin regenerate like this with no signs of scarring. His protective clothing saved most of his back. I can't believe he's still alive.."

"He must live." Arisada fed another injection of morphine and antibiotics into the saline drip.

The doctor noted fresh bloodstains on the back of Arisada's kimono. No use offering aid. The vampire had refused all treatment, declaring he had no time for it until the boy was out of danger.

The physician packed his bag before doing a final check of the readings on the heart monitor. "I've ordered more supplies on my private account. No one will know who they're for. I'll bring them tomorrow."

"*Domo arigatō gozaimasu, sensei.* Once again my apologies for the blindfold, it is for your own safety." Arisada offered a short, distracted bow, his eyes already travelling to the patient. Without another word, the doctor left the room.

Fornax lingered at the doorway for a moment, regarding his *Seisakusha*, the *kyūketsuki* he respected and loved.

"Fornax-san, please inform your Major that Cobb is alive but don't reveal his whereabouts." Arisada sat on the bed, hands cupped before his face as if praying.

"*Arigatō*, Saito-san. I didn't like that you ordered me to say nothing to the Major or the Lepers for so long. They are hardened men but they still grieve."

"*Wakatta,* there was no point in giving them false hope. I will bring the boy to the hunters as soon as he is well."

"You are in love with this human. He is the one, *neh?*" the smaller vampire asked without judgment or rancor.

"*Ha, hai.* He is the one. I would gladly give up everything, including my soul, to be sure he is safe." Arisada brushed a hank of damp hair from Tatsu's forehead.

"Sadomori will kill you for this."

"Perhaps. At least, he will try. The only way to ensure my *koibito's* safety is to for me to kill my *Seisakusha*. Once that is done, I will leave this city forever."

"What about the danger you pose the boy now?"

"Ironic isn't it? Even as I wish to protect him, I am the greatest threat to his life. I should have stayed away. To my shame, I could not. But I promise you, he will be safe in my care. As much as I detest it, I will feed every day."

"I do not envy you. A love like yours is a terrible thing." With a short bow, Fornax left the room. Like the doctor, he was astounded that the boy lived. For the past four days, Fornax had cared for Tatsu during the brief times when Arisada left the house to feed from the runaway indentured hiding at the other end of the island.

Fornax knew Tatsu disliked him, but as he dressed the boy's suppurating burns, he became impressed with the young man's courage. Perhaps Cobb-san was worthy of Arisada-sama's love.

Arisada ignored the agony from his own injured back as he washed Tatsu's sweat-covered body. He traced the puckered scars on Tatsu's throat and across his bicep. Obviously vampire bites, yet Tatsu had escaped infection. Of more concern was the tattoo over the youth's right breast. Arisada knew that *mons* well, yet he believed every member of that family had been eradicated.

His heart thrummed each time he regarded the strength and beauty in Tatsu's face. More than once, he stopped himself from kissing those sweet lips. The vampire felt no shame when his cock throbbed each time he cleaned Tatsu's buttocks and genitals. Arisada ached to feel the weight of those long, lithe legs on him while he buried his cock in Tatsu's core. But he knew it would never be. He sighed with desperate resignation.

Close to dawn, Tatsu awoke with a gasp and stared with uncomprehending eyes at Arisada. "My *koibito*, welcome back," the vampire whispered. Without saying a word, Tatsu slipped beneath the calm waters of his first real sleep.

Arisada laid his head by the youth's inert arm and wept with gratitude, giving thanks to whatever *kami* kept the boy alive. Tatsu slept on peacefully, his long lashes lying soft like a baby's against his pale cheek. One last glance back at his beloved, then Arisada left the room.

The vampire smiled while he showered. Tonight, he would send a message to Dr. Amos telling him his services were no longer needed.

Arisada bolted the steel door and set the primitive alarm at the head of the stairs descending to his basement bedroom. He lit several candles, not because he needed the light, but for the comfort from the flickering incandescence. Dropping his soiled yukata into a wicker basket, he dove with a grateful sigh under the steaming shower.

Exhausted, he fell onto his platform bed but he could not sleep. With a shiver of dread, Arisada considered Tatsu's tattoo. Ukita Sadomori wore an amulet with an identical design. The ancient vampire often bragged how he tore it from the neck of a woman he killed in Nagasaki. A woman Sadomori believed was the last of the Kurosaki house.

With a gasp, Tatsu jerked awake. Disoriented, he stared at the peach-colored ceiling. Where the hell was he? The infirmary? A hospital? What the fuck had happened to him? The pounding headache doing an imitation of a taiko drum in his head turned thinking into a major chore. Flashes of chasing after a white van, yelping dogs. Oh yeah, he'd crashed his bike. No, more had happened after that, but his pounding head refused to cooperate.

Nausea assailed him when he sat up and threw off the thin blanket. Thick bandages encompassed his left hand and more compressed his ribs. Their pressure hurt each time he moved. Sharp stabs of pain shot up his legs and back.

He scraped the crud out of his eyes and peered around. At first the room seemed familiar, comforting, as if he was home in Nagasaki. Vertical mahogany strips accented the soft yellow walls, which looked like they were made from thick rice paper. Even stranger, a clutter of medical equipment, including heart monitor, oxygen tank, dressings and medication, crowded together on a wheeled metal cart in one corner.

Despite the weakness making him shake, he swung his bare legs over the side of the bed. The movement rattled the stand next to his bed holding an intravenous drip bag feeding into his right arm. He fumbled off the tape holding the needle and pulled it out.

Tatsu slid from the bed and froze the second his feet hit the floor. The surface beneath his bare soles felt so familiar. He looked down at his toes curling over a *tatami* made from rice straw. Okay, definitely not in a hospital. But where?

The unmistakable urgency in his bladder said to forget about the where. He staggered into the adjoining bathroom. Pissing felt good. It also hurt like hell. The rawness around his cock slit told him he'd had a catheter in him.

By the time he got back to the bed, his muscles had the strength of overcooked soba noodles. The pain in his ribs screamed at him to rest, but he had to find out where he was and how he got here. *Kuso!* No sign of his weapons or gear. Cell phone missing too.

Beside his bed, he found a pair of black, rubber-soled slippers. He shoved his feet in, surprised by the shoes' perfect fit. Another mystery. A plain, cotton yukata hung over the end of the bed. He pulled on the garment and tied the obi.

Tatsu clutched his ribs with his uninjured hand and willed his wobbly legs to move to the door. He slid it aside before realizing it was a *shoji,* a Japanese sliding door. He stepped into a narrow hallway lined with light green *tatami* that complemented the smoky-grey walls hung with delicate Japanese prints. The house, if it was a house, reminded Tatsu of his home in Nagasaki.

"*Ohayō.*" He called good morning since he had no idea of the time of day. Heard no response, nothing in fact. "Just keep moving, Tatsu," he muttered. "Find some freaking answers."

He slid aside the door facing him, stepped over the threshold and stared, dumfounded. Thin light from the quarter moon filtered through the beveled-glass roof. It cast a silver wash over the perfect, rectangular *ikinewa*, a pond garden. Lines of groomed sand created a balanced symmetry among the rocks, night-blooming dragon-fruit and primroses. Off to one side, a waterfall trickled into a natural-stone pool filled with koi and water lilies.

Fighting nausea and weakness, Tatsu checked each room off the garden. One was *chashitsu*, a Japanese tearoom. The soft cushions around the low, teak table looked inviting to an exhausted Tatsu. Beyond it, he saw an alcove that held a modern kitchen. No windows, no exits. Another door from the garden opened on a second bedroom with an adjoining bathroom complete with modern fixtures and in-floor spa. Steam rose from the bubbling water. Again, no windows, no exits.

He entered another room. His breath caught at the exquisite beauty of the tiny *shoin,* a room used to display spiritual heirlooms. An exquisite painting of a sakura tree in full bloom covered the entire far wall. A *butsudan*, a small wooden cabinet with small front doors, held a clay bowl and scrolled paper *fuda*. He wondered who'd written the prayer on the scroll. Still, he refrained from touching it. *Fudas* bore sacred words for the *kami* of the petitioner.

Sticks of incense smoldered in a bowl of sand in front of the *butsudan.* A group of three rocks sat before a statue of Buddha Amida. A fission of grief lanced Tatsu. The three stones, perfect in their symmetrical placement, reminded him of *Ojii-san's* shrine, so far away in time and place.

Behind the statue, a floor-to-ceiling rack held a dozen beautifully decorated *katana*. *Hai,* weapons! Tatsu seized one, slid it from its saya and froze. Impossible! This sword could not be authentic. Yet the clear lines in the blade, the leather wrapping around the *tsuka* and the distinctive decoration of the guard, were unmistakably the design of the famous eighteenth century swordmaster Suishinshi Masahide. Tatsu had seen many paintings of this sword in books. This particular *katana* was long-considered lost. How was it here, in this house? Overcome with reverence, he returned the weapon to the rack. He checked the others. All were authentic, all were ancient. Despite his need, he felt utterly unworthy to take one, and turned his back on the precious treasure.

The building reminded him of the *shoin-zukuri* houses of the ancient samurai. However, unlike a traditional *shoin-zukuri* that sits within a garden, this house surrounded the garden. Also unlike a *shoin-zukuri,* this place had no windows.

Bullshit! There had to be a way out of this house.

Floor to ceiling murals covered the garden's end walls. He stared at a magnificent triptych of the Byōdō-in Phoenix Hall, the Buddhist temple in Kyoto. His tap on the center panel produced a hollow knock. There had to be a door behind it. Tatsu pushed and pulled on the panel with no luck. He smoothed his hands down each joint, but found no latch. More prodding over the frames of the two adjacent panels yielded no results. *Kuso*!

Clutching his ribs, Tatsu shuffled to the opposite wall featuring a stunning, life-sized mural of a *torii*, a traditional gate constructed from two wooden pillars and ornate, curved cross braces. Just beyond lay a small Shinto shrine. So realistic were the details of the shrine's gate that Tatsu reached out to push it open. A gasp escaped him when his fingers found the edges of a real *shoji*.

His increasing pain clouded his thinking. What kind of a paranoid idiot lived in a house with no windows or doors? A cold chill ran between his shoulder blades, dampening any excitement at the possibility of escape. He was surrounded by representations of two religions: Shinto and Buddhist.

Kuso, how could he be so *baka*? With a complete certainty, he realized all this beauty reflected the taste of a certain flame-haired vampire. Despite his injuries, Tatsu's groin responded with a distracting, totally out-of-place, throb of desire.

He turned to go back to his room. Muffled cries like an animal in agony came from the other side of the garden. Tatsu's concern about escape evaporated as he tore across the bedroom that led to the bathroom. When he pushed aside the door, he could only stare in horror, his throat closing on his offer of help.

Arisada stood trembling in the center of the steaming spa. His back was to Tatsu. Head bowed, the vampire's arms shook while pressing in clear desperation on the smooth tiles. The remnants of his glorious mane lay in short wet curls against the nape of his neck.

Huge, suppurating blisters covered his back from his shoulders to his clenched buttocks. Nothing remained of Arisada's beautiful tattoo. Tatsu knew the loss of that art caused the vampire far more anguish than any injury to his body.

With another agonized groan, Arisada lowered himself into the steaming water. He seemed oblivious of Tatsu standing frozen in the doorway.

A single memory burst into Tatsu's mind: That long, beautiful hair, flaring like flames in the wind as Arisada fought to reach Tatsu's side.

In that moment, looking at the *kyūketsuki*'s ruined back, Tatsu's heart broke. Waves of insane, irrational emotion gripped him. The tsunami caught him, sweeping away all other feelings except a powerful and undeniable love.

Stunned, Tatsu slid the door closed and staggered back to the sanctuary of his room. He fell onto the bed. Exhaustion claimed him. Tomorrow things would make sense, tomorrow—

A pounding beat woke Tatsu. Not the thumping of the migraine that had plagued him the day before, but the rhythmic sound of reggae. What the hell? Reggae? His nose caught the rich aroma of fresh coffee, distracting him from the music.

Puzzled, he sat on the edge of the bed. His bandages were gone. When he pressed on his ribs and leg, he felt only a twinge of pain. Creamy, healthy skin replaced the raw burns of only a few hours ago. He couldn't have been hurt that much. He sniffed. *Jigoku*, he stank. He needed a shower, like right now.

Resisting the heady lure of coffee or the mystery of the Jamaican rhythms, he stood for a long time under the bliss of steaming water. The scent of the sandalwood soap—masculine, sexy—called to mind Arisada. Tatsu toweled off, pulled a fresh *yukata* over his still-damp body and slipped his feet into the slippers left by his bed.

Dammit, he had to reach the Major, but first, answers. No, first, find the source of that coffee, then answers. Tatsu followed the tantalizing smell across the garden. He slid open the door to the dining room and stared at the exquisite *chashitsu,* a low table set for two.

Arisada turned to greet him from the tiny kitchen alcove beyond. "*Konban wa. Watashi no ie ni youkos.*" That friendly phrase welcomed Tatsu to the vampire's home.

"*Arigatō gozaimasu.*"

"Tatsu-san, it is good to see you're up, so to speak." Arisada smiled at his double entendre. He held up a glass coffee pot. "I have just made it fresh. Would you like some?"

The absurdity of seeing a vampire playing host hit Tatsu. He laughed. It made his ribs hurt like hell but he couldn't stop. "*Sumimasen.* I don't mean to be rude. I just didn't expect to see you making coffee."

"Why not? I enjoy the taste." Arisada smiled and handed Tatsu a steaming mug. "I hope you take it black."

Tatsu took a long, appreciative drink and lifted the mug in salute. "This is good." He stifled a laugh. "And, Reggae?"

Arisada shrugged as if to say, "why not?" then turned off the music. He waved toward the adjoining *chashitsu*. "Sit. No doubt you have many questions."

Tatsu knelt on the *zabuton,* placing his mug on the low table between them. "What the hell happened? How did I get here? How long? Where are my weapons? My cell? Where's Bana?"

"I am sorry, but Bana is dead."

The shock of Arisada's statement stunned Tatsu. No, not Bana. It couldn't be. Last Tatsu remembered, he and Bana had been fighting side-by-side. Partners.

"Bana's dead?" Tatsu couldn't believe it. "But he was trying to save those men."

Arisada held up one slim, elegant hand. With a deep show of reluctance, the vampire described the explosion. "I saw it, too, Bana's moment of humanity when you reached his side. But I saw his eyes change as he reverted to his vampire state. He fired at me when he saw I was killing *kyūketsuki*. He missed and hit the tank. I managed to fling you to safety before it exploded."

Tatsu's mind reeled. That Bana, a vampire, had died trying to save humans was a horrible injustice. That it happened six days ago made the death unreal. "He cannot be dead."

"*Sumimasen*, Tatsu-kun. The explosion destroyed the plant. I doubt any survived."

"No way, you're wrong." Tatsu's voice grated with suppressed grief. His skin turned freezing. He blinked rapidly, his eyes gritty as if full of dust. Then, details of that night flooded back—the theft, chasing a white van, the shock of Arisada's arrival, the screams of the mauled thieves, the staccato of Bana's automatics.

"Why were you there, Arisada?"

"I was summoned by my Daimyō. I knew nothing of the theft. Imagine my dismay when I saw you. The one you call Bana was fighting at your side, killing *kyūketsuki*. When he fired at me, his bullets punctured the tank. I had mere seconds to save you. No time to help any others."

The sick realization that Arisada had taken the full force of the explosion churned in Tatsu's gut. If not for that single act, he would be dead. Gratitude, fear, resentment, anger—a range of unwanted emotions rocked him.

"Why didn't you take me to the Colony? Why here?"

"Every *kyūketsuki* under Ukita's command is hunting for you. The Daimyō is hunting for the Leper Colony's location. My home is safer."

"I have to report in. My team... they think I'm dead."

"Do not be alarmed. Fornax informed your Major who agreed that you should remain here until you heal."

"The Major knows?" Tatsu felt a twinge of betrayal. He'd been left with this vampire at the Major's decision.

Arisada smiled thinly. "He gave his consent."

"Fuck that. Give me the keys to your car," Tatsu snapped and pushed himself to his unsteady feet.

"I cannot, you are far too weak to drive. And don't think about walking. We are on an island several miles from Seattle." He reached out to steady Tatsu but drew back at the boy's glare.

Tatsu snorted. One way or another, he was going to get out of this house of no-fucking doors. "Then give me your cell. I have to report in now."

The vampire shook his head. "Gladly, but it won't help. There is no signal. Dawn is too close. I promise, we will go tomorrow night." He felt a raw desperation to have Tatsu for a short time longer.

Weakness washed over Tatsu. His legs trembled, knees buckling. With a sigh of resignation, he dropped down, butt resting on his heels. "*Fakku.*"

Arisada smiled at the profanity. Adorable coming from that sweet bow of a mouth.

"*Wakatta.*" Tatsu's shoulders drooped. "Do you have anything to eat around here?"

The vampire bowed. "I apologize. You must be famished. Will miso soup and *oyako donburi* do?"

Tatsu's stomach rumbled and his mouth watered at the thought of the spicy rice dish. "*Arigatō,* it all sounds perfect. And tea, please."

At the boy's acceptance, the vampire relaxed. He went into the kitchen and began preparing the meal. Tatsu studied that profile haloed by its shorn locks. Remembered hearing those hideous groans of agony, seeing that ravaged torso, those suppurating wounds. He recalled with a terrible guilt how Arisada received those injuries. The urge to comfort the vampire, no matter how inadequate, overwhelmed Tatsu.

"I saw your back when you were in the hot tub."

"I know." Arisada put ingredients together, placing them into a saucepan. His actions were precise and elegant. Still, Tatsu saw the pain in the vampire's every movement.

"You were burned, your skin, such pain. And that beautiful tattoo, destroyed saving me. It seems inadequate, but *domo arigatō gozaimasu.*" He looked down at the table to hide the wet gathering in his eyes. "How badly was I injured?"

Arisada hesitated. He did not want to tell Tatsu of that night. He stalled by bringing the pot of tea to the table and pouring a cup for Tatsu. "You fractured three ribs. Also, you had a severe concussion and multiple stab wounds that caused internal bleeding. Burns. For a time, the doctor did not think you would live. But you fought hard. I have never known a human to recover so quickly."

"I always heal fast." *Really fast.* A Santa Fe doctor made remarks like "unnatural" and "inhuman" after Tatsu's rapid recovery from a severe beating at school. One more difference that added to his shame.

"Your combat clothes are truly remarkable. I have no doubt they prevented you from being severely burned."

No, you saved me from being burned, the thought filled Tatsu with a rush of gratitude.

"*Â, sō desu ka*, regardless of the reason, I thank the Buddha that you survived." To hide the emotion welling within him, Arisada went back to the kitchen. He returned with a tray of food. He placed a bowl of soup and a plate of steaming *oyako donburi* on the table. "Please, eat. I do not want to add the guilt of starving an honored guest to my many sins."

Tatsu, overwhelmed by the comfort in the invitation, dove into the soup. It was wonderful. He hadn't eaten food like this since he left Japan. He noticed Arisada taking a spoonful of rice. "I thought vampires didn't eat real... er... human food."

"It won't sustain us, but old habits die hard. I like the ritual of the meal, *neh*?"

Tatsu finished the soup and dug into the spicy dish. After a few minutes of silence, he pushed aside his empty plate. "*Arigato*. That was wonderful. I didn't know I was so hungry." He cocked his head to one side, a quizzical gesture he hadn't used since his mother died. "I'm grateful you have something to eat around here. I mean, besides me." Deep pink crept over his cheekbones.

"I am happy to be of service to you." Arisada smiled as his heart quickened at the boy's charm.

Tenderness for the vampire sitting across from him blossomed through Tatsu. With all certainty, he knew he loved

Arisada. Fighting the need to blurt out his feelings, Tatsu said the first thing that came to mind. "So this is your home? Isn't a Japanese house kind of obvious?"

"Only the interior is Japanese. The exterior is a typical, brick ranch, boarded up and long abandoned. It is quite safe."

"Yeah, safe all right. How the hell do you get out of here? Fly through the garden roof?

Unexpected laughter spilled from Arisada's beautiful mouth. "*Mochiron*. Of course! I am a vampire, after all. Rest assured, the entrances are completely hidden."

"And you built this yourself?"

"With help. The original house was designed around an indoor swimming pool. I simply rearranged everything with a little modification. Except for the garden atrium, the house is lightproof. And it is impregnable."

"Huh, some modification. How can you keep this place a secret from your own Master?"

"We are not all fanatical followers of the Daimyō's path. There are a few trusted *kyūketsuki* who keep my secrets as I do theirs. They are sick of Sadomori's pathological hatred; his sadistic torture of humans."

"Why did Sadomori steal the virus? Makes no sense."

The vampire poured them each a cup of tea before replying. "I am certain he plans to use it as a biological weapon. Create a vast army of vampires."

"An army for what?"

"To enforce his rule. He is a sociopath. Until he has complete power, he will not rest. Over the centuries, he has succeeded many times."

"*Jigoku*. I've got to let the Major know."

"Fornax has informed him."

Fornax; Arisada's Primary. Jealousy pricked Tatsu. "So, how much danger are you in?" he asked over the bowl held beneath his lips.

"Sadomori is seeking revenge on everyone including me. In saving you, I betrayed him. But I will never regret my choice."

The vampire cleared the table then brought a flask of sake and two tiny cups from the low sideboard. "This may help you relax." He poured the drinks. "You wear a tattoo also. Tell me about it." He silently prayed that the reason behind the design was superficial, a mere youthful fancy.

"It's the *mons* of my family, the Kurosakis. Why'd you ask?"

"Just curious. Most unusual design." He hid his shock behind a sip from his cup. He suppressed his fear that the day would come when Tatsu discovered Arisada had lied about knowing of Sadomori's vendetta. On that day, Arisada knew he would lose any chance of Tatsu's love.

To avoid further questions, Arisada rose and left the room. When he returned, he handed Tatsu three objects. "Your harness, *wakizashi* and *tanto*. I regret there was no time to find your *katana*.

Tatsu smoothed his fingers over the worn, familiar leather. Sadness from the loss of his *katana* thickened in his throat. "*Domo arigatō gozaimasu,* Saito-san."

"Perhaps you wish to dress. Your clothes are in the bedroom closet."

Tatsu pushed to his feet. The room swirled around him. His knees buckled.

Arisada's arms enfolded Tatsu, steadying him with warmth and strength. The vampire guided him back to his room and helped him ease onto the bed. Before the blackness rolled over Tatsu, lips brush his forehead. He heard a whispered, "*Ashiteru*, Tatsu-kun."

Fourteen hours later, Tatsu stood beneath a hot shower, flexing his arms and legs. Marveling at how good he felt, he slid his hands over his soap-slicked chest and belly. No signs of injuries. No scars either. When he stepped out, naked and dripping wet, an unmistakable, sex-filled murmur of appreciation startled him.

"I forgot these last night." Arisada held out fresh towels.

"Bullshit, you just want to check out my ass," Tatsu growled, but his skin warmed all over.

"Tatsu-kun, I have been *checking out* your ass, and the rest of you, for nearly a week. I am happy to say that it, and all other parts of you, grow healthier every day."

Tatsu opened his mouth to reply, said nothing. Arisada was standing behind him, settling a fluffy towel over his shoulders. "You missed a spot of soap," the vampire murmured with a gentle caress. Arisada smiled at the flurry of goose bumps popping out over Tatsu's honey-colored skin. "Let me dry you."

Before Tatsu could protest, the fabric was moving over his back, his buttocks and between his thighs. Want took charge of his brain. His skin begged for the vampire's naked touch. With a sudden and painful urgency, Tatsu's cock filled, jutting outward, a single pearly drop already beading on the head. *Fakku,* he wanted pull his cheeks apart and offer his ass to the vampire.

Arisada peered over that shoulder down the planes of the torso to the hard prick, visibly bouncing with every heartbeat. How he ached to slide his hands around those sharp hipbones, and stroke that hot pillar of flesh. His cock screamed for him to bend Tatsu over the sink, spread his butt-cheeks and core him hard and fast. Dangerous, too dangerous. Hissing with sheer frustration, the vampire stilled his hands.

Tatsu felt the mood that promised such possibilities suddenly evaporate. Confused, he snatched the towel, wrapped it around his waist and spun to face the vampire.

"*Domo,* I can dry myself." Arousal edged Tatsu's voice. He blushed at his hard-on tenting the towel.

"Of course you can." There was a slight note of petulance in Arisada's voice. The drape of his silk yukata could not hide his erection. "When you are done, please join me in the *chashitsu* for breakfast." Muttering about a cold shower and clothing with belts and zippers, Arisada fled.

"Breakfast? Rather have you," Tatsu muttered.

Half an hour later, they knelt on the cushions around the *chashitsu.* Arisada set a plate of adzuki buns on the table then stirred the tea. He yearned to lean across the small table, place one finger below Tatsu's chin, tilt his face up and kiss him. Offered a compliment instead. "You look quite regal in that yukata."

"Stop looking at me like I'm a girl," Tatsu snapped then glanced away in embarrassment.

The vampire's mouth quirked upward. "Believe me, Tatsu-kun, if you were a girl, I would not look at you at all."

"Whatever." Tatsu tried to sound disgruntled but it came off badly. "Have you always liked men?" he asked even as he yelled at his brain to "stop with the horny pictures."

A look of amusement lightened Arisada's countenance. "Yes. Women are charming and delightful. But, sexually, they never interested me."

"Have you loved anyone else besides this Nowaki?" Tatsu knew bluntness of his question bordered on being rude. Yet, he was desperate to know.

"*Hai*, I have shared my bed with dozens of others, but only truly *loved* the one," the *kyūketsuki* replied. "And he is you."

"Pretty convenient that my preference is men." Tatsu forced indifference into his voice, but knew he failed. He didn't have butterflies in his stomach; he had bats that flapped like mad each time he looked at the gorgeous creature before him.

"Convenience has nothing to do with it. You are the choice of Nowaki's *tamashii*."

"So, you're saying I'm your type?" Tatsu smiled, knowing the effect his dimples would have on the vampire—hell, on most gay men.

Then it hit him. What the hell was he doing? Flirting with a vampire over breakfast? No, he was flirting with a vampire that he was in love with over breakfast. The whole thing was fucking insane. He needed a distraction. "Don't suppose you've got a cigarette around here?" he said through a smile.

That smile disarmed Arisada. His eyes took on a lambent glow. He needed to remove himself from the temptation of the boy's aroused body. "No, sorry, I don't smoke. However, I have something else for you. Please, follow me."

Arisada led them across the garden to the *shoin*. At the rack of weapons, he selected a *kotagiri*, a sword longer and more curved than a traditional *katana*. With clear reverence, he unsheathed the blade. Candlelight sparkled off the steel.

"This was crafted nearly six centuries ago. It is my personal weapon and is superior only to the one I lost at Mii-dera." He bowed to the sword, sheathed it and placed it back in the bamboo rack. With a small frown, Arisada looked over the others. He lifted a *katana* sheathed in a black, lacquered saya and handed it to Tatsu.

The weapon fitted Tatsu's hands as if it belonged. Even in the simplicity of the ancient leather braid wound around the *tsuka*, Tatsu saw the sword's incomparable worth. He whipped the blade out. The *katana*'s perfection stunned him—the lines along the polished edge, the symmetry of the blood groove. With a gasp, Tatsu realized he held a sword made by the incomparable swordsmith Ikkansai Kasama Shigetsugu. A genuine Ikkansai hadn't been seen in more than a century.

"It's magnificent." Regret over the loss of his own *katana* stilled Tatsu's words of admiration. He snapped the sword back into its scabbard and handed it back to Arisada.

The vampire refused it. "No, please, keep it. Let it be a humble replacement for the sword of your ancestors."

Tatsu bowed before placing the weapon back in the rack. "*Domo arigatō*, Saito-san, it's a priceless gift. I would be honored to accept it, but I can't." He knew refusing such a gift could offend Arisada. But accepting the sword from the vampire, no matter how noble the reason for the offering, would be the ultimate insult to *Ojii-san*'s memory.

Disappointment clouded Arisada's golden eyes. "It will be yours when you are ready." He closed the *shoin* door, and they walked in an odd but comfortable silence back to the *chashitsu*.

The occasional brush of the vampire's shoulder sent heat sizzling over Tatsu's skin. He wanted to touch Arisada's hand, kiss him, anything. Confusion held him back.

Back at the dining room, Arisada fetched a bottle of sake, heated it and poured them each a cup. They sipped in silence. Tatsu tried to relax and let the liquor spread a warm lassitude though his aching body.

"Who is Sage?"

Tatsu's eyes widened at the abrupt question. "How do you know about Sage?"

Arisada shrugged, the silk of his kimono rustling over his shoulders. "You called for him many times during your delirium. Is he someone you love?" He did not mention the desperate longing in Tatsu's voice each time he uttered the name.

Tatsu put down the delicate sake cup hard enough to crack it. Then, he stared at it, as if fearing it would shatter. "*Sumimasen*," he muttered, smoothing one finger over the fragile porcelain. He didn't want to talk about Sage, about what he'd lost. However, under the vampire's gentle gaze, the words tumbled out.

"Sage was a boy at my school. I fell in love with him. I was only twelve, too young to understand it. Years later, we got together for a brief time. He didn't stay. I don't know why. End of story. He was my first...and only." Tatsu held a sob hard in his throat until the pain burned. Dammit, where was all this weepy shit coming from, anyway? He was trained to crush his emotions, hide them behind honor and duty. Sorrow warred with shame. Sorrow won.

"We never forget our first love. It is always the most precious no matter how brief or how it ends." Arisada moved beside Tatsu, wrapped strong arms around him and placed a soft kiss on the side of his head. The vampire offered solace the same way he soothed Nowaki-kun centuries ago. "There is no disgrace in grieving for what is lost."

Arisada's quiet wisdom promised comfort. Still, Tatsu pulled back, fearful of needing more. How could he take solace from this creature? "I don't understand what's happening to me. These feelings. You're making me *kuruwaseru*."

"I'm making you crazy, *neh*?" Arisada's slight smile hid the soaring joy in his heart. "Samurai are not robots. We are as moved by the exquisite perfection of *haiku* as that found in *seppuku*. We are fearless in the face of death yet weep freely at the right provocation. But I seriously doubt if you're crazy. Perhaps it is love?" Arisada's soft laugh chased away Tatsu's melancholy. "So, before either of us acts rashly, Tatsu-kun, meet me in the *ikinewa* in an hour. Then we will go to your Major."

Back in the bedroom, Tatsu pulled on his TAC pants, a thick roll-neck sweater and the new leather jacket left on the bed, regretting the loss of his old one. He grimaced when he strapped on his harness, feeling it list to the left without the weight of the *katana*.

With an impatient gesture, he opened the door to the *ikinewa,* bowed and then stepped in. Arisada, dressed in samurai garb, knelt before the small alter. His deadly *kotagiri* rested behind him on the floor. After a moment, he bowed, forehead to the ground, stood, fixed his sword in his *obi* and crossed to Tatsu.

Arisada's sun-bright gaze reflected only serenity. "Do you trust me?"

Tatsu eyes said he did.

"Have you fallen in love with me?" A playful glint danced in Arisada's burnished eyes.

"Yes. It makes no sense, but yes."

"Love does not have to make sense. It makes itself known, and we are its captives." Arisada handed Tatsu a small sandlewood box.

"What are we, engaged now?" Tatsu joked to squelch the want sending his mind and heart south to his prick.

"Perhaps? It depends on what you do with that." Arisada nodded at the box.

With a muttered, "Ah, what the hell." Tatsu opened the lid. A small jade ball mounted on a steel pin nestled in the white satin lining. "What's this?"

Arisada held up a thick needle. "A small favor? Pierce my tongue then I will insert the stud."

"No. You're out of your fucking mind. It'll hurt like hell." He closed the lid and pushed the box toward Arisada.

The vampire's deep laugh held only delight. "What do you mean hurt? The pain is nothing. I will heal in minutes. But this stone will represent a part of you I will carry inside forever. It will be our bond." Arisada picked out the stud and twirled it in the light so it reflected the pure color. "Imperial jade, very rare and precious. And the exact shade of your eyes."

"I won't. It's barbaric." Tatsu reiterated his refusal and moved to leave. Arisada's grip on his elbow stopped him.

"We live in barbaric times, *neh*? This is my choosing, please, honor it."

"It'll hurt like hell," Tatsu repeated, stubbornly trying to find a way out of this bizarre request.

"Not as much as my heart if you do not grant me this." Arisada crooked his head sideways. His golden eyes glowing with trust, he handed Tatsu the sharp needle. "*Kudesai,* please. Consider it payment for saving your life."

Tatsu shook his head. "Freaking blackmailer." So often he'd inflicted suffering and pain on others, yet this was different. "By Hachiman, I can't believe I'm doing this." His fingers trembled when he positioned the needle under the vampire's tongue. He took a deep breath and thrust, feeling the vampire's fang tips graze a knuckle before retracting.

Arisada snapped the barbell onto the ball and smiled. "*Arigatō*, Tatsu-kun, for making this bond with me. You have made me happy." He brushed his lips over Tatsu's forehead. "Now, we will go see your Major."

Tatsu clutched the needle with its minute drop of blood. Why did that word, *bond,* sound more like farewell?

Twenty-One

Unable to contain his agitation, the Major paced the confines of his small office. His eyes were hollow, his wispy hair disheveled. An uncharacteristic stubble covered his face. He clenched his jaw to control his frustration. He'd lost men before—courageous men who died protecting others—men he esteemed. Many had been friends. Until four days ago, the Major thought he'd lost one more; Tatsu Cobb. The news that Tatsu was alive brought the Major close to tears.

At his core, Major Blenheim abhorred the killing that always arose between different cultures, ideologies and now species. However, he was a realist. His military expertise meant less killing than if conflict was left to those who only lusted for power. Still, the death of any man under his charge hurt.

When they found Bana's charred corpse, Major Blenheim felt deep anger boil inside him. Even if no longer human, the Major still considered Bana one of his own.

Wyckes had cremated the Irishman's mangled body and the ashes were placed in an urn inscribed *Ireland Forever*. Phoenix's joke that it should say *Sod off you wankers* fell flat.

There was no way of determining if the youngster, Tatsu Cobb, lay buried beneath the massive piles of twisted, molten steel. The Major declared Tatsu missing in action, presumed dead. But he knew every Leper clung to the hope that the kid had survived.

Then that heartening call from Fornax. Tatsu Cobb was alive. He'd sustained life-threatening injuries, but was safe in a secret location. Against his better judgment, Major Blenheim agreed not to reveal the news to the Lepers right away, despite knowing how much it would lift their morale.

With a mental shrug, the Major combed his hair into place with his palms and entered the Pit. Every man fell silent.

"Gentlemen, despite our losses, we still have a contract to fulfill," the Major's voice grated. "No matter how all of you feel, we will not move out until we know Ukita's plans. Agreed?" Every Leper nodded.

"I'll tell you his plans." The slightly inflected voice startled the Major who spun around to see Arisada and Tatsu standing at the door of the Pit. Fornax hovered behind them.

"Welcome back, Mr. Cobb." The taciturn Englishman struggled to refrain from showing his joy at seeing his youngest operative alive and well. The Major's gaze shifted to the beautiful Japanese man standing calmly beside Cobb. A momentary shock flickered across the Major's weary face. Not a man; a vampire.

The sight of the unknown vampire next to Tatsu stilled the Lepers' exuberant reaction, but only for a moment. Bedlam erupted in the Pit when every the mercenary crowded around a stunned Tatsu. Kaiden cupped Tatsu's startled face in his hands and dropped a deep French kiss on his mouth. Chain stayed seated with a huge grin across his face. He winked when Tatsu, blushing deeply, looked at him.

"Little Bro," Phoenix bellowed and climbed over the top of the table to reach Tatsu. He shoved Kaiden aside. "I fixed your ride. Runs better than new." Phoenix wrapped Tatsu in a rib-cracking hug. Tatsu winced. "Crap, sorry man. Guess you got hurt, huh?" the biker mumbled. He backed away when he caught a warning flash in the red-haired vampire's eyes. For the first time in his life, Phoenix felt fear.

"Gentlemen, please, let's have a little order. Give Mr. Cobb and his guest a chance to enter the room." The Seattle Lepers resumed their seats but the Snake Eaters remained standing against the back wall, their hands close to their holstered weapons. They didn't hide their hostility toward the strange vampire in their midst.

"Are you the one Fornax told me about?" the Major asked.

Arisada bowed. "*Watashi wa* Saito Arisada, I believe I can answer some of your questions if—"

"How come the kid's with you?" Phoenix's growl was barely heard over the din of questions filling the room.

"I found Cobb-san at the power plant," Arisada replied, reluctant to acknowledge his part in saving Tatsu. Remorse filled the *kyūketsuki*'s face when he detailed the events at the facility, how Bana had fought to protect Tatsu. He omitted how Bana's bullets had caused the explosion. These honorable men did not need to know.

"I wish to help. It means I am betraying my own kind and my *Seisakusha,* who I have served for centuries, but I have my own reason for wanting to stop Sadomori." Arisada looked with open affection at Tatsu, now sitting in his accustomed chair.

The Lepers looked at Tatsu with awe. The kid not only had survived a massive explosion, but had become the boyfriend of one of the most powerful vampires in Seattle.

The Major frowned at Arisada's offer. This monster was clever, not to be trusted. Then Blenheim felt shame at his abrupt judgment. No, not a monster, more a brave warrior who had risked his life for the sake of a human, a Leper no less.

"Why does Ukita want this virus? What possible use is it to him?" the Major asked.

"Total domination." With those two words, Arisada irrevocably broke his oath to his *Seisakusha*. He felt the keen blade of his betrayal twist through him. The pain was as sharp as that caused by his own *tanto* centuries ago. Nevertheless, to protect the one he loved, he would endure far worse.

"Ukita Sadomori is obsessed with total power. He has conquered vast territories, slaughtered and oppressed millions of people. With this new strain of virus, he can create a vampire army; one large and powerful enough to control this territory."

"*Merde*, that's one fucking insane idea. What good are troops that can't move around in daylight?" Chain snorted.

"Daylight is not an issue when thousands of vampires can overrun a city within a single night. He will terrorize the surviving people into unquestioning obedience. Make no mistake, all survivors will obey Sadomori, either out of fear or misguided loyalty," Arisada replied.

Bell shook his head. "It makes no sense. Vampires can't

feed off each other so why destroy their source of blood by turning so many humans."

"There will still be enough left to feed the new vampires." Arisada replied.

"Why are you helpin' us bloodsucker?" Phoenix had moved beside the Snake Eaters lined up along the back wall. Making no effort to hide his mistrust, he held his shotgun in one hand the barrel almost trained on Arisada.

"Many Tendai vampires fear the Daimyō's ambition will lead to total annihilation of our species. I have sworn to prevent this even if it means betraying my Sire." No sign of emotion showed on Arisada's face, yet the crimson flickering in his eyes revealed the pain of his declaration.

The Major regarded Saito Arisada. If he didn't trust the vampire's reason for siding with humanity, he could trust the look of love whenever Arisada glanced at Cobb. The Major decided he'd be a fool if he ignored this offer. "I'll accept your help. And Saito-san, I'd like you to be Mr. Cobb's teammate until this matter is resolved."

Tatsu's glare bounced from Arisada to the Major. Trust an Englishman to describe the possible destruction of an entire population as a "matter." A moment later, Tatsu recognized his sarcasm as nothing but a reaction to his own anger. Tatsu didn't want a partner—of any kind. His last partner died, and Tatsu felt responsible.

"Your Kawasaki is in the motor pool. However, since you're in no condition to ride, perhaps Saito-san will take you home?" The Major nodded to Arisada before looking over the entire room. "Gentlemen, please put your affairs in order." Talking among themselves, the Lepers shuffled out.

Glaring at Arisada's back, Tatsu followed the vampire to the Audi. He climbed stiffly into the passenger's seat. "I don't need a partner. I can take care of myself," he snapped at the *kyūketsuki* sliding behind the wheel.

"*Honto*? Really? You think that?" Arisada leaned over and poked Tatsu in the ribs, forcing an involuntary grunt of pain. "You are not fully recovered, *koibito*. Now be quiet and fasten your seatbelt." He turned the key and the car purred. Tatsu thought it sounded too much like the smug satisfaction purring in Arisada's throat.

A day later, Tatsu was going crazy. Twenty-four hours of enforced rest had shredded every ounce of his patience. He paced from his bedroom to his living room and back, wearing a trail in the cheap rug. Frustration etched lines in his smooth, boyish face.

Earlier in the day, Phoenix had brought Tatsu's Drifter home. The biker had grumbled good-naturedly about having to ride a crappy rice-burner. Still, Phoenix couldn't conceal his pride in the overhaul he'd given the motorcycle.

Phoenix tossed Tatsu his keys. "Everyone's on the rag, man. This is heavy shit what with the stolen virus and all. We won't catch the fucking bug, but if it gets loose folks are gonna be royally screwed. I've told my brothers to go down to Oakie and hang out with the Disciples." On that note, the biker left to catch his ride rumbling in the street below.

A moment after the front door closed, Arisada slipped into the living room. He'd entered through the bedroom balcony.

"Can't you enter like a normal person?" Tatsu snapped to conceal his immediate arousal at the sight of the gorgeous *kyūketsuki*. The vampire wore leather pants. Slick and tight, they showed every bulge of Arisada's package. It was obvious Arisada wore nothing beneath. Tatsu felt his mouth water. *Kuso*.

The vampire grinned. "I'm not exactly a person, am I?"

"You know what I mean." Tatsu strode into his bedroom. "I need a smoke. Why are you here?"

"I need to see you." Arisada followed Tatsu's tense, retreating back. He draped his coat over a chair and bent over to place a wrapped object on the bed. The smooth leather stretched, molding his buttocks, revealing every muscle as if nude.

Needing a distraction from that all-too arousing sight, Tatsu fished a fresh pack of cigarettes out of his dresser drawer. He lit one and took a couple of drags. It didn't help. His belly started quivering and his blood rushed south, pooling into his groin. Crap, he was already half-hard. Pretending anger, he stubbed his unfinished smoke out in his ashtray.

Arisada picked up the still-smoldering butt, rolled it for a moment between his slim fingers and inhaled. The tobacco held a whiff of spearmint from Tatsu's toothpaste. Arisada extinguished it with odd care in the ashtray. He wandered over to the teak *kake* and traced his finger over the empty slot.

"You should not be without a worthy weapon." He unwrapped the cloth, and silently held the Ikkansai out to Tatsu who just stared at it.

The vampire lifted the boy's left hand, almost slapping the weapon in it. "You are Kurosaki, descendant of one of the most ancient Japanese houses. You should never be without a sword that honors your ancestors. Please, this time, accept it."

Tatsu stared at the marvelous sword as if for the first time. Unable to hide his reverence, he pulled the weapon from its ancient wooden *saya*. Truly, he wasn't worthy to wield a weapon of such esteem. "I already told you I can't." He snapped the sword back into the protection of its polished scabbard and held it out.

The vampire growled low in his throat, clenching his fists, refusing to take the proffered sword. "Will you dishonor me by rejecting my gift, Cobb-san?"

A mélange of conflicting emotions rippled through Tatsu. He was incapable of sorting them out. Flustered, he looked into those golden eyes, the pupils now ringed by tiny flecks of red. Within their depths, he saw hurt, yearning and pride. He knew the sword was more than a weapon. It was a symbol of love. How could he refuse such a gesture?

"*Domo arigatō gozaimasu*, your gift honors me." He bowed and placed the *katana* in the lacquered kake stand.

"I pray this weapon never fails you as I failed Koji Nowaki." Arisada stammered to a halt before the sudden confusion in Tatsu's jade eyes.

"I dreamed about him, about Nowaki. What he did to you."

"You dreamed about Nowaki?" Arisada stilled; an Arctic freeze in his quiet question.

Tatsu thought he would feel nothing with the telling of the

dream. Instead, his heart raced—he knew the vampire heard it. His armpits grew damp and his belly filled with liquid heat that spread into his shaft, plumping it, making it throb with need.

"It was so vivid, so real, not disjointed the way most dreams are. I know how it feels to be fucked by you. I felt every sensation. The touch of our fingers, our lips. How the tendons of my thighs stretched around your hips. My knees on the rock floor of the bath. And... and... when I thrust down on top of you, your cock utterly filled me. It hurt at first. But then every thrust became nothing but pure pleasure. We climaxed at the same time."

The tips of Tatsu's ears warmed. No way would he tell Arisada about how he woke up from the dream covered with cum and still hard. Or how many times he'd jerked off since then.

"You had a past-life memory, Tatsu-kun. Those events happened exactly as you described. How we made love in the bath, how possessively Nowaki rode my cock. I should have been more aware. When I returned from Nara, there was a change in Nowaki. There were many instances when I felt a distance between us, even while we coupled. But like any love-blind fool, I ignored it. It was inconceivable Nowaki would betray me. I believed he was my *unmei no hito*."

"Your soul mate," Tatsu whispered. He fetched the sketchpad from the bedroom closet and held it before Arisada. "Is this him?"

The vampire's expression changed from surprise to sorrow. "Oh, Nowaki-kun." The name slipped out with an incredible yearning. When he looked up from the drawing, tears filmed his eyes. "This is an exact likeness of him."

Tatsu reached for Arisada, intending only a gesture of comfort. Instead, he found himself cupping the vampire's face and claiming the startled mouth in a deep, possessive kiss. Arisada's lips parted at the probing of Tatsu's tongue. He dug between and lapped against his teeth, glided over the ridged channels housing their deadly weapons. When he swept over the ball of the piercing, he realized he enjoyed its smooth, perfect roundness against the underside of his tongue. Realized also how incredible that piercing would feel rolling over the lip of his asshole.

The sketchpad fell unheeded to the floor. The vampire's gasp dropped into a deep, husky moan. Tatsu released his kiss, stepped back and stared into the golden eyes for a second. Then, in a single fluid movement, he dropped to his knees, unzipped Arisada's pants, and dug out that fat cock. His mouth was around the slick crown in the next breath, and he sucked in his first blissful, oh-so-yearned-for, taste of Arisada's prick.

"No. You must not do this." Arisada grabbed Tatsu's thick hair and pulled him off. With fumbling fingers, the vampire tucked himself away and jerked up his zipper.

Tatsu climbed to his feet, the sting of Arisada's rejection clear in the glare from his eyes. He was angry, sure, but his mouth watered from the taste of that fine cock. "Don't do what? Suck your cock the way you did mine? Kiss you like you did me? What the fuck, Arisada? You started this."

Abruptly, Arisada's stance softened, tenderness suffusing his face. "That night in the Garden was a terrible mistake. It must not happen again. If I climax, I will not be able to stop myself from feeding from you. That time at the dojo, I barely stopped myself from killing you. Now, in my utter lust for you, I will have no control."

"That's bullshit. A vampire's bite isn't always fatal."

"Mine is. The virus in my blood has mutated, lethal to any human. You *will* die. Do you understand?" Arisada's voice turned brittle at the doubt in Tatsu's eyes. "I came here tonight to give you the Ikkansai and tell you after we stop Sadomori, I am leaving the city. We will never see each other again."

"*Fakku*! You say you searched for me for centuries, even say you love me. Hell, you swallowed my cum. Now you're gonna leave me? What am I? A toy for you to play with?" Tatsu's lips twisted with hurt and confusion.

"You know better. My love for you is the core of my soul."

"How dare you talk about feelings? You know only hate and death. You know nothing of love." Deep shame filled Tatsu. He was being cruel and knew his words were untrue.

"You accuse me of knowing nothing of love? I would have walked into the sun centuries ago if it were not for the hope that I would find Nowaki. True, my motive was *fukushū*. But the moment I saw you in that dojo, all that vanished, obliterated by love."

"And after all that time, you're going to throw it away? *Daisuki*. Don't you get it? *Daisuki!*" There was nothing tender in Tatsu's confession, just a terrible need.

Before the vampire had time to think, Tatsu grabbed Arisada's shoulders, hooked his foot around the back of the *kyūketsuki*'s knees and swept him flat onto the bed. Tatsu dropped onto the stunned vampire, straddling his waist and locked his knees against Arisada's ribs. He pressed his forearm across Arisada's throat, cutting off the air. Raw fury glittered from Tatsu's sea-dark eyes.

The boy's inhuman speed and strength stunned Arisada. His fingers clawed at Tatsu's forearm, fighting for breath. Then, in a wash of acceptance, Arisada ceased all struggle. So be it, let the boy kill him. It would solve everything.

Panting, Tatsu glared at the vampire. He wanted to kill the bastard. Or fuck him. Suddenly, shamefaced, Tatsu released his chokehold and sat back—right on the hard bulge of Arisada's groin. Tatsu was suddenly very, *very* aware of the press of his ass against Arisada's cock.

"I want you," Tatsu begged, looking into those golden eyes.

Arisada ached for this, ached so much his will dissolved to nothing. Even if he lived for another eight centuries, he would never be strong enough to deny this one moment.

"*Wakatta*, Su-kun. Take what you want."

In wonder, Tatsu cupped the vampire's face and fused their lips together in a deep, claiming kiss. A deep, primal sound rumbled in his throat when his tongue swept in and plundered Arisada's mouth, brushing over the wet inner cheeks, running over the channels that housed the deadly teeth. This was pure bliss. Still, Tatsu craved more. Hungry for the vampire's dick, Tatsu slithered back the vampire's thighs, dragged down Arisada's zipper and brought out his swollen prick.

"God, your cock is beautiful," Tatsu whispered. That turgid

member—the color of cream tea, filled his fist. The silky dome, already wet with precum, pushed out from the foreskin. He rolled his thumb over that perfect head, coaxing forth another slick flood. He tightened his fingers and began long, slow strokes.

But that hand's caress was not enough for Arisada. "*Dozo, koibito, dozo. Chinko no shaburu!*" he pleaded. "Suck my cock!" His words spilled from his mouth. His now fanged mouth.

Tatsu's "Oh yes!" blew out on a long breath. He engulfed the satiny head, savoring its smooth texture for only a moment before taking the entire prick in so fast it slammed against the back of his throat. He choked and pulled back, keeping his lips stretched tight and possessive around the crown. His tongue swept the weeping crown, drawing forth pearly juice and a long, harsh moan from Arisada.

Tatsu gulped, stretched his lips and opened his throat wider. Sucked every iron-hard inch down until his nose was buried in the surrounding nest of flame-red pubic curls. He drew back with a deep suck, rolling his tongue down the tender skin, lapping at the throbbing blue vein underneath. God, he loved it—the feel of that satin sliding over pulsing hardness, the sea-salt brine of Arisada's sweat, the musk of his readiness.

Fire raced through Arisada's body, destroying his doubt in a conflagration of pleasure. At the sight of his cock being fucked by Tatsu's mouth, Arisada gasped in wonder, shuddered with every sensation of his rock-hard flesh surrounded by wet heat. The deep suction back, an occasional light scrape of teeth, the roll of a warm tongue, then his cockhead hit the back of that gulping throat again.

His hands curled into Tatsu's hair, gripped hard, urging the youth on with deep, pleading groans and grinding hips. Arisada fought his need to fuck that demanding mouth, the denial adding fuel to his pleasure.

Clawing aside the obstructive folds of cloth, Tatsu cupped the heavy warmth of Arisada's sac. Tatsu fingered the fine brush of hair on the silky skin, palmed each orb, teasing at first then tugging harder in rhythm.

He pulled his mouth off Arisada's cock, nuzzled in to tongue the scrotum, sucking in one ball then the other. Moaned at how they filled him. Above him, he heard Arisada, begging in gutter profanity, to be sucked.

That tugging demand on his balls sent fire racing into Arisada's belly. A brief caress along his perineum. A finger circled his pucker, teasing the tight muscle open. That finger entered, followed by a second, digging deeper. Tatsu's knuckles curled against the walls. Electricity danced over the vampire's flesh, rocketed straight up his spine and spun out of every limb

Arisada bucked his ass, rocking between that hot, talented mouth and those driving fingers. He reached for his orgasm, climbing toward its crescendo, so close it maddened him.

"I'm not done yet." Tatsu pulled his fingers from the vampire's hole, and sucked greedily on them one at a time. The wicked glint in his eyes said he wasn't finished playing. Then he drove the wedge of his hand deep into Arisada's chute.

Arisada mewled with the rocketing pain and pleasure of it. He arched his back, clenching his ass muscle around the sweet invasion. Rode the wild sweep of sensation that flowed from his core to every nerve ending in his body.

The greedy depths of Tatsu's throat inhaled the vampire's cock again. And Tatsu's perfectly timed stroke vibrated over Arisada's gland.

Sweet agony engulfed Arisada. His inflamed nerves fired and fired again, sending his cum blasting from him in glistening ribbons. Uncontrolled, his fangs flashed out from their channels. Deep within his ecstasy, the feeding lust possessed him.

In desperation, he threw his arm against his mouth and bit into his own forearm, ripping through muscle and tendons. Gouts of hot blood splashed over his face. The pain lashed his orgasm even higher, spurting great, creamy jets into his lover's mouth. He clawed at the sheets as he ground his groin against Tatsu's mouth.

When Tatsu released that still-pulsing cock, cum spilled from his mouth, leaving a shiny trail down his chin. He swallowed then dove into the vampire's crotch, tongue lapping up the sweat slicking the wet pubic curls. He nibbled up the valley of Arisada's belly, over the arch of still-heaving ribs, tasting skin and sweat and sex, and slid his slicked tongue inside and reared back at the metallic taste of copper.

"Holy shit, what the hell did you do?" He stared at the blood covering Arisada's face and flowing from his arm.

"I nearly lost control. My body was the better choice," Arisada panted.

Babbling a string of *gomens,* Tatsu ripped off a corner of the sheet and wrapped it around the vampire's lacerated arm.

Arisada pushed up and leaned back against the headboard. He cleaned off his face. "That's the sixth *gomen* you've said. It is not necessary, I will be fine." He removed the makeshift dressing. The bleeding had stopped, the wound knitting closed. One-handed, he zipped up his pants. "And, for the record, you have the most talented mouth I have ever experienced."

Flustered, Tatsu climbed off the bed, walked over to the dresser, and stared for a long moment at the Ikkansai. When he looked at Arisada, his eyes had turned sea-green cold. "I want your word, your oath, that you won't leave the city. Give us a chance."

"My oath? I cannot do that. And there can be no *us.*"

"Yes, you can. That filthy *kono yarou* Sadomori tore an oath of fidelity from you. But I'm asking you to give it to me freely. If you love me, swear you won't leave. In turn, I promise never to touch you again. Just as long as I can be by your side, it'll be enough." Tatsu hadn't realized, until the words left his mouth, that he'd accept any conditions to be with Arisada.

"To my shame, I have been unable to stay away from you. Today, I could have killed you. I will not be responsible for taking your life. Because I do love you, I must leave."

Tatsu opened his mouth to protest, but only a croak emerged.

Gently, Arisada placed his hand against Tatsu's lips. "Do not ask me to stay. *Kudasai.* Please, allow me this."

"You gave your allegiance to a monster like Ukita Sadomori yet deny our love?"

"*Hai,* I am afraid it must be so."

For a single, horrible moment, Tatsu wanted to run the Ikkansai through the vampire. Instead, he turned his back. "Then there's nothing between us. Get the fuck out. The next time I see you, I *will* kill you." The threat burst from his lips and shattered like a mirror under the impact of a bullet. The shards of each word burst into the air, reflecting the lie a thousand times, multiplying it, raining it back onto him, shredding his soul.

"Arisada. *Yurushite,* forgive me. I didn't mean it." He spun around, outstretched hand reaching for Arisada. "*Yurushite,*" he cried again.

Too late. The vampire was gone. "*Yurushite,*" he whispered to the empty room.

Wearing only a towel around his waist, Tatsu stumbled into his bedroom from his shower. His mind felt trapped in an alien country filled with confused grief. How in the hell did things get so fucked up, so fast? From wrapping his lips around Arisada's gorgeous cock, tasting the sweetness of his spunk, to driving him away with threats of death

Years of training, of embracing only the art of the sword and denying all emotion for the honor of a samurai, crumpled before the overwhelming reality of his loss.

Jigoku, hell, he *had* to find Arisada, take back the destructive words. Even if it was the last time he spoke with the vampire, Tatsu had to obtain his forgiveness.

Cold air blasted from the open balcony door. His heart leaped with joy. "Arisada, *sumimasen,* I am so—".

An unknown form detached itself from the dark recess of the far corner. In a blur of motion, Tatsu snatched up the Ikkansai just when Fornax stepped further into the bedroom. The vampire's rain-wet curls plastered against his shoulders. His hands were tucked in the pockets of his full-length coat.

"What the fuck are you doing here?" Tatsu unsheathed the sword and shifted his weight forward, battle-ready.

The vampire ignored the deadly length of steel and stared down Tatsu's glare. "Be calm, Cobb-san. I mean no harm."

"*Neh*? You enter my place uninvited through the fucking balcony door? I'd hardly call that a polite way to visit."

"I am not your enemy," the vampire reiterated, frowning.

"So why the hell are you here?"

"It is imperative I speak with Saito-san."

"You forget how to dial a phone?" Tatsu recognized his animosity was unreasonable, fueled by his jealousy that the creature had been by Arisada's side, possibly in his bed.

"My information is for him alone. Where did he go?"

"How the fuck would I know?" Tatsu and placed the sword on the bed.

"He was here, I can smell him. His spunk is all over you."

"Not here now." Tatsu turned his back on Fornax, dropped his towel and bent to step into his jock.

That careless nudity caused a shiver of desire in Fornax, a visceral response he had not felt in years. He followed the sweet curve of Tatsu's spine down to the taut buttocks, that intriguing crease, the heavy scrotum dangling between strong, lean thighs. All the things Fornax loved about the male body. All the things forever denied him. Greedily, he watched the lithe, athletic body disappear beneath the layers of clothing. The covering of delectable parts was as arousing as the revealing of them.

Fornax snapped out of his reverie. "Do you love Arisada?"

"What's between us is none of your fucking concern." Tatsu's growl threw a fuck-you challenge at Fornax. The vampire ignored it.

"I helped Arisada-sama care for you after the explosion. I know you are in love with him." Fornax brought out his cigarettes, tapped one from the pack and lit it. His eyes flared gold with a painful brilliance in the flame. He exhaled a curling stream of pale smoke. "It will do you no good. Arisada belongs to the Daimyō. We all belong to the Daimyō. To do anything else is to be branded a traitor. Sadomori knows about you, who you really were. He will never permit you to have Arisada."

He took another drag on his cigarette. "Sadomori has sent a hundred rogues to destroy all Lepers. Before they left Tendai, he allowed each one to feed from him. His blood makes *kyūketsuki* insane with killing lust. They will obey his commands even to their deaths." He gave Tatsu a cold, level look. "Make no mistake, he *will* find you and Arisada. He will torture you both for weeks; let you watch each other suffer. Do you understand?"

Tatsu grunted. He sensed Fornax held something back. "Sadomori should watch out for his own ass. I intend to kill him. And no one, not even Arisada, can stop me."

"*Baka!* Foolish boy. Saito Arisada is oath-bound to the Daimyō. Your lover will be unable to cast that aside. He will protect his *Seisakusha* even knowing Sadomori will kill him."

"Arisada makes his own choices. And no matter what you or anyone else thinks, he no longer belongs to Sadomori." He's mine! The realization burst upon Tatsu, solid and real like the Ikkansai lying on the bed. He's mine!

With a mirthless smile, Fornax glanced down at the cum-splattered sheets. "Let me tell you why I fight with the Lepers. Years ago, I smiled at Arisada, flirting with him, not for the first time. He is my *Seisakusha*, and I love him. Before I drew a second breath, Ukita Sadomori threw me to the floor. With one hand, he tore off my clothing. He laughed when he said I would never flirt with another again because I would never fuck another again. Then, he ripped off my testicles."

The shock of the confession reverberated through Tatsu's senses. He stepped back, his eyes wide in shock. "Fornax-san. *Gomen, gomen nasai.* I...I had no idea." He fought the urge to drop to his knees in the ultimate gesture for forgiveness.

The vampire shrugged. A rueful smile tugged at the corners of his lips. "Now you do." Casually, with no show of the pain his confession caused him, Fornax flicked the cigarette butt over the balustrade.

"I *will* kill him," Tatsu snarled.

"There is no *killing* the Daimyō. He has survived countless wars, assassination attempts, even rebellion from his own kind. There was only one time when he came close to death."

"How? What happened? You owe me, Fornax."

The vampire took out his pack again and offered it to Tatsu, who shook his head. "I do not know the story. I only know the injury nearly severed his spine. Even his incredible healing ability could not prevent the scars on his back."

"When did this happen?" Tatsu's mouth felt like it was filled with grit. A sick foreboding crawled over his skin and coiled into his guts.

Fornax shrugged. "Thirteen years ago." Light flared for an instant inside his cupped hand. He drew a deep drag, then exhaled the smoke in a lazy, curling stream.

"Where?" Tatsu's eyes were jade-ice, the hard look filled with nothing but death.

A small shiver rippled over the vampire. Not fear but respect at the samurai spirit within this boy. "Arisada and I found the Daimyō in an abandoned farmhouse outside Nagasaki. I do not know how he survived until we arrived. We hid for weeks on one of the Ryukyu Islands. After Sadomori recovered, he kidnapped the most-skilled *horishi* in Nipon and forced the man to tattoo his entire back to conceal the evidence of his failure. *Mochiron*, of course, Sadomori killed him afterward."

Tatsu froze. Ukita Sadomori—the murderer of the Kurosaki family. Tatsu's vitals heaved, not with fear, but in a sick shock. Arisada had lied, denying knowledge of Sadomori's scars. Despite professing love for Tatsu, Arisada had protected his Sire.

Fornax interpreted the boy's stillness as fear. The reaction reassured him. *Wakatta*, Tatsu would wait for the Major's orders. Without another word, the vampire slipped over the balcony rail into the wet night. He was unaware he had just delivered Tatsu's death sentence.

"*Fakku!*" Tatsu raced across the room to the balcony door. He skidded in the puddle of rainwater, mute proof the vampire had indeed been there. "*Fakku!*" he spat out the invective again. Arisada—liar and traitor. A cold rage burned through Tatsu's grief and turned his love for the vampire to ash.

Tatsu paced his living room and fought to remember the discussion between the Major and Arisada. Tatsu had been exhausted. Lulled half-asleep by the conversation, he had missed many of the details. What had Arisada said? The Space

Needle. That Sadomori was obsessed with the monument, loathed it as a symbol of human superiority.

The fucker was there, Tatsu just knew it. He yanked on his tactical gear and slipped the *tanto* into his boot. He sheathed both weapons in his harness and strapped it on before tossing his dog collar on his bed. He didn't need it where he was going.

His reflection in the mirror caught his attention. Frenzied eyes stared back, wild with hurt and fury. Filled with death.

"*Su-kun*, before you face your enemy, give thanks for all there is." *Ojii-san's* calm voice in the back of Tatsu's mind halted his wild bolt out of the door.

He turned to the small *kami-dana*, the narrow shelf that held the few spiritual icons from his family. Drawing in deep, shuddering breaths he stilled his mind and brought everything into sharp focus. With hands together, he knelt, perhaps for the last time, before the tiny Shinto alter. He called upon every *kami* revered by his ancestors for the courage and wisdom to defeat his enemy.

"*Bushido* is the Way of the Samurai." he intoned. "*Bushido* is found in honor, loyalty, benevolence, courage. *Bushido* is found in death."

It was many minutes before he reached his *tanden*, that place in his heart where the rightness of all action dwelled. The purity of his purpose washed with a clear brightness through him His anger and despair over Arisada's defection melted, replaced by the cold steel of vengeance.

Without another thought, he charged down to the rain-swept street. He threw his leg over the bike, booted the kick starter and cranked the throttle wide open.

The motorcycle's angry roar reverberated in the narrow street. The back tire skidded once on the wet pavement before the bike leapt in the direction of the Space Needle.

Twenty-Two

Tatsu crouched in the jagged shadow of a concrete wall, the Ikkansai a comforting weight across his knees. A few steps away, the wreckage of the Space Needle reared up into the sky.

He felt alive, vibrant, as if the dawning day promised the excitement of a childhood adventure, not the real possibility of his death. He took a sip from his canteen, barely noticing the water, and licked his lips, craving a cigarette.

He continued to crouch, immobile, eyes sweeping from the perimeter to the base of the edifice and back. He filtered each moment with the patience of a lion stalking a herd of gazelle.

Beneath the crescent moon, the long shadow of the tower marked off the night. Tatsu cast his eye up to the top of the Needle five-hundred feet above his head. During the volcanic eruption, the methane torch at the top of the tower had exploded. For several minutes, the massive fireball and the erupting volcano were twins. The fire had immolated the top spire and raced down the elevator shafts before consuming the entire structure. Windows had exploded. Flaming lumps of glass rained like black hail over the city, killing hundreds.

The tower swayed, and many feared it would collapse. Through an engineering miracle, it remained upright. Now, it listed; a slight bend of two legs mid-center caused the dome to cant downward. Long metal spines—all that remained of the sundeck—cast a bizarre web of shadows over the weed-choked ground.

Tatsu took a long, deep breath, filtering out the scent of effluvia, decomposing vegetation, crumbling concrete and rusting metal. No human presence. No coppery blood signature of the vampire. Still, his nerves thrummed. Something evil hid in that tower. Something he would destroy without mercy.

A tremor of anguish shook him. Where had the real Tatsu gone? The young boy who once dreamed of becoming an artist and believed he could help better the world. Would killing Ukita Sadomori truly restore the Kurosaki name? Balance the scales of justice? The police reports claimed Tatsu's father did the murders. Who would know the truth? Unbidden, Arisada's warning about the soul-destroying consequences of revenge echoed in Tatsu's mind. Arisada, who'd experienced eight-centuries of suffering, said there was no place in life for vengeance. Said it destroyed all who touched it. Destroyed love.

If Tatsu would be the only one to know justice had been realized, why do it? He answered his own question. He must avenge his family name for the sake of his ancestors. It was they who souls bore the stain of dishonor. And if *fukushū* demanded Tatsu sacrifice love, so be it. Besides, he'd already turned his back on love.

Tatsu's heart lurched when he recalled his last cruel words to Arisada. The pain of Arisada's lie went deep deeper than *Ojii-san's* death, deeper than Sage's rejection. Tatsu wanted the vampire with a soul-deep certainty. Perhaps that was the problem, the utter improbability of an eternal love in the midst of this insanity. Or Tatsu's insane choice of a lover.

"*Baka*, you fool." He shook off his foolish musing. Who the hell was he kidding? He might die today but that didn't matter. All that mattered was taking the monster, Sadomori, with him into the Void.

Perhaps Arisada would grieve. Tatsu hoped for that much.

A breeze caressed his cheek, cooling it. Tatsu snapped out of his reverie. Pink tinged the tops of the Cascades. In the blossoming light, indistinct shapes took on substance. It was time. He picked his way through the black, molten glass that littered the blistered ground like so many rare jewels and slipped inside. Thin, pale shafts filtered down through the broken ceiling, illuminating the piles of smashed concrete and twisted steel covering the floor. He saw only the tracks of rodents in the dust. Tatsu stilled, learning the creaks and groans of the tower. Heard nothing unusual. Still, every instinct warned him that the deserted feel of the place was a lie; the silence hiding a trap.

With the stealthy tread of a samurai, he moved across the floor to the stairwell and peered down into the deepening dark. Dank air wafted up over his face. He smelled only the ubiquitous mildew and mold. Every sense searched for the most miniscule hint of danger as he descended into the depths of the tower. He checked each floor, finding nothing. Then he caught an incongruous whiff of wax coming from far below.

Although the lowest sub-basement was pitch black, Tatsu easily made out the entrances to three massive utility tunnels. He crouched for several minutes, letting the area speak to him. Caught the scent of wax, stronger now, coming from the central opening. Nothing. Just that out-of-place smell.

He stepped into the black-on-black hole. Rows of thick, mold-covered pipes and conduit snaked across the roof. Condensation dripped down the walls making the floor slippery. He reached a junction, listened and sniffed. The elusive waxy scent was coming from the right-hand tunnel.

He took four steps into the narrow branch when his temple exploded with pain. He staggered then dropped to one knee. A second blow crashed behind his ear, tearing through the lobe. Hot liquid flooded down his neck. A kick from the side caught him in his belly, flinging him over onto his back.

An oily voice slithered out of the black. "What do have we here? A nasty little *nezumi*. Nasty little rat, you shouldn't be crawling around where you don't belong."

"Daimyō, it's the one with two swords."

"Â, sō desu ka, the boy who believes he's a samurai. You shouldn't play with sharp objects." A shrill laugh, accompanied a driving kick into Tatsu's abdomen, cut through the silence, spinning him through the air. He crashed against a curved wall.

Bright lights danced through Tatsu's vision and his ears rang. He rolled onto his feet, staggering upright with his back against the wall. A second blow thudded into the side of his head. Dazed, he spun toward a movement and slashed his swords upward in a crisscross. The impact of the *wakizashi* through flesh reverberated along his arm. He lunged, cut left then right, and then heard a horrific scream ending in a strangled sob.

Suddenly, the air was thick with the sounds and smells of bodies. A shadow rose before him. He slashed sideways with the Ikkansai and felt the blade slice through flesh. Tatsu relished the wet sound of the death gurgle. A flash of silver and the glitter of red eyes materialized before him. He aimed for those red orbs. Then the impossible happened. Fingers wrapped around the razor-sharp blade. With a wrench, the weapon was torn away. Before Tatsu brought the Ikkansai into play, the wedge of a hand drove into his chest, nearly stopping his heart. The shock drove him to his knees.

"I've wasted too much time on this *nezumi*. Shoot him," that same malicious voice hissed.

Tatsu heard the click of the gun's hammer. *Yurushite*, forgive me *Ojii-san*, for my failure. A mere second for that last thought. Then darkness took him.

"Sir, listen to this." The quiver in Cooperhayes' normally implacable voice got the Major's attention with a snap. The second–in–command transferred the call to the building-wide speakers. Ragged panting and agony-filled moans echoed throughout the foundry. Every Leper heard it. Every man froze. They all recognized those harsh, gurgling wheezes. Whoever was on the other end of that call was spilling out the last of life.

"Mayday... Privet here... Alvarez dead." The voice ended in a wet gurgle.

"Mr. Privet, respond," Cooperhayes pleaded.

"Repeat, ambush... Benny dead... not gonna make it... trap." Guttural coughs broke up the man's cries. A coughing rattle preceded a ragged expulsion of breath. Then silence. Cooperhayes called repeatedly for a response from the man but received only a hissing silence.

"Do you think you can stop me? I eliminated two of your so-called fighters like the vermin you are. Soon, the rest of you will die beneath my sword." Pure vitriol spilled from the voice that slithered out of the speaker. In its tank, the cobra reared and flared its hood in an angry response.

"Who are you? Answer!" Silence met the Major's demand.

The Pit's double doors burst open under the rush of Lepers surging into the room. The bedlam from shouts of disbelief and anger drowned out his call for order.

"Fuck! Fuck! Fuck!" Phoenix punched the wall with every "fuck."

"*Merde*, who in hell is that?" Chain growled.

"Ukita Sadomori." Arisada stepped into the room and surveyed the hostile glares from the Lepers. "He is at the Space Needle. He will release the virus from its dome tonight."

"The fucking Space Needle?" Kaiden interrupted.

Arisada regarded the blond Leper. "Yes. He also captured Cobb-san this morning. He—" A chorus of "what the hells" drowned Arisada's next comment.

The Major restored order with one look. "Do you know if Mr. Cobb is alive?"

"*Hai*, he still lives. The Daimyō wants me to witness the boy's death." The vampire's expression revealed none of his fear that Tatsu was being tortured at that moment.

"Mr. Cooperhayes, bring me what we have on the Needle." The Major nodded toward his second who left the room without a word, returning a few minutes later with a roll of blueprints. He spread them over the conference table.

"Saito-san, how many vampires are with the Daimyō?" the Major asked, studying the diagrams.

"Three-hundred, maybe more. Recently, I discovered he has been letting many *kyūketsuki* feed from him, perhaps for months. His blood turns them rogue, makes them incredibly vicious and binds them to him. They will follow him to their own deaths. Think *kamikaze* of the last century's World War."

"We could wait for daylight. Give us an advantage," Bell suggested.

"No advantage. It is a misconception that vampires are strictly nocturnal. With effort, ancient vampires can remain awake during the day. Sadomori can do this with ease. So can his rogues after they drink enough of his blood," Arisada said.

"Does that also apply to you?" Major Blenheim looked at Arisada who nodded.

The Major turned back to studying the blueprints of the giant edifice. "Gentlemen, a night attack remains our best option. We'll need a diversion since Sadomori expects to lure us into a trap?"

Tracing one finger over the diagram, the Major outlined an assault plan. "There are two utility tunnels and a large storm drain leading into the Needle's lowest basement. The storm drain and the west utility tunnel collapsed in the quake. Mr. Jones, we'll need your expertise to clear them by the most expeditious means possible. To facilitate the best retreat, it may be necessary to demolish the tower. Can it be done?" The Major turned to his demolition man who looked like an eager, black bloodhound about to take to the trail.

Jones grinned and slapped his palm on the blueprint. "I can blow up anything, Major. Two of the tower legs are already far out of true. Joints have thousands of integrity cracks and the ground's unstable beneath 'em. Lot of fissures." He ran his truncated finger along the diagram. "I'll plant timed, low-grade fusion grenades. Open them tunnels wide. Since the blasts will be coupla hundred feet under, we won't have any radiation leaks. Also, got in some radical new shit better than Semtex. Set it under each tower leg. If the timing's right, we all get out before the whole fucking thing comes down."

"How long will you need?"

"Gimme Fornax and thirty minutes." At the Major's nod, Jones flashed a grin, then trotted off to the armory.

"Our priority is to retrieve the virus. But I also know you're all determined to rescue Cobb." No Leper would leave a teammate behind. "Four squads. Number one through the storm drain. The Chicago team into the west tunnel after it's cleared. Mr. Passebon and Mr. Galloway, take squad three through the northeast utility tunnel. Saito-san and all others will accompany me in a ground assault."

The Major's flaring nostrils gave him the appearance of an old foxhound about to give chase. "We're only thirty against a couple of hundred enemy. Not the most optimal odds but we are the elite. Gear up gentlemen. We'll move out in two hours."

Several muttered, "why not now?" and a few described how they would rip Sadomori apart. Knowing how his men thirsted to take on the monster, the Major ignored the insubordination and turned to Arisada. "Saito-san, how many *kyūketsuki* will follow you?"

"A dozen, perhaps a few more." Arisada reached for his cell phone.

"Good enough. Please let me know when you're ready." The Major grinned, not with any humor, but with a flash of excitement. "Mr. Cooperhayes, please issue the Israeli assault weapons. Mr. Chain, I know you prefer that bow of yours, but please take a firearm." He looked each man in the eye. "Gentlemen, I have every confidence in you. Dismissed."

In the armory, each Leper checked his weapons and readied packs for a full assault. One by one, they headed for the vehicles until only Kaiden and Chain remained. The Cajun settled two bandoliers of bolts across his massive chest and strapped a holster to his hip. "Gimme some of them .45 rounds. I'll take the Eagle for backup."

Kaiden pulled out several boxes before closing the locker with a quiet, deliberate click. He handed the ammunition to the Cajun standing by his elbow. "Partner, you know this one's gonna be bad?"

"Oiu, *mon ami*, but they've got our little brother." The Cajun's voice came out hoarse, his breathing tight and fast. A thin gleam of sweat beaded his brow.

Worried, Kaiden stared at his partner for a few moments. Chain had nerves of steel, reveled in every mission. Never got antsy. So why now? Kaiden turned back to the locker for more ammo. A large hand reached over his shoulder and slammed the door closed.

"Goddamn, Chain, you nearly broke my finger." Kaiden spun around to glare at his partner.

"Got something you want to share with me, *mon ami*?" The Cajun glowered, drilling his jet gaze into Kaiden's sky-blue eyes.

"What the hell are you talking about?" Kaiden glared.

"I saw the look on your face when that vampire said Cobb has been snatched. You fucking the kid?"

The warmth of Chain's breath brushed over Kaiden's cheek. "None of your goddamn business even if I was. But for your perverted information, all we were doing was range practice *per* orders."

"*Pardonnez moi*, was just concerned." He pulled back, but only a fraction.

"Forget it." Kaiden's resentment faded. In that same moment, he caught the deeper meaning behind his partner's anger. Chain was freaking jealous. An impossible hope filled Kaiden, and his heart climbed into his throat.

"What the fuck." If he was going to die today, Kaiden wanted one shot at the man he loved. He grabbed the Cajun's shoulders in a bruising grip and spun him, face-to-face.

"*Qu'est-ce tu fais?*"

"Just this." Kaiden gave himself no time to think. He reached up and cupped the back of Chain's neck, pulled him down and angled his lips hard onto that wide mouth.

Chain thrust Kaiden back. The blond's head banged against the cabinet door hard enough to dent it. The Cajun glared down. "What the fuck are you doing?" The look in his eyes was not one of anger, far from it. They glittered, silver-edge jet, as if from a, mind-blowing thrill.

"Seizing the moment. Maybe my only chance." Kaiden's impish grin lit his face but his cerulean eyes held a deep, wanting plea. Chain might kick him to the curb, might never talk to him again, but he had to taste that mouth just this once. Unblinking, he looked into that onyx gaze, saw in it a look full of realization and wonderment.

"Ah, what the fuck. At least one of us will die happy," he muttered. His large hands cradled his partner's face and he fused their mouths together. Kaiden's lips opened, and Chain swept his tongue deep into that welcoming cavern. A shock of fire sizzled straight into the Cajun's cock. He hardened but he didn't break the kiss.

The blond felt every iota of want between them. His heart

thundered against his ribs and an explosion of lust ripped into his body. He wrapped his arms around the wide back, molded his body into his partner and slaved his open lips against Chain's. Breath, spicy and exotic, tasting slightly of cigarettes, flowed into Kaiden's.

Kaiden ground his erection against the Cajun's groin. When Chain's palm slid down and cupped Kaiden's dick, they both let out a low moan of pleasure.

Chain had said it, if he was going to die, he would die happy.

A discreet cough shocked them into pulling apart. Unperturbed, Cooperhayes waved in the direction of the motor pool. "Gentlemen, it's time." Then, he executed a precise about-face and marched toward the waiting vehicles.

"Don't get killed, *mon ami*." Chain shouldered the heavy ammo bag. His fingers brushed Kaiden's shoulder.

Kaiden snorted. "You either, partner."

Twenty-Three

A pounding headache and the urge to vomit woke Tatsu. He licked his cracked lips, gagged on the vile tang in his mouth. Everything felt distant, hazy, his mind trapped in tar. He knew a tranquilizer moved its sluggish way through his body. Thick chains, fastened to his wrists, held him dangling from the overhead pipes. His toes dragged against the freezing, concrete floor. He was naked.

Tatsu pulled weakly against the restraints, the drugs robbing his muscles of any power. The plop-plop-plop of dripping water was a torturous reminder of his thirst. He pushed the need out of his mind and focused his blurry vision. In the light from dozens of candles placed around him, he made out the cracked curves of a chamber that formed the juncture for two massive drainage tunnels.

Another scent overrode the smell of wax. Ukita Sadomori materialized from the dark. In one hand he held Tatsu's swords, in the other a leather satchel, which he dropped to floor. "Finally awake, my pretty boy?"

"Fuck you," Tatsu croaked with feeble defiance. He jerked on the chains, his shoulders and elbows bellowing in anger. Good, anger would drive the fog from his mind. He realized the fact he was still alive meant the vampire wanted something from him.

"My, my. Such crudeness from the mouth of such a well-bred bishounen." He was armed with a long, lethal *nodachi*. The vampire moved so that his face hovered in front of Tatsu.

He smiled, revealing the wet, white gleam of fang tips. "So, you are the one?" He shrugged. "I knew my Primary would desert me the moment he found the reincarnation of his pretty, little lover. No doubt, he used thrall to seduce you, *neh*?"

"You don't know shit. What I gave him, I gave of my own free will. Vampire thrall doesn't affect me."

The vampire laughed. "That is where you are misguided, boy. I clouded your mind the moment you set foot in the Needle. How else can you explain why you never sensed me or my kind?" The vampire tossed Tatsu's *wakizashi* to the floor with a clatter. "What were you planning to do? Did you believe I'd be so intimidated by your so-called knowledge of *niten'ichi* that I'd surrender?"

"It was daytime," Tatsu sneered.

"*Baka*. Do you think we all become comatose at sunrise? *Kyūketsuki* that drink my blood can stay awake during the day." He laughed. "They are faster and stronger than any vampire you've ever faced. Still, I must admit, I have not seen skill like yours in centuries. Bravo. You took Nakamura's arm off with barely a flick of your wrist. Made him useless to me. I had to kill him."

Sadomori unsheathed the Ikkansai, held it up and turned it. The candlelight glittered off its lethal blade. "Ah, the incomparable Ikkansai." He slipped his thumb along the blade. Blood welled. Languorously, he sucked the cut clean. His yellow eyes turned an ugly vermillion. "Arisada must believe it will save you."

"You don't know shit."

The *kyūketsuki* grabbed Tatsu by the hair and jerked his head down so they were eye-to-eye, feral red drilling into sea-dark green. "I smelled him on you the moment you entered the tunnel. You are beautiful, I give Arisada that much. Did you enjoy his mouth around your cock? That tongue of his is quite talented. Did he make you scream?"

Tatsu jerked his head out of the vampire's grip. No matter what, he wouldn't give this monster the sick satisfaction of a response, especially one concerning any details about Arisada.

Sadomori shrugged. "No matter. It is my turn to make you scream," Sadomori hissed. "Since you stole my Primary from me, I will take you from him. I know he has not fucked you. He would have taken your blood and killed you. The virus in him is lethal. Mine is, too." He released his punishing grip and placed the Ikkansai beside his own sword. "You know he will come for you. When he does, I will kill him."

"Asshole, you're wrong. We fought. There's nothing between us." *Please, Arisada, don't throw away your life on a foolish rescue. Stay away, far, far away,* Tatsu prayed.

"Seems you don't know my Primary as well as you think. His foolish, romantic heart will not let you die. I made sure he knows of your capture." Ukita removed his sword and *obi*, folded the silk sash and placed the weapon on top. With languid grace, he shrugged out of his elegant clothes, dropping them one by one to the filthy floor with careless disregard. Sadomori stripped off his *fundoshi*. He stroked his cock, the gesture made obscene by the absence of expression on his face. The pale organ stayed soft.

Tatsu snorted with derision.

Anger flickered across the vampire's face before he turned to light more candles. The intricate art covering his back jumped and rippled in the flickering light. Dozens of scenes merged into each other in a kaleidoscope of colors. Yet the layers of ink failed to disguise the ugly ridges of keloid that crossed from shoulders to waist.

The sight of those scars shredded Tatsu's mind. "You fucker! You slaughtered my family." He jerked at the chains, twisting around in a futile attempt to reach the vampire.

A malicious smile creased Sadomori's lips. "Interesting how the wheel of life revolves. I would never have dreamed you were the same little *nezumi* who escaped me in Nagasaki."

"Why?" Tatsu croaked, slumping against the torturous drag of the chains.

"That *mons* you wear on your breast is the reason, boy. The crest of Kurosaki no Gitako, once my beloved Emperor. He betrayed me and annihilated the Ukita house. By the time I discovered it, I was *oni*, a demon, unable to father children. I vowed to wipe the Kurosaki name from memory. I thought my *fukushū* complete fourteen years ago but that meddling fuck of an old man interrupted. At least my sword took his life."

A biting laugh erupted from Tatsu's split lips. "You failed. Grandfather lived."

"No matter, I have you now. I shall slice that cursed badge from your body with Arisada's own sword." He glared at Tatsu through eyes turned scarlet with rage. Sadomori's fingers clamped down on the top of Tatsu's head, forcing it down in the direction of his crotch. Sadomori's organ hung soft and unstirred between his thighs. "But first, *I* will fuck you."

Tatsu wrenched his head up and spat in the vampire's face. "Not with that limp dick. You are *okubyomono,* a coward. You're—"The vampire's fist sent him reeling in the chains.

Sadomori wiped the spittle from his cheek and smeared it on his now-stirring cock. He sauntered behind his prisoner, trailing his fingers over the straining muscles of Tatsu's shoulders.

Tatsu suppressed a shudder of revulsion at the touch of those sharp nails trailing over his body. He risked another blow and sneered, "You mean you're an impotent fuck."

"Interesting, your defiance excites me." Sadomori traced over each knob of Tatsu's spine down to the clenched buttocks, grasping each cheek and forcing them apart. "Now, this is a delicious sight."

Tatsu twisted away, ignoring the humiliation.

"Struggle all you want, my lovely boy. It just excites me more." The vampire licked the tender skin behind Tatsu's ear before driving a fist against that same spot. Stunned, Tatsu collapsed against the tearing pull of the chains.

"Pity, I do not have more time for foreplay," Sadomori mused, and pulled Tatsu's glutes far apart. The vampire sniggered, a sick, demented sound at the sight of that dark hole. He grasped his cock and rubbed the head against the exposed anus. But his member refused to harden.

With a snarl, Sadomori turned to the satchel and pulled out a long, leather whip tipped by steel. Tiny needles embedded into the tightly braided thong glinted wickedly in the flickering flames. He stalked around until once again he stood before Tatsu and hefted the coiled length of the whip.

"This is *Senkirikizu,* the deliverer of a thousand cuts. Such an elegant instrument of death." Sadomori stroked the handle as if it were his cock. "I shall flay you alive. You will beg for my mercy. Then, I will tell Arisada of your cowardice before I kill him," he purred and strolled behind Tatsu.

"Go to hell," Tatsu spat, steeling himself against that first lash. He did not fear death, but to break and grovel before this vile monster, to bring shame to his family name, filled him with terror. Never by all *kami* would he allow that to happen.

Sensing Tatsu's resolve, Sadomori flicked the whip, kissing Tatsu's ass with a touch lighter than a breeze. The delicate brush left a scalpel-thin cut. The boy, every muscle rigid, didn't flinch. The vampire grunted with satisfaction. "Admirable self-control. Let's see how long it lasts."

"*Fuck you!*" Tatsu spat. An arc of fire scorched across his shoulders as the whip kissed his back again.

Lash after lash, each one landing a hair's distance from the last, flayed his skin with the delicate touch of an artist's brush on canvas. Tatsu ground his teeth against any outcry, refusing to thrash against the chains. Dimly, he sensed the blood and sweat running in ropy rivulets down his buttocks and thighs. He took his mind deep into *tanden*, and moved beyond the pain. But how long before his body went into shock?

As terrible as it was, the flogging wasn't the worst of the torture. Between each lash, Sadomori described in excruciating detail his sexual torture of his Primary. How Arisada, drenched in blood and cum, begged for the subjugation. Descriptions of the pain-driven writhing of that lean body, the musk of his sphincter, the rich taste of his spunk spilled from Sadomori's with vulgar relish.

That repulsive voice painted images so degrading that Tatsu wept for his beloved. He forced his mind to recall that vision of Arisada, hair radiant, limned in a halo of moonlight, and knew that was the moment he'd fallen in love with the vampire. Tatsu infused that memory into his *tanden*, the core of his being, and felt its power run like living fire through him. But his love for Arisada wasn't enough.

Tatsu's body jerked when stroke after excruciating stroke cut into his skin. He felt the world graying out. He knew he wouldn't last much longer. He prayed, offering his soul to the *kami* of *fukushū* in payment for granting him revenge. And the *kami* answered. It roared into Tatsu with the fury of a dragon, melding with his pain, forging it into a ribbon of living hate.

Tatsu's *ki* grew with the spirit and strength that seemed to flow directly from his ancestors—the Kurosaki samurai. With supernatural strength, he pulled himself erect and bellowed his utter defiance.

Sadomori gasped with disbelief. The whip stuttered and missed. The boy should be nothing more than a sobbing, begging shell; his courage stripped from him as his body was stripped of skin. But this human scrap was not only alive but uncowed.

Enrage, Sadomori shoved the whip handle into the cleft between Tatsu's buttocks. "I should castrate you for loving that monk. But this will have to do." With a vicious jab, he drove the thick leather rod into Tatsu's sphincter.

Tatsu bellowed. He bucked, twisted and tore at the chains. Continuing to roar, he took the violation, changed it and forged it into a weapon.

Stunned, the Daimyō flung the whip aside. No creature, human or vampire, had ever endured this much from his hand. Most died before the twentieth lash. Sadomori strode in front of Tatsu, and gasped at the pure, unalloyed hate radiating from the boy's green eyes.

Dread rippled through the ancient *kyūketsuki*. For the first time in millennia, he saw the certainty of his own death in the face of another.

The ancient vampire covered his fear with a semblance of a snarl. "*Wakatta*, it looks like the little *nezumi* bit his tongue." His foul breath washed over Tatsu's face. He grabbed Tatsu's chin, and licked the blood and spit from his lips. Then, twisting Tatsu's head sideways with a brutal wrench, the vampire struck, burying his fangs in the soft jugular where the life pulsed strong and rich.

With every ounce of strength he had, Tatsu drove his knee into the vampire's crotch.

Sadomori reeled back clutching his injured testicles. His blood-covered face contorted with pain, his breath hissed out ragged and short.

"You will pay for that!" He unsheathed the *nodachi*, spun and drove it with incredible accuracy toward Tatsu's breast.

Tatsu stared straight into those demented, scarlet eyes, took a deep breath and accepted his death.

A muffled boom rocked the tunnel. The floor heaved. Sadomori stumbled, his sword slicing along Tatsu's ribs.

The vampire lowered his weapon. "Looks like this will have to wait. I believe your lover has arrived."

A second explosion, louder and closer, opened giant cracks in the wall, showering them with chunks of concrete. Smoke billowed into the chamber just ahead of five vampires.

"Daimyō, we're under attack. Hunters!" they all shouted at once. Another explosion rocked the tunnel, drowning out their confused cries.

"Cowards, why are you wasting my time?" Sadomori screamed. He jabbed his finger at the four of them. "Summon every *kyūketsuki*. Kill the human vermin." They ducked their heads in frightened acknowledgement and dashed away.

The Daimyō barked at the huge bull that had remained. "Take this little rat to the roof. I'll meet you there." His insane laughter receded down the tunnel.

The monster vampire undid the chains. Tatsu's knees gave way and he sagged toward the floor.

"No, you don't," the beast growled and grabbed Tatsu's wrists. Tatsu bit back a scream at the pain when his arms were jerked behind him and tied. The vampire tossed him over one shoulder like a sack of rice and trotted to a tunnel that led to the tower stairs. Acrid bile flooded Tatsu's mouth each time his head slammed against the bull's meaty back. Too weak to struggle, Tatsu was overcome with dizziness at the upside-down view of their climb.

At the top of the spiral staircase, Tatsu was dropped to the floor. When he staggered to his feet, his knees buckled from the pain from his bruised insides and flayed back.

The big vampire snarled as he kicked open a door. He slapped Tatsu between his ravaged shoulder blades, propelling him onto the moss-covered slope of the dome.

Tatsu stumbled, fighting for balance on the slippery curve of the halo. A freezing wind soothed the blaze across Tatsu's ravaged skin. His vertigo passed and his vision cleared.

Patches of rust, mold and seagull shit formed a psychedelic collage on the torn metal of the dome. He looked up at the clear, obsidian sky, the glints of stars, the moon dancing silver across the water of the Sound. Far off, he saw the checkerboard pattern of the city's lights. The city about to die.

From hundreds of feet below came the distinct chatter of the Israeli automatics, the booming of a shotgun, the shouts of men, incomprehensive and indistinct. Tatsu's heart surged with hope.

Sadomori stepped through the door dressed in the traditional robes of the samurai. An elegant, sleeveless outer coat with wide, stiff shoulders draped over his black samurai's garb. His *obi* held a long *nodachi*. In one hand, he carried the Ikkansai; the steel biocontainer was in the other. He set the case with its lethal cargo against the wall of the scorched spire.

The ancient *kyūketsuki* acted as if the battle below was of no concern. Instead, he stared with a predatory lust at Tatsu's genitals. That enviable cock, now tucked up from the cold, yet still substantial, those large testicles. "Pity to kill such a gorgeous boy," he said to himself.

"You're fucking insane. Killing me, I understand, but why everyone in the city?" Tatsu tensed, ready to move his feet into combat stance. The bull sensed it and tightened his grip on Tatsu's neck.

"Why? I would think it is obvious. I require an army. Young, newly-made vampires bound solely to me. Soon, this area will be mine."

"No way. Hear that below? Those are my friends. They're gonna eat your vampire army alive and spit out the fangs."

"Ignorant whelp. You think that pathetic human rabble can stop me? This is not the first time I've conquered a land. Who do you think led the Mongols? Who do you think was the prince of that confused little country in Eastern Europe? No one can stop me."

"*Yarou.* Bastard. I will." Tatsu threw his cold conviction at the arrogant vampire.

"I seem to recall only a few minutes ago that I had my way with you. Hardly a position of strength, my dear boy."

"You call shoving that silly toy up my ass having your way? I've taken butt plugs twice that size," Tatsu taunted. "You are *eta!*" He spat out the vilest insult to any Japanese. *Eta.* Outcasts who handled offal and animal skins. Reviled as unclean. Ignored as if they had no existence.

The insult made Sadomori recoil with shame and fury. With visible effort, the old vampire regained control and strode to the edge of the dome. He squatted on his haunches, the Ikkansai resting across his knees. His nostrils flared, testing the air.

"This night is perfect. Soon, the wind will be in the right direction." He rose and faced Tatsu. "But we still have time to play. How elegant. Arisada will be here shortly. He will witness my triumph before I take both your lives." He smirked and nodded toward the bull. The monster freed Tatsu's arms, bowed and then lumbered through the door to the stairs.

Tatsu massaged his wrists, forcing the feeling back into his numb hands. "Like I said, *konjo nashi*," Tatsu jeered, trying to buy time.

"Ignorant whelp. I *have* the balls. I will enjoy ripping yours off much like I did to that whore Fukashima. The one who calls himself Fornax." Sadomori expelled a cold, pitiless laugh. His thumb pushed the *nodachi* a mere inch out of its *saya*, ready to draw.

Tatsu's genitals hiked up in blinding, primal hate. *Jigoku* no matter what, he had to kill this monster. He looked around for any advantage, and focused on the treacherous curve of the dome. If nothing else, he would hurl the psychotic vampire off the roof, even if they went together.

The Daimyō sneered at the hate rolling from the boy. He indicated the dome's edge with a casual wave. "Perhaps I will throw you off this roof. Fittingly dishonorable, *neh?* But I will wait. My Primary climbs this tower even now."

He brayed with laughter at the dismay in Tatsu's eyes when they flicked toward the door. "You fear for your lover's life. *Wakatta.* I'll give you a chance to save him, you little *izumi.*" Without warning, he tossed the Ikkansai toward Tatsu.

In one flowing move, Tatsu caught the spinning sword and

pulled it free from its black lacquered sheath. Power flowed into his body. He had been given this ancient weapon just for this. For revenge.

Before Sadomori drew his next breath, Tatsu lunged, slicing the vampire from shoulder to hip. The *kami* of vengeance bellowed its approval.

Instinct and supernatural reflexes saved Sadomori from that death cut. The rents in his clothing fluttered when he danced back. His sword flashed out before Tatsu brought his blade down again. With a scream of rage, the Daimyō launched a furious counterattack, plying the heavier *nodachi* as if it weighed no more than a fan. Their swords clashed, sending sparks to be snatched away in the wind.

Knowing it would be his only advantage, Tatsu sought the *kami-hasso,* the spirit, of his sworn enemy. Found it in the way *kyūketsuki* shifted his body, moved his feet and held his blade. In the evil cunning in his scarlet eyes. That knowledge flowed into Tatsu's *ki*. His entire life's purpose came down to this one fight. The honor of the Kurosaki house—and yes, his love for the *kyūketsuki* Saito Arisada—all rested on the next few minutes, perhaps the next few seconds.

They fought across the slippery, curved dome. The unending rings of steel on steel drowned out the sounds of the battle below. Left, right, left, pressing each other across the expanse of the halo. And all the while, Tatsu prayed Arisada wouldn't come through the door.

Sadomori expelled a guttural bark of astonishment at the boy's knowledge of the most ancient ways of sword fighting.

"So, you stole the secrets of the Seikanjito Shinden?"

"No, I learned them from the *kensei* Shiniichiro Kurosaki. My Grandfather."

For a moment, Sadomori recoiled. Then his scream of, "Kurosaki scum!" shattered his restraint. But before his sword moved, Tatsu attacked. With blindingly fast cuts, Tatsu drove the creature back until his foot rested an inch from the dome's edge.

The cunning old *kyūketsuki* rallied. "Stupid boy. You think to trick me?" In a blur of speed, his sword flashed back and forth, forcing Tatsu to retreat up the curve toward the center of the halo.

Silence enveloped them save for their panting and the ring of steel on steel. Tatsu didn't sense the passing of time, just the execution of every cut, delivered with only one intent—kill this vile beast. Yet he knew his tortured body was failing. Sweat poured off his skin, flooded his eyes and, made every step wet and treacherous. His lungs heaved in an effort to gain air. Every muscle, deep in oxygen debt, burned with pain. The Ikkansai fought him, its weight dragging against his arm.

He considered the unthinkable. He was going to lose.

Soft and dreamlike, he heard the voice of his Grandfather. *"Su-kun,* remember the four principles. The foundation of every samurai's faith: Eye, footwork, courage, strength."

Those four simple words sent power surging through Tatsu's exhausted body. He risked everything in one radical move. A move he learned from Arisada. He stepped under the high sweep of Sadomori's blade. Singlehanded, Tatsu cut his sword upward, blocking the *nodachi.* His other hand, fingers folded into a wedge, drove into the vampire's chest with enough force to stop the heart.

For a heartbeat, Sadomori faltered, fanged mouth agape, seeking to pull air into his punished lungs. Then he rallied. With a great sucking gasp of air, he raised his sword, legs braced, and brought the blade down in blur.

Tatsu rolled out from under the vampire's cut, leaped up and slashed his blade tip across the Daimyō's elbow. Muscle and tendons parted.

The vampire screamed, flipped the *nodachi* to his uninjured hand and drove toward the center of Tatsu's exposed abdomen. Tatsu spun. The blade tip left a scalpel-thin wound. Tatsu, ignoring the pain, lifted the Ikkansai high and stepping forward. But his bare sole caught on a razor-sharp rent in the steel roof. Agony lanced deep into his foot. He staggered, throwing his descending blade wild.

"Now, you will die!" Sadomori screeched in triumph. He leapt high, spinning in the air. His foot lashed out, catching Tatsu across the temple. Tatsu crashed backward, the back of his skull slamming onto the dome. His vision went black.

The Daimyō swept his *nodachi* down in a blinding arc. Just in time, Tatsu blocked with the Ikkansai. With a clang of angry steel, the heavier blade caught Sadomori's weapon, skidded down its edge and locked *tsuba* against *tsuba*. Sadomori grunted with surprise, grabbed the Ikkansai by the back of its blade and tore it from Tatsu's grasp.

"Say hello to your dishonorable ancestors," Sadomori hissed. He lunged, driving death toward Tatsu's exposed abdomen.

The tower door burst off its hinges and crashed on the roof. Saito Arisada, his *kotagiri* raised above his head, stepped onto the dome. The war cry of the Mii-dera Sōhei rent the night air. In it was centuries of injustice.

"He belongs to me!" Fanged mouth wide and snarling, Arisada leapt, reaching the fighting pair in the time of a single heartbeat. He drove his blade between Sadomori's descending sword and Tatsu's naked belly. Steel screamed against steel as the two weapons collided. Arisada saw Tatsu roll, Sadomori's *nodachi* missing the boy's spine by a hair's width.

With a berserk scream, Sadomori turned to face his Primary. The two supernatural creatures, twins in skill and strength, clashed. One fought for hate, the other for love. Blade struck against blade, over and over again, in a maelstrom of steel, fire and hate.

But even the finest weapons made by human hand are no match for vampire strength and fury. At the same moment, both swords shattered. Arisada stepped back, holding only an inch of blade. But Sadomori held more than a foot of deadly steel.

Screaming in victory, the older vampire drove the truncated blade into Arisada's abdomen. In bizarre parody of their first meeting centuries earlier, the Daimyō twisted the weapon. Arisada screamed. Then Sadomori buried his fangs into his Primary's throat.

Tatsu heard a gurgling cry. He stared up in horror at the two creatures locked in mortal embrace. Then a hot stream of blood splashed over on Tatsu's face. Arisada's blood!

In desperation, Tatsu rolled out from under the feet of the two vampires. He scrabbled about for the Ikkansai, found it and grabbed it—by the blade. No time to shift his grip to the leather-clad *tsuba*. No time to think about the sword severing his palm.

With a yell that came from the deepest part of his *ki*, Tatsu swept the *katana* sideways, ignoring the agonizing bite from its naked edge. A wailing shriek rent the air as a fountain of ichor drenched Tatsu. He scrambled to his feet and stared in shock. Somehow, his desperate cut had severed Sadomori's leg at the knee.

"*Arigatō*," he whispered to the *kami* of revenge.

Off balance, the old vampire staggered inches from the dome's edge. Arisada reached for him. "*Seisakusha*, my Sire. No."

Sadomori finger's curled into Arisada's *keiko-gi*. "Even in death, you belong to me." With an evil smile, Sadomori took them both off the roof.

In rank desperation, Arisada reached out and caught one of the protruding beams of the sundeck. Their fall halted with a jerk that nearly tore his arm out of its socket.

"Fool! We die together!" Sadomori growled through blood and spittle. His eyes shone with a maniacal hatred. He raked his fingernails over Arisada's wrist, trying to loosen his grip. Sadomori's other hand clutched the sword imbedded in Arisada's guts. The blade's dragging pull sent fire lancing through the younger vampire's body.

Arisada thrashed in agony. His knee caught Sadomori's swollen groin. The old vampire shrieked and let go of Arisada's arm. At that moment, the broken sword tore free.

Sadomori tumbled into the dark below. His howl of rage was drowned in Arisada's cry of loss.

Horror seized Tatsu as the two vampires tumble over the dome's edge. He flung himself over the rim, hand extended in a futile reach that encountered only air. Off balance, he nearly followed Arisada into the dark. For a heartbeat, he reveled in it. But his life belonged now to the *kami* of death.

He rolled back onto the dome, gasping for air, body shuddering with exhaustion and shock. Lay there while seconds, minutes, years of unendurable grief passed.

"Tatsu. Help me." A choked whisper from below brought him scrambling to his knees. A cry of joy spilled from him when he saw two hands clutching the rim. Sobbing with relief, he grabbed the vampire's wrist, but his injured hand had no strength. His grip on Arisada slipped. Tatsu leaned further out, the metal ridge digging painfully into his naked stomach. He caught the vampire by his *obi,* and with a yell of fury, heaved his lover onto the dome.

Mind soaring with relief, moaning, "You're safe, you're safe." Tatsu rolled onto the dome. He crushed Arisada against his chest. But his relief last only a second. Blood gushed over him. Tatsu struggled to his knees, cradling Arisada while he pulled off his *obi*. He pressed it with raw urgency to the *kyūketsuki*'s stomach. The cloth blossomed dark red, the stain spreading with ominous speed.

"Don't take him, don't take him," Tatsu begged the *kami* of death. The words repeated in his head like a mantra. He pressed and prayed for what seemed like eternity, his eyes darting from the blood pumping from the vampire's abdomen to the ragged hitch of his chest.

Arisada's breathing stuttered then halted.

"*Iie!*" Tatsu's wail rent the cold, night air. He crushed his beloved against his naked chest. "Don't leave me, *koibito*, please," Tatsu begged, rocking back and forth with ragged, grief-stricken motions. Unbelievably, he felt a quick, struggling gasp, then another. Heard a hoarse cough.

The vampire's golden eyes fluttered open. "*Koibito?*" he whispered, wonder coloring his voice.

Tatsu hurt, oh hell did he hurt, body and spirit. But his beloved was safe in his arms. As he hugged Arisada, Tatsu couldn't stop running his hand up and down the vampire's back, seeking reassurance that his lover was alive. In a rush of relief, Tatsu turned to kiss him.

The vampire's backhand flung Tatsu flat. Shocked, he stared up at the *kyūketsuki* looming over him. The lover,

Arisada, was no more. Tatsu faced only a mindless predator—all reason, all emotion, all sign of humanity gone.

Arisada snarled and bared his fangs.

Tatsu stared at the face contorted with an animal's viciousness. Vicious, yes, but still beautiful and perfect. He was Tatsu's love for all eternity, and Tatsu trusted him with his life.

"Go ahead." Tatsu offered his throat. "I won't stop you."

The acceptance in that voice obliterated the vampire's blood-lust. He pulled away from the youth and scrambled a dozen yards backward until he hit the blackened wall of the spire. Cowed, he turned his face to the wall. "Leave me! I beg you, leave now!"

Tatsu stared at the stricken vampire crouched against the wall. "How can I leave you, Arisada. We are soul-joined."

With one hand pressing into his bleeding side, he crawled across that endless expanse of roof until he reached Arisada, touching the bowed head.

"Please, go." Arisada trembled with the effort not to seize the boy, pierce that tender neck and drain his blood. He closed his eyes and shrank further away. A tender, warm caress brushed down his tear-wet cheek. The back of Tatsu's fingers delivering a tender affirmation of the boy's love. Steel-strong fingers clamped under Arisada's chin. An insistent pull demanded he turn his head.

"Saito Arisada, look at me."

Arisada groaned with desolation, turned and looked. He wanted to close his eyes against the terrible compassion in Tatsu's emerald gaze. The blood rage drained from his body. His fangs slid back into their channels.

"*Watashi wa kimi kara isshou hanarenai yo,*" Tatsu whispered. "I will never leave you, beloved."

A wisp of breath caressed the vampire's forehead. Warm, pliant lips touched each eyelid, landed light as a bird on his rigid mouth, the moist tip of a tongue tracing along the seam.

The sheer wonderment of it all left Arisada breathless. He fused his lips to Tatsu's mouth in a deep, life-affirming kiss.

"Cobb! Cobb, answer me, man." Chain charged onto the

dome, sweeping the area with his bow, Kaiden right behind him. The Cajun spotted Tatsu caught in the arms of a vampire, both surrounded by pool of blood. He sighted his weapon and squeezed the trigger.

Tatsu saw the big Leper out of the corner of his eye. He flung his arm over Arisada's bowed head.

"Bro, stand down!" The barrel of Kaiden's gun knocked Chain's weapon upward. Three bolts wasted themselves on the night sky. In seconds, Chain had already re-armed his bow.

"Where's Sadomori?" Kaiden sheathed his guns. His eyes swept the expanse of the dome.

Tatsu nodded toward the rim. "Over the edge." Still mistrustful of the Cajun's intent, Tatsu held Arisada.

"Virus?"

"There, by the wall." Without warning, Tatsu's eyes rolled up, and he collapsed. Thin arcs of blood pulsed up from the holes in his neck. Arisada cried out, clutching Tatsu's shoulders, trying to lift him from the cold metal.

In a single movement, Chain tossed his bow to Kaiden, scooped up Tatsu's limp body and threw him over his shoulder. "Let's go. Major says we've got three minutes before the place comes down."

"C'mon, Arisada. Move your vampire ass!" Kaiden slung the bow over his back, grabbed the biocontainer and charged down the stairs after his partner.

Mind still reeling, Arisada picked up his *kotagiri* and the Ikkansai and staggered after them. He saw Tatsu's arms flop against Chain with every step. The Cajun's back and thighs were drenched in blood. The sight of Tatsu's flayed skin filled Arisada with despair. He knew nothing could save Tatsu from being Sadomori's last kill.

A dozen synchronized explosions ripped the Needle's bowels apart. The edifice groaned and swayed on its fractured supports as if reluctant to give up its life. One by one, its steel beams bent then snapped like rotten timber. Amid a mind-shattering roar, the sixty-year-old edifice collapsed, pulverizing everything along its path. Great, running fissures swallowed men and vampires. Thick, blinding clouds of dust billowed into the sky and boiled over several blocks, turning everyone and everything cement grey.

Arisada staggered over ground that bucked beneath his feet. A piece of flying concrete smashed between his shoulders, knocking him down. He lay stunned on the shuddering earth. After an unknowable time, he struggled to his knees, peering through the tornado of dust and grit. He searched with raw desperation for the huge man carrying Tatsu. Finally, Arisada saw the Cajun lay the pale, inert form onto the ground next to one of the Colony's vehicles.

Someone yelled for Wyckes. The man limped over to Tatsu and crouched beside the still youth. After an endless moment, the doctor shook his head. "No good. He's dead."

The scream of an animal ripped from Arisada's throat while the world narrowed into those two immutable words. He stumbled toward them, calling for his beloved. Unmindful of the vampire, Kaiden and Chain lifted Tatsu's limp body into the Humvee. Without a backward glance, the two men jumped in the cab. Doors slammed, tires spun and the truck tore away amid the acrid stench of burnt rubber.

Arisada's gore-soaked hand reached out—imploring and futile. Abruptly, he collapsed to his hands and knees, unable to hold his head up. He heard the Major call for Fornax, heard a reply that the vampire was dead. Hands grabbed Arisada and helped him stand. He stepped in the direction of the two vanished men. An iron grip on his shoulder halted him.

"We take care of our own." Major Blenheim squeezed once, a fleeting gesture of consolation then strode toward the last truck. In seconds the site emptied save for the vampire dead.

Mindless with grief, Arisada staggered to his car. His eviscerated belly pumped out his life force. One by one, his organs went into shock, his limbs turning numb. He knew healing was beyond his superior vampire abilities. He cared not. Let his life leave him. It was only fit. His heart so recently full of love was now dead. The loss defied all understanding.

He did not recall driving from the devastation. When he halted, he stared without comprehension at the indentured wandering the sidewalks of the Alki Compound. Why were they milling about like frightened sheep, gesturing toward the massive plume of smoke and dust obscuring the night sky?

A visceral savagery possessed him at his first sight of sustenance. His fangs tore through cartilage and arteries as he bit into throat after throat with mindless gluttony. For the first time in centuries, he felt no guilt for their deaths. His grief obliterated all rationale, all remorse and all morality.

Twenty-Four

Kyuketsuki Saito Arisada was mere hours from his death. He embraced it with gratitude. In the morning, he would walk through the forest, stand on the beach and watch the sun's first rays dance over the waves. Although not the honorable act of *seppuku*, this death would be fitting. He had lost his *nunmei no hito*, his soul mate, and with it, all reason to live.

"Oh, *koibito*, forgive me. I failed you," he cried, recalling his desperate search for Tatsu. The dust from the Needle still blanketed the city when four days later Arisada had visited Tatsu's apartment. His footsteps echoed in the empty rooms. Likewise, the vast building that housed the Leper Colony was also deserted. He caught the scent of freshly cremated remains. In that hollow place of the dead, Arisada's soul shattered. He collapsed on the cold, damp floor, dropped his head into his hands and keened.

First, a ritual bath, the symbolic cleansing of the mundane world from his body. For a time, he sat in the *ikinewa* gazing fondly at each plant and flower. He recalled his life, savoring each tender memory before casting it away to drift like cherry blossoms in a spring breeze. In his death poem, he asked for forgiveness for his sins and paid homage to Nowaki and Tatsu—his two lovers, one beautiful soul.

"*Namu Amida Butsu*." One-hundred eight times he recited it while moving each onyx stone of his mala through his fingers. Time had worn away the engraving of infinity on the beads, yet its meaning remained etched in his heart. One-hundred-eight times he avowed his veneration for the compassionate Amida Buddha.

Sunrise and the end of his suffering was an hour away.

A faint vibration like the gathering of a violent wind invaded his awareness. A wild, unreasonable hope flared through him. The rumble grew into a roar before the motorcycle engine stuttered into silence. He'd never moved that fast in his entire existence yet it seemed to take an eternity to dash through the mud to the garage. He skidded to a halt, struck immobile by the sight of Tatsu dropping the Drifter onto its kickstand. Arisada continued to gawk in stunned silence while a thoroughly drenched Tatsu dismounted from the bike. He shook his tangled hair, flinging water in all directions.

Arisada's heart hammered high into his throat. It was as if he were seeing the youth for the first time, unknown and exquisitely innocent.

"You are alive?" Arisada's incredulity drowned in a sublime wash of happiness. Enveloping Tatsu in a crushing embrace, Arisada's thinly clad body pressed against the cold, clammy leather of the motorcycle jacket. "I was certain you were dead." Arisada's choked voice vibrated against Tatsu's wet neck.

A tiny huff of contentment slipped from Tatsu. He curled his arms tight and hard around the quivering shoulders, his cheek rubbing against Arisada's head. "Dammit, you're hard to find. I've been riding around this island all night in this fucking rain."

Abruptly, they disentangled and stepped away, distancing themselves an arm's length from each other and the intensity of their feelings.

"How are—?"

"I'm freezing, and I've been through hell. But I'm better than you. Do you know you're naked?" Tatsu interrupted with no sign of teasing on his face.

Hapless in the clutches of his emotions, Arisada silently waved them into the house. But when he followed the boy into the *genkan,* fear shredded Arisada's euphoria. There was no denying those edgy movements and small uncertainties that turned Tatsu's gliding samurai walk into a parody of its former elegance. That rigid back and the locked shoulders said the boy was using every iota of his samurai discipline to hide an unspeakable violation.

Tatsu removed his boots before stripping off his wet chaps

and jacket, hanging them on hooks. He dug out the pack of Kings, pulled one out with his mouth and flicked his lighter.

Arisada's quivering fingers plucked the cigarette from Tatsu's lips. "Let me give you something better." He drew Tatsu close and crushed their lips together.

For one, long hungry moment, Tatsu leaned into that kiss. He chased his tongue in deep, relishing Arisada's taste. Then, he snapped his head back and stepped away, staring at the vampire through jade eyes turned as cold and hard as their namesake.

Arisada lowered his head. "*Sumimasen*. Cobb-san."

Tatsu ducked his head once but his gaze remained empty. Still, even this polite gesture was precious to Arisada. With a sudden conviction, he knew the horror Tatsu had experienced at the hands of the Daimyō. Knew it because he'd lived in the same horror.

Feeling utterly helpless under the weight of his insight, Arisada waved toward the bedroom where he'd nursed Tatsu back to health. "Please, you are wet and cold. You must be exhausted. Warm yourself under the shower. There are clean clothes in the closet. Join me in the *chashitsu*. I will make tea." He kept his invitation impersonal that of addressing a casual visitor instead of his life's love. But his sad gaze clung to Tatsu's stiffly retreating back, only turning away when the door closed.

A moment later, the innocuous sound of running water broke Arisada's self-control. He bowed his head and wept. His *koibito* was alive! No matter the boy's reason for seeking him out, even if only to revile him, Arisada's beloved lived. For that alone, his heart soared with indescribable gratitude. He breathed prayers of thanks to the Buddha Amida.

The simple acts of getting dressed and preparing the refreshments calmed Arisada's mind. His movements were excruciatingly careful when he arranged the tea things on a tray and carried them into the tearoom. Afraid his control would shatter at any moment, Arisada focused on the exact placement of the teapot, utensils and cups on the table.

He plumped the cushions and arranged them in the

position of host to guest, opposite each other. Then, he sat back on his heels facing the door, folded his hands in his lap and waited.

A few minutes later, Tatsu, dressed in a black, silk yukata, entered the room, bowed then knelt stiffly on the *zabuton*. "*Domo arigatō* for your gracious hospitality, Saito-san." He felt detached; body and mind so numb he was unable to offer anything more than the polite formality of strangers.

Arisada immersed himself in the calm, deliberate motions required for the proper serving of tea. Not shirking or hurrying a single step, the vampire prepared the teapot, blended the powder into a paste, added hot water and brought the tea to life with quick stirs of the whisk. His face reflected only the serenity that comes with the gentle art of *chaiki*.

The last time Tatsu sat for *chaiki*, a tea ceremony, was with his mother a few weeks before she died. Now, in that same time-honored ritual, a vampire offered him a porcelain *chawan* filled with a fragrant liquid.

Tatsu accepted the delicate cup, inhaled the bouquet coming from the steam before taking his first sip. The warmth spread through his chilled fingers. A shimmer of emotion stirred behind that stone wall he'd built around his heart during the last few days. Tatsu didn't know if he felt sorrow for his lost past or fear about his future. He sipped the tea then lowered the cup with deliberate care. "I need your help," came out in a choked whisper.

"I know." Arisada nodded, understanding reflecting in his face. "But before you speak, I have something for you." He rose and left the room with a rustle of silk. When he returned, he handed the Ikkansai to Tatsu, who stood to accept it with silent gratitude and shaking hands. He bowed then knelt again on the *zabuton,* placing the sword behind him in the position of total trust. He lifted his cup. It quivered in his hand.

After a few sips, Tatsu looked into Arisada's eyes, startled to see the shimmer of tears. There was also unmistakable love in the golden orbs. The rawness of that emotion scared Tatsu.

"I heard Dr. Wyckes declare you dead," Arisada's quiet tone belied his roiling emotions.

"Think a few stabs could kill me?" Tatsu's tried a false bravado that he certainly didn't feel. "What about you? Sadomori ran a sword into you."

"My injuries were not severe." Arisada caught Tatsu's frown, realizing the boy could read the lie. "Many were not so fortunate. My dear Fornax is dead. Some of your teammates."

"*Hai,* three of the Seattle team, six of the Snake Eaters. Bell's still in a coma. Cooperhayes is dead. The Major was devastated. Guess they were really special to each other. He shut the company down, went back to England."

"I discovered the foundry deserted. At that moment, I truly believed you were dead. Sadomori fed from you. How is it you live?"

"Hell, Arisada, I'm a Leper." Tatsu coughed a mirthless laugh.

The vampire looked confused. "*Wakarimasen?*"

"Aha, finally something you don't understand." Tatsu snorted. "I'm immune to the virus. Sadomori infected me the night he killed my family. Don't know how, but I survived it and stayed human."

"*A, sō desu ka.*" The vampire's pale face flushed and he dropped his eyes in embarrassment. How could he not know of this condition, this Leper immunity? A heartbeat later, his next thought nearly devastated him. In a voice that grated as if he had swallowed gravel, Arisada forced out the question. "Did Sadomori...?"

A terrible, bruised gaze turned those green eyes to stone. "He tried, couldn't get it up. Just used the whip handle." Tatsu thought he could just say it, utter the unthinkable, but the words turned to poison in his mouth. Since he regained consciousness, he'd planned this moment—being able to tell Arisada of the torture, simply saying it, getting it out of the way. Tatsu was sure the hate consuming his soul would dissipate with the telling. He was wrong.

Tatsu's unemotional reply horrified Arisada. He reached for Tatsu's cheek but dropped his hand at the impotence of the gesture. "Oh *koibito,* beloved. I am ashamed that I could not prevent this atrocity against you."

"While he did it, he described everything he did to you, thought it would break me. Didn't work. Made me so fucking angry. I thought only about killing him. And then I did." Within his cold, clinical voice, Tatsu heard a desperate plea for understanding. He'd dreamed of the relief he would get from telling his story. Instead, raw panic overtook him. He was going fucking insane, nothing made sense any more.

Suddenly, he had to get away from the very person who, moments ago he looked to for succor. "I should never have come here." Tatsu lurched to his feet, staring blindly around the room, no longer aware of his surroundings, seeing instead that chamber and Sadomori's hate-filled face.

"Come." Arisada picked up the Ikkansai, stood and gripped Tatsu's elbow. He steered the boy through the garden into the *shoin,* and guided him to the far wall that opened to reveal a fully equipped dojo.

In silence, Arisada unsheathed the Ikkansai, placed the blade in Tatsu's hand and pointed to the *makiwara*. The line of tall straw targets stood like sentries awaiting their duty. He gave Tatsu a slight push then leaned against the wall.

What Tatsu did now would determine their future together.

Tatsu stared at the silent row bisecting the *shiaijo*. He looked down at the naked sword as if just now realizing it was in his hand. In an ungainly lurch, he approached the first target and froze. The weight of the weapon dragged his arm down. He wanted to drop it and run. Numbly, he looked back to Arisada. The *kyūketsuki* offered nothing, only folded his arms across his chest and nodded once.

So ingrained was Tatsu's training that, without thought, he, bowed beneath the sword, bowed to the vampire then to the *shiaijo*. He moved into the familiar the two-hand position and swung at the first *makiwara*. He missed, lost his balance and stumbled past the target. In that clumsy step, the wall around his grief fractured. His anguished cry tore its way up from the depths of his soul. He spun back to the target and cut. For six seconds, the two parts of the target stayed together before the top slid slowly down to the floor.

Six seconds. A good cut, but not perfect, Arisada thought.

Tatsu's cries escalated into roars as he attacked, slicing left, right, left, step, step, step, faster and faster. His rage, his grief, and yes, his fear poured from him as he cut each *makiwara* into perfectly proportions sections.

And then it was done. For a moment, he swayed, drenched in sweat, hearing only his harsh pants. The Ikkansai dropped unheeded from his hand. The room and everything in it faded. Weak as an infant, he folded to the floor, wrapped his arms around his knees and buried his face. The anguish ripped out of him in great keening wails as the true horror of his violation engulfed him.

Arisada rushed to Tatsu's side and gathered the boy in his arms. "Oh, Su-kun, *gomen nasai, gomen nasai.*" Blood-red tears flowed down the vampire's cheeks. He cried for Tatsu—his childhood innocence taken by the murder of his family. And the vampire cried for the orphan Nowaki—destroyed before he really had a chance to live.

In that moment, Arisada forgave Koji Nowaki. And forgave himself.

Tatsu's wracking sobs faded to exhausted shudders. Murmurs filled with love penetrated his tortured mind, pulling him from that deep, dark place into a world made safe by the enfolding embrace of Arisada's arms. There, wrapped in the assurance of love, Tatsu surrendered that desecrated part of himself to the Universe.

"*Watashi wa okubyōmonodesu.*" Tatsu's voice rasped with exhaustion.

"No, Tatsu-kun, you are *not* a coward. You have never been a coward." Arisada felt the coward. How easily would he have ended his life and leave Tatsu to face his demons alone.

For many minutes, they remained locked together grieving, consoling—two wounded doves that might never fly again.

Tatsu finally stirred, gripped Arisada by the upper arms and forced the vampire to look at him. "Can I share your bed? We don't have to do anything, just be together. I really need this. *Kudesai*. Please, Arisada-san." Tatsu's voice cracked desperation. He wouldn't be able to take it if Arisada refused him.

"*Wakatta, koibito.*" Arisada concealed his joy. He helped Tatsu stand, gripping the boy's hand as if fearing he would vanish.

The vampire guided Tatsu to a hidden door leading down to the basement bedroom. Arisada lit several candles. Their yellow glow filled the room much like the first rays of the morning sun. The sun he came so close to embracing.

"This simple bed is all I can offer you," Arisada bowed.

"It's beautiful," Tatsu licked his lips and stared at the large, platform bed with its black silk duvet and simple white cotton sheets.

"I can light the fire if you are cold." Arisada indicated the gas burner in one corner.

"No, I'm fine." Shyness made Tatsu stumble over his words. He plucked at the lapel of his kimono as if unsure of what to do next.

Tenderly, Arisada took Tatsu by the shoulders and kissed him. The light press of his lips deepened and Tatsu opened his mouth. Their tongues slid into yielding warmth, accepted the truth between them—the truth of eternal lovers.

Arisada stepped back and shed his *yukata*. Naked, he faced Tatsu. "We will sleep. That is all, beloved."

For one second, Tatsu feared the sight of Arisada's pale skin under the guttering candles would be a brutal reminder of Sadomori. But Arisada's body glowed with a satiny, living beauty. Lean, muscles hugged the curves of each rib, the slight indents of the chest. Large pink areoles surrounded pale nipples. The hollow of the belly curved down to the nest around the root of a proud cock—a cock that rapidly lengthened under Tatsu's hungry stare.

"You are exquisite," Tatsu breathed. Damn, his moth watered for that prick. He wanted to kiss the ripe crown, savor the salty taste of its precum dripping from the bulbous head, engulf the entire length of that shaft until it hit the back of his throat.

He'd asked only to lie beside Arisada, nothing more. But who was he kidding? He wanted the vampire to fuck him into oblivion. Then fuck him again.

Afraid of revealing the force of his desire, Tatsu turned away from the tantalizing sight of Arisada's sex and hurriedly stripped. He bent and stepped out off his jock, not realizing that revealing his tight crack was the most erotic act the vampire had ever witnessed.

Behind him, Tatsu heard a gasp of dismay when he sat on the futon. Warm fingers brushed his back.

"He marked you." Arisada traced the ruby-red crisscross of scars. How intimately the *kyuketsuki* knew that defilement. Knew how it destroyed courage and faith, and tainted the soul. How would his beloved live with that?

Tatsu rolled on his side and touched the fine white lines beneath Arisada's eyes. It was a moment before Tatsu found his voice. "He marked both of us." He held Arisada's cheek. "He said I would bear the scars of shame. He was wrong. These scars are proof I restored my family's honor. Sadomori boasted I'd never kill him. He was wrong about that, too. The fucker tortured me, fed from me but he's the one who's dead. We beat him."

The quiet conviction in Tatsu's voice stilled Arisada's fears. He breathed his thanks to the Buddha Amida for protecting his beloved. And no matter what the future held, he knew Tatsu's courage would sustain them both.

As if knowing Arisada's thoughts, Tatsu pressed closer. "You and me? We're going to make it." His words came out in calm conviction.

"I'm *baka*, an idiot, for doubting us."

Tatsu dropped his gaze to their hard cocks pressed between their bellies. His face suddenly dissolved into a genuine, dimpled smile. "Yes, you are *baka*. You owe me, big time. Only one payment I'll accept." He gave a little grind against Arisada.

The vampire's nearly lost his mind at the raw need in that blatant motion. He groaned with frustration, felt the shake of Tatsu's laughter.

"Sleep first. We need this time to heal." He took Tatsu into his arms, fitting their bodies together.

Expelling a disappointed huff, Tatsu buried his face against the crook of the vampire's neck. He wriggled into the hard press of Arisada's hipbone, maneuvering about until Arisada's cock nudged against his thigh. He took a possessive grip on that cock.

"When we wake up, I want you to give me a new memory, a memory of love." A small huff of contentment and then he was asleep.

That grip, erotic and comforting at the same time, reassured the vampire of Tatsu's love as much as any words.

Arisada inhaled Tatsu's distinct fragrance; sweat-damp hair and human-boy skin with its whiff of cigarettes and motorcycle oil. He tangled his hand in Tatsu's unruly hair before slipping into a deep slumber unlike any he'd known for centuries.

The day flowered then withered while they slept.

Twenty-Five

A few seconds after sunset, a delicious anticipation woke Arisada. His arm curled over Tatsu's chest, one hand cupping the tattooed pec. When he eased back, Arisada immediately regretted the cold that filled the space between them. He propped his head on one hand and stole a long moment to take in his *koibito's* back.

Many of Tatsu's wounds had already healed but a few would leave angry, red scars forever marring that honey-kissed skin. Sorrow over his lover's torture caught dry as ash in Arisada's throat.

Gently, he traced over the jut of Tatsu's hip bone, smoothed over the flank and one cheek. He slipped his hand into the slight dampness of Tatsu's crack. Lifted it to his nose and inhaled the distinct scent of his man.

Tatsu made a deep, about-to-wake sigh and rolled onto his back. He looked up at Arisada through heavily-lidded eyes. "*Konban wa,* Arisada-sama." Tatsu stretched with the fluid grace of a jungle cat. His hard-on thumped against his belly, the dusky crown leaving a sticky blob. He pushed onto his elbows and looked around. "Ah...*otearai?*"

"Behind the screen." Arisada pointed then snapped on the bedside lamp.

Tatsu scrambled off the bed. A minute later, the toilet flushed and then the shower hissed. The thought of Tatsu, standing naked beneath that hot spray, skin foamy with soap, made Arisada's loins throb. Damn, this was not the time no matter how he ached for it.

"What a good little monk I am," he muttered with a wry smile. He dressed and went upstairs, returning minutes later with tea and adzuki-bean buns.

Toweling his wet hair, Tatsu padded in from the bathroom. A few drops of water beaded his skin and clung to his wiry pubic hairs. His fat erection swayed between his lean hips as if to say, "Now?"

A fine trembling seized Arisada at the sight of that length of hard male flesh. So arousing, so beautiful, so eager for him. He tore his gaze from Tatsu's cock, and looked in the direction the low nightstand. "Breakfast?"

"*Domo*, but there's something else I'd rather have." No doubt in Tatsu's very deliberate, very dimpled smile.

"You are temptation beyond words. But for both our sakes, I must leave for an hour. I have not fed for many days. Please, drink your tea." Arisada dropped his *kimono* and opened the closet door. Tatsu's arm wrapped around his chest and pulled him back. He felt the nudge of a hard cock along his crack. "Arisada, face me." The murmur tickled against Arisada's nape. Reluctantly, he turned within that embrace.

Want blazed from Tatsu's emerald eyes. "When I said to make a new memory, it included all things between us. Take my blood."

"I cannot. It is too dangerous." Arisada needed to leave yet his body refused to obey.

"*Baka*. Where's your faith? Leper, remember." A whisper of breath blew between them before Tatsu pressed his lips against Arisada's. It was a perfect kiss, a touching, shy declaration of love. After a seeming eternity, Tatsu pulled away. "You know I'm yours in *every* way."

"*Wakatta*. But later, Tatsu-kun. At the right moment."

"So, let's make that moment happen." Tatsu did not wait for a reply but tumbled them onto the bed, landing astride the vampire's narrow loins. Tatsu's balls pooled against the root of Arisada's erection. Their cocks rubbed against each other.

Everything Tatsu wanted lay beneath him. He nuzzled into the pale skin beneath Arisada's jaw line, and caught a distinctive scent of spices and sweat. Gently, kissed over fluttering eyelids and down that scarred cheek, pressed each corner of Arisada's lips before slaving their mouths together. With a soft moan, the vampire surrendered.

Tatsu drove his tongue in, touched the wet cheek, the jade stud, the ridges of the palete. When he traced over the channels and hard bone beneath, a scorching heat flared through him. The arousal so demanding he'd thought he'd burn up.

Breaking off the kiss, Tatsu pressed their foreheads together. "Arisada, I know you'll never harm me."

Under that blazing conviction, Arisada's resistance crumpled. "Oh, koibito, I am *baka* for fearing this."

"*Hai, hai*, stupid, alright. Now can we fuck?"

"Rude boy, you will pay for that," Arisada laughed. In a blinding move, he rolled Tatsu onto his back. "Su-kun, I want nothing more than to fuck you until you scream with pleasure. But not until I taste every part of your lovely body."

With hands and lips, Arisada explored the beautiful country that was his beloved. He sucked in a whorl over honey-kissed skin, kissed under the jaw, left wet trails over the collarbone. He grazed over each nipple before taking in one brown nub, teased it to hardness, moved over to the other. He tasted the damp underarm hair, traced over the ribs of Tatsu's heaving chest, down the ridges of Tatsu's abdomen, before combing his teeth through the wet tangle of pubes. He nosed at the root of Tatsu's shaft, breathing in its smell.

Never before had Tatsu felt such tenderness, such affection. Unbidden, images of jet-dark eyes and a wide, laughing mouth drifted on the edges of his mind. Sage! Their desperate, frantic couplings had been the only way Tatsu knew how to love. Until now. Sorrow and joy caught in his chest, making it tight. His eyes stung with unshed tears.

Needing the reassurance of touch, he caught a strand of Arisada's silky hair, and wrapped it around his finger.

At Tatsu's embrace, the vampire raised his head and smiled through kiss-swollen lips. He crawled between Tatsu's tension-splayed legs, and lifted one foot. Arisada pressed the calloused pad to his cheek before kissing the arch. Tatsu twitched and giggled, all sadness forgotten.

"Ticklish?"

"Oh, yes. But, feels so freaking hot."

Arisada kissed the sole again before taking each toe, one at a time, into his mouth. He moved up each leg, placing butterfly kisses over ankles, calves, the hollow behind the knees, along the thick tendons inside Tatsu's locked thighs to the straining juncture of leg and groin.

Warmth throbbed deep through Arisada's loins at the sight of Tatsu's vulnerable genitals. The pebbled skin stretched tight over the two hard nuts, the ridge of dark skin leading to the tight pucker, the dusting of dark hair around its rim.

He nuzzled into the soft scrotal mound, rolled his tongue over each ball before sucking in one then the other. Gave them small tugs with his lips. Relinquishing those heavy globes with a *pop*, Arisada sat up. His gaze traveled up Tatsu's tea-colored shaft to the swollen purple head begging for attention.

"Your cock is so beautiful." He licked his lips,

Tatsu blushed but held a smoldering gaze on Arisada. He grabbed the cock in question and gave it a slow stroke, pressed into the slit. The glide of his thumb pulled out a thin, sticky ribbon. He slicked it down his shaft, before toying with his balls, never taking his seductive look from the vampire. "Want a taste?"

"Such impertinence, *belovedo*. Now, let go and give me that pretty thing." Taking Tatsu's erection, he blew cool air over the heated head. A thick glob of fresh juice oozed from the slit. Arisada spread it slow and easy down Tatsu's prick.

"Tell me how you want it."

"Harder. Faster. Love my balls pulled. And palm the tip. And...Oh... *Fakku!*" Because at that moment, Arisada brushed his palm featherlight over the oh-so-sensitive tip. He began pumping, slow strokes at first, then harder and tighter with a twist just below the ridge. Tatsu, writhing under every stroked, panted out a stream of "So goods," and "Just theres."

Arisada cupped Tatsu's large balls, giving them a hard tug in perfect time perfect with every twist on his cock. Arisada's thumb dragging against Tatsu's perineum made his ass bunch and quiver. A teasing rub over the wrinkled pucker made him arch off the bed.

Ragged mewls escaped Tatsu's lips at those perfect, gonna-come-now strokes. The thumb pressing into that sweet spot under the ridge of Tatsu's foreskin danced lightning up his spine. Too soon that frosty ache spread from his sac up his cock, climbing, climbing, climbing. So close, so-freaking close. He closed his eyes and reached for that sizzling burst.

A cum-stopping squeeze around his root choked off his orgasm. "What the fuck—"

"Not yet, *bishou*. I want you in my mouth." Arisada planted a quick kiss on the turgid, ready-to-spill helmet.

"Then get sucking. Now." Grabbing Arisada's head, Tatsu dragged those mobile and oh-so-talented lips against his throbbing member. A laugh vibrated against the skin as wet heat ran up the thick vein on the underside. Then, almost total shock when that mouth swallowed every meaty inch of his dick.

Holy shit, Arisada had to be the master of cocksuckers. Tatsu sucked in air to say it but his brain-to-mouth connection was lost somewhere in the hurricane roaring through his skull.

Arisada vibrated his lips and tongue over Tatsu's thick rod, playing it like a delicate instrument, pulling out every note of pleasure. The jade stud rolling up the large vein gave its own unique pleasure. He remembered the flash of ecstasy in the vampire's eyes when that ball pierced his tongue. Now, that same ball was driving ecstasy into Tatsu's ass.

And then a needle-sharp pain pricked against his shaft. With no warning, his prick went supernova, blasting out its load in briny gouts. He arched into Arisada's mouth, aftershocks sizzling over his body from every swallow.

The vampire pulled away with a loud *smack*. A satisfied smile played over his swollen, cum-slicked lips. He crawled up Tatsu's shaking frame, feeling the thunder of the boy's heart beneath his heaving ribs. Tatsu gulped for air between wide, pink-flushed lips.

"You are adorable," Arisada said before locking his mouth onto Tatsu's and giving him the sea-salt taste of his own cum.

They held that kiss, mouths locked, groins grinding together. Tatsu hardened again. He broke the kiss with a deliberate and loud *smack*.

"*Kuso*, that was fucking amazing. But I didn't ride around this damn island in the rain for a blowjob."

Arisada did a slow rub of his prick along Tatsu's. "Did I not satisfy you, my *bishou*?"

"Yes. No...I mean...I want your cock in my ass."

The vampire's golden eyes flared with joy for a single heartbeat before washing dark. "No. It is too soon. You are not fully healed."

"*Fakku*, you've waited eight centuries. You going to wait another eight? I've got news for you, *vampire*, I won't be around." Tatsu hadn't been fucked in years. Knew it would hurt like a bitch. He didn't care. He just needed Arisada to pound into him. Needed that burn which would turn into the sweetest pleasure a man could ever feel.

"Tatsu-kun. I cannot endure the thought of causing you a single second of pain." The refusal contradicted Arisada's blatant need pressed between their bellies.

"I finger-fucked myself every night, thinking about you." He grabbed the vampire's erection. "Thinking about this!"

Then Tatsu saw the fear emanating from those golden eyes. "What are you afraid of?"

Shamed, Arisada turned away. "When I come, I will kill you."

Tatsu took the vampire's chin and turned him. "Believe in me. Believe in us."

Arisada heard the undeniable trust in those words. "I am such a fool. How could I have doubted you?"

"Again, *baka*." Tatsu smiled, his dimples melting the last vestige of Arisada's doubt. "Now, open me up."

Arisada dismounted from Tatsu with a smooth roll. "*Wakatta*, my *bishou*. Not like this. Turn over."

"Finally!" Tatsu laughed, low and sexy, before flipping onto his belly. He planted his knees and elbows on the mattress, lifted his ass and spread his cheeks. His balls swayed below with the motion.

Arisada's breathe caught at the uninhibited presentation of that pert rump and its brown, wrinkled hole. "You've got the most adorable backside I've ever seen."

"Stop admiring and start fucking." A hitch followed Tatsu's lust-ladened growl. "Wait! Lube?"

"No need, precious boy." Ignoring Tatsu's impatience, Arisada kissed a slow tease over each knob of Tatsu's spine down the dip above his ass. The vampire kneaded each globe until they quivered beneath his hand then thumbed them apart. He pushed his face into the crack. Before he could stop, he had nipped the creamy skin. A single drop of blood fell onto his tongue and flooded his taste buds. Seconds fled while he fought to suppress his hunger.

The musk of sweat and sex surrounded him as he licked down the crack to Tatsu's tight, brown pucker. Lapping at that clenched iris, Arisada coaxed it open. So sensitive, twitching and vibrating, beneath the lightest brush of his tongue, the hard roll of the piercing.

When that entrance softened, Arisada pushed inside, savoring the musty taste he'd craved for eight centuries. His tongue flickered against the wet walls. Each dip drew needy little whimpers from Tatsu. Arisada wanted to make his own needy little whimpers but his breath was trapped somewhere in his chest. *Koibito*, my precious *koibito*. The mantra pounded through Arisada with every beat of his heart.

Desperate to keep from touching his prick, Tatsu clawed at the sheets. His cock throbbed, so hot and hard, so freaking ready to blast its load. *Kuso*, one more dip of that tongue and he'd come—again. He tore his spit-slicked bud from Arisada's face.

"Stop. Want you to fuck me,"

Arisada gave that quivering entrance one final lick before sitting back on his heels. His throbbing rod, the head leaking precum, jutted over his thighs,

"Patience, my *bishounen*, patience." *Kuso*, he was the one who needed the patience. Want turned his voice into a husky growl. "I think you said something about wanting to fuck. On your back."

"*Hai, hai.*" Tatsu flipped over and locked his legs over the vampire's shoulders. He squirmed close until their groins pressed together. Arisada's iron-hard rod rode down his crack.

Taking that cock in one hand, Tatsu ground the head against his pucker. "*Dozo*, now!"

And Arisada froze, every muscle locked in fear.

Despite his near-blinding desire, Tatsu knew the vampire's fear had nothing to do with killing and everything to do with betrayal.

"Arisada, let me take your pain."

Featherlight, Tatsu moved his hands up Arisada's chest, over the trembling shoulders to massage the nape of that rigid neck. His touch held nothing but his love as he mapped the hideous mosaic of scars down Arisada's back. He kneaded those clenched buttocks until they turned buttery soft. Taking a firm hold of one cheek, Tatsu steadied the vampire's cock against his hole.

"Arisada, I give you my oath. I will never betray you. *Never!*" With that, he impaled himself on that rigid length. Pain, intense and high, shot through his belly. Ignoring the instinct to reject that thick invasion, Tatsu bucked again. He moaned, loving the sting as his rim stretched to take in the wide base of the vampire's prick.

All Arisada's fear was obliterated by the primal demand of the body surging beneath him. In one blinding moment, his cock was sucked deep into Tatsu's scalding core. The muscle quivered and pulsed around him.

"Make it messy, make me hurt," Tatsu begged.

And Arisada made it messy, pumping that sweet burn through Tatsu's chute and up into his skull. Thrust so deep, Tatsu thought Arisada's cock would hit his heart.

Tatsu whimpered for Arisada to fuck him faster and let him come. He rocked onto that invading rod, taking it so deep he thought it would bump against his racing heart. Each time Arisada's cock gave him an oh-so-perfect rub that sent electricity through Tatsu from his well-sucked toes all the way to his gasping-for-air mouth.

"*Yate! Yate.*" With a punishing grip on Arisada's hips, Tatsu pulled the vampire into him with every "fuck me."

All hint of tenderness vanished as they slammed together in primal fury. The *slap, slap, slap* of flesh against flesh punctuated their rhythmic grunts and groans. The thick smell of sweat ladened with sex and ass filled the room.

Arisada's glutes bunched and rolled as he pistoned into the depths of Tatsu's willing ass. Arisada lost himself in the slide of raw skin against raw skin, the clench of that pucker as he pulled out, the accepting yield with each driving thrust. He gave himself over to the exquisiteness of Tatsu's ass, slammed in with primitive fury until his orgasm burst out in long pulses.

At the crest of his release, Arisada's blood-lust tore free.

Tatsu's eyes, hidden behind closed, sooty lashes, flew open. He stared at his lover's face—the gleaming fangs, the crimson eyes. The face of a beautiful, savage creature. Vampire or man, it did not matter, Arisada was his.

Ignoring those gleaming fangs, Tatsu dragged Arisada down and fused their mouths together in a claiming kiss. The taste of his own blood spilled into his mouth. Heat flamed through his cock, his balls, his ass, in sweet blasts that spiraled higher and higher. And Tatsu knew what he needed—what they both needed. He threw back his head and bared his throat.

"Arisada, now! Take my blood."

The vampire struck, claiming his lover in the most intimate, deadly way. He fastened his lips to the punctures and sucked. Oh such bliss, the richness of that coppery nectar sliding down his throat and filling his starved body. He kept feeding far beyond the point of satiation. Even when he felt Tatsu's pulse stutter, Arisada was unable to stop. A small part of his mind gibbered with horror, knowing he was killing his beloved. But his blood-lust wanted everything Tatsu offered— his body, his life, his *tamashii*.

Tatsu knew he was dying. Even the incredible healing power of his Leper body could not overcome such a rapid loss of blood. He heard the thuds of his heartbeat grow softer, the intervals between longer. It didn't matter. He would accept his own death if it came from his lover.

The beckoning Void promised peace and an end to his sorrow. He reached for it.

A face—its harsh planes softened by love—drifted behind Tatsu's closed lids. "*Atsili*, you've found him, the one your soul belongs to. But if you die, he dies also. And my sacrifice would have been for nothing."

A despairing sob tore from Tatsu. How could he so easily surrender to death and abandon Arisada to suffer more heartbreak?

Bushi damashi, Tatsu's samurai's warrior spirit rose but not toward death. Seeking, seeking, seeking, it spiraled through the Void until it found the nebula of Arisada's *tamashii.* Tatsu's *ki* enveloped that tormented spirit, flowing and swirling until the two energies melded into an ethereal whole. All anguish, all guilt, all pain vanished as their souls became one.

A power, gentle as a dove yet stronger than samurai steel, surged through them both. Crying Arisada's name, Tatsu wrenched away from death.

The ravenous beast in Arisada fled. With a sob, he tore his mouth from his bloody feast. His horror turned to wonderment when he stared into Tatsu's eyes so wide-blown that only a thin green line edged the black pupils.

"How is this possible?"

The joining of their spirits seemed unbelievable to Tatsu yet he accepted its truth. "Perhaps after so much suffering, Buddha has granted you compassion and made us *unmei no hito,*" he said barely above a whisper from his ravaged throat. "*My* soul mate." Then he proved his conviction by kissing the vampire's bloody mouth.

The *kyūketsuki* nearly wept at that simple gesture. Never had he loved the boy more than in that moment. "*Aishiteru, koibito.*"

"*Aishiteru,* Arisada. My soul mate." With a happy sigh, he dragged Arisada down against his chest covered with cum, sweat and blood. Peace filled Tatsu. They were joined as one spirit, nothing could separate them. Not even death.

Hours later, they curled against each other in the center of the bed. Tatsu touched the healed wounds on his neck, proof he was Arisada's in every way. A small smile curved Tatsu's kiss-swollen lips.

The speed of his recovery was no surprise. What did surprise him was at the first surge of strength, he'd dragged Arisada to the shower, and fulfilled the vampire's not-so-secret fantasy of blowing his cock blown beneath the streaming water. No loss of vampiric control this time, no neck biting or blood drinking. Just Arisada bucking and crying while he spewed jizm down Tatsu's throat. And after that, they'd fucked—again. Now, even though his ass burned, the silky leak of spunk sent a delicious stirring all the way through him.

Lulled by the measured beat of his lover's heart, Tatsu drifted half-asleep. His sigh ruffled a strand of Arisada's hair.

"What troubles you, Su-kun?"

"When I was about to embrace death, Sage came to me. Told me not to waste his sacrifice."

"Your Navajo lover was wise."

"*Hai*, he showed me *how* to love. But it is you who showed me *why* to love. My *koibito*."

"You called me *koibito*."

Tatsu tightened his arm around Arisada's chest. "*Koibito*, it feels good coming off my tongue."

"There is another thing that feels good coming off my tongue." Arisada stroked Tatsu's semi-hard cock.

"Oh, gods, yes! But give me a moment." He heard his own voice, rough, like he'd swallowed gravel. No, not gravel; Arisada's creamy cum. Gouts of it. Damn it was sure no myth about a vampire's libido.

"How many times have we fucked?" Shit, the delicious ache deep in his belly, the pulsing rawness of his spent cock told him how many.

"You know. Don't be so smug about it, sexy boy."

"Boy? Technically, I'm only a year younger than you."

"Age is immaterial. *Sumimasen*. I know you are sore. I've fucked you five times."

"I love how you say *fuck*. For an ancient Buddhist monk, you sure talk dirty." Tatsu shifted closer, nudging his prick into the vampire's groin, loving the feel of it. And loving the pain in his throbbing, oh-so-very-fucked ass that he figured he wouldn't be sitting on for days.

Arisada's laugh reverberated against Tatsu's chest. "I may be an old Buddhist monk, but I'm no celibate."

Suddenly, Tatsu wanted to know everything about Arisada. Good and bad. "How did you learn to speak English?"

"From a British cabin boy. The poor lad had visited a pleasure house and passed out from too much wine. When he awoke, his ship was many hours gone. I found him huddled in a doorway, soaking wet from the rain, sobbing his heart out. *Mochiron,* I took him home. At first, he was inconsolable. Not only had his crewmates abandoned him but he was deeply in love with his captain and feared he'd never see him again."

Tatsu knew how that young boy felt leaving home, family, everything familiar. "How old was he?"

"He arrived during *uzuki,* April, in 1610. He was seventeen and had been aboard ship for five years."

Tatsu propped himself up on one elbow, and traced delicate whorls over Arisada's chest. "Did you love him?"

"I was fond of him. He taught me his language, and I taught him the many ways men could love each other." Arisada brushed a tangle of hair off Tatsu's forehead, noticing the small frown between his jade eyes. "There is no need to be jealous, Su-kun."

"Not jealous. Just sad for him." He snuggled back into the crook of Arisada's arm. "Did he know you were *kyūketsuki?*"

"No, he believed I belonged to an eccentric religious order, and my duties took me away during the day."

"Did he find his captain?"

"His ship never returned. He died of a fever."

A stab of sorrow caught Tatsu. "You couldn't save him?"

"I was gone for several days. By the time I returned, it was too late. I mourned him. He was precious to me."

"Have you had many like that? Precious, I mean?"

"Just that boy and two others, including Fornax."

"Your Primary." A statement not a question. Tatsu had seen love in Fornax's eyes when he spoke of Arisada.

"Fornax was a gentle man who followed the Eight Fold Path. He did not deserve the fate I gave him. I should have given him a peaceful death but soldiers interrupted me. After he became *kyuketsuki,* I made him my companion."

"Were you his only lover?"

"Oh, no. He had many lovers—vampire and human alike—before he was mutilated. Recently, I sensed he'd given his heart to someone, although I do not know who."

"His body wasn't found. Maybe he survived."

"*Tabun,* perhaps. I am not ready to accept his death."

Tatsu tightened his arm around that too-slim waist. He wished he could take the vampire's grief just as he took his fear. "I'm not going away. Ever."

The vampire sighed. He wanted to believe in the promise, in those words, but, oh, their precious naïveté. The harsh reality of their true natures lay between them. Tatsu's lifespan would be a handful of decades. Arisada could live for centuries. No, not centuries. Not even one day longer than his beloved. He would commit *seppuku* within the hour of Tatsu's death.

"Can you make peace with time, Su-kun? How it is different for us?"

"No one can predict the future. We take each minute as it is offered. I'm at peace with that." He sat up again so he could look at Arisada. "And I know we will have a lot of time. I just wonder what's going to happen in Seattle. Things could get ugly. And Tendai has no Master."

"Yes, it does. I am the natural successor to Sadomori." Arisada sounded as if the idea was distasteful.

"*Wakatta,* if you become king, I'll be queen." Tatsu laughed. And in that, all his hurt from years of hatred and bigotry vanished. How wonderfully queer to experience such healing from the love of a vampire!

"There is one solution. As a couple, human and vampire, we could forge peace between Seattle's two races. Restore the balance and rebuild the city."

Tatsu's jade eyes sparkled. "I have a degree in bio-engineering. There are so many improvements I—"

The vampire interrupted by pulling him down against his

breast. "I believe this is how our *karmas* will atone. Arisada turned off the light and drew the sheet over them. "Enough talk, sweet boy. *Nete, kudasai.*"

Arisada listened to his lover's breath deepen into sleep. He traced his forefinger over his lover's sleeping mouth, lips parted around the tip of a pretty, pink tongue.

Quietly, the vampire reached over the side of the bed and found Tatsu's discarded kimono. A smiled flickered over Arisada's lips when he dug out the hidden lighter and pack of Kings. Sometimes, his beloved was so predictable. Arisada lit a cigarette and took his first puff in decades. A mild rush of nicotine hummed along his nerves. He watched the lazy curl of smoke as he wondered about the end of his life with Ukita Sadomori.

He was not convinced Sadomori was dead. Old, cunning and paranoid, the Daimyō always had an escape plan. And even if dead, Arisada knew he and his *koibito* would be haunted by Sadomori's legacy of torture and rape.

But, for now, Arisada let peace flow into him. His soul mate lay wrapped around him, clinging tightly even in sleep. Arisada had journeyed for eight-hundred years and finally found his refuge in the arms of this human boy.

After extinguishing the smoke, Arisada fitted his body against Tatsu. Prayers to the gentle Buddha Amida flowed through Saito Arisada's mind. He blessed *Bushido*, the Way of the Samurai that kept him on the path of honor. He gave thanks for the virus that contaminated his body, for only as a monster could he have lived long enough to find his *unmei no hito*.

Tears slipped down his face. Tears of joy for his lover, Tatsu Cobb, whose beautiful *tamashii* had restored the honor of Koji Nowaki.

辰

B. D. Heywood, 2012

ABOUT THE AUTHOR:

Born and educated in England, B. D. Heywood lived in several countries before moving to the United States. Heywood earned a Bachelor's in English and a degree in Secondary Education-Language Arts. On the way to a career as an award-winning journalist, Heywood worked as a researcher, teacher, lecturer and construction estimator with a short side trip into demolition.

Heywood's study of Buddhism and martial arts evolved from a long-time interest in the culture and history of Japan. The Battle of Mii-dera in Japan in 1180 inspired the story for *Eternal Samurai*. A love for all things samurai and vampire coupled with the desire to give gay readers a hard-hitting, male-on-male erotica story, led to the creation of this unique, cross-genre story.

Heywood is working on a second novel, *Eternal Warrior*, an anthology of erotic gay stories, and a coming-out play for local theater. Any spare time goes to training horses, advocating for gay rights, supporting several community organizations including one for at-risk GLBTQ youth, and an equine-rescue operation. Heywood lives in Arizona with family and several assorted horses.

Sometimes, when the summer heat is so high it can fry an egg on the sidewalk, Heywood will haul people and horses up to a quiet town in the forest of Northern Idaho.

To reach the author, please e-mail:
icinibooks@yahoo.com

ISBN-13: 978-0988300002

Made in the USA
Charleston, SC
07 August 2013